Dance

IN THE

Dark

Dance in the Dark
Dance with the Devil #2
By Megan Derr

Edited by Samantha M. Derr
Cover designed by Natasha Snow

Third Edition November 2019

Printed in the United States of America

Author's Notes

Johnnie is fond of spouting off quotes, and a handful of characters quote lines right back at him. Because I am nowhere near clever enough to know dozens of fitting quotes off the top of my head, I cheated. Credit where credit is due, the following books were used in the course of writing *Dance in the Dark:*

The Oxford Dictionary of Quotations by Subject
Edited by Susan Ratcliffe
ISBN 978-0-19-860750-2

21st Century Dictionary of Quotations
Edited by The Princeton Language Institute
ISBN 0-440-21447-5

Grimm's Complete Fairy Tales
Barnes & Noble Books edition
ISBN 0-88029-519-8

Doctor Faustus by Christopher Marlowe
Edited by Sylvan Barnet
ISBN 0-451-52779-8

William Shakespeare: The Sonnets and A Lover's Complaint
Penguin Classics
ISBN 0-140-43684-7

Riddle Me This: A World Treasury of Word Puzzles, Folk Wisdom, & Literary Conundrums by Phil Cousineau
ISBN 1-56731-649-2

Twentieth Century Russian Poetry
edited by John Glad and Daniel Weissbort
ISBN 0-87745-365-9

Dance
IN THE
Dark

2

MEGAN DERR

Case 001: The Devil in Glass Slippers

Johnnie straightened his black and silver tie, thumb sliding over the rose-shaped tie pin made of diamonds set in silver. The suit was bespoke and the equal, if not the superior, to that of any snob in the room. Already a few people had cast inquisitive, nose-up glances his way, sensing a normal amongst their powerful, abnormal throng. They could not dismiss him entirely, however, not when he had clearly been invited, since there was no other way to get into Jesse Adelardi's parties.

He might be a normal, but in every other way he fit the part, right down to his costly clothes. His suit was a smoother black than his ink-dark hair, which was razored so the ends fell in jagged wisps around his face. His eyes were a dark charcoal gray, hard as he looked at the man beside him. "So, now are you going to tell me why you insisted I come? You know I hate costume parties."

"Masques," Rostislav corrected, smoothing his own playboy fine hair. If Johnnie was a shadow, Rostislav was sunshine. If Johnnie strove to be a good little human, Rostislav was an abnormal troublemaker born. "They're called masques."

Johnnie shrugged. "A rose by any other name would still be just as annoying."

Rostislav slid him an amused look, gold eyes glinting. "The Ice Queen vexing you again?"

"As though he ever does anything else," Johnnie

replied with a slight grimace that was quickly smoothed away. "I really do not feel like discussing him right now. Tell me why you dragged me here, or I am leaving."

Rostislav sighed at him, long and pointedly. "We are here to find a pair of shoes."

"I am leaving," Johnnie replied, and turning sharply on his heel, strode from the balcony where they had been watching the ball down below, out into the lobby of the casino where the party was being hosted. It was a beautiful building; his father often used it to conduct business or simply spend time with friends. The Last Star, it was called. It had the finest ocean view around, for those who could afford the rooms where that view might be obtained.

Generally, Johnnie loved being at the Last Star. Right then, he wanted no part of it. Masques creeped him out. Maybe he should learn to let go of childhood trauma... but, no, he really did not feel like it. The worst part about costumes was the not knowing. He did not see the fun in it. People were hard enough to understand, and abnormals harder still, without the additional challenge.

"Wait, wait, wait—" Rostislav grabbed his arm and forced him to a halt. "Come on, Johnnie. Don't stomp off in one of your hissy fits."

Johnnie ignored that. "I am not going to dig you out of whatever mess you have gotten yourself into this time, Rostiya. Do it yourself."

"Please?" Rostislav said, golden eyes pleading. "It's not what you think. I didn't start this mess."

"Start from the beginning," Johnnie said. "Tell me everything, and if you leave anything out, I am going home and will ignore you for a very long time."

Rostislav winced, knowing the words were no bluff. "All right, all right. I was asked to consult on some old junk."

Old junk being Rostislav's rather flippant term for magical artifacts. The abnormal world was rife with magic-imbued objects that were never properly cared for or deactivated. Most were harmless, but too many were not. Rostislav, a witch of no small ability, consulted on the various objects people found and helped to render them harmless, or at least find the person who could render them harmless. "In with the mess was a pair of shoes. Dancing shoes, made of glass."

"Cinderella slippers?" Johnnie asked, immediately intrigued despite himself. History was rife with ways for abnormals to hide themselves amongst humans and from each other. To save energy, many abnormals put spells into clothing, jewelry, or the like, that cast an illusion—a glamour—over the wearer.

Old legend held that a particularly powerful abnormal—no one knew what kind—had placed a spell in a pair of slippers made of glass. Ostentatious and stupid, but abnormals excelled at nothing so much as showing off while hiding in plain sight. "So we are looking for missing glamour shoes?" he asked. "That should not be too much of a problem."

"They aren't just glamour shoes, unfortunately," Rostislav replied. "Examining them revealed they were actually holding a demon. I put them in a spell cage while we went to lunch. When we came back, the shoes were gone."

"Wonderful," Johnnie said and returned to the balcony, staring down at the people below, lips pursed in thought. "So somewhere down there, a demon is wreaking havoc with some Cinderella." He looked at Rostislav. "I do not see why this concerns me. You are the witch. Find them and destroy them."

"I can't find them," Rostislav said, blowing out a frustrated breath. "I've tried. I finally told Jesse—"

"Jesse?" Johnnie demanded. "You are helping Jesse Adelardi?"

Rostislav glared at him. "Yes," he hissed. "Business is business, and I don't need you to lecture me. The shoes are what matter, and right now I need your help, all right? I didn't get a chance to determine what the demon had to do to break free of the shoes. All I know is that they are Cinderella slippers and this is Jesse's ball, so we need to find them soon."

"Let us hope that we figure out which tradition was used by the sorcerer who put a demon in a pair of slippers." He looked out over the crowd again and murmured softly, "Shake and quiver, little tree, throw gold and silver down to me."

"So does this mean you'll do it? I promised Jesse that I knew a clever little detective who could help us."

Johnnie rolled his eyes. "I am no detective. Finding the odd missing object and such for people does not a detective make."

"If you say so, Johnnie," Rostislav said with a smile. "Let's find the slippers. It's entirely possible they're not even here."

"No," Johnnie said, eyes still on the crowd. "A demon in Cinderella slippers would find no better place to be than a costume ball. So let us go find Cinderella and hope we do it before the stroke of midnight." He glanced back at Rostislav and sneered at the gold half-mask Rostislav was sliding into place.

"Didn't you bring a mask, Johnnie?"

"I do not wear masks," Johnnie replied. "You know that."

"Yeah, yeah. You really need to learn to mellow."

Johnnie ignored him and turned away, sliding into the role of finder that he seemed to have acquired over the years. He looked over the crowds of people again, murmuring softly to himself again as he caught sight of a woman with a particularly extravagant coiffure. "Riddle me, riddle me, what is that; over the head, and under the hat?"

Rostislav frowned at him. "What?"

"Nothing," Johnnie replied. "Just nonsense. Make yourself useful, witch, and see if you cannot pick out bits of Cinderella style spell work. I doubt we can detect the demon itself, but the spells and effects employed with Cinderella slippers are more or less rote. Hunt them out, or at least try."

"Oh, yeah." Rostislav made a face. "Because illusions, love spells, and enchantments are so bloody uncommon at a bloody masque."

Johnnie regarded him coolly.

"All right, all right," Rostislav replied, throwing up his hands. "What are you going to do?"

"Examine shoes," Johnnie replied, striving to keep his voice even and unaffected and not let out the bitterness that always came with the knowledge that he had no abnormal abilities to draw upon. He was the quintessential ugly duckling, and heaven and hell forbid anyone let him forget it. Already he could see the looks, feel the curiosity. Some knew him and would tell those who did not. Others would simply figure it out for themselves. Everyone wondered why his father had adopted him. Nearly all pitied him. Many regarded him as potentially amusing. All looked down on him. "Shoes and people."

He pointedly dropped his gaze to Rostislav's shoes, which were as perfect and golden as the rest of the man and ensemble. Rather than a fancy costume, Rostislav simply wore a suit and domino mask. Looking up again, he said, "I suppose your shoes are in order."

Rostislav laughed. "I hope we find them quickly, Johnnie. Thank you for coming to help me. You'll be home soon enough, I promise."

Johnnie shrugged dismissively and stifled a sigh. What waited for him at home but another fight with Elam? Home was seldom a welcoming place at the best of times, and worse still when the Ice Queen was in a foul mood and eager to take it out on his unwanted brother.

Gods above, he wished the day would come when he stopped hoping for Elam to return just some of what Johnnie felt for him. Shoving the thoughts away, focusing on the task at hand, he watched as Rostislav descended the grand staircase and rapidly vanished into the throng below.

Johnnie stifled another sigh, then finally descended the stairs himself. Immediately the press and crush of people began to irritate him. The stench of sweat, perfume, smoke, and the underlying bitterness of too much magic in too small a space gave him a headache, and he fought his way through it until he at last found a bit of free space near the main bar.

He skimmed the crowd, looking absently at shoes where he was able, but mostly looking for a possible Cinderella or the 'prince.' As it was Jesse Adelardi hosting this event, he should be the 'prince' for whom the demon would have to seek to fulfill the Cinderella strictures.

It was an ever raging debate, which had come first—the slippers or the tale. Most held the tale had come first and many an abnormal had been inspired. Others held that the slippers had come first: that once upon a time, an abnormal placed a spell or trapped a demon within a pair of slippers in order to win her prince and obtain freedom from an evil stepmother.

Johnnie had always thought that was close, but did not believe it had played out quite that way. The various mothers, that was the key. A dead mother, a stepmother, and then the 'fairy' godmother, which in some versions was simply the spirit of the 'good' mother.

The closest he ever came to being a true abnormal was by studying them incessantly. The only thing he excelled at more than finding things was knowing things. Reading, research, talking to those who would indulge him...

His private theory in regards to the Cinderella slippers was that it had never been Cinderella herself who obtained the slippers through positive means. Far more likely, he had always thought, that some girl's over-ambitious mother had plotted to see that her plainest, most lackluster daughter landed a successful marriage. Possibly her only daughter, or perhaps her youngest, but whatever—she could not or would not be what her mother wanted.

So, bring in magic. A mother who placed a spell or spells in... a new pair of slippers? A favored pair? And suddenly her daughter was far from plain, far from ordinary. Attract the prince, ensnare him, and the deed is done. A glamour, a love spell, tied together just so to make a happily ever after. Such things had been done since the beginning of time.

"Master Desrosiers," said a cool voice.

Johnnie nodded at the vampire, acknowledging and then dismissing him. He did the same as several others greeted him. He was not here to socialize, and they were only acknowledging him because they did not dare offend his father. Turning away from the crowd, he glanced at the bar for a potential place to sit.

Oddly, the bar was occupied by only the bartender and four other guests. Two of the guests wore masks, and two did not. One of the masked was a sharp looking figure in green, and Johnnie sensed he should know the costume, but he did not. The other masked figure was some sort of yellow bird. Of the two unmasked, one was a beautiful woman dressed mostly in diamonds. The other was a plain looking man dressed in simple black, with nothing to cut or soften the severity of it.

Johnnie passed his eyes over each—the two masked figures avoided his gaze, the woman met it and immediately dropped her gaze, and the plain looking man met it, smiling politely before returning to his drink.

No Cinderella candidates here, then. They lacked... something, though, as usual, he could not put a finger upon what was off. He simply knew they were not right. Well, beauty obviously. The point of Cinderella was that 'she' would be the most beautiful at the ball. The woman in diamonds was stunning, but there were others more stunning. The plain man, obviously not. The two masked figures were not remarkable enough of costume to fit.

Approaching the bar, he sat between the two unmasked figures, a barstool of space on either side.

"Vodka rocks," he told the bartender. The bartender nodded and turned to pour the requested drink, and Johnnie turned slightly so that he could look out over the crowd again, carefully maintaining an air of boredom. He was looking now solely for Adelardi—if he could find the prince, Cinderella would present eventually. It was only just past nine; Cinderella would not make herself known to the prince before ten.

Where was Adelardi? He should be around and highly visible, even in costume. This was his fête, so where was he? It occurred to Johnnie then, he had never asked Rostislav the purpose of this party. Odd Rostislav had neglected to mention it, but perhaps he had simply forgotten.

Not his annual charity ball. It was the wrong time of year. Not a holiday, though that would have fit a costume ball. Birthday? The ball did not seem to fit that, though. It was possible, but he did not think that was it. He turned to the diamond-encrusted woman. "I beg your pardon, do you know the reason for this fête? I am afraid a friend brought me, but he did not tell me the purpose."

The woman shrugged and turned slightly away from him. Johnnie lifted a brow at that, but said nothing.

Before he could turn and ask the man on his other side, the very one he sought suddenly appeared. "Master Desrosiers," Jesse said with a smirk. "I am honored you deigned to attend my little fête. You look quite stunning, as always. I shouldn't doubt more than a few here would love whatever taste you were willing to give."

Johnnie ignored him. He did not *deign* to respond to such unclever taunts.

Jesse laughed softly. "Johnnie, Johnnie, as cold and beautiful as any vampire, but it took you only twenty-six years. Dance with me."

Finishing his drink, Johnnie placed his hand in Jesse's and followed him to the crowded dance floor. Immediately people moved to give them plenty of room, and Johnnie felt the prickle of eyes upon him, the heat of envy and the cold of contempt.

More than a few vampires disapproved of the way a Dracula had not only taken in a human, but worse, adopted him. Humans were prey, not kin. The only thing worse would be if he and some vampire dared to take up together.

Thinking that, of course, led to thoughts of his brother, but Johnnie stubbornly ignored them. He focused, instead, on Jesse Adelardi. Not a Dracula, but wealthy and powerful enough in his own right that he was counted high amongst the elite. There were always rumors floating around about that he was set to marry this daughter or that and be made an Alucard, eventually to take up Dracula.

So far, none of those rumors had come to pass, and the lack of marriage always created further rumors. Jesse was, of course, heartbreakingly beautiful. His was a handsome beauty, in contrast to Elam's more androgynous features. His hair and eyes were a deep, soft gold set in flawless sun-kissed skin. It was little wonder that he could get Rostislav to do whatever he asked. Johnnie had tried to tell Rostislav a thousand times the futility of being a human and loving a vampire, but they had always had stubbornness in common.

"I suspected you were the help that Rostislav mentioned," Jesse said, smoothly leading the dancing, hand warm where it curled around Johnnie's hip. How many people, over the hundreds of years of Jesse's life, had fallen victim to his warmth and charm and beauty? "I do thank you for coming."

Johnnie ignored the thanks and simply replied, "He neglected to mention the purpose of your masque."

"Oh?" Jesse asked. "It's the one hundredth anniversary of my hotel. I've never managed to stay so long in one place; it's quite exciting for me. The day it opened, I threw a masque." He pulled Johnnie closer, turning them neatly, moving gracefully across the dance floor. Beautiful, so close to perfection, but Johnnie remained unmoved. He possessed no special ability to resist vampires, he simply had grown up with them, amongst them, and the lure of that wicked beauty had lost its shine along the way. "Naturally, another masque was the only suitable option."

"Of course," Johnnie said, turning his head, following a pair of handsome blue high-heeled slippers. No. He turned back to Jesse. "You are careless."

"It was not my spell cage that failed," Jesse replied.

"Mm," Johnnie murmured, "but you did possess a pair of Cinderella shoes. You are no necromancer, but neither are you a fool." He pulled away as the dance ended and sketched a half-bow that was only just barely polite.

Jesse's mouth quirked in amusement, but he said only, "Thank you for the dance, Master Desrosiers."

"My lord," Johnnie murmured in reply, then left him, moving through the ballroom, surreptitiously examining shoes. After half an hour, he decided to try something else. He searched around for Rostislav—

and paused, frowning, when he finally saw Rostislav tucked into a discreet, shadowy corner with Jesse. What they were doing, he could not determine.

But he could guess.

He turned away in anger and contempt—and envy. Vampires *never* took humans as lovers; it was beneath them to have truly amorous relations with their food. If Jesse was doing anything, he was toying with Rostislav, and Rostislav knew that.

But Rostislav had always loved Jesse, the same way that Johnnie had always loved Elam. Stupid, to fall for vampires, but they had fallen all the same.

Rostislav was apparently wearing the mask of a fool for the ball, Johnnie thought as he glanced toward that dark corner again. He watched them a moment, quoting softly to himself, "So true a fool is love, that in your will/Though you do anything, he thinks no ill." Turning away again, he climbed the stairs he had earlier descended.

Away from the crowds, standing in a dimly lit hallway, he weighed his options. He should have had Jesse or Rostislav give him access to the spell cage in which they had tried to bind the shoes. Going back down into the crush below was not worth it, however. Not when he had other means to try first.

Moving to the lobby, he pressed the button on Jesse's private elevator. Though he possessed only ordinary senses and laid no claim to special abilities, one could not live his entire life amongst abnormals without some effect. He could almost always feel magic, unless it was very slight or too subtly cast. He could also smell it, when it was strong enough or, like downstairs, there was simply a great deal of it.

He felt it now, like a prickle across his skin, as he

stepped into the elevator. Glancing at the control panel, he immediately saw where a special key was required to access the very top floors. Jesse's rooms occupied the top three floors of the hotel.

The thing about the more powerful abnormals, Johnnie had learned over the years, was that they stopped worrying about normals. Instinct drove most normals to avoid abnormals like Jesse Adelardi. Over time, Jesse and his ilk, Johnnie's family included, become accustomed to being avoided. They largely ceased to notice normals.

As a result, they seldom bothered to incorporate wards against normals in their many and varied defensive spells. All the wards and spells blocked all levels of magic and mischief—except good, old-fashioned normal mischief.

Reaching into an inner pocket of his jacket, he extracted a suitable lock-pick and made quick work of the penthouse access. Tucking the lock-pick away again, he pushed the button and leaned against the back wall as he rode to the topmost floors with a slight sneer on his face.

The doors opened without a sound a moment later, and he stepped out into the first of the three floors. This floor was the living room, dining room, kitchen, and a beautiful patio complete with garden and fish pond. He knew from two previous visits that the second floor was equal parts library and museum; all the long-lived abnormals had a penchant for books, antiques, pieces of the long years behind them. The top floor was Jesse's exclusive domain. It obviously contained his bedroom, but beyond that, Johnnie did not know. No one else went there, ever.

Crossing the room, he slipped into the study and

immediately found what he sought. In one corner of the room was a large, round oak table, stained dark. The table top was not wood, however, but set with black chalkboard. On one end of it, pieces of chalk were neatly laid out. A sorcerer's table.

At present, the board was covered with an elaborate spell cage, the kind that took years to be able to draw without errors. Rostislav was an excellent witch, though. Johnnie felt the usual twinges of bitterness and jealousy. Being the adopted son of a Dracula only made him more acutely aware of all the special abilities he did not possess. He was quite literally nothing, minus that his last name was Desrosiers.

The closest he would ever come was to read and watch and learn. He would never be able to make a spell circle that would work, but he could read them as well as any sorcerer. A lifetime of relentless study was the only reason he was able to hold his head up in a room full of people who would be his superiors if not for his surname.

On the table before him was a spell cage: a double circle of intricate, high-level runes woven together to trap whatever object was placed inside the empty circle within the inner band of runes. Rostislav had been thorough; breaking it should have been difficult for anyone other than Rostislav.

Johnnie studied the circle more closely, examining every meticulously chalked rune, every stroke and curve. It was perfect, exquisite work, except... he bent over the table as far as he dared, hands carefully braced on either side of the circle, looking more closely.

There.

A break in the inner circle, no wider than the edge of a razor. That would have been enough to ruin the spell cage and render it ineffective. But once a circle was set, or activated, breaking it was not as simple as smearing the chalk—protections against such things were automatically put into all spell circles. In order to sabotage it, the break must have been done before the circle was activated. Even Rostislav might not have noticed such a minute gap. Johnnie probably would not have, had he not been looking for such a flaw.

Rostislav should have been looking for flaws as well. Hmm. Knowing Rostislav, and knowing Jesse, no one else would have been anywhere near this room when the shoes were brought out and the work done. Rostislav would have done all the work, obviously, but Jesse would have insisted on observing.

Once they realized something had gone wrong, Rostislav would have gone over the cage with a fine-toothed comb. He should not have missed the flaw; he was a better witch than that. "Man is practiced in disguise; He cheats the most discerning eye," Johnnie quoted softly, and turned away from the useless spell cage, picturing Rostislav in his elegant suit and the perfectly matched shoes.

He remembered Rostislav and Jesse tucked into that dimly lit corner while people danced and laughed around them, oblivious.

What was the game? Why bring him into it and yet not into it? Why would Rostislav lie to him? That upset him the most. Why would his friend lie to him?

Frowning in thought, he left the study and strode to the windows in the living room. Beyond the lights of the casino and hotel was a great deal of nothing. Here and there, where the moonlight slipped through the clouds, he could see the never-ending motion of the sea. Otherwise, it was only black. The casino was in a carefully selected middle of nowhere; even the locals who worked in the casino were either abnormals who lived there, or normals who lived at least half an hour away.

The Last Star drew hundreds of thousands, and the taxes Jesse paid to the Dracula were no small part of the reason that the Desrosiers territory was one of the wealthiest.

Leaving the window, he strode back to the elevator—and halted halfway, the glitter of gemstones just catching his eye. He knelt and reached under the couch, picking up a ruby bracelet he knew well; he had given it to Rostislav two years ago as a birthday present. It was a long standing joke between them that he always gave Rostislav such nonsensical, ostentatious gifts.

Kneeling in front of the sofa, he could now smell traces of Rostislav's citrusy cologne... as well as traces of *exactly* what he had been doing on Jesse's sofa. Johnnie sneered as he stood. So Jesse and Rostiya were definitely having an affair.

Why? A vampire caught in such dalliances with a human would turn himself into a laughingstock. Even a vampire as powerful as Jesse stood to suffer, and suffer greatly, for committing such a taboo. What did Rostiya stand to gain from such a hopeless arrangement, whatever the precise nature of the arrangement may be?

Nothing. Nothing but pain.

Hitting the button for the elevator, Johnnie stepped inside and pushed the down button, brooding as he returned to the lower levels. When the doors opened, he left the elevator slowly, still lost in thought. He stopped halfway, deciding that he did not want to confront Rostiya until he knew for certain what was afoot.

Turning around, he returned to the elevator and rode it up to the floor housing the Desrosiers suite. Though he had made no plans to come here, and would not have come except it was Rostislav who had asked, his father and brother were frequent visitors, and so Jesse always kept their suite ready.

It opened immediately to his keycard, the lights flicking on as they sensed movement. Removing his jacket and tie, he strode to the bar tucked into the corner of the room and poured vodka over ice in a crystal rocks glass.

He had just taken a sip, enjoying the ice cold bite of good vodka, when all the lights went out, leaving him in absolute dark. His skin prickled, and on the air was the sudden scent of myrrh and musk roses. Someone was in the room. That should have been impossible. The room was so heavily warded, a demon would sweat trying to break through. None but the Desrosiers and Jesse could walk in here without permission.

Johnnie reached out slowly, carefully, and set his drink back down upon the bar. He could see nothing; it was the most absolute dark he had ever experienced. Even the windows gave no light, though he knew very well that lights from the casino and the parking lot should have been filtering through the curtains. "Who are you?"

No answer immediately came, but Johnnie did not lower himself to repeat the question. There were eyes upon him. He could feel them like a touch. He could always feel eyes upon him.

"So you are the infamous human child of the Dracula Desrosiers?"

Johnnie said nothing.

Fingers slid down his arm, warm through the fine linen of his shirt, curling briefly before dropping away, and Johnnie only just barely kept himself from showing any reaction. The man was behind him and had not once made a single sound until he'd spoken.

Definitely a man, to judge by the hot-toddy voice, the shape and feel of those fingers. They touched him again, those fingers, and Johnnie spun sharply around, the back of his hand swinging up and cracking hard—

But only against the hand that caught his. The hand that did not let go, but only lightly squeezed his fingers and held fast.

"Unhand me," Johnnie said, voice cold. "You have no business touching me, or being here at all, and I will not tolerate it."

"In all the places I've been," the man said, "never have I encountered one as breathtaking as you."

Johnnie froze, momentarily startled by the words.

"Beautiful, elegant, graceful, but also cold, haughty, and proud. You could be a vampire but for the lack of fangs."

How much easier his life would be if he did have the fangs. "You will explain to me your purpose here. Fangs or not, I am a Desrosiers and will not tolerate your crass behavior. You will unhand me and tell me who you are."

Soft, deep laughter brushed across Johnnie's face, smelling like some sort of sweet, fruity candy. "I saw you downstairs and was captivated. I wanted a closer look."

"There is not much to see in the dark," Johnnie replied.

"Not for you, perhaps," the man replied, squeezing Johnnie's hand again—then his thumb brushed over Johnnie's bottom lip.

Johnnie jerked his head back and hissed, "Do not touch me." He glared at the man he could only feel and hear and smell, but to judge by the soft laughter, it had no effect.

"You're truly the most captivating person I've ever met," the man replied, and abruptly let Johnnie go.

Johnnie flexed the fingers of his suddenly free hand, wondering why it felt so strange. It tingled, as though it had fallen asleep and was just beginning to wake up. So too his lip, he realized. He frowned and lifted his other hand to touch his lips.

All the while, he felt the presence of the stranger, but he refused to ask again who the man was. Instead, he asked, "What do you want?"

"To be with you in hell," came the reply.

Johnnie jerked in surprise, not having expected that reply. He had never encountered anyone besides Rostiya who could quote Russian poetry. Intrigued now, though he knew he should be frightened or at least still angry, he gave the next spoken line of the poem. "It would seem your words/Bode neither of us any good."

A hand cupped his chin, the man's thumb rubbing along his lip again. "Tell me how men kiss you. Tell me how you kiss."

The words hung there in the air, thick and heavy, and Johnnie could not quite repress an unexpected shiver. He asked again, though he hated to lower himself, "Who are you?"

"An admirer," the man replied. "I admired you standing beneath the hard shine of the lights. I admired you dancing across the floor. I think I admire you most here in the dark, where I alone can see you."

"How can you see me?" Johnnie asked before he could bite the question back. "How well can you see me?"

"Perfectly," the man said. "Dark is as day to mine eyes."

Johnnie frowned at that. Nearly all supernaturals could see well in the dark, but he knew of nothing that could see *that* well, except perhaps ghosts. This man was no ghost. He did not know what the man could be, and that annoyed him. He should know. The stranger must be exaggerating, and his magic was simply good enough to overcome the wards. "Why can I not see you, then? Why must I remain in the dark? Afraid that if I know your face, you will be made to suffer the consequences of your actions?"

The man laughed. "Consequences? No. I've nothing to fear from consequences."

"Then why—" Johnnie was cut off by soft, warm lips, a mouth that tasted like sticky-sweet fruit candy. He tried to draw back, offended and infuriated, but one hand cradled the back of his head, sank gently into his hair and grasped a firm hold while the man's other arm wrapped around his waist and held fast. The man took his mouth more firmly, plundering it with a boldness that no one would *ever* dare display towards a son of a Dracula.

Johnnie did not mean to react—he did not want to encourage the abominable behavior—and yet he realized after a moment that he *was* responding.

It was the kind of kiss he'd always wanted. The kind

of kiss he'd never gotten from the few attempts he'd made to find lovers when he was younger. But those he'd considered dating had only wanted to amuse themselves with the Desrosiers human, or use him to get more prestige. And all of them had been doomed to failure anyway because they had not been Elam. His only lovers had all been forgettable one night stands. Even his first lover was a woman whose name he could not recall, a witch he'd met while out shopping one day who'd invited him back to her room for a few hours of fun.

Why could he not be kissed this way by Elam?

The stranger pulled away the barest amount, drawing a breath. His lips ghosted softly over Johnnie's, then his tongue was lapping where his lips had just been, and then Johnnie was being kissed thoroughly again, and even thoughts of Elam momentarily fled.

When the second kiss ended, the stranger drew back. Johnnie drew a breath to speak—then realized he was alone. Orange-yellow light slipped through the curtains, a sliver of light peeked from the bottom of the door. Johnnie licked his lips, tasting a stranger on them. No one dared treat him in so crass and familiar a manner. *He* chose who to kiss, and when, and how. He licked his lips again, tasting fruit candy and a hint of dark beer.

Annoyed with himself, he resisted an urge to lick his lips a third time and picked up his vodka. Draining the glass, he set it down again and went to retrieve his jacket and tie. He restored his clothing quickly and checked his appearance in the bathroom mirror. Johnnie scowled at his reflection and smoothed his mussed hair. Unfortunately, he could do nothing about the fact that it was clear he had just been well and thoroughly kissed. A rush of sudden, unexpected heat washed through him.

Johnnie turned sharply away from the mirror, furious with himself. He was angry, and only that. Whatever else he was or was not, he was a Desrosiers, the youngest son of a Dracula. He would not tolerate such insults upon his person. *He* chose who to kiss, and when they proved unworthy, he cast them out. How dare some shadow act so—so crassly, so presumptuously.

Leaving the suite, he made his way to the elevators and back downstairs. He thought of the strange encounter, the kiss, the possessive grip in his hair, around his waist. He thought of Elam, tried to imagine Elam holding him in such a way, kissing him that thoroughly. His gut twisted with an old, familiar ache. It was so impossible a situation, he could not imagine it. All he could see was Elam's perfect, beautiful face, the cold eyes that dismissed him as carelessly as they would a servant. Elam, who would not lower himself even to Jesse's level and use him in a dark corner.

Johnnie frowned, mind pulled back at last to the real problem at hand. What did he really know about this situation? Rostislav had called him to help find a pair of Cinderella slippers. The spell cage to contain the slippers had been purposely broken, rigged to fail. He supposed it was possible that someone else had done it, but the chances were slim. That razor thin cut had been as meticulously placed as every rune. That aside, Jesse was no fool. He must have had some suspicion as to the true nature of the slippers. Until they were completely safe, he would not have permitted anyone not strictly necessary anywhere near them.

So which of them had sabotaged the shoes and why?

Johnnie worried his bottom lip in thought, but immediately stopped when he tasted hints of fruit candy and dark beer. Rostislav, he needed to focus on Rostislav. He would solve his own sudden personal mystery later. What if Rostislav had broken the spell cage? He could have done it before the cage was activated, or after.

So, going with the idea that Rostislav had been the one to sabotage the spell... Rostiya would know that wearing the shoes would mean that he had cast a love spell on Jesse, the 'prince' of the ball. Given only he and Jesse had been around the shoes, there was no one else who would have wound up wearing the slippers.

In breaking the ward and wearing the shoes, he would have gotten Jesse to love him, after a fashion. Jesse would love him, and likely for a very long time, because breaking a love spell was no easy task.

Love spells were one of the few things universally frowned upon by abnormals. Though not forbidden, except as individual territories dictated, when those casting them were caught, they were most often heavily punished. It was complicated, dangerous magic because it manipulated a person completely—mind, emotion, and body. Forcing the breaking of a love spell almost always broke the victim.

If Rostislav had chosen to wear the shoes...

But that did not fit Rostislav. He loved Jesse, but resorting to such a spell would be dishonorable in Rostiya's eyes. Neither would he ever view it as real love, and that he would find unbearable. He would also be punished severely for casting such a spell on so powerful and influential a vampire.

So that theory could be discarded.

That left Jesse. So what if Jesse was behind it? That made even less sense. Jesse stood to gain nothing by arranging for his own succumbing to the love spell. He would likely be afflicted the rest of his life—well, the rest of Rostislav's life, which was still too long by vampire standards, and there was no telling how it would affect Jesse when Rostislav died.

Johnnie laughed. No vampire would ever tolerate such a thing. The only way Jesse would even risk it was if he knew it would have no effect, and the only way to properly block or break a love spell, and so cause no harm, was *real* love, and that was impossible. Vampires did not love humans.

But the back of his mind whispered, unable not to see the logic, what if he did?

Society would not stand for it. If Jesse ever admitted to loving Rostiya, he would suffer for it—rejection, isolation, loss of standing, possibly even violence. He would be fortunate if the Dracula did not oust him from the territory.

Unless...

Unless it was a convenient accident. Hardly the first time a mistake was made and a dangerous object was not properly warded. Should the whole thing be nothing but a tragic accident, then Jesse would merely become an object of pity, a delectable bit of gossip, shunned by society but not treated as harshly as he would have been otherwise.

It fit. It explained everything neatly—except that it must be wrong. In all he had ever read, all he had ever heard, not once had he ever come across a case of a vampire who fell in love with a human, never mind one who chose to love a human *openly*.

Down below in the ballroom, everything had gone still. The guests formed a circle of gawkers around the center of the dance floor, where three figures stood locked in quiet, but clearly tense, conversation. Johnnie's chest went tight, twisting with longing and pain, as he stared at the third figure, who spoke with obvious anger to Jesse and Rostislav.

Elam: beautiful, pale, delicate, and cold Elam. Tall, slender, with grace in his every movement. The perfect smile, the perfect voice—perfect in every way. Perfectly uncaring whenever he deigned to acknowledge his detested little brother. "The love that lasts longest is the love that is never returned," Johnnie murmured softly.

Rostislav glanced up and saw him. Seeing his attention distracted, Jesse and Elam followed the direction of his gaze. Johnnie simply stood and stared back. He cocked his head the slightest bit, indicating they should come upstairs and leave behind the gawkers surrounding them.

He waited, still and patient, as they made their way up the stairs and toward him—two beautiful, flawless vampires and a handsome, striking witch. As they reached him, Johnnie looked up at Elam, meeting the pale blue eyes he loved and hated in equal measure. "Good evening, Ellie."

Elam regarded him coldly, immediately irritated by the despised nickname. "John."

Brotherly greetings exchanged, Johnnie turned to Rostislav and recited, "What is it that is too much for one, enough for two, and nothing at all for three?" Rostislav smiled faintly and shook his head, acknowledging without words that he knew Johnnie had figured out their ruse—and that he would keep the secret. That settled, Johnnie spared a glance for Jesse, who only stared back and said nothing.

Elam broke the silence, his voice perfectly modulated to freeze. "Why am I not surprised to see you here? What do you have to do with this mess, John?"

Johnnie ignored him. "Shall we discuss this matter in private?" He turned away and led them to one of the many conference rooms on that floor. When they were all inside, and the door closed and locked behind them, he leaned against the wall and folded his arms over his chest, and said, "Now, then. Ellie, I assume you are here about the Cinderella slippers and the unfortunate love spell that is part of them. No doubt it is woven with the demon bound to them to make it unbreakable." He looked to Rostislav for confirmation of this theory and received a slight nod.

Elam's mouth twisted with sneering disgust. "I was summoned here because Adelardi was caught consorting amorously with the witch. Lo, I arrive and find he reeks of magic, with a known troublemaker of a witch—and you."

"You know I like a problem to solve," Johnnie replied. "Are you hoping to burn a witch, brother?"

Elam regarded him coldly. "That isn't funny. I am hoping that we have not, in fact, lost one of our most valuable citizens to the machinations of an unreliable witch," Elam replied. "You will forgive me if I doubt anything you might say in defense of your questionable friendship."

Johnnie ignored the jibe; his brother had never approved of his friendship with Rostislav, but Johnnie would not give it up, not even for a chance to please Elam. "It was an accident. Rostiya asked me to come here to help him when the shoes went missing. I have been investigating."

Elam sneered, and Johnnie fought against the same hurt, the same bitterness, that he always faced when his brother so coldly dismissed his abilities. It was not much, his store of knowledge and his knack for solving problems, but it was something. But he was normal, and Elam would never believe that a normal could adequately solve abnormal problems. "What did you supposedly uncover?"

"I examined the spell cage Rostiya built to contain the shoes, upstairs in Jesse's study. They miscalculated the power of the demon bound in the shoes and the love spell woven with it. Naturally, once placed within an inadequate spell cage, the shoes woke from their dormancy and immediately sought out the nearest suitable Cinderella—Rostiya. After that, there was nothing that could be done. The nature of the slippers precludes the wearer knowing he is the victim. The 'prince' too would know nothing until too late. I was brought here to find the slippers before irreparable damage could be done, but it was done before I even arrived."

"An accident," Elam repeated with scorn. "You are telling me that Adelardi is a victim of a love spell because of a slight miscalculation?"

Johnnie laughed, his scorn the equal of Elam's, for it was Elam who had unwittingly first taught him scorn. "What do you suggest? That Rostiya would sacrifice his own reputation and standing to attach himself to a vampire? How would he profit, living the rest of his life as a taboo? It would do him more harm than good. Oh,

I know. Perhaps Jesse engineered it, bored out of his mind and curious to see if living in what amounts to exile would prove more interesting."

"Perhaps some enemy is at work," Elam snapped.

"No," Jesse said. "Those shoes have been in my unwitting possession for years, part of a collection of artifacts I've always meant to go through. I brought Rostislav in to help me sort them and properly ward them. When we realized the nature of the shoes, we immediately sought to cage them until we could summon a sorcerer to banish the demon. We underestimated them. I got cocky, and cocky is the same as careless."

Johnnie nodded and quoted, "A bad beginning makes a bad ending."

"Indeed," Jesse said, shooting him a wry look.

Turning to Elam, Johnnie asked, "What do you propose to tell father?"

"That Adelardi is a fool and the witch a greater fool, but there is little to be done about it, as it would seem that it was an accident. However," he said, turning to Jesse, "you and the witch are under house arrest until my father says otherwise. In your current state, you cannot be trusted and so shall not be. Play in your casino, but do no more. I will tend to your guests downstairs. Until such time as we can find an effective way to break the love spell, I am afraid you are quite useless. Johnnie, say your farewells if you must, then come home. We will no longer be spending our time here."

As he finished speaking, Elam called up his magic and vanished, as cold and clear a dismissal as Johnnie had ever seen. Silence fell with Elam's departure before Rostislav finally broke it. "You figured it out."

Truly annoyed for the first time all night, Johnnie said in his chilliest tones, "Of course I did."

Rostislav merely smiled. "Of course. How?"

"Your behavior in the dark corner beyond the columns by the buffet lines. The razor-thin break in the spell circle. The smell of sex and cologne. This," he finished and tossed Rostislav the ruby bracelet. "Why?"

"I'm surprised you have to ask," Rostislav said, looking at the bracelet in amusement.

Jesse cut in, "What in the hell were you doing in my rooms, and how did you get into them?"

"None of your business," Johnnie replied. "I refused to believe the reason that first presents. Vampires do not love humans, and they certainly never sacrifice their livelihoods—their lives—to be with one. Why drag me into this mess?"

"To lend the story credence," Rostislav replied. "You made it true. Everyone will believe now that it's an accident, that we are in this situation because of a mistake. It's not ideal, but it's better than keeping our relationship a secret."

Johnnie shook his head and said again, "Vampires do not love humans."

Jesse laughed. "Vampires don't like to admit it happens, which isn't the same thing. I'd rather love openly and be reviled than be accepted and love in secret, however great a fool that makes me."

"Makes us," Rostislav said and took Jesse's hand, and the look they shared was one not even Johnnie could sneer at, though he tried. Johnnie could only watch them. He hated that Rostislav had lied to him, had used him. Envy was bitter in his mouth, that Rostislav had what he so badly wanted.

Mostly, he was just sick of the matter and sorry he'd wasted his evening on being manipulated and betrayed. "Enjoy your house arrest," he finally said, not bothering to keep the curtness from his voice because, on top of everything else, Elam had forbidden him to see Rostislav again, and their father would undoubtedly stand by it. Rostiya had clearly not considered that possibility when he had decided upon this scheme and on using Johnnie to authenticate it. "I am happy that I could be of service to you, Rostislav. Should you require my services again, however," he finished bitterly, "you will have to pay for them." Brushing by them, he stalked toward the door.

"It wasn't like that!" Rostislav said, sounding hurt. Johnnie paused but did not turn back around. "I was trying to protect you, Johnnie. You're my best friend. If this scheme failed and blew up in our faces, how would it have looked for the son of the Dracula Desrosiers to be party to it? I'm selfish in doing this, but not so selfish I would truly betray a friend."

"But still selfish enough to sacrifice a friendship, since now it will be all but impossible for me to see you," Johnnie replied. He looked over his shoulder and added, "You made your choice, Rostiya, and now you must live with the consequences."

"Wouldn't you do the same damned thing?"

Johnnie turned back toward the door, not deigning to look at Rostislav as he replied, "Elam would think better of me if I conformed more. If I stopped dabbling in my mysteries, if I ceased to speak with you of my own free will, if I spent more time helping him and father instead of following my own whims and desires. Yet I have done none of those things, so the answer is no. I would not have done the same damned thing."

"So like a vampire, to expect everyone else to bend to you," Jesse said. "I meant what I said downstairs. It takes us decades to achieve the cold, arrogant pride that you wear so easily after only twenty-six years. If vampires look down upon you, it is because they are jealous you are already superior in so many ways."

Ignoring the comments, for that was all the attention they deserved, Johnnie said, "You are both fools."

"God damn it, Johnnie," Rostislav said. "Don't be this way. We're friends. I won't let you break it off."

"You made your choice," Johnnie snapped, "and apparently part of that choice was lying to me and sacrificing our friendship. You are the one who did the breaking. The next time you decide upon so mad a scheme, keep in mind that house arrest means losing *everything*."

He pushed the door open and left before anyone could speak further, angry and hurt and miserable—but he would not bend. Perhaps love was worth any and all sacrifice, but that love was of no comfort to those who *were* sacrificed.

Turning slightly to close the door, he caught a glimpse of Jesse holding Rostislav tightly. They looked beautiful together, and miserable together, and for a moment, Johnnie almost wanted to say something comforting.

Instead, he closed the door and walked away, reciting in quiet, bitter tones, "There they go, there they go. No blood's in the shoe. The shoe's not too tight. This bride is right."

Case 002: The Riddling Tale

Johnnie knew it was going to be a bad day when he woke up in the dead hours of the morning and was unable to fall back asleep. He stared at the ceiling for several minutes, anyway, willing himself to go back to sleep before at last conceding defeat.

Climbing out of his enormous four-poster bed, he padded naked across the hardwood floor of his bedroom and into the cold-tiled bathroom. It glowed a faint blue-white from a small nightlight plugged in near the door. Not bothering to turn on the overhead lights, he simply headed to the shower and turned it on. Another pale, blue-white light turned on as the water started, all the light Johnnie needed and wanted.

When the water was hot, he slid into the shower and closed the glass door behind him. Steam billowed over the top of the door, making the dark tiles glisten in the dim light. Beyond the splashing of the water, there was no sound. The clock on his nightstand had read 2:17 a.m. when he had finally climbed out of bed.

He wished he could go back to sleep. It was all the more frustrating for not having a reason for his sleeplessness; not even something as trivial as nightmares could explain it, for he did not dream.

Even worse, once he was awake, he did not sleep again the rest of the day. He had never managed to take even a nap. Reaching out, he snagged his soap and washed thoroughly, rinsing off and then washing his hair. He had never really had to bother with shaving. Finally, he dragged himself from the shower, shutting off the water and pushing open the door. He grabbed a towel from the hooks off to the right and toweled off lightly before returning to his bedroom.

Crossing the room, he went into his dressing room and reluctantly flicked on the sharp, bright overhead lights. Looking over his not inconsiderable wardrobe, he weighed his options, taking into account who might be visiting, what he would be doing, where he might go, if he would be back in time to change into evening dress, or if he would have to dress in something to accommodate night and day...

But his day was supposed to be a quiet one, and his father had announced no visitors for the day. Johnnie had no visitors, not since his only friend—

Sharply dismissing that thought, he focused on his clothing and finally settled on dark gray slacks with black pinstripes, a dark, smoky lavender shirt, and a vest to match the pants. From his jewelry case he chose a set of amethyst cufflinks. He set the matching tie pin aside, then went to his tie racks, pulling down a paisley tie in shades of gray and purple. He tied it in a Full Windsor, then arranged it properly with the vest and fastened the tie pin in place.

Going to the drawers and shelves for shoes and socks, he pulled out black for both and finished dressing. Last, he combed his hair and dabbed on a bit of his cologne, hints of apple and opium wafting through the room.

Leaving his bedroom, he walked down the hall, then down the winding stairs, and finally toward the northeast corner of the house, passing by the main library to his private library just off it. Throughout most of the house, the lights were set to work automatically. Johnnie hated it; any room that was exclusively his, he controlled the lighting himself.

Even here, in his library, no lights came on, and he most often chose to use only the barest amount required. As the room had no windows, to protect the books, he often required a great deal of light, but he contained it to where he was working.

He moved through the absolute dark with ease, as familiar with his library as he was with his own reflection. Reaching the chair where he had been reading just a few hours ago, he turned on a rose patterned Tiffany lamp.

Sitting down, he picked up the book he had been working through the past week, as well as his reading glasses. Sliding them on, he began to read. The book was, for all intents and purposes, a bestiary of abnormals. Naturally abnormals resented such a thing, but it was infinitely useful to normals who were dragged, willingly or otherwise, into the supernatural world that teemed below the surface. He owned several such compendiums, but this one was by far the most thorough and reliable. Obtaining it had put a nice dent in his savings, but the expense had been worth it. Every book he owned was worth it.

Granted, too many of the abnormals listed had nothing by them save *little or nothing is known,* but it still contained more information than any other bestiary he had obtained. Johnnie was reading it from beginning to end, despite the fact he had the contents all but memorized. Despite his efforts, in this and a few other books, he still could find no clue as to the stranger who had stolen two kisses in perfect dark.

Kisses he still remembered with crystal clarity,

though he tried to forget them, be repulsed by them. It was the mystery of it that got under his skin, the audacity of it. "What lies lurk in kisses," he muttered to the empty room. He wanted to know who would dare treat him in such a manner and laugh at the idea of facing consequences.

The wards and the vision were the key. But the wards... the wards he had checked out. As he had already known, they protected the suite from everything, even those things normally neglected, ghosts and other such creatures, which were the only ones that could see in absolute dark with such perfect clarity.

So he had not a single clue as to who had taken liberties in the dark.

Irritated all over again, he focused once more on his reading. If this bestiary turned up nothing, he would resort to other books, though as of yet, he had not decided what those would be. He might have to go in search of the proper books if nothing in his own collection or the household library proved useful.

He read the bestiary until the clock chimed five, then set it aside and moved to his work table. As tempting as it was to pursue the matter of the stranger relentlessly, obsession hindered more than it helped. A cool, collected mind served better than a feverish one.

Settling at the table, he opened his latest journal—then paused, scowling when he saw he had mistakenly opened it, not to a blank page, but to the last personal entry he had made. He used his journals for everything, from research to recounting his days to empty his mind to whatever he fancied, really. The last entry was an accounting of his assisting Rostislav. In a moment of self-mockery, recalling the way Rostislav had called him a detective, he had given the entry a mock case number and name reminiscent of a bad detective novel.

That debacle had been three weeks ago. He had neither seen nor heard from Rostislav since. No doubt that was how Rostislav preferred it, tucked away in exile with his precious vampire.

Refusing to give in to the urge to throw the journal across the room, Johnnie flipped open to a blank page and marked it with date and topic, which was a continuance of his translations and studies of a set of alchemical journals he had acquired a couple of months ago. He had found them by chance in a normal bookshop that purported to sell books pertaining to witchcraft and other such things that amounted only to normal nonsense. The books he had found amongst all the nonsense, however, were authentic, and sold for a pittance because they were old and poorly cared for, and the normals had believed them to be only junk.

As was typical of such journals, the alchemist had not put his name anywhere in it—at least, not anywhere or any way that was obvious. The contents were also written in a complex code. It had taken him the better part of a week to crack it, and he was still only halfway through translating the second of three books.

He would never be able to make practical use of what he was learning, but he had always liked learning simply for its own sake. So he worked and learned, making elaborate notes until the door opened right as the clock began to chime six.

"Good morning, Master Johnnie."

"Good morning, Lila," Johnnie greeted, pausing briefly in his work to look up and nod at his favorite of his father's servants. "Thank you for the tea."

"Of course, Master," Lila replied. "Your father said to tell you that he'll be in the morning room around ten and would like you to join him and Lord Elam there."

"Very well," Johnnie said, stifling a sigh and only smiling politely. "Convey to him that I will, of course, see them at ten." Nodding, Lila departed. Johnnie returned to his work, pausing only for the odd sip of tea. By the time the clock chimed nine thirty, he had managed to finish translating one more experiment. It was a more popular experiment amongst alchemists—the mystery of the Snow White Poison.

The exact nature of the poison used, no one knew, only that it was capable of killing nearly any and all abnormals. One of the greatest witches ever born had been killed by a single bite of poison-laced apple. Her death had been such a tragedy that the poison had forever after borne her name. Like every other alchemist who had tried to recreate the infamous poison, this one had failed, but Johnnie admired the effort and thought the man had clearly put into his work.

Sighing, he closed his journal, tidied up his work table, then slipped his glasses into their cloth case and tucked the case into a hidden pocket of his vest. Checking that every fold of fabric and strand of hair was where it should be, he left his library and walked through the halls to the main part of the house.

The morning room was heavily favored by Ontoniel Desrosiers, for it had been his late wife's favorite room. Johnnie hated the room for the very same reason; he wanted as little to do with the woman who had killed his real parents as was possible. Things tended to get very awkward indeed when they were all forced to remember that he was a Desrosiers only because the late Lady Desrosiers had gone blood crazy and killed his parents and Ontoniel had adopted him out of guilt.

His father and brother sat at the table in front of the bay window that took up most of the main wall. Ontoniel was reading the paper, while Elam studied pages of sheet music, humming softly beneath his breath. No doubt he was preparing for his recital next month. He did very little beyond play Alucard and his precious piano.

"Good morning," Johnnie greeted. "Father. Ellie."

Elam spared him a brief, withering look, and said nothing.

"John," Ontoniel greeted, folding his paper and offering Johnnie what passed for a smile with him. "How are your studies?"

"Well enough," Johnnie said cautiously, unpleasantly surprised. His father never asked about his studies. Vampires naturally admired knowledge and the pursuit of it, but Elam had informed him on several occasions that he had surpassed dedication and tipped over into crass obsession. Johnnie ignored him, especially since he had more than once provided an answer or solution when no one else could. "What is this about?"

Ontoniel sat back in his seat, folding one leg over the other, sipping specially treated blood from a gold-rimmed teacup. "I have been in negotiations for some time to find Elam a suitable bride. The matter was finally settled last night. We will be holding the betrothal ball in a few months. I wanted you to be the first to know."

Johnnie kept his voice under control, but only barely. He looked at Elam, so beautiful it hurt, so out of reach it was crushing. "Congratulations, Ellie. Who is the lucky woman?"

"Lady Ekaterina Salem," Ontoniel replied. "They're a good family: respectable lineage, affluent, well-liked and admired. I believe she and Elam will be happy and more than capable of handling the expanded territory the union will bring."

"I have not the slightest doubt all will be as you say," Johnnie said, managing to smile. He knew the name, but nothing in particular about them came to mind. That was all to the good, of course, because the less said, the less scandal, but all the same... "I assume she will be visiting soon?"

Ontoniel nodded. "Next week. She is coming with her family to stay for the weekend. I expect both of you to present yourselves at your very best. None of your usual walking around buried in books and sheet music, no gallivanting off on your strange riddle-solving trips, John, and none of your moodiness, Elam. You both know what I expect. This is the rest of your life, Elam. Treat it accordingly. John, I want them to admire you and regard you as the fine addition to the household that you are, so do not hide away with your books."

Johnnie bit back anything he might have wanted to say to that and said only, "Yes, Father."

"Yes, Father," Elam echoed.

Unable to bear another moment, Johnnie said, "I will have to begin looking for a suitable gift for the bride to be, as well as one for the newly betrothed couple. If you will pardon me, Father."

"Of course," Ontoniel replied, but absently, already focused on lecturing Elam further.

Married, Johnnie thought bleakly as he left. Elam was getting married. Bad enough that Elam barely noticed him, bad enough he could not break his love for Elam no matter how hard he tried—now he would have to watch and endure as Elam married and had children, raised his family. At least being normal had the advantage of a short life. He would not have to endure the misery for centuries, merely several decades.

He stopped halfway back to his library, the entire house suddenly stifling. Turning around, he took the stairs quickly, returning to his room to fetch a proper jacket and a light-weight coat. He was going out, and he would stay out for as long as possible.

When he was ready, he called down to have a car brought 'round. He then went downstairs and to his library, retrieving his journal and the bestiary. He lingered a moment longer to write a note for Lila to deliver to his father, then finally departed.

Outside, his personal chauffer waited patiently beside a dark gray Rolls Royce Phantom, sleek and elegant, not as ostentatious as the limos his father and brother more often used. The chauffer held the door open, then closed it behind Johnnie before walking around the car and sliding into the driver's seat. "Where would you like to go, Master Johnnie?"

"Into the city, please," Johnnie replied, staring out the window as they drove down the long drive.

"As you wish."

'The city' was four hours straight north, technically at the heart of his father's territory. But Ontoniel preferred his privacy, and so lived four hours away from the city where he conducted most of his business and social engagements. When Johnnie traveled with his family, the distance did not matter. By himself, however, the four hours must be driven.

He did not particularly mind most of the time, content to be alone with his thoughts; right then, he definitely was not, but hopefully the bestiary would distract him a bit. He really did not want to find himself thinking about Elam the whole time. His gut twisted, and he snatched up the bestiary and pulled out his glasses, desperate to distract himself from the pain. Why, he thought miserably, staring at a page discussing firebirds but not at all comprehending the words. Why must he love someone he all too often did not even like? Why must he love someone who did not even care enough to hate him, merely regarded him as an annoyance to be endured?

Why, he wondered with growing despair, did he not have anyone to turn to with his pain?

Because Rostislav had counted him amongst those things that could be sacrificed, and Johnnie could not forgive that. He stared out at the landscape, the ocean and fields passing by, muttering to his reflection in the window, "I am in that temper that if I were under water I would scarcely kick to come to the top."

"Did you say something, Master Johnnie?"

"Only to myself," Johnnie said. "My apologies. Notify me when we are a quarter of an hour away."

"Yes, Master Johnnie."

Thanking him, Johnnie looked again at the bestiary in his lap and made himself actually read it. Unfortunately, even forcing himself to read slowly and meticulously, he finished the book well before they reached his destination. Stifling a sigh, he stared out at the scenery and tried to solve the riddle of his mysterious, so-called admirer.

Heat struck, sudden and unexpected. Perhaps he was spending too much time alone of late if being all but assaulted in the dark left him flushed with stirrings of lust. He should be angry. He *was* angry. But he also remembered that hot toddy voice reciting poetry, the warmth and sticky-sweet flavor of a bold mouth taking his like the man had every right. The way he'd never really pushed further than Johnnie had allowed.

Shaking his head, he muttered, "Insanity is often logic of an accurate mind overtaxed."

Except he was not overtaxed. Quite the contrary—he was bored out of his mind and frustrated by problems he could not solve. Normally, Rostislav would appear with some puzzle or mystery for him; he had been good at distracting Johnnie and giving him interesting ways to apply all the things he knew.

But he refused to think about Rostislav, just like he refused to think about Elam. Restless, irritable, he waited impatiently for the trip to finally end. Just when he thought he could not endure a single minute more, his chauffer spoke. "Fifteen minutes away, sir."

"Drop me off downtown, by the fountain," Johnnie said. "Retrieve me there in the morning at nine o'clock."

"Yes, Master Johnnie."

"Thank you."

Twenty minutes later, Johnnie stood alone in the heart of the city. There were places aplenty he could go. No door was closed to a Desrosiers. But he did not want the clubs and restaurants and private suites and cocktail bars. He was sick of it all, sick unto death. All he wanted right then was to avoid the life that was currently making him miserable.

Abandoning the heart of downtown, he walked the streets aimlessly. People looked at him askance, especially as he reached the more questionable portions of the city, but no one bothered him. It was close to five when he finally grew sick of walking and started looking for a place to rest for a bit.

He was at the very edge of downtown, well away from any of the 'safe' portions of the city. It could be dangerous for abnormals. Normals who happened to be in the city steered clear, kept away by pure instinct.

Crossing the street, he met the eyes of three vampires watching him with obvious intent. They wore small silver pins on their jackets in the shape of a triad of roses. Visitors, rather than citizens of the territory. "Gentlemen," he said, and smiled with stiff politeness as he kept walking, hiding his smirk when he saw surprise ripple across their features as he effortlessly resisted their Venus flytrap beauty. He had not gone three steps past them when they moved, one blocking his path in front, the others coming up at his sides, hovering just so to block his retreat. Johnnie's smirk faded.

"What are you?" the ringleader asked.

"Only a normal," Johnnie said.

"You're lying, pretty boy," said one of the others, reaching out to touch Johnnie's hair.

Johnnie did not react to the touch, refusing to encourage them by showing his displeasure. Instead, he only laughed and quoted, "In heaven an angel is no one particular."

"Who are you?" the ringleader demanded again.

Johnnie shrugged and slowly lifted his gaze to meet the vampire's eyes. The man was taller, more heavily built; they all were. It would not be hard for them to do whatever they wanted to him. But he could see in their eyes that they had already figured out he was far more than he appeared. "Leave me alone," he said, "and you will not have to find out."

In silence the vampires withdrew, and Johnnie resumed his walking. Near the end of the block, just as he was considering turning around and taking a different street, a bar sign at the corner caught his eye. *The Bremen* it said, and the name appealed. Reaching it, he pushed the door open and slipped inside.

The bar had an old time pub feel, warm and discreetly lit, with old wood, leather, a fireplace in one corner and a beat up jukebox in the other, adding a touch of eclectic to the atmosphere. He ignored the momentary silence that greeted his arrival, hanging his coat and jacket up at the hooks by the door before striding to the bar itself.

He slid onto a barstool and glanced surreptitiously around. The bar was mostly empty, only eight people total including the bartender. Two men sat at a table in the center of the room, talking in low tones, a bit of anxiety in the voice of the human; the other figure was an imp. A young vampire stood at the jukebox. To judge by his appearance and manner, he could not be older than eighty, quite possibly as young as fifty.

Two more men stood at a pool table, lazily making shots and drinking beer. Another man was at a corner booth, baseball cap pulled down over his face, slumped in such a way that he was probably fast asleep. Johnnie could not tell what he was, or if he was anything at all. One other man, a witch of modest power, to judge by the feel and smell, sat several stools down at the bar, nursing a beer and chatting quietly with the bartender.

The bartender, of all things, was a lone wolf. That was a definite rarity in vampire territory, but he wore a gold rose pin that said he was an approved citizen. "Vodka rocks," Johnnie said when the bartender came over to him. He pushed money across the bar and pulled out his journal, flipping it open and pretending to read while he eavesdropped on the imp and alchemist at the table a couple of yards away, drawn by the agitated tone of the conversation.

The alchemist was clearly deeply upset by something, and the imp was trying to soothe him without real success. "I'm never going to find her," the alchemist said, fighting tears. "He's taken her, and every night he torments me with that fucking apparition—"

"It's just a stupid cane," the imp said. "Give him the damn thing, Micah."

"No!" Micah said. "I can't. If he's willing to do all this to get it, then letting him have it is a bad idea. And giving it to him doesn't mean he'll give her back. I just don't understand—it doesn't fucking do anything. It's just a cane."

The appeal of a problem to solve brushed along Johnnie's skin like a lover's touch. He took another sip of vodka, then said, "I beg your pardon, but who is 'she' and what is this cane that somebody wants badly enough to resort to kidnapping?" Around him, the bar went still again. Johnnie merely took another sip of vodka and waited.

"Who the fuck are you?" the imp at the table demanded. "You're too high-priced for a dive like this."

Johnnie ignored that. "Someone has been kidnapped; by your wedding ring and the fact you are here and not at home, I would say a wife. Given the trouble to which your assailant has gone to obtain an innocuous cane, I can only surmise it is not, in fact, innocuous. You are an alchemist, so the cane must be alchemical in nature and useful to abnormals. To judge by the condition of your clothes and your exhausted state, I would say this has been going on for weeks. Your tormentor is obviously powerful and arrogant, and he is probably a witch, a sorcerer, or an alchemist."

The alchemist stared at him, then said, "Three weeks. My wife was kidnapped three weeks ago. He can't get into my house, so he took her while she was going to work. The cane is something of a family heirloom, given to my great great great grandfather, though it's of no real use to alchemists. Uh. My name is Micah."

"Shut up," the imp snapped. "Haven't you learned by now one of his ilk is never anything but bad news?"

Micah just stared at him. "I'll take whatever help I can get." He turned back to Johnnie. "Who are you, stranger? If you do not mind my asking."

Johnnie took another sip of his vodka, then stood up and moved to the table. At the last minute, he decided not to use his real surname, and on impulse, reverted to the name he had given up shortly after turning nine. Extending his hand, he said, "Johnnie Goodnight."

"That name sounds familiar," the bartender said thoughtfully. "Dunno why."

Johnnie did not bother to jar his memory.

The imp sitting with Micah sneered. "What do you

care about our plight, Mr. Goodnight?"

"I like puzzles," Johnnie replied. "I am very good at solving them."

Surprisingly, Micah laughed. "That's as honest a reason as I've ever heard. If you want to amuse yourself by solving my problem, by all means, have a seat. Can I buy you another drink?"

"That would be most generous, thank you," Johnnie replied. He sat down and made himself comfortable, leaning back in his seat and folding his arms over his chest. "Start at the beginning and tell me everything. Leave no detail out, no matter how inconsequential it may seem."

The bartender came then with their fresh drinks, and Johnnie thanked him, handing over a generous tip because the man served excellent vodka, ice-cold even before it was put on the rocks and served in crystal. He took a sip, then repeated to Micah, "Tell me everything."

Micah nodded and took a long swallow of his beer, then started to tell his story. "Two months ago, a man came by inquiring after this old family heirloom. It's a wooden cane, painted black with a silver head carved with runes. According to family legend, it can travel across planes."

"I see," Johnnie said, seeing very well indeed. 'Across planes' meant the cane could travel to every shadowy corner of the supernatural world—earth, hell, dreams, and so forth. Normally, items did not travel with a person; not even clothing. Rare was the object which could travel all the planes. "I take it the secret to making the cane was lost?"

"Yes," Micah replied. "That is how it came into my family's possession. It's always been our task to figure out the riddle of the cane's making."

"Tell me about the man who wants it."

Micah eyed him, cautious but also amused. "Beggin' your pardon, sir, but he had an awful lot in common with you."

Johnnie smiled in amusement and quoted, "As long as there are rich people in the world, they will be desirous of distinguishing themselves from the poor."

Micah flushed. "I didn't mean—"

"No offense was taken, I assure you," Johnnie said. "So a wealthy abnormal, well-dressed and arrogant. Human?"

"A witch," Micah clarified. "I'm fairly certain he's up to some sort of darker magic and thinks the cane will help, but I don't know for certain."

"He would not be the first witch to try and cross planes," Johnnie said. "You refused to give him the cane, and so he resorted to other methods."

"Yes," Micah replied and drank more of his beer. "Every day he came back and tried to get it—money, pretty promises, and finally threats. I kept refusing. Then, three weeks ago, my wife never showed up for work. All I found when I rushed home was a note informing me that until I handed over the cane, I would never see her again—except her apparition comes to me every night and simply sits in her chair, from ten to two. Every night, for those four hours, I sit there and try my damnedest to learn something, anything, but..." He did not bother to finish the sentence.

He did not need to finish it. Apparitions were 'ghosts' of the living, most often appearing under times of duress. Some of the more dramatic stories involved apparitions appearing when the person had been buried alive, or was otherwise trapped. They could also be forced to appear, in situations like Micah's, to wear down the victim. Forcing apparitions was hard work, however, even for a highly skilled sorcerer.

Johnnie took another sip of his vodka, then another, before he stood up. "Let us go see your home, then."

"What—" Micah cut himself off and only nodded, finishing his beer, then stood and grabbed his coat from the back of his chair. He shrugged into it, then said, "Of course. I live about five blocks away."

Johnnie nodded and strode to where his own jacket and coat hung, pulling them on and then going to the bar to fetch his journal.

"You don't mind walking, do you?" Micah asked.

"Not at all," Johnnie replied.

"I'm coming, too," the imp said. "No way should you be trusting another fucking noble, Micah. I don't trust him."

Johnnie smiled, slow and razor sharp, then said, "To stop a demon, get another demon." It was part of an old abnormal saying, in reference to the more powerful supernaturals. The entire phrase went: "To stop a werewolf, get a witch/To stop a witch, get a sorcerer/To stop a sorcerer, get a vampire/To stop a vampire, get a dragon/To stop a dragon, get a demon/To stop a demon, get another demon."

"You're a normal," the imp said scathingly. "Suits and manners and arrogance don't make you abnormal. You shouldn't even be here, let alone acting like you're one of us."

"Tell me thy company, and I'll tell thee what thou art," Johnnie said. "I am what I am, accept it or not.

Your opinion means nothing to me. Micah, let us go."

Nodding, Micah led the way out and then north five blocks, until they were well out of the city proper and into the outlying townhouses. He stopped in front of a house that was blue and white, complete with a white picket fence and a pretty little stone path leading up to the house, lined with rosebushes the entire way.

Johnnie eyed all the flowers thoughtfully, pausing on the stone path leading up to the house. "You said you had protections on the house?"

"Yes," Micah replied. "It's perfectly safe—"

"What of the yard?" Johnnie asked.

"No," Micah replied. "Not really. It's damned hard work, maintaining wards and all outside. The only things I've done out here are spells to help Lisa's roses."

Johnnie smirked and indicated the rosebushes lining either side of the walkway. "Once upon a time, there were three women who were cursed, turned into flowers in a field. Over time, though, one of them was able to return to her own home at night. Then, one night, shortly before she had to return to the field before daybreak, she told her husband that if he came and picked her that afternoon, she would be forever free of the curse.

"And so that afternoon, the husband went to the field and looked upon the three flowers. They were in every way exactly alike. After a moment, the husband picked one of the flowers, and then he took his wife home."

Looking over his shoulder, Johnnie said to Micah and the imp, "The question is, how did he know which flower was his wife?"

They looked at him as though he had lost his mind, and Johnnie laughed softly. Cupping one of the roses on the bush that had caught his eye, he bent to smell it. The faintest hints of magic tickled his nose. "It rained heavily last night. I remember the sound of it, starting when I went to bed at eleven. When I first woke up at one-thirty, I could still hear it, but by the time I got out of bed after two, it had stopped. Yesterday's weather report said that it stormed here. These rosebushes all show signs of it—broken stems, strewn leaves, the soil in which they are planted is still quite damp even now, and in the curls of petals where the sun cannot reach, water remains. Except this one bush; it looks as though it has not been affected by anything for days."

He released the rose he held and turned to face Micah. "Someone turned your wife into a rosebush, which is clever. It could have been done so quickly, no one would have noticed a thing, and being so close to the house means the witch does not have to force the apparition to travel a great distance. Being close to the house also means that the residual magic of the wards kept you from feeling the magic emanating from this rosebush. "You or your friend can, I am certain, break the spell easily enough."

Looking stunned, disbelieving but so painfully hopeful, Micah reached into his jacket and extracted what was often called an alchemist's travel kit. It contained all an alchemist needed to do the most basic and common of spell work. He knelt in front of the rosebush—

"I would not do it quite yet," Johnnie said. "There is something rather curious about all this that I do not think you have realized."

Micah frowned and reluctantly stopped what he was doing. "What do you mean?"

"A sorcerer or a witch might be able to change the shape of something, but it would require a spell circle, and as whoever it was changed her here, there should be evidence of a spell circle on location—but I see no chalk, no remains of work in the grass and dirt, nothing. Not many abnormals are so magically powerful they easily can change the shape of something. Demons certainly, a good enough necromancer or sorcerer... and imps."

"What—"

Johnnie ducked as the imp swung, then threw his arms out and caught the imp at the legs, sweeping the imp off his feet. Reaching into his coat, he pulled a small silver dagger and held it to the imp's throat. Without looking away from the imp, he said to Micah, "How long have the two of you known each other?"

"A-a-couple of months," Micah said, staring wide-eyed, looking confused and hurt and uncertain.

"Do not move," Johnnie said to the imp, "and I would not try magic if I were you, either. One nick of this dagger will cause you a great deal of pain."

The imp stared at him. "How did you know I was part of it?"

"I would wager you are all of it, actually," Johnnie replied. "The plan was never to hand the cane over to the wealthy man you pretended to be. I would wager that, as Micah's friend, you eventually would have convinced him to give it to you for safekeeping or some such. Am I right?"

"How did you know that?" the imp demanded.

"You are an imp," Johnnie replied. "Any self-respecting imp would have seen that rosebush was false. I have no magical ability whatsoever and I knew immediately something about it was off. There was also the way you encouraged him to give up the cane; that is not typical of any abnormal when it comes to objects of power. Abnormals have killed and died to protect far less than a plane-crossing cane. The only thing I do not know is why. Perhaps you are not a free imp, as I first thought. Perhaps it is simply money."

The imp snarled at him. "Do you know how much someone would pay for an object that can travel the planes? The chance to unravel its making is worth a fortune."

"Money, then," Johnnie said lightly. "But you would not work for months to obtain something on the chance you could sell it, so you must have been paid in advance. Who is paying you?"

"That is none of your business," the imp snapped. "Kill me, go ahead, but I promise that you will regret it."

Johnnie threw his head back and laughed, then abruptly withdrew his dagger, sheathed it, and reached into his pocket to extract one of his business cards. He dropped it on the imp's chest and stood. "Take that and give it to your master. Inform him that if I want to kill his imp, I will do so at my leisure and do not care if he takes issue."

Frowning, the imp sat up and looked at the card—then went pale. "You said your name was Goodnight."

"I lied," Johnnie replied lightly. "You may go, on the proviso that you never trouble anyone in this city again."

The imp fled.

Micah stared after him, then at Johnnie. "I—I don't even know what to say. I thought he was my friend."

Johnnie's mouth twisted with bitterness, and he agreed by quoting, "An open foe may prove a curse/But a pretended friend is worse." He motioned to the rosebush. "I would save your wife, now."

Though he nodded in agreement, Micah made no move to do so. "Who are you?"

"Johnnie Goodnight," Johnnie replied. "But he will trouble you no more, though I suspect the cane you hide is worth a great deal of trouble."

Micah stared at him a moment, frowning pensively. He abruptly spun around and strode toward the house, calling over his shoulder, "Wait one moment, if you please." Curious and amused, Johnnie obeyed. Three minutes later, Micah returned, holding a long, thin wooden box. Opening it, he presented the box to Johnnie. "This is what he wanted."

Johnnie took the cane, unable to refuse the offer, utterly captivated. It was precisely as Micah had described—smooth wood, painted black. The top of it flared out slightly, a solid silver handle carved all over with ornate runes. The very tip was silver as well, and though it was clearly old, it obviously had been well cared for over the years.

It also had a strange weight and heft to it. Studying the runes thoughtfully, Johnnie then pressed down on one of them and gave the top of the cane a sharp twist—and drew out the hidden blade, cutting the air sharply. "A cane sword. That does better explain why they so badly wanted it. A sword that can cross the planes is infinitely more valuable than a mere cane. Exquisite. Thank you for permitting me to see it."

"Keep it."

Johnnie paused and looked at Micah, for once wholly and genuinely surprised. "It is a family heirloom, and a valuable and dangerous one. You have known me not more than an hour. Why would you tell me to keep it? I thought you studied its secrets."

"I know how to make such items; my family has always known," Micah said. "We lie because the price of the making is too high. I am sick of the damned thing. It nearly cost me my wife. It suits you; no one else who ever saw it deduced its true nature, but you figured it out in a matter of seconds."

"Then I thank you," Johnnie said. "I will keep it close, and promise that never will it fall into the wrong hands."

Micah waved his words aside. "Thank you for finding my wife. Nothing I can give you can repay that."

"We will call it even, then," Johnnie replied and smiled. "I will leave you here, to restore your wife. I bid you good day." Sketching a half-bow, he lifted his new cane in farewell, then turned and walked away, heading briskly back to the Bremen.

Removing his coat and jacket, he kept the cane and returned to the stool in which he had first sat. Without a word, the bartender brought him a vodka rocks. "Micah gave that to you."

"Yes," Johnnie said, sipping his drink. "He and his wife are fine now. The imp will not be returning." From his vest, he extracted his glasses and a pen. Taking another sip of his drink, he then began to write out all that had happened that day, recounting the 'case' in detail.

He did not stop until he was finished and fully satisfied with the results. When he finally closed the journal and looked up, he realized the hour was late and the bar deserted save for himself and the bartender.

"You've been busy," the bartender said. "Did you want another drink?"

"Just water," Johnnie said. "You have a very nice bar."

"Thanks," the bartender said. "Name's Peyton Blue. It's taken me all night, but I finally remembered where I know your name. You're the adopted son."

Johnnie sipped the glass of water Peyton gave him. "I prefer to be called Johnnie."

Peyton nodded and smiled. "Johnnie it is, then. Everyone who wanders into the Bremen is welcome."

"Thank you," Johnnie said. "Can you recommend a decent room for the night?" He really did not want to go back to his part of the city until tomorrow morning.

"You can have the rooms upstairs. Just threw out my last tenant, finished cleaning them up yesterday. They're good as new. Micah called while you were writing, told me all you did. For that, you can have the room free."

Johnnie started to argue, but then left it alone. "Thank you. I believe I will head that way now, then."

"Go on through that door to the back room, can't miss the stairs."

Thanking him again, Johnnie followed the directions, climbing a small flight of stairs up to what proved to be a small but handsome apartment along the same look and feel of the bar below. There was a large main room that was kitchen and living area combined, a bathroom in one corner, and two doors leading to what must be bedrooms.

He moved toward the nearest of the two rooms—

Then everything went pitch black. Johnnie's skin prickled, the scent of myrrh and musk roses filling the air, and he could not help but draw a sharp breath. "You again."

The hot-toddy voice washed over him, making him shiver despite himself. "I could say the same; I did not think to see you once, let alone twice."

"What do you hope to gain by all this presumptuous, melodramatic behavior?" Johnnie asked coolly. The man laughed again, and Johnnie realized suddenly that they were only a step apart. Fingers glided across his face, and he reached up to smack the hand away, furious with both of them when his hand only wound up captured.

Warm lips pressed a firm kiss to the back of his hand. "I admit I thought to see you once and never again, and sought only to play a bit with you, steal a kiss or two. But I find myself obsessed and in want of more kisses. I think what I hope to gain by all this presumptuous, melodramatic behavior is the sound of you screaming in pleasure while I fuck you."

Johnnie jerked back, ignoring the way the words affected him, not quite certain he ever wanted to face how the words affected him—but to no avail, for the stranger was stronger than he, and clearly determined, and only pulled Johnnie flush against him. Then Johnnie was being kissed, hard and sure and possessive, held fast by arms that were like bands against a hard chest, and he did not know what to do except hope the assault ended soon.

Except it did not really feel like an assault, and it was all too easy to return the ardent kiss that affected him in ways no other ever had. The few people he'd bedded, he'd been just as content to see leave again. He should be pushing this man away, demanding apologies and punishment. But his mouth was hot and talented and Johnnie could not entirely deny he was intrigued and turned on. As the man's arms loosened so hands could roam, Johnnie could not keep himself from shivering. He tried to picture Elam's face, match the shape of the shadow with the form of the man he loved, but Elam's image slipped away with every new touch.

"Why do you hide in the dark?" he managed, flinching at the breathless quality of his own voice. "Are you too cowardly to face the light?"

The stranger only kissed him again, until Johnnie could scarcely breathe and was left panting and unsteady on his feet when the kiss finally broke. "Greedy," the man murmured. "I want to be the only one who sees you."

"That does not explain why you will not let me see you," Johnnie replied. "You have something to hide."

"Only myself," the stranger said, and abruptly grabbed hold of Johnnie's coat and shoved it off his shoulders, then did the same with his jacket, until Johnnie was trapped in a tangle of fabrics, arms pinned by the clothes and the wall against which he was pressed. His mouth was taken with ravenous force, and he could do nothing but go along with it. He should have been fighting the assault, struggling to get away, but every time he thought about it, he was kissed again and all ability to think shattered.

He moaned softly, unable to bite back the sound, letting his head fall to the side as a hungry mouth attacked his throat. "Are you Eros, sneaking around the dark and hiding yourself until a moment of your choosing?" In his arms, the stranger went suddenly stiff and still. Johnnie frowned and started to speak—but then realized he was alone in the room, threads of city light slipping through the curtains, and then the overhead light flickered back on.

What had that been about? What was going on? Damn it, he would figure out the mystery of his shadowy, amorous visitor if it was the last thing he did. It did not help at all that the man's abrupt departure had left him hard and aching, and why was he so willing to let a stranger in the dark consume him when his every waking moment was filled with trying not to think about Elam?

Balling his hands into fists, he slowly righted his disheveled clothes and trudged into the bedroom, body still tight and hard with thwarted passion, mind in shambles, and feeling more alone and rejected than ever.

Case 003: The Bremen

Johnnie took a sip of tea as he perused his newest book. It was not answering the question preying most upon his mind, but it was teaching him other things, so it was not a complete loss. He took another sip of tea, enjoying the book, the morning sunlight spilling through the bank of windows on the eastern wall, the warm calm—the peace.

He might have been getting less and less sleep, and he might have been going mad between watching Elam and his fiancée and thoughts of that second encounter with his strange Eros, but mornings like this, it was easy to enjoy the moment and pretend everything was fine.

Who was Eros, damn it? More importantly, *what* was he? Johnnie did not know anyone or anything that could bypass wards and come and go so easily. It was maddening that he had so little to go on. Beyond the strange magical abilities, he knew his assailant was educated, bold to the point of insanity, magically powerful—and as much as Johnnie hated to admit it, the man could kiss.

He could do a great deal more than kiss. Johnny was more disappointed than he liked to admit, given the entire situation, that he had somehow driven the man away before he could enjoy that great deal more. His body ached with want if he thought about that thwarted night too long. What did it say about him that he had enjoyed those strange encounters that he should have feared?

Closing his book with a snap, he dropped it on the table and finished his tea, shifting to stare out the bank of windows to the flower garden beyond. He needed to stop obsessing. He needed to stop wishing it was Elam because it definitely was not. He needed to stop feeling as though he were betraying Elam, and his feelings for Elam, because the truth was that Elam could not care less about him.

Stifling a sigh, he poured more tea and picked his book back up. It was infuriating that he could not find an abnormal that fit the description. Sipping his tea, he resumed reading. He paused several minutes later when the sound of the door opening drew his attention. He stared in surprise. "Good morning, Father."

"John," Ontoniel greeted and took a seat caddy-corner to Johnnie. "You have been more reserved than usual lately; not to mention we scarcely see you anymore."

Closing his book again, Johnnie set it aside and took a sip of tea. "My apologies? I am attempting to stay out of the way while Ellie courts his fiancée and the wedding plans are begun. My presence is only superfluous. That aside, I have been consumed by a particularly tricky puzzle of late. Did you require something?"

"No," Ontoniel said, regarding him pensively. "I wanted only to see how you faired. You are family; you should be part of everything."

"I am certain I shall come in handy should someone misplace a ring or a glove," Johnnie replied. "Until then, I doubt I am missed overmuch."

Ontoniel frowned. "I am not convinced you are at

ease. You seem troubled of late."

"Only my puzzle causes me trouble, Father," Johnnie assured him, more than a little discomfited by the show of concern. It was not typical for Ontoniel to worry about him. He must want very badly indeed for the wedding to go well.

"What is this puzzle?" Ontoniel asked.

Johnnie hesitated, but whatever his motives, his father had asked after him. It would not kill him to discuss the matter with someone else, even if he preferred not to consult others unless strictly necessary. "I am trying to determine what manner of abnormal can come and go with a thought. I mean quite literally appear and disappear in the span of a heartbeat. He can also bypass wards without effort, no matter how thorough and strong they are, and can see in the dark with daylight clarity."

Ontoniel was silent, obviously lost in thought. Finally, he asked, "Have you met this abnormal, or is this one you have only heard about?"

"I have met him twice," Johnnie said. "Always in absolute dark; he seems to have some sway over that as well.

"I see," Ontoniel said, brows lifting. "That... sounds only like a creature that does not actually exist. Even abnormals have their myths and legends. Every race has its fictional monsters to explain what cannot otherwise be explained or to romanticize the truly frightening and make it easier to bear. What you describe sounds like a legend, a being from another plane, one who can move between planes with impunity."

Which was practically impossible. Once moved across planes, creatures tended to stay put, or remain only for a brief stay. One classic example was the dream plane: those who entered it only stayed for a brief time. But those who dwelt in the dream plane, succubi and the like, never left it. Hell was another well-known example: demons left, summoned by those who would harness their power. But once out of hell, they rarely went back. Angels, too, were often pulled from their plane and given corporeal form.

Precious few were the abnormals who could move across the planes as they chose. They were called Walkers, those who could walk across the planes, and of those, only one had ever actually been confirmed—Black Dogs, and very rarely did anyone encounter one of those. Otherwise, it was all myth and legend and unconfirmed sightings.

So he was being molested by something that did not exist. The thought should irritate him. He *did* find it frustrating, but like all real mysteries that fell across his path, it only made his blood run hot in thrilled determination. It was as heady as the kisses he could not forget no matter how hard he tried. "So he is merely clever. That was my conclusion, but it still leaves me wondering what he is that he could seem to be something that does not exist." Perhaps he would be better served to find the true motive for the man's behavior and then deduce from there what he was—yes, that was perfect.

"He is not merely a clever human?" Ontoniel asked. "Give that lot magic and they can be too crafty for anyone's peace of mind."

"No, he was too powerful magically to be even a sorcerer; I could smell it on him. He had to be on a par with at least an imp." He drummed his fingers on his book.

Ontoniel seemed to hesitate, then said, "What about a half-breed? The history of abnormals is rife with the consequences of mixing races."

"I am considering that, but his abilities should still be present somewhere, and so far I have only found abilities that come close. I suppose I should better factor in how those that are close might alter if crossed with other races." His head hurt thinking about it.

Silence fell for what seemed several minutes, but could not have been more than a couple, before Ontoniel said, "More than likely, this stranger of yours is an imp or something. However..."

"However?"

"However, demons and angels are not the only ones to have forever crossed their planes and settled here. I once heard of a succubus who managed to leave the dream plane and become a normal human. The degree of veracity to the tale, I could not tell you, but in light of such an outlandish description, I suppose the possibility must be considered."

Johnnie frowned pensively at his book, then quoted, "How often have I said to you that when you have eliminated the impossible, whatever remains, however improbable, must be the truth?" He looked up. "I will need better books. Where did you hear this tale of the succubus turned human?"

"Ages past, and I believe I was still buried somewhere in Eastern Europe at the time," Ontoniel said. "I cannot even recall who told me. More than—" A knock at the door made him pause, then call for the knocker to enter. The door was opened by a servant, who approached and gave a letter to Johnnie.

Rostislav? But even as he thought it, Johnnie dismissed it. Letters were not Rostislav's style. If he had any interest in seeing Johnnie, he would simply have shown up somewhere, sat down next to him, and ordered a drink. If had been nearly two months now since his falling out with Rostislav; there definitely was nothing coming from that quarter. Accepting the letter and thanking the servant, he examined it. Cheap paper and ink, and he was immediately caught by the name on the front of the envelope: *Johnnie Goodnight*. Opening the envelope, he pulled out the letter.

Johnnie,

I'm sure this is presuming, but I'm at my wits end. I send a letter to be as discrete as possible, since I know enough about vamps to know that would be appreciated.

I don't have any right to ask, but I also don't have anywhere else to turn for help. You helped Micah out, and so I was kind of hoping you'd help me. These past two weeks, someone has been harassing me, vandalizing the Bremen, roughing up my customers. I think someone is trying to shut me down, but I don't know who or why. None of my efforts to figure it out have come to anything.

Any help you can offer would be appreciated, and I would certainly pay you back to the best of my ability.

~Peyton

Johnnie folded the letter and slid it back into its envelope, then tucked the envelope into an inner pocket of his black and silver checked vest. He stood up. "I am sorry to depart so abruptly, Father, but there is a problem requiring my attention."

"A problem? Who is in trouble that would go directly to you instead of through me? Is it Rostislav—"

"Not Rostiya," Johnnie said, then could have kicked himself for using the diminutive of Rostislav's name, as though they were still friends and he could still do that. "This is something else entirely, and a trifling. My presence is not required here today, anyway. It will give me a good reason to stay out of the way. If I am to be absent overlong, I will send you word. Thank you for assisting me with my puzzle." He pulled his jacket down from where he had hung it on a hook near the door, smoothing the black fabric into place, adjusting his dark aquamarine tie. Then he tucked his reading glasses away and retrieved his cane from where he had propped it against the table.

Striding to the house phone at the edge of the buffet table, he picked it up and said, "My car, please. Tell Lila to see that an overnight bag is packed for me. I will require the sapphire, forest, dark crimson, and turquoise ensembles. Thank you."

Ontoniel frowned. "Where are you going? It is not like you to run off."

"Someone needs my help," Johnnie said, "and you know I like a good mystery. I cannot imagine I will be gone longer than a day, two at the most." Departing, he strode to the front door and slipped into the coat a servant held out for him. He stepped outside and waited patiently as the car was brought around and Lila arrived with his clothes and travel case, packing it all in the car with utmost care. "Thank you, Lila."

"My pleasure, Master Johnnie," Lila replied, smiling at him. She was the only other person permitted to touch his clothing, and only because she had taken care of it when he was still too young to know what he was doing. Closing the trunk, Lila bustled back into the house—pausing to give a hasty bow as Ontoniel suddenly appeared on the steps.

"Father," Johnnie said, pausing just in front of the car door being held open by a servant.

"I do not like this gallivanting off," Ontoniel said.

Johnnie considered his reply and finally settled on, "Please all, and you will please none. We are both unhappy with my current state, father. At least by doing this, I will be happier with myself."

In reply, Ontoniel only sighed. "I should forbid it, but I will only order you to take utmost care in regards to what you say and do. They are not married yet, and I will not have you jeopardizing the engagement with this eccentric behavior."

Johnnie nodded and managed to say, "I have no interest in seeing Elam's future demolished, most definitely not by my actions. Good day, Father."

"John."

Sliding into the car, Johnnie waited impatiently as his driver was sternly admonished by his father. Finally, however, they were off, and he gave orders to take him into the city. The four-hour journey was interminable; once whetted, his appetite for a mystery ached to be sated.

When they finally reached the city, however, he resisted the temptation to have his driver take him straight to the bar. The less his father knew, the better, and Johnnie was no fool—the servants were required to report everything to Ontoniel.

Once the car was out of sight, with instructions to deliver Johnnie's belongings to his family's city lodgings, he quickly left the heart of downtown and made his way north to the more derelict sections, headed straight for the Bremen.

When he reached it, the acrid smell of smoke was the first thing to greet him, though it was clear the fire that had caused it had been extinguished. The second thing to greet him was a collection of startled, disbelieving faces. They were all the same, minus one backstabbing imp: the young vampire, Micah smiling in greeting, the two men at the pool table, the man in the corner with baseball cap pulled low, the witch at the bar, and Peyton. "Johnnie!" Peyton greeted eagerly, breaking into a smile. "You—did you get my letter, then? I can't believe—thank you for coming!"

Johnnie acknowledged the words with a nod and removed his coat and jacket, hanging them on the hooks by the door before moving to the bar and taking the same stool in which he had sat before. Reaching into his vest, he pulled out Peyton's letter. "I did receive it. Your bar smells like there was a fire in the kitchen; the fire is related to your note."

The words were more statement than question, but Peyton nodded in answer anyway. "Yeah, it's only the latest problem plaguing me." He slid a crystal glass across the bar toward Johnnie.

Nodding in thanks, Johnnie took a sip of the chilled vodka, then said, "So tell me everything."

Wiping his hands off on a rag at his waist, double-checking his other customers were set, Peyton moved closer to Johnnie and recounted his problems. "Started just a few days ago. Small things at first:

orders going missing, shit in the alleyway torn up. Then a few of my regulars here were harassed on the street, advised to stay away. Yesterday, I came in early like always and found every last piece of glass in the place completely shattered, minus the windows. The guys pitched in and helped me clean up, else I'd still be working on it. This morning, the stove caught on fire when I tried to use it. Barely got out of the way in time. If not for Walsh," he motioned to the witch at the end of the bar, "I wouldn't have a bar. I'm afraid that harassing my regulars will soon turn into assaulting them."

Johnnie drummed his fingers on the bar. "You have no idea why someone would do this? An angry customer? A competitor? Someone interested in buying you out?"

Peyton laughed. "Buy me out? This place ain't worth that much effort. I love her dearly, but the Bremen was barely making ends meet when I bought her off Lynette five years ago. I make enough, but not much more than that. When I first bought it, I renamed it and had all sorts of plans for improvement, but I haven't been able to get anywhere with them. Nobody would want this place, not unless they went forward with my plans or some of their own, and frankly, there are better spots in the city."

He did not have to bother saying that most of those better spots would not be available to a lone wolf who had probably been kicked out of his pack. Given he had said his last name was Blue, though, and all the trouble that pack had endured over the past several years... but even with the Dracula granting him citizenship, some people would never unbend.

"What were your plans?" Johnnie asked, curious.

"To buy the empty building next door, expand the whole place, add a stage. I'd get more business with a larger dive that did live music." He shrugged. "It's definitely not going to happen now, not when I've got glassware to replace and a kitchen to redo. That's why I wrote to you. I need this to stop before I'm left with nothing."

Johnnie nodded. "I will certainly do my best. If no motive is immediately present, then we must widen our scope. Have you heard of anyone else having such problems?"

Peyton stared at him in surprise. "Hadn't thought of that."

"Then we shall start there," Johnnie said, not relishing the thought because it would get back to his father that much faster that he was wandering around the less savory parts of the city solving mysteries.

"I can do that," Micah said. Johnnie frowned because wandering around town might be a bad idea, but he was capable of it. Micah sat down next to him and grinned. "They're more likely to talk to me than you, Mr. Fancy."

Johnnie rolled his eyes, but conceded the point. "The help would be appreciated. In the meantime, I will see what I can learn from the fire and the other attacks."

Micah stood, then motioned to the witch at the far end of the bar. "Come on, Walsh. You can help. You know the east corner better than I do."

Rolling his eyes, Walsh nevertheless finished his beer and stood up, raking back his shaggy black hair and shrugging into an old, beat up, brown corduroy jacket. Waving to Peyton, he nodded to Johnnie as he passed, pulled on an equally worn flat cap, and followed Micah out of the bar.

Turning back to Peyton, Johnnie asked, "May I see the kitchen?"

"You can have the run of the place," Peyton said. "Whatever you need."

"Thank you," Johnnie said and stood up. He stopped as he turned away and turned back again. "I do not suppose someone would be willing to fetch my belongings? I brought them along, in case this took me longer than a few hours, but I was forced to leave them at my rooms in the Hummingbird Building."

Peyton snorted in amusement. "Sure. You want the upstairs room again?"

"If that is possible," Johnnie said.

"Of course it's possible," Peyton replied. He turned and called out, "Hey, G-man. Wake up!"

Over in the corner, the dozing man stirred. He sat up slowly and shoved back his baseball cap, revealing a rather plain-featured, clean-cut man. His eyes were still foggy with sleep as he grumbled out a rough, "Huh? What?"

"Run me an errand, man," Peyton said. "Hoof it to the Humm-B and fetch the belongings of Johnnie Goodnight."

"Give them this," Johnnie said and held out one of his business cards, his signature on the back so they would know it was definitely upon his request.

G-man blinked at Peyton, then at Johnnie, then slowly stood up. He removed his hat, raked his hair back, then shoved the cap back on. "Fine," he grunted, "but I want a beer when I get back." He did not wait for an answer, just took the business card and left

Peyton chuckled at Johnnie's expression. "G-man is always like that. Don't mind him. He's a huge help around here."

Johnnie shrugged. "It makes no difference to me. I appreciate his assistance. The kitchen?"

"Through that door. Call if you need me."

Nodding, Johnnie strode through the indicated door and into the kitchen. He wrinkled his nose at the stench, grimacing at the wreckage. Really, only the process of elimination and Peyton's comments about the fire starting with it allowed him to identify the wreck as the stove. The fire had spread to the counters, the floor, scorched the ceiling... It was painfully clear that if Walsh had not been on hand to stop it, the fire could have very well succeeded in destroying the entire bar.

He knelt as close to the mess as he dared get and closed his eyes, breathing in the smells. Smoke, charred metal, melted plastic, traces of food and grease... and a hint of magic, so faint that he almost thought he was imagining it. There was the possibility it was traces of the witch magic that had stopped the fire, but he did not think so. He had smelled chalk and magic in the bar, so Walsh had probably used a spell circle to stop it. There was also the fact that the smell of magic seemed tangled with the fire, not laid over it.

So there was definitely an abnormal behind the attacks. Not that it was a surprise, or narrowed down possible motives, but at least abnormals he knew. For all that he was technically one of them, he knew absolutely nothing about normals.

Opening his eyes and standing up, he looked around the kitchen and weighed his options. Walking toward the back, he opened the door and glanced out into the alley. He winced for his shoes and slacks as he noted the amount of filth and grime, but ventured out anyway. Reaching the dumpster, he used a handkerchief to open the lid and then lift out a trash bag that proved to be filled with broken glass.

Throwing the bag on the ground, he opened it and examined the shards of glass. Unfortunately, if magic had been used in the breaking, it did not show in the shards. But it would not, necessarily. Whoever was behind the vandalism had needed to be present to set the fire but had been good enough to break the glassware from a distance.

Frowning thoughtfully, Johnnie returned the bag to the dumpster, then picked his way gingerly through the muck and back inside. Once there, he found a clean place to sit down and tried to salvage his shoes. Damn it. He much preferred drawing room mysteries that did not get suspicious substances all over his person. When his shoes were as clean as they were going to get, he strode back out to the bar proper.

"Hey, Johnnie," Peyton greeted. "G-man just got back. I told him to take it all upstairs. Walsh called to say they found one other place, but were still looking around. I was going to order pizza, would you like any?"

Johnnie blinked. "What is pizza?"

Peyton's jaw dropped. "What do you mean *what.* You've never had pizza?" Johnnie just looked at him, not bothering to voice what everyone was clearly thinking: that someone of his position did not eat the same things they did.

Over by the jukebox, the vampire snorted and wandered over to the bar. "You're stamped 'vampire elite' in sparkly fluorescent pink ink, pretty boy. The clothes, the airs, no concept of real food? Not to mention the pretty. There's only one normal I've ever heard of who could pass as vampire nobility, and his last name sure ain't 'Goodnight'."

Johnnie regarded him coolly. "So far as anyone here is concerned, that is my last name."

The vampire lifted his hands in surrender. "Hey, man. I didn't say it was a problem. It ain't. I'm just saying it's sad you've never had pizza." He extended one hand. "Name's Heath Rochester. Call me Heath."

Johnnie shook hands. "A pleasure to meet you."

Heath grinned. "You really could be a vamp; it's sort of spooky." Johnnie dismissed the words with a shrug. Heath smiled ever so briefly, as though amused by something, but only motioned to the guys at the pool table. "That's Chuck and Nelson. I think you more or less met everyone else. It's cool you came to help—don't know many of your lot who would."

His lot. Johnnie almost rolled his eyes at that, but in the end let it go.

"So, pizza?" Peyton asked.

"Totally," Heath replied and clapped Johnnie on the shoulder. "Order up a good variety, Peyt. Let's see what our new friend likes." New friend, ha. It was unfortunate that both Heath and Peyton knew who he was, and chances were that if those two knew, by now everyone knew, and so he probably should not come here again.

But it had been nice, he acknowledged with a burst of sad wistfulness, not to be seen first as Ontoniel's adopted human son. He was regarded as a rich, haughty pretty boy here, but he had left a greater impression in the way he had helped out Micah. He liked that.

Reclaiming his barstool, he took a sip of the vodka still sitting there. "It was definitely an abnormal who set the kitchen on fire. Given the nature of the attacks, I would say it was the attacker himself who did the fire, rather than hiring someone else to break in and do it. Hopefully Micah and Walsh will bring back useful information."

Peyton sighed. "I hope so."

"So how did you decide on the name of your bar?" Johnnie asked.

Peyton grinned. "I can see you already know the answer. It was about six years ago, now. I'd just quit Blue because of crap that went down and was going to keep going down. That pack went bad a long time ago. Anyway, I was drowning my sorrows in beer with my last twenty when I met this guy named Jack. He'd just ditched a problem situation of his own, was looking to follow his dream of being a singer. I could strum a guitar well enough; it was about the only thing I hadn't yet pawned. He had a gig, was good at getting them, so we palled around together for a bit. Wasn't really my thing, but hey, it was better than moping. A couple months later, we met this guy Roosevelt. He did drums, needed a new band. He also had a bassist friend, called himself Cat. So we played for a bit together, did all right. It was my idea to call us Bremen Town, 'cause it was a lot like the old story, yeah?"

"Then what?" Johnnie asked, as obviously the band had not stayed together.

"We came here," Peyton said. "We weren't real big, so we had odd jobs to supplement what we made when we got a gig. I worked here, serving drinks and bouncing the occasional problem. Cat fell into music tutoring. Last I heard, he'd gotten a degree and was a proper teacher and shit. Roosevelt owns a bed and breakfast; it's just outside the city on the west side.

We all found things we'd rather be doing, and our hearts just weren't in the music anymore. Eventually we broke up. We were all cool with it, except Jack. He always hated us, claimed we were just using him and all." Peyton shrugged. "I hear about him from time to time. Last I heard he was still singing and doing well for himself. Me, I like serving beer."

Heath laughed. "You like lording it over the six drunks who keep you in business. Speaking of, business must be booming with Mr. Fancy Pants here ordering vodkas all over the place."

Peyton flipped Heath off. "This places closes, jackass, you'll have to find a new watering hole on which to waste your trust fund."

Making a face, Heath only said, "Water me."

Rolling his eyes, Peyton moved to a special cooler below his shelves of liquor and pulled out a bottle of dark green glass wrapped with a black, green, and silver label. Blood wine, Johnnie recognized. Vampires had a million and one ways to enjoy the only sustenance they required, even if the traditional method remained the favorite.

Setting the bottle and a wine glass in front of Heath, Peyton took the twenty Heath held out, then moved down the bar to refill drinks, including a fresh vodka for Johnnie. He also set a fresh beer on the bar, two stools down from Johnnie.

A minute later G-man appeared and moved immediately to the waiting beer. "Thanks," he told Peyton.

Johnnie half-turned to face him. "Thank you for getting my belongings."

G-man shrugged. "Forget it. Wasn't doing anything else, and the way they tried to get information out of me, I can see why you didn't want to go yourself."

Johnnie nodded in agreement. "I have no doubt they are under orders to keep me there once I appear."

G-man rolled his eyes. "A blood sucker tried to tail me, but he sucks at it. I lost him down on fourth."

Lifting one brow, Johnnie said, "You have experience with being followed?"

Peyton and the others laughed. "Yeah, he's good at that shit. He's like some secret agent, government spy type. That's why he's G-man."

"I see," Johnnie said. "So what—" he stopped as the door opened and a man came in bearing boxes that clearly contained food. The pizza, he supposed.

"Set'em on the tables," Peyton ordered and handed over the necessary cash. "Thanks, man." The delivery man nodded and departed, and Peyton set Chuck and Nelson to squaring everything away, including bringing Johnnie a plate. Acutely aware of all eyes on him, but somehow amused rather than annoyed, Johnnie obediently picked up a piece as he saw someone else do, and took a bite.

It certainly was not the four-star cooking of his father's chef, or anything like the food at the restaurants and cafés where he infrequently dined. It was greasy and salty and seemed made of nothing but cheap cheese and questionable meat. But he did not hate it. "Not bad," he finally said, setting the piece down and wiping his hands on the napkin Peyton offered him.

Laughing, the others dug into their own food, demanding more beer from Peyton. Johnnie slowly ate own pizza; the one with vegetables was so far his favorite of the options provided. He watched his companions surreptitiously as they all ate—Peyton at the bar, eating between replenishing drinks, G-man back in his corner, cap pulled low as he nursed a beer and slowly work through the pile of pizza on his plate, Nelson eating enough for three though he was half the size of everyone else in the room, Chuck barely eating at all, Heath nibbling almost playfully while he drank his wine.

Throughout, they talked and laughed and joked. Clearly they were all good friends, despite their colorful mix of races. In his circles, vampires did not mingle with lone wolves, never mind imps and low-level alchemists and witches.

Johnnie's stomach clenched at the thought of witches. Try as he might, he missed Rostislav. Being a much more powerful witch, Rostislav could have helped with the case. The bar would have amused and pleased him. Johnnie wished he were there. He would have been vastly amused that Johnnie had a 'case' at all. "The more he looked inside the more Piglet wasn't there," Johnnie muttered the quote to himself and tossed back the last of his vodka. "Water," he said when Peyton shot him a silent query. He finished off the last few bites of his vegetable-laden pizza and pushed the rest away.

Micah and Walsh would be back soon. Unfortunately, there was not much more he could investigate. He could ask about the harassment, but he sensed he already knew where that ended, which was in nothing useful. "So who was harassed and by whom?" he asked the room.

"Me," Nelson replied. "Walsh and Micah, too. I guess they thought we would be easy targets. Just came up, shoved us around a bit, told us if we didn't stop coming to the Bremen, we'd regret it." Nelson rolled his eyes. "Different guys for each of us, just a few Joes hired to harass. We can probably hunt them out, but I doubt it would go anywhere."

Johnnie shook his head. "No, guys like that are just paid to do a job. They do not ask the details, and no one gives them. We will wait and see what Micah and Walsh have to say."

"Probably not for a couple more hours, if they're playing gumshoe," Peyton replied.

Nodding, Johnnie stood up. "I am going to go situate my belongings. Call me immediately if they return or if something else happens."

"Sure," Peyton said and waved him off.

It should have felt strange, really, striding with such familiarity through the bar to the back and then up the stairs to the apartment above. But he only felt oddly proprietary—and despite repeated admonitions to himself, the beat of his heart increased with anticipation. Like the suite in Jesse's hotel, he could not think about the rooms above the Bremen without thinking about Eros.

He pushed the door open and slipped inside, closing the door behind him again. He looked around the space. It really was a tidy little set of rooms. The living area was generous, the bathroom adequate, and he did not care about the kitchen because he had very little use for one. It could all use a bit of touching up, some cosmetic changes here and there, but overall...

What was he hoping, that he could live here? He had pressed his luck as it was, defying his father just that morning. If he dared to tell Ontoniel he was moving out and planning to live above a bar in the worst part of the city... And it was a bad idea, anyway.

Peyton and Heath knew who he was, which meant *everyone* knew who he was, and he sincerely doubted they would want him there much longer than it took to solve the case.

The idea appealed, however, no matter all the reasons it shouldn't. He could all too easily imagine his belongings there. If he fronted the money for the expansions Peyton wanted to make, he could expand the upstairs as well, meaning there would be more than enough room for his books and clothes and whatever else he brought with him.

He strode across the living area to the rightmost bedroom, the one that contained no windows. It would make an ideal library, and the second room would be his bedroom. He stood in the middle of the room, imagining, wishing there was a way to make the dream a reality. Now that he had thought of it, he very badly wanted it.

The light flicked off, and Johnnie whipped around right as the door clicked shut. Hands sank into his hair in the next breath, and before he could say a word, a mouth took his in a ravenous, bruising kiss. Johnnie meant to push him off, get some space, resolve this strange matter once and for all—but his fingers only gripped the soft cotton of the man's shirt. Johnnie kissed back hungrily, even though he should not, even as it ached because he was so tired of living with someone who barely acknowledged him and wanting someone who would only kiss him in absolute dark.

But what a kiss. The few one-night stands in his past, desperate attempts to banish Elam from his mind, had never felt anything like Eros's kisses. Johnnie should have been afraid, angry, or at least offended, but it was hard to think of anything except the hot mouth plundering his like he belonged to Eros. Johnnie wanted to know how the hands gripping his hair would feel on the rest of his body.

Eros finally tore away, and Johnnie had trouble gathering his thoughts. All he could focus on was his breathing. Finally gathering enough air, he said, "I did not think I would encounter you again."

Angling Johnnie's head, Eros nipped his ear, nibbled along the column of his throat until he reached the collar of Johnnie's shirt. "I did not intend to visit you again, but my resolve vanished when you reappeared. You are more than you seem, human child of the Dracula. Too beautiful to be truly normal, too warm to be a vampire; every lordly order you hand out is matched by a gesture of kindness."

"I have no idea what you are talking about," Johnnie said, genuinely baffled. Too beautiful? Too warm? Lordly? Kindness? None of those fit him, not really. His looks were barely passable for his strata, and he was hardly 'lordly'—more like simply reserved. Eros chuckled and sank his fingers into the hair at the nape of Johnnie's neck, tilting his head for another plundering kiss. Johnnie moaned despite himself, fingers still tangled in the cotton shirt Eros wore. But then Eros slid his free hand down Johnnie's back to finally rest on his ass, jerking them flush.

It reminded Johnnie that though he could not see, he could still touch. Loosening his fisted hands, he splayed them across a chest that proved to be impressively muscled beneath the cheap fabric of his shirt. He moaned again as Eros continued to kiss him senseless, and shifted his own arms to wrap tightly around Eros's waist.

He broke the kiss briefly, startled as his back met

the wall and the arm around his waist suddenly became a hand grabbing him through his pants, fondling with a boldness that would normally have had Johnnie reaching for his dagger. Instead, he thumped Eros hard on the chest, wishing he could *see*. "Do not mess up my clothes—" He bit at Eros's lips as he was cut off, eliciting another chuckle before the kiss grew deeper.

Eros shoved a hand inside his pants and boxer briefs, grabbing firm hold of Johnnie's hard cock. Johnnie jerked, hips moving of their own volition, and really, it had been far too long since he had had any attention but his own. Eros's laugher was warm against his skin, and his tongue warmer still as he lapped at Johnnie's throat just above the collar of his shirt. "I want to see you naked, spread out on your bed and begging me to take you."

Johnnie felt his way up Eros's body, then sank a hand into soft, soft hair, tugging hard. "I want to see you, period."

"That would spoil the fun," Eros murmured, then kissed him again, cutting off Johnnie's reply, eventually making him forget what he had been going to say.

Suddenly he was no longer pressed against Johnnie—but in the next moment, belt and button and zipper were undone, and the hottest mouth Johnnie had ever felt engulfed his cock. Johnnie only just barely bit back a shout. He clapped one hand over his mouth, the other one sinking into Eros's hair and holding on tightly as Eros sucked him off like their lives depended on it.

Only the fact that everyone downstairs would hear him held back another shout as he came in Eros's mouth. He was still attempting to catch his breath when Eros rose and kissed him. Johnnie made a sound that might have been a whimper as he tasted himself in Eros's mouth. The scent of myrrh and musk roses was heavy all around them, tangled with the smell of sex and sweat, making him dizzy and hungry for more despite the fact he was thoroughly spent.

He faltered in the dark a moment, but at last found what he sought. Eros jerked in surprise, grunting as Johnnie fumbled through fabric and finally got hold of his cock and stroked it as hard and sure as he could manage with absolutely no visibility. Eros kissed him again, kept him pinned against the wall, and there seemed something urgent, even desperate, about his rough-edged kiss.

Eros's cry was soft, further muffled by Johnnie's mouth, and he shuddered quietly in Johnnie's arms. His kiss softened, a little clumsy but somehow sweet. "I want to see you," Johnnie repeated in low tones, releasing Eros's cock, gripping Eros's shirt, feeling like a clinging child. Pathetic, pleading was too much like begging for his taste, but...

"See me once, and you'll not want to see me again," Eros replied. "Spy by candlelight, and the dripping wax will stir me."

"But of all the senses," Johnnie quoted, "sight must be the most delightful. Is that all you ever plan to do? Steal pleasure in the dark and vanish again when sated?"

Eros brushed a soft kiss across his mouth, then recited, "Stolen sweets are always sweeter/Stolen kisses much completer/Stolen looks are nice in chapels/Stolen, stolen, be your apples." Another brief kiss, and then as suddenly as that, Johnnie was alone again.

He swore softly in the dark, the only shred of light the sliver between the closed door and the floor. "The pleasure is momentary, the position ridiculous, and the expense damnable," he quoted with a sigh, furious with himself but not as sorry as he should have been. If it was the last thing he did, he would figure out the mystery of Eros—and *he* was not foolish enough to let the candle wax drip.

Pushing away from the wall, he fixed his clothes and combed his fingers through his hair. He had just reached the bedroom door when he heard footsteps in the living area beyond. Pulling the door open, he saw Peyton. "Oh, there you are," Peyton said. "Micah and Walsh are back."

"Good," Johnnie said. "Actually, Peyton, there was something else I wanted to discuss with you."

Peyton looked at him, faintly puzzled and a little worried. "What's that?"

"I was wondering if you would take me on as a silent partner," Johnnie said. "I will front the money for the renovations you want to do, as well as the repairs you need to make now, if you cut me in on the profits and give me the rooms upstairs."

Peyton's jaw dropped. "What—but—*why?* You—you're the son of the Dracula, Johnnie. Why would you want to bother with this crumbling dive?"

Johnnie fought the sudden, crushing, unexpected weight of disappointment. He drew himself up. "Of course if you are not interested—"

"You get haughty when you're upset, don't you?" Peyton laughed. "It drops over you like a blanket, or maybe like a switch got flipped. I didn't mean no, I only meant you could do so much better than this place."

Relaxing slightly, Johnnie shrugged and said, "I like it here. I would like it to remain open. I would like to see it do well."

Peyton grinned, "Then by all means. The rooms are yours, man. I'll dig out all my plans and paperwork and crap."

"Send it all to this man," Johnnie said and pulled out his card case. Flipping briefly through it, he extracted one for his lawyer. "He will take care of everything."

Laughing, Peyton took the card and put it in a pocket of his jeans. "Sure thing. Never had a fancy lawyer to do all the work before."

Johnnie shrugged. "It is convenient. If we are to be business partners, he will be our lawyer as well. At some point, we will all have to go to dinner. Now, however, I want to know what Micah and Walsh have learned."

Peyton nodded and led the way downstairs, back into the bar proper. Walsh and Micah were at the bar nursing beers They looked tired but triumphant. "Hey, Johnnie," Micah greeted.

"Hello," Johnnie said and sat at his own seat. "What did you find?"

"Three other places have been hit recently, vandalizing and harassment of customers, just like Peyton. The weird thing is that each has nothing to do with the other—this place, a bed and breakfast just outside of town, an upscale bar on the west end, and a fancy steakhouse on the east end. We found out about the steakhouse and the B & B by sheer dumb luck," Micah said and finished his beer, motioning Peyton for another one.

Johnnie latched onto that last bit. "What dumb

luck? Tell me precisely what you learned, leave no detail out."

Micah nodded around his beer, but Walsh spoke before he could set it down. "We left here and started working our way south, stopping at every bar, restaurant, and other dives we came across. Someone in the Blue Dove tipped us to the bar uptown, heard it from a friend of his who worked there. The manager at the upscale bar, Blood & Lace, told us they'd been having the same problems Peyton's been having—broken glassware, fires, harassed customers, a few other things. *He* told us that the owner of Blood & Lace also owned a steakhouse on the other side of town, and *it* had been having the same problems. So we went there, and the manager there told us something else—"

"That a friend of his, who owned a bed & breakfast, was also having the same problems," Johnnie said.

Laughing and shaking his head, Micah said, "How did you know?"

"Deduction," Johnnie said. "Peyton, that friend of yours who was a teacher—does he have a lover or spouse who is in the restaurant business?"

Peyton frowned in thought. "He was dating a manager at a diner we haunted for ages. They'd been going out for months when we split; they were still together when we went our separate ways. What was his name, Roger? Something like that. He had ambitions to own his own place. He always was jealous I beat him to the punch with this bar."

"What did you deduce?" Walsh asked, curious.

"Peyton told me earlier that he was in a band," Johnnie said. "The lead singer resented the band's breaking up. One of the band members went on to run a bed & breakfast, just outside of town. Acts of violence that randomly hit that place as well as this one? It could be coincidence. However, the upscale bar and the steakhouse are owned by one person, which means only three people are being affected, and we know for a fact that the owner is friends with the man who runs the bed & breakfast. So we have Peyton, Roosevelt, and Cat's lover all being harassed and their properties vandalized."

"But Cat doesn't own them," Peyton said, frowning again. "His lover does."

"Hitting the school where Cat works would draw too much attention," Johnnie replied, "and teachers do not make a lot of money. The four of you became a band because you were united by hard times. I would not be surprised if your friend reappeared here shortly, looking to restart his band, or perhaps he is simply exacting revenge."

Micah shook his head. "How did you even think to make that connection?"

"If the attacks were truly random, more buildings in the vicinity would have been hit," Johnnie said. "As that was not the case, the attacks must be personal. We needed only to determine why." He turned back to Peyton. "This all would have been discovered sooner if you had contacted your friends, or your friends had called you."

Peyton shrugged. "We weren't tight man. I mean, Cat and Roosevelt were old friends, but otherwise we just worked together, you know? I'm downscale to their upscale, so it probably didn't occur to them. Didn't occur to me. They may yet call, and I could always dig up their numbers if I had to."

"Not yet," Johnnie said.

"So what do we do?" Micah asked.

"I think we will wait until he approaches Peyton," Johnnie said. "Unless, of course, there is another incident, in which case we will have to find him and end the matter." He stood , picking up his journal and cane. Reaching into his pocket, he pulled out his phone and speed-dialed his father's office, ignoring the anxiety that fluttered in his chest.

Ontoniel answered the phone, which meant his assistant must be on break. "John?"

"Father," Johnnie replied. "We need to talk."

"About what?"

"A great deal," Johnnie said. "I am downtown. Where shall I meet you?"

"The Garden," Ontoniel said. "Half an hour."

"Forty-five minutes," Johnnie said and hung up. He turned to Peyton and the others. "I will be gone a few hours." He pulled out his card case and extracted one of his own, sliding it across the bar to Peyton. "Call me at that second number should you need me."

Peyton snorted in amusement and tucked the second card away with the first. "Oh, the money I could make selling your private line. I'll give you a ring should I need, but I doubt anything else will happen today."

Nodding, Johnnie said, "Call the Hummingbird and tell them to send my driver, if you please." Laughing again, Peyton obeyed. Johnnie left the bar and strode upstairs. In his future bedroom, he saw that G-man had already neatly arranged his clothes in the closet, with the cases holding his shoes and accessories stacked neatly on the floor.

He perused his choices. The Garden... that limited him to the turquoise and the red. As he was dining with his father, and they would not finish until roughly midnight, the red would be the most appropriate. Stripping off his clothes, he pulled on black slacks with a slightly stiffer cut than the ones he had just discarded. His shirt was a crisp, sharp white, over which he pulled a vest of deep crimson with a subtle crown and roses pattern. Then he knotted a black silk tie embroidered with the Desrosiers triple-rose and added a tie pin and cuff links of rubies set in gold.

Over all he pulled on his formal black wool coat, which fell to just below his knees. Last, he pulled on a black fedora with a gray band, then retrieved his cane and went back downstairs. He strove to ignore the looks everyone gave him as he returned to the bar.

"Fancy, fancy," Heath drawled, grinning. He lifted his wine in a mock toast. "Enjoy dinner with the Dracula." Johnnie glared at him. Heath only snickered.

Nodding a farewell to the others, hoping he had not just lost his new partnership, Johnnie left the bar and slid inside the car that stood waiting with door open for him. When the driver was situated, Johnnie instructed, "To The Garden, please."

They reached the restaurant in the heart of uptown several minutes later. The lobby was true to the restaurant's name: all exotic plants, stained glass in matching floral patterns, and even the floor was composed of rich green tiles with subtle floral touches.

"Master Desrosiers," the maître d' greeted. "Your father called; I've arranged his favorite table. Right this way." He snapped his fingers at one of the doormen, who came forward to take Johnnie's coat and hat.

"I will keep the cane," Johnnie said when the doorman tried to take it as well. Bowing off, the doorman vanished and Johnnie was led to Ontoniel's preferred table—up on a dais and shaded by plants, tucked into one corner of the room. It was the perfect place to see without being seen. Johnnie sat down and immediately told the waiter who appeared, "Vodka rocks. Also bring a scotch, neat."

Johnnie sat down and stared at the runes on his cane, trying to compose in his head what he would say to his father. There was no easy way to announce he was moving out—and to an area of which Ontoniel was certain to disapprove.

He had finished half his vodka before Ontoniel arrived, exactly on the one hour mark. Sitting down, Ontoniel ordered their food, then sipped at his scotch. Though it did nothing for him, Ontoniel liked to drink it for the sake of some nostalgia he had never explained past saying it had to do with an old friend.

They said nothing until the soup arrived, blood broth for Ontoniel, a lobster bisque for Johnnie. After several sips of broth, Ontoniel finally said, "What is this about, Johnnie?"

Johnnie looked at him, then finally simply said, "I am moving out."

Ontoniel said nothing, only continued to sip his broth. Johnnie worked on his own soup, knowing better than to push or press. They finished the soup, and it was taken away and replaced with the main course. Ontoniel waved his off, but Johnnie accepted a swordfish steak, potatoes and vegetables. Oddly, amidst the high-quality drinks and food, all he could think about was greasy pizza and the old, scuffed bar.

"Why?" Ontoniel finally asked, breaking the silence, drawing Johnnie back to the matter at hand.

"Because the house should be free for Ellie to build his own family. He does not need his eccentric little brother underfoot, especially as more and more guests arrive. I should find my own feet."

"Where?"

Johnnie hesitated, for this was the sticky point. "I have some rooms above a bar down on second street."

"No," Ontoniel said. "We have several vastly more suitable places available. You are not living in the damned slums."

"*You* have places," Johnnie said. "I do not want to live in *your* houses. I want to live in a place that is mine."

"Some tacky dive owned by god alone knows what?" Ontoniel demanded.

"Owned by a lone wolf with a citizen pin," Johnnie countered. "He wears Dracula gold, so you approved his presence here, despite his lone status. He cannot, therefore, be all bad. Anyway, I am to be a silent partner in the bar. We will begin renovations the moment the paperwork is signed and the weather warms up enough to permit it."

Ontoniel shook his head. "If your reason is to help your brother, I fail to see how moving to live in practically the slums is helping."

"I am doing it as much for myself as for Ellie—and I am not using my real name, if that reassures you any. I have no plans to embarrass the Desrosiers."

There was a beat of silence, then Ontoniel said quietly, "You are using your birth name."

"Yes," Johnnie said. "I cannot promise it will always work—"

"You should be careful," Ontoniel cut in. "You are in a position of great power and authority as my son. Using your birth name will deflect some attention, but not all of it. People still remember that name, that tragedy. That alone could draw more attention than you like, and out of my immediate sight—"

"I will take care," Johnnie said.

"If you were interested in taking care," Ontoniel said, "you would not be moving out to live in one of the worst parts of the city. I do not like it."

Johnnie nodded. "I knew you would not, but it will not stop me."

Ontoniel sighed. "I know. I never told you this, and perhaps I should not now, but I met your mother on three occasions previous to her death. I can honestly say that you are at least as stubborn as she."

"What—" Johnnie said, staring at him, jolted by the fact Ontoniel had known his mother and all the ramifications of that. "How—that is not possible. We were a completely normal family."

"No one living in my territory is completely normal, other than those in the bronze district. Your family did not live there."

Johnnie stared at him, feeling as though the rug had been yanked out from beneath him. "I do not understand. I am completely normal; there is not one single drop of abnormal in me."

"They left the abnormal world behind," Ontoniel said. "They wanted to be normal—they wanted *you* to be normal."

"I see," Johnnie said, and he did. It was far from unheard of for abnormals to try and live completely normal lives, free of the magic and treachery and further complications that filled the abnormal world. Humans, especially—the alchemists, witches, sorcerers—tried to retreat to normalcy when they found that the previously unseen world they had discovered was too much to bear.

So they walked away, tried to go back to life before they knew the monsters were real. But once aware, it was hard to live blind again. Most still settled in supernatural territories and simply tried to live on the fringes of it, safe and as normal as they could manage.

"Who—who was what?" Johnnie demanded.

Ontoniel grimaced but said, "Your father was an alchemist. They never told me, but my impression was always that your father managed some experiment that terrified them. So they gave it all up and gained my permission to live here." He sighed. "Then my wife..."

They both winced at that, perfectly mirrored expressions. Ontoniel hastily moved on. "I am ordering you to leave the matter alone. You know all there is to know about your parents now. If you insist upon moving out, to live in this slum bar of yours—and I very strongly protest it and will continue to do so—then I insist upon contact information and I want you to call at least once a week. You will also visit at least once a month. Last, if I *ever* demand you return home immediately, you will do so without question."

Johnnie wanted to argue, but he knew how to pick his battles with Ontoniel. "Yes, Father. Thank you."

Waving the words aside, Ontoniel asked, "So what are you going to do, owning a bar and living above it?"

"It is something new to learn," Johnnie said. "I will, of course, continue my studies and translations." He hesitated, then slowly added, "I was thinking I might devote more serious attention to solving mysteries and such. You said I could not, living at home, with the wedding looming, but well away, I see no reason I could not pursue that path."

Something flickered across Ontoniel's face. It was

sad and pensive and too many other things for Johnnie to pick them all out. "You seem determined to put yourself in danger, Johnnie."

Johnnie lifted one brow. "No 'case' I have ever solved has involved danger." The imp who had tried to hurt him had failed so thoroughly it scarcely counted.

"Such a line of occupation always runs into violence," Ontoniel said sharply. "That little dagger I gave you will not protect you from everything, and neither will that cane sword. Try not to do anything too foolish, Johnnie. Even my name cannot save you from everything."

"I will be careful," Johnnie said stiffly.

Of all things, Ontoniel smiled—only the barest bit, just the slightest upturning of one corner of his mouth, but a smile all the same. "Your mysteries always find you. I am certain that trouble will follow in their wake. When do you plan to move?"

"Soon," Johnnie said. He should really wait until the renovations were done, but he was too impatient, and he wanted to do it before he changed his mind or something prevented it.

Ontoniel grimaced. "Very well. I will inform you if I alter my decision about permitting it."

Johnnie bit back his initial response to that, not wanting to make a tactical—fatal—error. Their main course was taken away and dessert brought. Tense discussion over, and far more smoothly than he could have anticipated, Johnnie shifted the conversation to Ellie and the wedding, ten months away now, and by the time dessert was finished and drinks brought, they were discussing books and articles they had both read.

It was, Johnnie realized with surprise, nice.

~~*

It was just past midnight when he returned to the Bremen.

"Hey, Johnnie," Peyton greeted. "Didn't expect you back this soon. Family discussions usually last forever."

"My father was called away," Johnnie replied. The bar was almost completely deserted. Besides himself, only G-man remained, slumped in his corner, a half-finished beer in front of him, baseball cap pulled down low. To all appearances, he was fast asleep. Johnnie wondered if he had anywhere to go but did not ask. "How was everything here?"

"Quiet all night. Cat called, of all things. I told him I'd been having trouble, too, but he didn't seem to make the connection, just noted it was weird we were all having problems. Roosevelt called too, about an hour ago, and I asked him about Jack. Said he hadn't heard from Jack in years, but there were always rumors that he had wound up in a big city not too far from here."

Johnnie nodded. "I think he will show himself soon: tonight, tomorrow, not longer than the day after tomorrow. It would not surprise me to learn he needs a band and is clinging in his desperation to how good the four of you used to be together. People often cling to the past when everything else seems to let them down."

Peyton sighed. "Man, we were always up front about not wanting to do it forever. It was just a way out of a hole, for us. We always told him that, and he said he understood, but I guess he wanted to believe we would change our minds." He shrugged.

"For what a man would like to be true, that he

more readily believes," Johnnie quoted.

In reply, Peyton only sighed again. "Would you like a drink, Johnnie? Oh, I dug out all my paperwork and such and sent it on to your lawyer."

"I got a call from him," Johnnie said, "and told him what to do, what we want. He will move the necessary funds to a new account and set up access for both of us. I will probably move in over the next few days, though I no doubt will have to move again when the renovations begin."

Peyton laughed. "Whatever, man. We'll see how it plays out when we get there. I can't believe you're doing this—especially this dive, especially with me."

Johnnie shrugged. "I like the Bremen." He started to say more when the door opened.

At the bar, Peyton froze in obvious shock. But in the next breath, he was smoothly pulling a beer and sliding it across the bar to the new arrival. "Long time no see, Jack."

Jack coughed, then sipped the beer before finally saying, "You too, Peyton. How's life?"

"Rotten, but I think you know that," Peyton replied coolly.

Jack frowned. "Come again?"

Johnnie spoke before Peyton could. "You are ill, your clothes are in poor condition, you are thin enough that you clearly have not eaten properly for a long time. Your hand is bandaged, and you smell like burn cream. Underneath that I can also smell chalk: the classic tell of a sorcerer or a witch. You further reek of magic, and very strongly, which means you have either cast a strong spell very recently, or have used a great many spells over the past several days—probably both. There is a cut on your left forearm that is bleeding through bandages and your shirt—did you have to break into the steakhouse, the Bed & Breakfast? Blood & Lace? Or did you have to be on location to break the glassware of one of them, lacking the familiarity to do it from a distance?"

Jack stared, pale-faced, anger in his eyes. "I beg your fucking pardon?"

"You have been vandalizing the various establishments of your former band mates," Johnnie said. "Are you hoping to get them back?"

Jack snarled and shoved his beer off the bar, forcing Peyton to jump back. He lunged for Johnnie—

—Only to find himself grabbed by the throat by G-man. Johnnie jerked in surprise, nearly dropping the dagger he had half-pulled from his hidden sheath.

"You have admitted to your crimes by your actions," G-man said. "Why?"

"They ruined my life," Jack said bitterly. "I wanted to ruin theirs."

"Next time, be more clever about it," G-man replied. "For assaulting citizens of the Desrosiers territory and attempting to harm the Dracula's son, you are under arrest."

"What—" Peyton exclaimed, dropping the pieces of glass he had just picked up.

Johnnie scowled. "You are an Enforcer." In his father's territories, the closest the abnormals had to a police force were his father's Enforcers. But no one knew who they were, or even how many there were, save for the Dracula and the Alucard. They wore no uniforms, had no real known headquarters, but they were always there, shadowing around the city, upholding the Dracula's law.

G-man's hand flashed out, knocking Jack hard, and

he then let Jack fall unconscious to the floor. He reached inside his jacket and pulled out a badge: the Desrosiers triple roses, surmounted by a pentacle with an 'E' in the middle. "Enforcer Bergrin, Master Johnnie," he said with a smirk that livened up his plain-pudding features.

Johnnie swore. "You better not have been—"

"Ordered to watch you?" Bergrin interrupted. "Yes, I'm afraid. You showed up the first time, I had to report it. You showed up the second time, I was put on bodyguard detail."

Swearing again, Johnnie yanked out his phone and hit the speed dial for his father's cell phone.

"John?"

"I do not need a bodyguard," Johnnie snarled.

Ontoniel laughed. "So my Enforcer played his hand. That means you were in danger."

Johnnie snapped, "I was fine."

"You have always been capable of defending yourself, Johnnie, but I am not bending on this matter. The dangers you have encountered thus far are piddling things, and I am not going to leave you to face even worse alone. Whatever you might think, you do not have the experience. You will tolerate the Enforcer, or you will be dragged home and locked in your room. Am I clear?"

Johnnie snapped his phone shut and shoved it in his pocket. He shoved Bergrin—G-man, whatever his name was now—out of the way. "I do not require a babysitter." Not waiting for a reply, he stalked through the bar and up the stairs to his new accommodations. He would sleep, and tomorrow he would begin to pack his things, and he would be damned if he tolerated a babysitter.

Case 004: The Fishwife

Johnnie laid his cards down on the scuffed tabletop and tossed back the last of his vodka. "Fold." Over at the bar, Peyton looked at the empty glass in query. Johnnie nodded as Walsh claimed his winnings and Micah gathered up the cards to shuffle them.

Across the table, Nelson pulled out a small cedar box, extracted a cigar, and passed the box around the table. Johnnie took one, amused. The same cigars were in his father's study; he knew exactly what they cost. He doubted Nelson had paid that price. Once his own was properly lit and sampled, Johnnie asked, "So did you pay full price for these?"

Nelson snorted his own amusement. "I paid for them, but that's about all I'll say."

"I see," Johnnie said with a smile. He thanked Peyton, who had arrived with his drink. "Deal the cards, Micah."

"As you command," Micah said cheerfully, but his hand froze in the process of tossing Johnnie his third card, eyes on the door, where everyone else's had gone.

Johnnie did not bother to turn around—he would know the scent and feel of that magic anywhere. It was like sunflowers and snow, a contradiction in scents that suited their owner perfectly. Footsteps drew closer to him, but Johnnie ignored them. He set his cigar aside, took a sip of vodka, then finally dragged his eyes slowly up to meet the familiar blue eyes quietly watching and waiting. "Rostislav."

"Johnnie."

"What do you want?"

"To talk."

Tossing back the rest of his vodka, Johnnie stood and said, "Upstairs." He led the way to the back of the bar, scowling at Bergrin, slumped in his corner like the harmless, lazy bar bum he pretended to be and not the odious, obedient-to-the-Dracula-only, aggravating babysitter that he was.

Leading the way up the stairs, Johnnie opened the door, motioned Rostislav inside, then closed it again behind them and threw the lock. "So talk."

Rostislav did not immediately reply, but strolled around the living area, filled now with all the furniture from Johnnie's sitting room. He glanced into the open doors of the scaled-down library and the bedroom, then turned slowly around to face Johnnie again. "So it's true—you left Ontoniel's house. Why in the world are you living *here?*"

Johnnie was really getting sick of that question, even if he could see Rostislav was merely amused. "What do you care?" he asked coolly. "How is life with Prince Charming?"

"Fine," Rostislav said with a sigh. "It's not the same without you. I swear, Johnnie, I never meant to sacrifice you. It never occurred to me."

"I would say actions speak louder than words," Johnnie replied. "You left me out; you lied to me for *years* about your relationship with Jesse. You made it painfully clear that you do not trust me. Then you used me like a pawn, knowing full well that at the end of it all, I would be forbidden to see you and that there was no easy way to defy my father. The very *least* you could have done was tell me the truth. You did not. I feel that is all that needs to be said."

Rostislav looked miserable. "I'm sorry, Johnnie. I never saw it that way—I never imagined you would take it that way. I swear to god, I was trying to protect you. We never told you because it *wasn't* years. It's only just now been a full year since we figured everything out. We were both worried sick about who might get hurt by knowing about us. Your father is still furious, and everyone else who ever called us friend no longer has anything to do with us. It's lonely, Johnnie, especially for Jesse. He loves his parties, his dinners, and his casino gets by only because the normals continue to pour in. But it's nothing like it used to be, and it's heartbreaking for him.

"It never once occurred to me you would actually walk away. My only mistake was in being so selfish and presumptuous that it never occurred to me you would obey your father's edict. I took it for granted that you would defy him, even knowing how much you look up to him. I just assumed you'd always be there, so I thought I would protect you as much as I could for as long as I could."

Johnnie started to protest the idiotic idea that he looked up to his father, then decided that was an argument for another day and stifled the words.

Rostislav, however, never missed a trick. "You *do* look up to him, Johnnie. No matter what he says, what you say, what either of you does—you look up to him, and he dotes on you."

"Shut up," Johnnie said sourly. "I do not, he does not, and that is the end of the matter."

Laughing, Rostislav said, "If you say so, Johnnie."

Making a face, Johnnie strode to his brown leather

sofa and sat down, hands shoved in the pockets of his slacks, dark brown with cream pinstripes. "How did you find me here, anyway?"

"Elam told me," Rostislav replied. "He comes to check on us every couple of weeks. Jesse has been trying to get him to thaw, but to no avail." He shrugged, and for a moment, looked sad and tired.

Johnnie could not stay angry. Hell, he had probably started thawing the moment he realized Rostislav was in the room. "Throwing Elam into a volcano would not get him to thaw. Ellie cannot stand anything that breaks the status quo because it interferes with his piano time and we cannot have that."

Rostislav laughed, and Johnnie smiled slightly, and that was that. Sitting down next to him, Rostiya asked slyly, "So I noticed you lost that last hand of poker. Losing your touch, Johnnie?"

"It is only natural, given how seldom I play these days," Johnnie said.

"I just bet," Rostislav replied. "Next you'll try to convince me you suck at chess now, too."

Johnnie shrugged. "No doubt I am rusty. I have not played since I defeated you a few months ago."

Rostislav hesitated, then said, "You could come over, sometime. To the Last Star, I mean. We could play chess, and Jesse would love some non-frigid company. He does genuinely like you, you know. He was almost as upset as I when you walked out." He paused, then added, "Unless it really will cause you too much trouble—"

"Oh, shut up," Johnnie snapped. "I would have come all along if I thought I would be welcome. You are the one who has been holed up in that casino for months with not so much as a letter."

Rostislav frowned. "If I had thought you would see me, I would have come sooner. I wanted to see you and apologize every goddamn day, Johnnie. You're my best friend. It was knowing you would have my back that helped give me the strength to throw everything away for Jesse—but I never meant or wanted to lose you."

Johnnie nodded and said gruffly, "We die as often as we lose a friend."

Smiling faintly, Rostislav said, "I actually thought reconciling would be more difficult. I don't think I'll even have to use the peace offerings I brought along."

"Peace offerings?" Johnnie asked, and reached out to pick up his cane from where he had left it on the coffee table.

"That's a handsome piece," Rostislav said. "When did you start affecting a cane?"

Johnnie smirked. "Since it did *this."* Springing the release, he drew the sword and held the edge close to Rostislav's throat. "What peace offerings?"

Rostislav laughed. "Impressive. Who was foolish enough to give you a sword stick?"

"Micah, he is the alchemist you probably noted downstairs. It was my payment for saving his wife and scaring off the imp who had turned her into a rosebush."

"Why did the imp do that?"

"For the cane sword," Johnnie said. "It can cross the planes."

Rostislav's eyes snapped open wide. "Shit."

Johnnie frowned. "What?"

"It's a whisper I've been hearing—well, was hearing before I was grounded indefinitely. Someone's been hunting plane-crossing objects and creatures. No one knows who or why, though I'm sure it's the usual motives."

"No doubt," Johnnie said with a grimace. The ability to cross the planes at will was the abnormal equivalent of finding the Holy Grail or discovering Atlantis. Being able to traverse *all* the planes, to know once and for all how many existed, would grant the abnormal who did it unprecedented knowledge and power.

It was all balderdash, a fool's quest. There were better odds on finding the Ring of Solomon. "I would keep that thing close, or put it somewhere extremely safe," Rostislav said. "If even half the rumors are true, you and your friend downstairs could have been killed."

"I am not so easy to kill as that," Johnnie said dismissively, not adding that anyway, he had a damned babysitter downstairs. "No one would dare infuriate my father by killing me." Ontoniel would consider any assault on his family an insult to his authority and power.

Rostislav smiled faintly. "This is true. Ontoniel would be heartbroken, and I bet he would burn his own territory down if that's what it took to find your killer."

The idea of Ontoniel *heartbroken* over anything, least of all Johnnie, was too ridiculous to take seriously. "So are you going to give me my peace offerings or not?"

Snickering, but wisely saying nothing further on the matter, Rostislav snapped his fingers and caught the box that fell into his hands. Dark-stained wood, smooth and glossy, embossed with a symbol Johnnie knew well. "This is the first one."

Accepting the box, Johnnie opened it and admired the pen and inks inside; they were his favorite, and he did not have any of the colors nestled inside their velvet cubbies. "Thank you."

"The second offering was a mystery to solve, unless, of course, you've got too many other cases to manage right now, Detective Johnnie Goodnight."

"Please do not say there are rumors circulating," Johnnie said. His father would kill him.

"I have no idea," Rostislav replied, looking briefly sad again. "Your brother told me everything; I'm honestly not certain why. He certainly is the same as ever, otherwise. You're not though." He frowned thoughtfully at Johnnie. "You seem... looser. Perhaps living here is good for you." He grinned and teased, "Or maybe you're keeping a boyfriend secret from me, now."

"No," Johnnie said, though that was not exactly true—neither was it exactly false.

It was complicated, that was what it was. He did not know what Eros was, beyond the hot, hard shadow that had appeared in his room every night since Johnnie had moved in two weeks ago. Every night, when the bar was closed and only Johnnie was around, Eros came to him. He drove Johnnie mad, touching and teasing, fucking him senseless—then left him exhausted and enthralled, frustrated and lonely, and more determined than ever to solve the mystery of his shadowy lover. Yet he continued to drag his feet on the matter. Perhaps the risk of dripping candle wax gave him pause after all.

"Johnnie?"

"Hmm?" Johnnie asked, shaking off his thoughts of Eros.

"I think you *do* have a secret boyfriend," Rostislav said, teasing again.

Johnnie frowned.

Rostislav's eyebrows lifted sharply. "Johnnie—"

"I do not know what I have, besides a mystery," Johnnie said tersely. "When I understand the matter better myself, I will discuss it further with others."

"That isn't like you, Johnnie. What about Elam? I thought—"

"I do love Ellie," Johnnie said. "I do not know what is going on, and that is all I intend to say on the matter for now."

Rostislav nodded reluctantly. "Let me know if I can help."

"So what is this mystery you mentioned?"

"An innocuous case of a runaway husband," Rostislav said and pulled a folded section of newspaper from his jacket. Unfolding it, he tapped on the front page story. "A local paper, from the next city over going east."

Taking the paper, Johnnie read quickly through the story. It was about a woman who claimed that her husband of twenty years left her because she lost the necklace he had given her when they first met. The necklace, she said, had been around her throat since the day they met. It was lost when she was mugged one night on her way home from work. She went on to say that her husband had comforted her, helped her when the police came, but seemed more upset about the necklace than anything else. The next morning, he was gone. The events had happened three weeks prior to the article's printing. The woman was begging her husband to come home, for the mugger to return the necklace even if she had to pay for it—she just wanted her husband back.

There were two pictures printed with the article—one of the couple on their wedding day, and a more recent one showing them at the beach. Johnnie stared thoughtfully for a moment, then said, "Innocuous? Not in the slightest. Her husband is a selkie; that necklace is his skin." He looked up at Rostislav and added, "But you already knew that."

"Only the same way you did—by reading the article and looking at the pictures. I wanted to see if you came to the same conclusion, confirming my suspicions." Johnnie nodded at his words and glanced at the necklace again—a simple trinket really, except it was made of pure gold and far more than a simple, silly golden fish charm.

Normals had legends aplenty involving selkies: the way they laid their skins out and how greedy humans snatched them up and forced the selkies into slavery, matrimony, and so on. The reality was that selkies were not that foolish or careless. They could not live far from their skins, and so always turned them into something that could be kept close without attracting notice. More often than not, that meant a piece of jewelry.

"She is normal," Johnnie said.

"I believe so, yes. The city has a small abnormal community, but they lived several blocks from it. No doubt he worked there, but my impression is that she has no idea what her husband really is."

"If she did, she would not have agreed to the article," Johnnie said. "That means she definitely did not steal the necklace and ward it so that he could not remove it. The only real question, then, is whether the mugger wanted the selkie, or simply a bit of jewelry and her purse."

"Selkies fetch a handsome price on the black market," Rostiya replied. "They're not as impressive and versatile as imps, but slave labor is slave labor, and it's easier to hide a skin than to spell an imp."

Johnnie nodded and threw the paper on the coffee table. "I am surprised you did not simply solve the matter yourself."

"I'm not supposed to be leaving the Last Star," Rostislav said. "I'll be lucky if I don't catch it for not only leaving, but coming to see the Dracula's little boy."

Johnnie hit him on the leg with his cane. "Shut up. You are definitely out of luck. Did you see the man asleep in the corner downstairs?"

"Yes ..."

"He is not asleep. He is the Enforcer my father has set upon me."

Rostislav rolled his eyes. "I should have realized you would have one of those skulking about. No way would daddy dear *really* let you out of his sight."

Johnnie grimaced in agreement. "The men downstairs do not know, other than the bartender, Peyton. They call him G-man. He calls himself Bergrin."

"Huh," Rostislav said. "Guess that means I'm in big trouble. I really should have thought of that, but I was more concerned that you would refuse to have anything to do with me."

"Shut up," Johnnie repeated. "Let us go back downstairs." Keeping hold of his cane, he led the way back down to the bar. He paused at Bergrin's table, striking one leg of it with his cane.

Bergrin slowly looked up. "Yes, Highness?"

Ignoring that, Johnnie asked, "So have you already

ratted out Rostislav?"

Something like annoyance flickered across Bergrin's face, gone as quickly as it had come. "I'm not your enemy."

"Babysitter," Johnnie replied. "Same thing."

"I have not spoken to your father today, Highness. I had no plans to. No one in this bar is on the list of people not permitted near you."

Johnnie scowled. "There is a bloody *list* about who is and who is not—" He cut himself off and tamped down on his anger. "We are going to Belle City." He really did not want to share that information, but he was not stupid—if he pushed back too hard, his father would follow through on the threat to drag him home and lock him up.

"We three?" Bergrin asked.

"So far as I am concerned, it is a party of two, but I suppose you will do as you please."

Bergrin smirked and tugged on the brim of his cap. "Yes, Highness."

Turning sharply away, Johnnie strode to the other end of the bar, where the poker game had disbanded in favor of another round of oohing and aahing over the finalized blueprints that had arrived two days ago. Micah looked up with a smile. "Who's your heavy-hitting witch friend?"

"This is Rostislav Petrov."

"Oh," Walsh said. "I know that name. You're the one they call the Cursebreaker."

Rostislav laughed. "The very same." He held out a hand to each man in turn as they went through introductions.

"He has brought us a case," Johnnie said as the introductions wrapped up. "Over in Belle City."

"Oh?" Peyton asked.

"Yes," Johnnie said and held out his hand to Rostislav, who obediently handed over the newspaper. Opening it, Johnnie spread it out on the table and spun it so they could all read.

"That's a selkie or I'm a cat," Peyton said after a few minutes. "Poor woman doesn't know it, I'd wager my best vodka on that."

Johnnie smiled. "Correct on both counts. Rostiya and I are going to Belle City to find him."

"The abnormal sector there is clustered around the docks," Walsh said. "I started out a beat cop there, long before I knew anything about abnormals. It's rough trade for normals, even rougher trade for abnormals. They trade in imps, goblin food, and worse. Place got shook up a few years ago when some demon consort tore through it, but it's seedier than ever now, I hear."

"Good to know," Johnnie said. Goblin food—that meant humans, most often normals, were being sold to the goblins, who loved nothing better than a nice slice of tender human.

Imps were the poor man's genie: powerful enough magically to do damn near anything. They sold for extremely high prices on the black market. Any place that dealt in worse than slavery and illegal foodstuffs... Johnnie grimaced at the thought. It was certainly nothing he needed to be concerned about—and he most definitely did not need a bodyguard—but it was bothersome.

"Call if you need us," Micah said.

"I will," Johnnie replied. "Rostiya, I must go back upstairs to get my things."

Rostiya nodded, and they headed back up to

Johnnie's rooms where he pulled on a brown blazer to match his pants, a brown fedora and long brown coat, and a paisley scarf that was a duplicate of the brown, cream, and pink paisley pattern of his vest, the same shade of pink as his tie.

Pulling on cream gloves, he picked up his cane again and said. "Shall we?"

"Always so immaculate and pretty, Johnnie," Rostislav said in amusement.

Johnnie ignored him and simply gripped the arm Rostislav held out, keeping firm hold as Rostislav cast his spell. Traveling by abnormal means was so much easier than normal. Johnnie was ever bitter at his own inability to travel by such means.

They arrived in Belle City in front of a bakery, the smell of fresh bread and cinnamon washing over him, mixing with the less pleasant odors of a busy city street. "The woman and her husband live a few blocks that way," Rostislav said, pointing. "This was the closest I could get, working from my memories of the city. They've got some nice beach front property; it must have cost a small fortune."

"My father's beach houses certainly cost a tidy sum each," Johnnie said. "Lead the way, then."

Looking amused, Rostiya obeyed. "So do you think you have a little shadow?"

"No doubt I will eventually," Johnnie said sourly. "I do not know the extent of Bergrin's abilities. He definitely has magic, but that is all I have been able to determine. Hopefully it will take him some time to follow us here, and then find us."

"Hopefully," Rostislav agreed. He glanced around the street corner on which they stood, then said, "This way." They walked another ten minutes, as the houses grew more and more sparse, until they reached the beach front proper and the small smattering of mansions overlooking it. "Oh, there she is. How handy," Rostislav said and pointed.

A woman stood on the edge of the beach, the tide lapping at her ankles as it raced up the shore. She was dressed in a blue and green sundress with only a heavy cardigan to ward off the chill and a wide-brimmed straw hat protecting her face from the sun. Though she must have been nearly forty, she was prettier by far than all the girls half her age who struggled for the grace and poise this woman naturally possessed. She turned as she heard their approach, eyes widening slightly as she took them in. "You're not more reporters."

"No, madam," Johnnie said. "I am a private investigator, of sorts."

"Of sorts?" she asked, seeming uncertain whether to be amused or annoyed.

Johnnie nodded. "I do not charge for my services, and I take only those cases that interest me."

She laughed, sad and tired, but irrepressible hope flickered in her eyes. "Of what interest is a runaway husband? Millions of people every year wake up to find their spouses gone."

"But very few lose them because of a stolen necklace," Johnnie said quietly.

The woman lifted a hand to touch her throat where the necklace had once been, tears falling down her cheeks. "He loved me. I cannot believe I was wrong about that for twenty years, not after all we have been through—" She burst into tears, sobbing into her hands.

"There, there," Rostiya said, moving forward and

sliding an arm across her shoulders. "Is your house the blue one? Let's go inside, then." He continued to soothe and comfort her as they went inside her home. He sat her down at the kitchen bar and prepared a cup of tea after a couple of minutes of searching around.

The woman laughed softly as she cradled the hot mug in her hands. "It is the height of stupidity to let strangers do all that I have let you do, yet being around you is similar to being around Mark. I'm not sure why. Thank you for the tea."

"Of course," Rostislav said.

"I do not believe your husband is gone because of the necklace," Johnnie said, quietly grateful that the crying had stopped. He removed his hat and set it on the counter. "Not the way you think. Your name is Pearl, yes?"

"Yes," Pearl said softly. "My family has always been involved with the sea. My father does research pertaining to jellyfish. My brother owns a cruise business. Family legends hold we started out as pirates. I met Mark when I was seventeen, vacationing here visiting friends while my father did his research. Five hours after we met, Mark gave me that necklace and told me that it meant he would grant my every wish. He didn't have much money then, and my parents were furious I would take up with a poor boy with nothing to his name but a leaky fishing boat. He owns his own fleet now, and we just bought this house last year. It's our fifth one, because every time I get bored with one house, he obediently buys me one that's bigger and grander.

"My every wish, he's always granted, and he never once minded that I'm an entitled brat. I like fine things, expensive things, and I'm used to getting them. I have never denied I am spoiled rotten, but Mark never minded, no matter what I demanded, because he always knew I loved him best." Tears began to trail down her cheeks again. "I guess losing that necklace was too much for him, but I swear—I didn't mean to—I'd give up all of this just to have him back. He's gone, and it's all my fault."

"It is not your fault you were mugged," Johnnie said.

Pearl sniffled. "I suppose. I mean, I know. I volunteer at the aquarium three days a week, and every evening I walk home, the same way, the same times. It's a safe stretch, though; there have never been any problems. I tried to get away, but I just couldn't. You should have seen his face when he realized my necklace was gone. It was like someone had died." She pressed the heels of her hands to her eyes. "I've never seen him look that way, not in all the years I've known him. I just don't understand."

Johnnie could feel a headache coming on—there was nothing quite as difficult as telling a normal there was so much more to the world than they had ever imagined, and they had to do it now by telling her that her husband had likely been sold into slavery.

Rostislav motioned to him. "Why don't you go start at the docks, Johnnie? I'll finish up here."

More than happy to leave the tricky matter to Rostislav, Johnnie nodded and stood. Replacing his hat on his head, he tugged at the brim in farewell and departed. A quick call was all it took to bring a car, and as he slid into the back seat, Johnnie said, "To the docks."

"Begging your pardon, sir," the driver said, looking at him in the rearview mirror, "but you don't look the sort what should be going alone to the docks."

Johnnie smiled, amused. "I am safer than a pup who smells like blood and old booze and is still sporting Pit wounds. To judge by the teeth marks on your wrist, I would say you wound up on the wrong side of a goblin. Take me to the docks, little wolf."

"Yes, sir," the driver muttered and drove off. Twenty minutes later, they pulled to a stop in front of a coffee shop that looked like it was in business only because it bribed the health inspector. "Be careful, man," the driver said.

"I will, thank you," Johnnie said and tipped him. He turned toward the docks—and swore.

Bergrin smirked and tugged on the brim of his baseball cap. "Hello, Prince."

"Go away," Johnnie said and strode past him, headed toward the docks proper. When Bergrin fell into step beside him, Johnnie ignored him.

"You could just accept it gracefully, Highness."

"My name is neither Highness nor Prince," Johnnie said. "I do not require a babysitter."

Bergrin sighed. "Look—I have better things to do with my time than dance attendance upon you—"

"Then do them."

"*But* you're not the one paying me, and you're not the one who will cut off my balls and make me eat them if you so much as nick yourself shaving."

Johnnie rolled his eyes and did not deign to respond to that. "So I am stuck with you, no matter my feelings on the matter?"

"No matter *our* feelings on the matter," Bergrin said. "You could just go home like a good little prince and stop this whole rebel against daddy thing."

Too furious to respond to that without losing his

temper, Johnnie settled on pretending Bergrin was not there and turned his full attention back to the mystery at hand. If Mark had been taken to be sold off to some abnormal as a magic slave, then he probably was being sold at auction. There were private sales, but auctions brought in more money. The likeliest place for such auctions would be the Pits. His driver had been a fighter in the Pits, so they were local. So small a city, however, would not have the full range of Pits. Likely they had only A through C here; D-Pits attracted a great deal of attention, more than such a small city could endure without attracting the notice of normals.

So probably one of the warehouses around the docks hosted the Pits. He was jarred from his thoughts when Bergrin groaned. "I hate that look in your eyes, Prince."

Gods above, he really hated the stupid, mocking names Bergrin used. "What look?"

"The one that says you've reached some logical conclusion that's going to lead you into doing something stupid."

"Stupidity is the result of not thinking," Johnnie quoted. "I have thought very carefully."

"The need to be right—the sign of a vulgar mind," Bergrin quoted in reply.

"It is not enough to have a good mind; the main thing is to use it well," Johnnie countered. "I use mine very well, and my deductions tell me I am going to the Pits."

Bergrin heaved a long sigh. "Do you even know how stupid an idea that is? You don't even know where they are."

"You probably do, though," Johnnie said. "Not that I intend to waste my time asking you. I do not require your help. I do not require you at all."

"But you're stuck with me, Highness."

"The game is not over yet," Johnnie said icily and stalked off to go in search of the Pits. It did not take him long to figure it out, either. A half-hour of observation and a brief conversation with a woman who thought him pretty, and he was on his way.

"I really do not think the son of a Dracula should be visiting the *Pits*," Bergrin said sourly.

"I really do not care what you think," Johnnie said. "We will not find Mark by avoiding the Pits."

"It is not your balls on the chopping block, Highness," Bergrin said. "I like my balls right where they are, if it's all the same to you. If you did not insist upon doing things like this, you would not require a bodyguard."

Johnnie motioned impatiently with his cane. "I have never had a bodyguard before."

Bergrin smirked. "Are you sure about that?"

Spinning sharply away, infuriated beyond all reason and how he *hated* the way Bergrin smirked and taunted and relished rubbing salt in Johnnie's wounds. Ignoring Bergrin as he reappeared at Johnnie's side, Johnnie strode to the side entrance of a dilapidated looking warehouse where the Pits were located. The guard there eyed him, clearly trying to decide if Johnnie was a buyer or a joke.

"I require admittance," Johnnie said.

"Good for you," the man said. "I don't give a damn."

Johnnie smirked and murmured, "The employer generally gets the employees he deserves." He pulled out one of his business cards and flipped it to the guard. As always happened, the man's eyes popped wide open, and he hastily opened the door.

"I will take that card back," Johnnie said, and when the man made no move to return it, reached out and plucked the business card from his fingers. He motioned to Bergrin with his cane. "He is with me."

Inside, it was just as foul smelling and looking as he had anticipated. Bergrin made a face. "If I'm not able to get it up for my date tonight, Prince, I'm going to kill you myself." He removed his baseball cap and shoved it away inside his old, beat-up corduroy jacket, then raked a hand through his shaggy, curly brown hair in a futile attempt at taming it.

"You could always resign," Johnnie said.

"Perish the thought, Prince."

Biting back choice words that would only encourage him, Johnnie walked on until he came to a man directing the flow of people. "Auctions."

The man stared at him, saw money, and asked, "What are you in the market for?"

"Help around the house," Johnnie answered.

"That way, down the hall, yellow door off to the right," the man said, then turned to help the next person.

Johnnie walked on. The yellow door, when he reached it, was guarded by a brawny werewolf in a black tank top. The muscles were most certainly impressive, but the haggard, angry face was decidedly less so. The wolf glanced at Johnnie with disinterest, but his eyes sharpened as he looked at Bergrin.

Leaving them to their staring contest, Johnnie walked on into the auction room. It was a small, amphitheater style; he could see where they had removed the cage and other such elements that turned it into a fighting ring. The air was thick with the stench of blood, piss, expensive perfume, fancy cigars, and cheap cigarettes. There was also so much magic in the air that Johnnie sneezed three times into a handkerchief he barely pulled out in time. Pulling the brim of his fedora low, he took a seat in the first row, grimacing when Bergrin almost immediately joined him. "I fail to see what you think you will accomplish here—"

"Besides the incurrence of my father's wrath and the loss of your balls?" Johnnie cut in. "I want to see what is on the market, who is buying, and quite possibly, if a selkie is up for sale."

"He was kidnapped three weeks ago," Bergrin said. "He's long gone."

Johnnie shook his head. "No, I do not think so. Auctions are hard to arrange—the people, the goods, the space, the money. On average, they are held once a month, and sometimes only every two months. I was not even certain there would be an auction today, except it is the end of the month, selkies are not often captured, and the woman I spoke with said something about today being a particularly busy day. Taken together, that means an auction. However, if we did happen to miss him, then this will at least provide an opportunity to deduce who might have purchased him.

Bergrin sighed. "I suppose you have theories on that as well."

"Not really," Johnnie said. "My money would be on a collector since, as I said, selkies come up rarely. However, any alchemist or witch with sufficient funds would find a selkie of interest." He looked over the small crowd of potential buyers, grateful that his eyes were long accustomed to the dark.

Wealthy men and women, though several looked more like stewards sent to stand as proxy for their employers. By the look of them, not a single person present would be able to outbid him easily. Ontoniel had always been very generous in seeing his sons had more than sufficient funds because once they came of age, they were largely responsible for their own finances.

Johnnie had taken particular care in learning finances. Unless he did something phenomenally stupid, which was impossible, money was no object. He glanced toward the arena where the auctions would be held and saw from the equipment being set out by assistants that money was to be by wire transfer. That made things easier.

Bergrin shifted impatiently beside him, but Johnnie said nothing. He was just starting to get bored himself, though, when the lights went down and the bidding finally began. Johnnie listened with disinterest to the opening comments, and the information rattled off about the first item up for bid—but his attention was arrested as they dragged the imp in question out to the arena floor.

He was in a terrible state. Clearly the imp had not gone down without a fight. One horn was broken—that would decrease the value—a wing was torn, and he was bandaged in half a dozen places. They had not even given the imp clothes to wear; he stood shivering beneath the harsh spotlights.

Johnnie's anger grew as, around him, the other men and women began to bid with an air of privileged boredom. The bidding went on, his anger increasing as rapidly as the price. When the bidding finally seemed to stall out at $100,000, Johnnie called out,

"$110,000."

A startled silence fell, then the auctioneer called for more bids. When none came, he closed the bidding. Johnnie leaned over and murmured several numbers in Bergrin's ear. Without ever saying a word, Bergrin stood and moved to the tables where money was to be paid. While Bergrin did that, Johnnie turned his attention back to the bidding, where another imp was on the block.

He bought that one as well, and every abnormal to come after that. Finally, the auctioneer announced the final bid of the evening—a selkie, middle-aged but in extremely good health, strong physically and magically, handsome and quiet, should not be too hard to train.

The bidding on Mark started at $25,000. It quickly climbed to $200,000. Selkies were less powerful than most other abnormals, but they were rarely seen on land and because they excelled at hiding their skins, hard to capture.

When the bidding seemed to settle at $300,000, Johnnie raised it to $310,000. Across the room, a man raised it again, and fought Johnnie all the way up to $750,000. Sneering, Johnnie took the bidding to an even million.

"Just who the hell does he think he is?" The man across the room loudly demanded, shaking his head in refusal when the auctioneer looked to him to raise the bid. From the seat above him, a woman in a sleek gray suit bent and murmured something in his ear, causing the loud-mouthed man to blanche and fall silent.

Johnnie winced to think what his father would do to him when he learned that Johnnie had just dropped a cool two million buying up would-be slaves. Because no matter what he did, his father would find out—between the other bidders and his bodyguard, there were too many people who would love to chat with his father right now.

The bidding wrapped up, and Bergrin returned from where he had remained by the payment table to see that only the proper amounts of money changed hands. "They said they'll have your goods waiting by the loading dock out back."

Johnnie nodded, spinning his cane in his hand. "Then let us go pick them up." He pulled out his cell phone and hit the button for his car service. "Send three cars," he said and gave the address. "Yes, I said three. Thank you."

Returning the phone to his pocket, he strode from the arena, back through the building, and around to the loading dock, Bergrin a silent shadow at his side. They were stopped halfway around the building by a group of disgruntled men, including the one who had loudly demanded to know who the hell Johnnie was. "So, what?" the man demanded. "You think because you're some Dracula's kid that you can just come in and buy up everything?"

Shrugging, Johnnie replied, "He who pays the piper calls the tune."

"What the fuck does that mean?" one of the other men muttered.

"It means yes," Bergrin said, stepping forward, pushing Johnnie slightly back. "Back off unless you want trouble."

The man sneered. "I'm not scared of you."

"I will show you fear in a handful of dust," Bergrin quoted.

"What's with all the stupid, snotty lines?" Another

man complained.

Movement caught the corner of Johnnie's eye, and he turned his head slightly to see that his cars were arriving. Turning back to the group of men, he said, "I do not to have time for this. If you are offended by the fact I have more money and power than you, by all means take it up with my father. Bergrin, it's time for us to go."

Bergrin nodded and stepped forward, the men parting around him. Johnnie walked on—and saw too late the man that came up from behind him. He brought his arm up to deflect whatever attack was coming, other hand going to the catch on his cane—but then the spell struck him.

In the next moment Bergrin moved, but almost immediately he froze again, staring at the witch who had thrown the spell at Johnnie. He lay on the pavement, struck by his own spell when it rebounded off Johnnie. "What the fuck?"

Johnnie was equally confounded. He should not have been standing unscathed. "The spell rebounded. That should not have been possible." Noise distracted him briefly, and he watched as the rest of the men had fled. They were likely in no hurry to find out what else might rebound. Well, at least that solved one problem, even if it created others. He glanced back at Bergrin.

Bergrin glared at him. "So I take it you *don't* have magic defenses no one mentioned to me?"

"No," Johnnie replied. He knelt alongside the man who had tried to attack him. Magic filled his nostrils, stirred goose bumps on his skin. The man was twitching slightly, as people did when they dreamed; his mouth was twisted in a grimace of fear.

"Nightmare curse," Johnnie murmured, eyes

sliding to meet Bergrin's equally pensive gaze. "Why would they try to cast a nightmare curse? That is a parlor trick, a child's prank."

Bergrin scowled. "I'd rather know why the fuck it *bounced off you."*

"Yes," Johnnie agreed and rose. "I suggest we figure it out later, though."

"For once, we agree," Bergrin replied and stood. He grabbed Johnnie's upper arm and dragged him along.

"Unhand—"

"Save it," Bergrin snapped. "This is my job and I'm doing it, Highness. If I must knock you out to do it, I will."

Johnnie rolled his eyes, but let himself be dragged along like an invalid. At the back of the warehouse, the seven abnormals he had purchased stood waiting. They had been given clothing, thankfully. They eyed him warily, but before Johnnie could reassure them he did not keep slaves, more men came rushing up from behind them. Bergrin shoved Johnnie toward the nearest car, then drew a wicked-looking knife and lunged, steel flashing beneath the streetlights as he attacked the closest of the half-dozen men.

Swearing as he slammed into the car, Johnnie whipped around and brought his cane up. "Get in the cars!" he called to the huddled abnormals. He turned to face the men coming at him, springing the release on his cane and drawing his sword just as one of them swung a knife. Steel rang against steel as he caught it against his sword.

The man was abruptly ripped away, and Bergrin towered over him and snarled, "Get in the car!" Taken aback by the tone, the flash of something—anger?

Fear?—in Bergrin's hazel eyes, Johnnie got in the car. As he slammed the door shut behind him, he heard screams of pain that were like nothing he had ever heard before.

Then there was abruptly nothing but silence.

Another moment passed and then the cars were moving. Johnnie punched the button to drop the glass between the passengers and the driver. "Where is Bergrin? My bodyguard?"

"He ordered me to go, Master Johnnie," the driver replied. "He was clearly not going to tolerate anything but 'yes, sir,' so I said 'yes, sir,' and drove."

Johnnie closed the glass again, then sat back in his seat and sheathed his sword. He fumed silently, scowling at his missing bodyguard. What was Bergrin doing, staying behind like that? How melodramatic, and he would only exacerbate it all later by heaping on the 'I told you so'. Johnnie really wanted to do something violent to the bastard, but of course, he was nowhere to be found now because he was stuck fighting, and Johnnie hoped he was not dead. Was all of this really because he had spent money? That was too illogical to believe, and so he must deduce the real reason.

The spell, the answer had to be in that stupid, waste of time spell they had tried to cast on him—and which had rebounded. Why in the hell had a spell rebounded? That should only happen if there were heavy wards upon him, or if he had some relic that served essentially the same purpose. Neither was the case, unless there was something he did not know.

But that was unlikely. His father was over-protective, but he would not have had spells cast on Johnnie without telling him because it was extremely dangerous for a person not to know the spells cast upon him, and therefore what people might try to do.

A nightmare curse was a cheap little trick used to scare normals and annoy abnormals. It was not fun, but generally being forced to endure a nightmare for a short period of time was *only* annoying. So why bother? As displeased as those men had been, the entire affair had not been worth all that had just transpired.

"Um—sir?"

Johnnie stirred from his thoughts and glanced at the man who had addressed him. Around his neck, the man wore a collar, from which dangled a gold necklace sealed in a warded mesh bag. So he was close to his skin, but not able to actually use it.

"You are Mark," Johnnie said.

Mark looked at him in surprise. "Yes. How—"

"There was an article in the newspaper about your disappearance; your wife has been most distraught. I realized what was going on when I read the article and came to find you."

"I..." Mark stared at him, wide-eyed. "And the others?"

Johnnie looked at him in brief annoyance. "Was I supposed to leave them there?"

"Uh—no, of course not. I didn't know if you were looking for them, too," Mark replied.

The other man in the car, an imp, stirred and looked at Johnnie. "Doubt he knew about us; I appreciate it all the same."

Johnnie shrugged but said, "You are welcome."

"So is it true, what they were saying?" the imp asked. "That you're the son of the Dracula Desrosiers?"

"Yes," Johnnie said. "I am his younger son. Once Mark is reunited with his wife, and my companion has broken the wards upon all of you, the cars will take you wherever you want to go." As he finished speaking, they pulled into the driveway of Mark's house. Rostiya and Pearl came out a moment later and stood waiting on the front porch.

Mark sighed softly, eyes on his wife. "She knows now, doesn't she?"

"Yes," Johnnie replied.

Sighing again, Mark seemed to gather himself, then opened the car door and climbed out.

Johnnie glanced at the imp. "Best collect your companions and inform them of what I have told you," he said. "I will speak with Rostislav about your wards." When he climbed out of the car, Pearl was shouting and crying and pounding her fists on her husband's chest—but when Mark pulled her into a tight embrace, she did not protest. Moving to join Rostislav on the porch, Johnnie saw Rostislav smirk and snapped, "What?"

"What did you do, purchase every abnormal who went up for bid?"

"Why does that seem so strange?" Johnnie demanded. "What was I supposed to do, let them all be sold into slavery?"

Rostislav just laughed and shook his head. "Of course not. I guess you need me to break their wards?"

"Yes," Johnnie replied and dismissed the matter, content to leave it to Rostislav and turn his attention to the problem at the docks. Where was his babysitter?

"What has you frowning so hard?" Rostiya asked when he returned a few minutes later to find Johnnie still scowling.

Tersely, Johnnie explained all that had transpired at the Pits. "That... that doesn't make any sense," Rostislav said. He reached out and splayed a hand on Johnnie's chest, eyes falling shut as he concentrated. He opened his eyes and withdrew his hand a couple of minutes later. "Nothing; there is nothing on you other than the residue of living your entire life surrounded by abnormals. Does your cane have protections of some sort?"

"No," Johnnie said, but he handed it over for Rostislav to examine. "Neither does my dagger."

"I am at a loss," Rostislav said, returning the cane and shaking his head. "I think you will have to ask Lord Ontoniel."

Johnnie winced at the mention of his father. Of course, it also reminded him that Bergrin was still nowhere to be found, and really, why had he not reappeared to yell at Johnnie and start in with the 'I told you so'. Had the idiot actually gotten himself killed? The thought turned Johnnie's blood cold, made his gut twist. Surely he had not—

"Johnnie?"

"Hmm?"

Rostiya was frowning at him. "Are you all right?"

"Fine," Johnnie said. He started to ask if they could leave, but Pearl and Mark approached before he could get the question out.

"I can't thank you enough," Mark said, extending his hand.

Johnnie shook it. "No thanks are necessary. I am glad I was able to help. Hopefully you will be troubled no further."

Mark nodded. "We will probably move, find a

quieter beach where I don't have to hide as much." He looked at his wife, who scowled but squeezed his arm. "Really, whatever I can do to repay you, just ask. I thought I was going to spend the rest of my life as some alchemist's slave. You've saved my life."

"I saw a mystery in want of solving," Johnnie said. "I am glad all will be well."

Pearl stepped forward, nervous and curious and determined. "So—uh—is it true you're a vampire? I'm sorry, this is all so new—"

Johnnie shook his head. "No, I am not a vampire. I am a normal, much like you. My father, however, is a vampire. He adopted me when my parents were killed."

"Oh," Pearl said—then suddenly turned and thumped her husband's chest again.

Mark grimaced, but said nothing.

"We will leave you in peace," Johnnie said. "Do call, however, if there is further trouble with you or the others."

"Sure," Mark replied. "I'll see they all get where they need to go. It's the least I can do. Thank you again, for helping all of us." Johnnie nodded. Mark hesitated, then asked, "Is your friend okay?"

"Yes," Johnnie said, though he was not at all certain of that. "Bergrin is very good at taking care of himself." He hoped. Fervently. There never should have been such a threat to his person, and if he had thought there would be, he would have... Well, he probably would have done the same thing. Why had it all gone wrong? Nothing he had bid on—

Him, of course, Johnnie realized, furious with himself. They had probably thought to kidnap him, thinking Ontoniel would empty his coffers to get his son back.

Except...

Johnnie's gut twisted, sharp and painful. He ignored it and focused on the facts.

Ontoniel's wife had murdered Johnnie's parents. A sense of guilt, and probably duty, had driven Ontoniel to adopt Johnnie. As Ontoniel was very traditional, and held much stock in protocol, this had been a very earth-shattering thing for him to do.

He had raised Johnnie like a real son, but the truth was that Johnnie was *not* his real son. He would never marry another vampire, he could never contribute to the family the way Ellie did, he would never hold a powerful position in the supernatural world. He was, in short, a burden. Even his little talent for solving mysteries amounted to nothing, so far as everyone was concerned—including his father.

So would Ontoniel pay a ransom for him?

Johnnie could not see a practical reason that he would. He had set Bergrin on him to avoid these problems, and Ontoniel did care—but only to a point. So this entire mess, and possibly Bergrin's life, had been for nothing. Ontoniel's honor would demand blood, but it would not require a ransom.

Ellie would require a ransom, not Johnnie.

Unable to continue thinking about it, he bid Mark and Pearl a last farewell.

"I'll stay here and help," Rostislav said, smiling. "Did you want me to send you home?"

"No," Johnnie said, "I will take a car back."

"Come over later this week," Rostislav said.

Johnnie nodded. "I will." He turned away and strode to his waiting car and slid into the back seat. As the car pulled away, he leaned back in his seat and closed his eyes.

"So have we learned something from all this, Highness?"

Johnnie jerked, eyes snapping open to see Bergrin sitting in the far corner of the opposite seat, so ensconced in shadows that it was little wonder Johnnie had not seen him. "When did you get here?" he snapped. "When were you going to let me know you were here and not dead or bleeding out—" He cut himself off. "You are truly obnoxious, babysitter. Nothing but growling and sniping and skulking about and vanishing dramatically."

"Maybe the next time I tell you that something is a bad idea, you'll fucking listen to me!" Bergrin snapped.

"Their behavior was illogical," Johnnie said. "Attacking me over the auctions was disproportionate to my actions."

"Criminals don't have to make sense!" Bergrin snarled. "You hurt their pride, you snatched up goods they've been eying for weeks, if not months, and you *flaunted* your power. Of course they fucking tried to kill you!"

"The first group, maybe," Johnnie said. "But the second group was looking to capture."

"Yes," Bergrin said.

"You took care of them."

"Yes."

Johnnie was silent, then slowly said, "I am sorry."

Bergrin grunted, then said just as stiffly, "You were trying to do the right thing. Forget it."

"Are you hurt?"

Bergrin smirked briefly. "Only scrapes and bruises. They never stood a chance."

Johnnie shot him a withering look. "You have a

great deal of nerve getting on me for arrogance."

"I don't flaunt it to the point of suicide, Highness," Bergrin retorted. "Even you did not think I was more than a local drunk."

Preferring not to think about that, Johnnie moved the conversation along. "So did you inform my father?"

"I thought I'd see if you were going to face the music."

"No," Johnnie said, "but it little matters. Someone else will have already scurried along to tell the Dracula that his silly little adopted human was throwing around money in the Pits." His father was going to *kill* him. Really, though, what was he supposed to have done? Left them all to be bought up by the very same men who had just tried to capture or kill him? Johnnie stifled a sigh and looked out the window, wondering if there was *any* possible way to convince his father not to drag him home and lock him in his room.

"So what did you do with the others you bought?" Bergrin asked, breaking the silence.

"Mark is going to see they get to where they want to be. I left the cars to assist," Johnnie replied. "Hopefully they will not be recaptured."

Silence fell again, and Johnnie resumed staring morosely out the window at the passing glimpses of night-shrouded scenery. He wanted to be back home at the Bremen, playing cards or reading, enjoying a glass of vodka.

Instead, he was minutes away from his father's wrath. He was surprised Bergrin was not yelling at him more than he had.

"So you can actually use that fancy little sword stick of yours?" Bergrin asked. "I thought you just enjoyed having it for show, but you seemed to have some skill back there."

"Of course I can use it," Johnnie said. "My father is quite traditional about such things. I am well-schooled in swordsmanship, as well as other things. My father would not have given me my dagger if he did not believe I could properly use it."

Bergrin only murmured a thoughtful, possibly doubtful, "Hmm."

Johnnie almost snapped at him, but caught himself. He did not know what Bergrin had done to make his assailants scream like they had, but he knew even his dagger and sword, impressive though they were, could not begin to compare.

"So how does one become an Enforcer?" he asked instead.

Bergrin stirred from wherever his mind had taken him and glanced at Johnnie in surprise. He smiled faintly, bringing his plain face to life and making Johnnie think of the Cheshire Cat. "One goes down the rabbit-hole."

"One falls into it?" Johnnie asked dryly. "That seems rather... lax, for so important a position."

"Well, it's not exactly the sort of job one finds in the wanted section," Bergrin replied. "It was your brother, years ago. Slinking off to where you shouldn't go seems to be a family trait. I saw him, I knew who he was, followed him. Some men were ready for him—but they weren't ready for me. I got him back home, left him there. Three days later, your father offered me a job. I was hired on a trial basis for one year, then made a full employee, if that's even the word for it."

Johnnie's curiosity was well and truly piqued now, despite himself. "So do you usually play bodyguard?"

"No, though I have done that a time or six for your brother. Usually I do find and retrieve style work. I have a knack for finding things people don't want found."

"Somehow, that does not surprise me," Johnnie said, and realized with annoyance that he wanted to smile.

Bergrin smirked.

Scowling, Johnnie asked, "So why were you switched to watching me?"

"Your father trusts me more than some of the others. He does not want so much as a single hair harmed on the head of his golden boy."

Johnnie snorted at that. Elam was Father's golden boy. Johnnie was a constant reminder of past tragedies. He was a duty Ontoniel felt obligated to attend.

"You don't believe me?"

"It is illogical," Johnnie replied. "Father dotes on his real son." Not the human one he'd had more or less forced upon him.

Bergrin shrugged and said nothing. Johnnie resumed his staring until the car finally pulled up in front of the Bremen. Climbing out of the car, thanking the driver, he waited until Bergrin was with him, then led the way inside. A group of wide-eyed, silent, pale-faced men greeted him. Johnnie frowned at them. "You all look like a group of normals who have seen their first ghost."

"Uh—worse," Peyton said and pointed one finger to the ceiling, indicating Johnnie's rooms. "We just saw a Dracula."

Johnnie froze. His father was *here*? He pinched the bridge of his nose, then managed a brief, "I see. Excuse me, please." Striding across the room, he quickly climbed the stairs and opened the door to his apartment.

Ontoniel sat in a leather chair in the living area, reading a book by the light of a tiffany lamp. Johnnie recognized the book as one of his herbalists. His father removed his reading glasses and looked up as Johnnie arrived, his mouth quirked with amusement when he said, "If you want to be a philanthropist, John, there are less dramatic ways to go about it."

"I knew they would not waste time running to you," Johnnie said in disgust.

"My secretary fielded no less than thirty phone calls," Ontoniel replied and picked up the cup of tea on the side table by his chair. Johnnie recognized the smell of it—rose tea, another of his father's favorites. But Johnnie had not brought any of it with him. Ontoniel had brought tea?

He could not determine what that meant. "I am sorry they caused you so much trouble. I did not intend to cause such a ruckus."

Ontoniel looked at him a long time, expression shuttered, making Johnnie want to fidget. At last he sighed and said, "Sit down, John. Tell me what transpired, beginning to end."

Johnnie nodded, but instead of sitting, he strode to his bedroom and put away his jacket, hat, and other bits of going-out clothing, making certain it was all neat and properly hung and not yet in need of cleaning. In just his shirt sleeves and vest, he returned to the living area. Settling down in his favorite spot on his leather couch, he recounted everything, from Rostiya's arrival to his return to the Bremen. Silence fell, thick and oppressive, as he finished.

Finally, Ontoniel said, "You have absolutely no real comprehension as regards your actions, do you?"

Johnnie bristled. "I am fully aware of my mistakes, Father."

"I do not doubt you believe that, John," Ontoniel said. "You have always been a quick learner; you learn too quickly for anyone's peace of mind, especially mine." Not certain what to say to that, Johnnie said nothing, only continued to scowl. Ontoniel sighed. "You *were* stupid, John. I do not assign bodyguards because I think you weak or ill-equipped or any of the other things going through that head of yours. I give you bodyguards because people know you are no fool and will use means beyond your ability to counter."

"Which is essentially all things abnormal," Johnnie said, not quite able to keep all the bitterness from his voice.

For a moment, something like gentleness flickered across Ontoniel's face. It quickly vanished beneath his more familiar sternness. "John... if tragedy had not struck, even now you would be completely normal. It is not so bad a thing to be. *Non omnia possumus omnes*."

We cannot all do everything. Johnnie shrugged irritably, quoting, "And oftentimes excusing of a fault/Doth make the fault worse by the excuse."

Ontoniel sighed. "I am not making excuses for you Johnnie. You are hardly normal, in the end, for all you may not possess any particular abnormal traits—"

"What about the way that spell rebounded?" Johnnie demanded. "Why in the hell did it do that?"

"I do not know," Ontoniel said. "I think it best to leave the matter alone for now. You are alive and safe. That is all that matters to me."

Johnnie looked at him. Ontoniel was lying. He started to say that, then thought better of it. If he wanted to play games, then games they would play. Johnnie would figure out why Ontoniel was lying by himself, just as he always did.

"Your parents wanted you to be normal," Ontoniel said with the firm voice of a Dracula. "I defied their wishes when I adopted you. That you flourish the way you do, never hampered by your lack of abnormal abilities, speaks all the better of you. I suppose you will only see that with time.

"But," he continued, "it was not to your mistakes I referred when I said you did not comprehend your actions. I can see you will tread more carefully and better remember to have a care for poor Bergrin."

Johnnie nodded stiffly. The bastard was insufferable and arrogant and *smug*, but Johnnie did not want him dead.

"Good," Ontoniel said. "I was referring to the fact you spent three million—"

"Two million," Johnnie corrected.

Ontoniel smiled in that razor way of his, and Johnnie realized he had been played. "Two million dollars on buying up abnormals simply because it was the right thing to do. Sariah—" He stopped for a moment, then said quietly, "Sariah was given to much the same propensities."

Johnnie stared at him in shock. Ontoniel *never* discussed his late wife if he could possibly avoid doing so, and he had definitely never compared Johnnie to her.

"You need to be more careful, John," Ontoniel continued. "Here, on your own, away from the safety of my homes, it is harder to keep you safe. Though

Elam is Alucard, you are by far the better prize to capture."

Johnnie frowned at that because it made no sense—but then he saw it, and wondered why he had not seen it before. He was normal, one hundred percent boring, unremarkable human. Weaker, and less important to the wider community. If anyone dared to harm the Alucard, they would bring down far more than the Dracula on their heads. But for one adopted human? He was the better—easier—catch, though he still was not convinced that Ontoniel would or even should pay a ransom for him.

But he could not bring himself to ask. "Yes, Father," he said stiffly.

Ontoniel sighed. "I am not going to order you home, John, not unless I feel there is no other choice. I do not like you out here in the open, and in so dangerous an area, but if this makes you happy, I will put up with it. Simply try harder to have a care. Recklessness is a predominant trait with you, and it is a dangerous trait. Even your remarkable intelligence will not temper your recklessness much. I had hoped, and still am hoping, that Bergrin will provide a calming influence."

Johnnie sneered inwardly at that, but at the look his father gave him, did not voice his thoughts.

Chuckling, Ontoniel said, "Perhaps he is already doing so. At any rate, he is a quieter presence than Rostislav."

"Yes, about Rostiya," Johnnie said, "Bergrin mentioned before that Rostiya is not on the banned list." Ontoniel laughed. "So there is such a list?" Johnnie demanded.

"Yes," Ontoniel said. "It is a standard list for my

entire household, with one or two unique additions per person. Six hundred years is a long time, John—plenty of time to acquire enemies." He stopped, then added dryly, "Though I did not have half so many as you do at your age."

Johnnie pointedly ignored that. "Why did you not add Rostiya?"

Ontoniel snorted. "Jesse and Rostiya are not evil; they are merely scandalous. If that was all it took to be blacklisted by me, we would have no friends or acquaintances at all. Everyone is kicking up a fuss now, but it will ease over time. Six hundred or so years is also plenty of time to forget these sorts of things have and will happen."

"Ellie was rather harsh—"

"Your brother is young and inflexible," Ontoniel said. "Much of that is my fault, as I used to be far more traditional about certain things than I am now. He was spoken to, I promise."

Johnnie unbent slightly. "Rostiya said it was Ellie who told him I was at the Bremen."

"Interesting," Ontoniel said, looking surprised. "Perhaps he has relaxed more than I realized. So I trust that for now you will stop trying to get yourself and Bergrin killed and giving me heart attacks?"

Johnnie snorted at the absurdity of Ontoniel having a heart attack, but dutifully replied, "Yes, Father."

"Then I will leave you to rest," Ontoniel said. "I also brought a couple of boxes of things that Lila insisted you should have."

"Thank you," Johnnie said. "I am sorry to have bothered you, Father."

Ontoniel shook his head. "It is not that you

bothered me, but I expect that is the only way you would see it."

"What does *that* mean?"

"Good night, John," Ontoniel replied, and then was gone.

Grimacing, Johnnie gave up thinking about all of it. Striding back into his bedroom, he stripped off his clothes and set them aside for dry-cleaning. Retrieving a towel from its hook in the closet, he left his bedroom and crossed the living room to the bathroom, turning out lights as he went. Only the orange-yellow glow of the street lamps and the blue-white nightlight in the bathroom kept his apartment from absolute dark. Turning on the shower, he waited until the water turned steaming, then climbed inside and began to scrub away the day.

Several minutes later he climbed out, reaching for his towel and drying off roughly before he returned to his bedroom. He dried off more thoroughly, then threw his towel in a hamper. Moving to his dresser, he combed out his hair, then strode to his bed and slipped beneath the covers.

He had just closed his eyes when he felt an awareness that had become far too familiar. Johnnie opened his eyes and sat up. Predictably, he could see nothing. But he could smell myrrh and musk roses. He could *feel* the magic prickle along his skin. He could feel Eros's eyes on him, more deeply and thoroughly than he would shortly feel Eros's touch.

Johnnie drew breath to speak—a mouth covered his and a long, hard body pushed him down into the bedding. A hand captured both of his, pinned them to the mattress. Eros's mouth was rough, almost aggressive, bruising Johnnie's mouth. His free hand was no better as he tore away blankets and mapped Johnnie's skin.

Grunting, Johnnie bit hard at Eros's lips, gasped for breath when Eros pulled back. "What—"

"Shut up," Eros muttered and attacked his mouth again, not relenting until Johnnie was hot and dizzy and incapable of remembering why he had been angry. Eros withdrew with a last biting kiss to trail his mouth down Johnnie's body, freeing Johnnie's wrists only so he would have both hands free to touch, torment, drive Johnnie wild with need.

Johnnie gasped and jerked as two fingers shoved inside him, abrupt and unexpected, but warm and slick. He obediently spread his legs wider when Eros silently ordered it, scrambling for purchase in Eros's soft hair, the sweat-slick skin of his well-muscled body, desperate for more as he was thoroughly finger-fucked.

Tonight was different. Eros was usually gentler, more thorough, a slow and steady burn. Tonight was more like a flash fire, and Johnnie sensed he would be feeling it for days. He groaned as the fingers withdrew and Eros began to push inside, hard and hot, stretching and filling him. Johnnie's head fell back, digging into the pillow. He reached out to grab hold of something, crying out as Eros rammed all the way in with a single hard motion.

His nails dug into Eros's back, and he clung for dear life as Eros rode him hard and fast, setting a punishing pace. When he finally came, Johnnie bit his lip to keep from screaming loud enough to draw attention from downstairs.

He barely held back a whimper as Eros pulled away, both of them panting heavily in the dark. When he could finally speak again, Johnnie asked, "What was that all about?"

Eros kissed him hard. "I don't approve of your behavior. There is no pleasure in knowing you could have been kidnapped or killed."

Johnnie drew back—or tried to, but for his efforts only found himself tangled quite thoroughly by blankets and Eros, who pinned him by half-draping himself along Johnnie's body. "Why am I not surprised you know?" Johnnie said.

Eros laughed softly, breaths warm against Johnnie's skin, stirring goose bumps. "Of course I know. You are far too reckless for anyone's peace of mind."

He was really getting tired of hearing that sort of thing. First he was too intelligent for peace of mind, now too reckless? Which was it? "Reckless implies a lack of thought," he said coldly.

Eros laughed again. "You're reckless because you're too smart for your own good, Johnnie. You're so busy examining trees, you never notice who else might be in the forest or what they're doing."

Johnnie freed himself enough to drive an elbow back into Eros's gut. In response, Eros only laughed again—then moved, pinning Johnnie face down on the bed, spreading his legs wide and settling between them. "Get off me," Johnnie snapped, even as his body betrayed him by shuddering and trying to move even closer to Eros.

"No," Eros said in his ear, then bit it. Johnnie jerked, but could not move away. Eros put teeth and tongue and lips elsewhere, exploring Johnnie thoroughly from throat to ass, and Johnnie *hated* how easy it was to forget *everything* when Eros was touching him, fucking him. How had he allowed these nights to become a habitual part of his life? How had he allowed even one?

Eros released him, but only to move Johnnie so he was on all fours on the bed. Johnnie folded his arms to pillow his head, muffling his sounds in the bedding as Eros wasted no time shoving back inside him. Johnnie gasped at the overstimulation to his already thoroughly used hole, but pressed back seeking more.

The fucking was slower the second time, but still just as thorough. Eros drove in deep and paused briefly before pulling out and shoving back in. Johnnie suspected he would be spending the next day moving as little as possible, but he could not seem to make himself sorry about it.

Johnnie smothered his cries in the blankets as he came, only barely hearing Eros's much quieter cries above him. They collapsed on the opposite side of Johnnie's bed, and he was too exhausted to protest when Eros bundled him close, tangling them together. Their scents mingled in the air, on their cooling skin, and Johnnie noted irritably that he would never be able to smell myrrh and musk roses without getting hard. "So am I ever going to be permitted to see you? Spend time with you in daylight?" Johnnie asked when the silence stretched on.

Eros's only reply was more silence. Every night they went through the same conversation. Johnnie did not know why he bothered to bring it up over and over again, except that persistence was all he had. Whatever, whoever, Eros was, he was beyond Johnnie's abilities to counter. "So does it please you to have me this way?" he asked bitterly. "Does it thrill you to keep Desrosiers's son as your dirty little secret?"

The arms around him tightened, nearly to the point of pain, Eros's face buried in the cradle of Johnnie's neck and shoulder. "That—no, Johnnie. Never. I—that's not it at all."

"What then?" Johnnie asked. What was the point of a lover he had never seen, did not truly know, who did not trust him? Did not want or care enough to even let Johnnie see his face.

Eros sighed softly. "I can't have you in daylight. It's not allowed, or wouldn't be allowed, and now I'm afraid it's too late, anyway."

Johnnie was so very tired of the excuses, the cryptic answers. "So why can it not be *our* secret?"

"Because candlelight will not reveal an Eros, but quite his opposite," Eros replied. "I am no beauty, no noble—I am nothing."

"You are a coward," Johnnie snapped.

"I cannot deny that," Eros said. "If you do not want me to come—"

"I want you to—kiss me in broad daylight," Johnnie said, furious with himself over what he had nearly said instead of 'kiss.' He twisted free, turned away, put his back to Eros, though he could not quite make himself pull entirely out of the arms that still held him.

Eros kissed the side of his neck, his cheek—then he was simply gone, and Johnnie sighed, staring bitterly at the orange-yellow light of the streetlamps now bleeding through the curtains. He had no idea how to be a normal, but he was still too normal ever to be a proper abnormal. His father had adopted him out of guilt, his brother—

Johnnie's thoughts faltered.

He had not thought of Elam in days—weeks, even.

Between his new life, his new friends, his cases, his babysitter, and Eros... He balled one hand into a fist and pounded it into the bedding. He was furious and shaken and lost because he had barely caught himself in time to say 'kiss' instead of 'love.' *I want you to love me in broad daylight.* Bad enough he kept begging Eros to stop keeping secrets. Bad enough he kept letting Eros fuck him, use him, night after night. Bad enough he only had a family due to guilt. Bad enough he was normal.

He would be damned if he *begged* for a cowardly shadow to love him. He was not yet that pathetic. Disgusted with himself, too awake now to sleep, Johnnie threw back the blankets and climbed out of bed. He grimaced at his state: sticky, sore, well and thoroughly used.

Refusing to think any more about it, he fetched a fresh towel and went to get another shower. Then he would read, study, investigate, because his father was lying to him, and Eros was a coward, and he would uncover their damned secrets if it was the last thing he did.

Case 005: Snake Leaves

Johnnie sunk another ball, then another, quickly and neatly clearing the pool table.

Around him, the bar was oddly quiet, save for the empty noise of the TV above the bar. Outside, the rain poured relentlessly down in heavy sheets, the pounding, drumming sound of it seeming to drive out the energy of all who heard it, broken only by the odd burst of thunder.

Stepping back, Johnnie picked up the shot glass Peyton had brought him a few minutes ago and knocked back his vodka. He lifted the glass to Peyton, signaling for another, then motioned to Walsh. "Rack'em." Obediently Walsh fetched the balls from the pockets and set them up again. He stepped back and motioned for Johnnie to proceed. Returning to the pool table, Johnnie bent and began to sink the balls.

"I'm starting to think we should get a second one," Peyton said in amusement as he brought a fresh shot.

"So buy it," Johnnie said dismissively, sinking three more balls. Outside, thunder ripped through the sky, crashing and booming, then fading away slowly while the rain continued tirelessly on.

Peyton laughed. "Going stir crazy, Johnnie? You do nothing but read and write and shoot pool."

"I am bored out of my mind," Johnnie replied and sank another ball. "I am tired of trying to find something that does not exist." He sank the last ball, then accepted the shot Peyton still held, tossing it back in one smooth motion. He handed his cue stick to Walsh, then returned to the pile of books and papers he had left on one of the tables.

"What are you trying to find?" Micah asked from where he sat at the bar, steadily working through beer and nachos while he chatted with Nelson about whatever sports game was on the TV. Johnnie shook his head, not willing to discuss either Eros or the riddle of rebounding spells. Micah smiled in understanding and said only, "I think you need a break."

Nodding in agreement, Johnnie flipped open his latest bestiary; it was a joke, a ratty old thing full of nonsense and wishful thinking. Even in the supernatural world, some things simply did not exist—birds with tears that could heal all wounds, ghosts that could wander freely, horses with wings. The list went on and on, and every word of it was useless. He did not know why he bothered. If he was this desperate for a solution, it was time to stop. Shutting the book again in disgust, Johnnie stared angrily at his pathetic one page of notes. There was precious little about Eros that he actually *knew*, and really, most of it was educated supposition.

Powerful. Fearless. Myrrh and musk roses. Was able to bypass most, if not all, wards. Lower to middle class. That was a strong supposition, but Johnnie was confident about it. Not beautiful. Another supposition, but Johnnie had a *very* strong hunch that Eros hated that name because he was not beautiful. 'Quite his opposite' had been the exact words. What was the opposite of love? Hate? That made no sense. So it must be a matter of beauty.

He believed one hundred percent that Eros *must* be a half-breed of some sort. Given how unpredictable the results of such things could be? There was no telling who or what had combined to give birth to Eros. Johnnie was beginning to despair of ever solving the mystery. He could solve others, but he could not solve the mystery of Eros.

Neither could he seem to solve the mystery of the rebounding spell. Rostislav had confirmed there were no spells upon him, and his parents had wanted to live a normal life, so they would not have cast spells upon him. Ontoniel would have told him if he had done it—yet Ontoniel was keeping a secret.

"You look as gloomy as the weather," Peyton said, pulling him from his thoughts. Glass clinked as Peyton set another shot on the table.

"Thank you," Johnnie said and tossed the vodka back. "I do not like secrets."

Peyton nodded. "Secrets always cause more problems than they solve."

Johnnie grunted in agreement.

Thunder cracked and boomed, hard enough to shake the bar. Lightning lit the place up clear and bright as the middle of day for the span of a heartbeat. Then the bar returned to normal, lit only by a few old lights overhead and the lurid brightness of the TV screen. Outside, the rain fell harder than ever, and even Johnnie began to wonder if it would ever stop.

He had not seen Eros in nearly a week, too stubborn to give his secretive, cowardly lover—fuck toy—an opportunity to visit. But there was no use denying privately that half his current tension was purely for want of a fuck. Sighing at himself, Johnnie slammed all his books shut and stacked them neatly to carry back upstairs later. Though he had absolutely no desire to go out in such foul weather—

The sound of the door banging open drew his and everyone else's attention, and they looked up to see Heath step inside amidst a torrent of rain. He looked like nothing so much as a drowned rat, and oddly somber as he removed his things and hung them up.

Peyton slid him a glass of blood wine without a word, and Heath murmured a silent thanks. He drank half of it, then walked to Johnnie's table and sat down across from him. "Ever heard of these?" Heath asked and reaching into his pocket, pulled out a small, clear plastic bag in which were three small, long, sharply-pointed, dark green leaves.

Taking them, Johnnie examined the leaves, then recited, "After a while a second snake crept out of the corner, but as soon as he saw the other lying dead in three pieces, he went back and quickly returned with three green leaves in his mouth. Then he took the three separate portions of the snake, placed them together and laid a leaf on each wound, and no sooner were they joined than the snake raised himself as lively as ever, and went away hastily with his companion."

Heath rolled his eyes.

Johnnie drew one of the leaves from the bag and twirled it in his finger. "But they are only legend. No leaf can actually bring the dead back to life. Nothing can. Dead is dead."

"Tell that to my friend Carrie," Heath said. "Her father died last year. About a week ago, she received a plant in thanks from one of her customers—she doesn't know who, but that sort of thing happens a lot. She planted it in her garden. A couple of days later, she woke up to noise. She went downstairs and saw someone ransacking her father's study. Only when the intruder turned around, she saw it was her father. He came toward her, and Carrie fled. She's refused to go back to the house since. I only just learned about all this a couple of hours ago."

Johnnie nodded. "Did you go to the house yourself?"

"Yes," Heath said. "I think her father wasn't the only one to ransack the place."

"Did you linger long enough to see her father? Did he bear all the marks of the draugr?"

Heath smiled and shook his head, chuckling softly. "You knew the moment you saw the leaves."

Johnnie twirled the leaf he held again. "This plant is largely believed to be extinct, but abnormal records reliably prove that it is still around, if extremely hard to find. Something about the scent of snake leaves calls to the dead and raises them from their slumber. Alchemists and magic-users find them useful in necrotic workings. The reason for calling them snake leaves is lost, though theories abound. The most popular one is that the man who first discovered their peculiar ability bore a white snake as his crest."

Heath laughed again. "You're a piece of work."

Shrugging, Johnnie said, "If you are here and telling me about the draugr, you did not destroy it."

"Oh, I destroyed it. I also destroyed the snake leaf bush. See, it's not that which is bugging me. I told you—someone else has been in there. They were looking for something. I think they hoped raising ol' Mike as a draugr would lead them to it. I don't know if they got what they wanted or not, but I do know Carrie is still too terrified to go home. She's a good friend. I need you to figure out who did this and why."

Johnnie nodded. "Address?"

Heath reached into his pocket and pulled out a business card that had somehow managed to stay dry. "Her father was an alchemist; this is their home. I told Carrie that I would get someone to help and that you might be stopping by to see her. She's staying with a friend. That address and phone number are on the back."

Taking the card, Johnnie tucked it away in the pocket of his black, blue, and silver striped vest. Then he returned to staring at the snake leaf he held, once more twirling it back and forth, pondering it.

"You're already thinking hard," Heath said. "Do you think it's that easy a case, or that difficult?"

Johnnie did not take his eyes off the snake leaf as he quoted, "Singularity is almost invariably a clue. The more featureless and commonplace a crime is, the more difficult it is to bring it home."

Heath sighed. "And that means?"

"It means—" Johnnie was cut off by a resounding sneeze from across the room. He looked toward Bergrin and called out, "You are to be seen and not heard."

"Get rid of that damned snake weed, then," Bergrin groused. He stood up and crossed the room and took the other empty seat at Johnnie's table. He scowled at the snake leaves. "I'm allergic as hell to those damned things."

Johnnie quirked one brow but put the leaves back in the bag and sealed it. "You are allergic to a rare, imported plant that most believe to be extinct?"

"Yes," Bergrin snapped. "My father is an alchemist, too."

"Ah," Johnnie said, then added with exaggerated politeness, "As we will be likely running into more of them, perhaps you should remain here."

Bergrin smirked in that way Johnnie hated. "Nice try, Highness, but no dice."

Making a face, Johnnie stood and went to go get dressed for going out, already dreading the rain that would ruin his clothes and leave him feeling wet for days. It took him only a few minutes to pull on a plain black blazer to match his slacks, hiding the smooth gray of his shirt save where it was visible behind the striped vest. He shrugged into a long, heavy, weather-proofed trench coat and pulled down a black fedora with a gray band. Last he pulled on his rain boots, grimacing again as he thought about what the weather would do to his clothes. Still, he would endure it for a mystery—anything to distract him from the difficulties of Eros and rebounding spells.

Returning downstairs, he saw that Heath was nursing a full bottle of wine, and Chuck and Nelson had reclaimed the pool table. Bergrin leaned against the wall by the front door, patiently waiting. Normally, he wore browns, greens, blues—muted colors and shades that blended in, went unnoticed. Bergrin was *very* good at being invisible, as much as Johnnie hated to admit it.

Today, though, he seemed as dark and gloomy as the weather, as everyone else who was sick of the unending rain. He wore dark denim jeans and black work boots, a tight-fitting, long-sleeved, black t-shirt, over which he had pulled a black leather jacket. Even his baseball cap, usually blue and white, had been exchanged for a rather new-looking one. It was all black, the front stitched with a cartoonish looking grim-reaper, complete with flowing robes, scythe, and bright red eyes. It was ridiculous looking.

"Nice hat," Johnnie said. "Is that new?"

"Yes," Bergrin said, scowling, looking defensive. "My mom gave it to me for my birthday."

Johnnie had prepared a taunting response, but the unexpected words drew him up short. "Your birthday? When was your birthday?"

"Yesterday," Bergrin replied shortly.

"Hmm," Johnnie said. "I suppose it is better than knowing you picked it out yourself."

"Shut up," Bergrin said, "or I'll shove you into a puddle and ruin all that pretty, expensive silk you're wearing, Prince."

Ignoring him, Johnnie retrieved his umbrella from its hook on the wall and said, "Shall we, babysitter?"

"After you, Highness."

Bracing himself, Johnnie threw open the door and dashed for the car Peyton had called while Johnnie got dressed, Bergrin close on his heels. Throwing themselves into the car, Bergrin pulled the door shut while Johnnie told the driver where to take them.

"About an hour drive, sir," the driver told him.

"That is fine," Johnnie replied. He glanced at Bergrin and said, "So what do you know about draugr?"

"The after-goers, those who walk after death," Bergrin replied, tugging on the brim of his cap. "Draugr wake when those things and persons they love are threatened. They also wake when forced to, most often by a sorcerer or magic user of similar caliber. Death-black and corpse-pale; the longer they wander, the stronger they grow. One of the few creatures that can naturally shape-shift, if allowed to grow that strong, though their forms are limited to cat and raven. To destroy a draugr, one must decapitate it and then burn the remains. The normals have a popular story that recounts the defeat of one terrible draugr called *Hrómundar saga Gripssonar.*"

Johnnie looked at him in surprise, something about the way Bergrin spoke making his skin prickle. Then he realized what was odd about it. "You said that beautifully. The Old Norse was perfectly pronounced."

Bergrin actually looked embarrassed. "Uh—I was crazy about mythology as a kid. Normal, abnormal. The Norse stuff was my favorite."

"I see," Johnnie replied. "Here I thought you must have spent your formative years learning how to skulk and impersonate drunks."

Bergrin bared his teeth. "Instead of learning how to sip tea and the difference between silk and linen?"

Johnnie smirked. "Incidental lessons. My primary focus was learning how to ignore bothersome shadows."

"What a coincidence: I was learning how to be a bothersome shadow."

Johnnie made a face and removed his fedora, setting it aside with his umbrella and cane on the seat beside him. When, he wondered, had he and Bergrin slipped from open hostility to almost friendly banter? It drove him mad, but he could not seem to stop.

"I wonder what I am getting us into today," he mused aloud. "With alchemists, it could be everything or nothing."

Bergrin grimaced and said, "Philosophy is odious and obscure/Both law and physic are for petty wits/Divinity is basest of the three—/'Tis magic, magic, that hath ravished me."

Johnnie looked at him, reluctantly impressed. "Quite so. History is rife with magic users who could not leave well enough alone, many of them alchemists." Something flickered across Bergrin's face, a flood of emotions too tangled and quickly gone again for Johnnie to properly catch them all—but he saw pain and love and something he thought was loneliness. He swallowed and tried to pretend he had seen nothing. "You said your father is an alchemist, yes?"

Bergrin nodded. "Not a very good one. He likes thinking and writing about it more than actually doing."

"Where do your parents live?" Johnnie asked, more startled than he knew he should be to hear about something as common as parents from Bergrin.

"In Sable Brennus's territory, just outside the city proper," Bergrin replied. He seemed to hesitate, then continued with, "It's an old house, a little cottage type place that's belonged to my dad's family for generations. My dad is only the second abnormal to come out of the family, and the first one was a great-great-great uncle who was declared insane and locked away.

"I see," Johnnie said. "That is unfortunate."

Bergrin shrugged. "At least my dad was smart enough to keep his mouth shut."

"So how did you wind up all the way out here? Brennus's territory is hours away by plane ride, days away by car."

Bergrin laughed. "Why do you live above a seedy bar?"

"I concede the point. What does your mother do?"

"Mostly, she just stays at home with my father, but she used to find things. Family business, I guess."

Nodding, Johnnie tried to think of something else

to say, but he could not come up with any other questions to ask that did not seem too intrusive. He did not know why he had asked the ones he had, except he was always curious and Bergrin was unusually forthcoming. "My father was an alchemist, as well," he finally said, though he was not quite certain why.

Bergrin raised his brows. "I thought your parents were normals, though I suppose I only know the same stories all the nosey gossips know."

Johnnie smiled briefly at that and admitted, "I did not know until very recently myself. My father only told me about—" He broke off, annoyed with himself over the clumsy sentence, "My father only told me a short time ago."

"Yet you have no alchemical ability?" Bergrin asked.

"No," Johnnie said. It was not unusual, though. Of all humans capable of some measure of magic, alchemists were the weakest. They relied heavily on components, supplemental magic by way of science, rather than pure, internal force like more powerful magic users. It was not unusual for the ability to miss generations, or fade out completely. "What about you? You have magic, but I cannot tell what you are."

"I'm good at finding things," Bergrin said.

Stifling his disappointment, not even certain *why* he was disappointed, Johnnie asked, "So what do you most often find?"

Bergrin did not immediately reply, but eyed Johnnie pensively. "People, mostly, but objects too—books, magical items, jewelry, whatever."

"I guess that explains why I am ever stuck with you," Johnnie said.

In reply, Bergrin only smirked. Johnnie made a face and looked out the car window, where he could see nothing except the odd bit of light bouncing off water to show waterlogged trees and dark buildings.

Shortly thereafter, the driver pulled to a stop in front of a barely visible, two story little home. "We've arrived, Master Johnnie."

"Thank you," Johnnie said. Bergrin slid out of the car first, and Johnnie followed after, sending the driver off to await his call. The front door, when they reached it, was locked. A quick examination proved all the doors and windows were locked.

"We could break in through the back door," Bergrin suggested. "Since I doubt you will take no for an answer. In this weather, no one will hear the noise."

"I have a less noticeable method," Johnnie replied. "Keep that umbrella over me." Kneeling, he examined the lock as best he could in the porch light, then reached into his jacket and pulled out his lock-pick set. Selecting the appropriate tools, he set to work. Only a couple of minutes later, he stood and tucked the tools away again. He turned to face Bergrin, braced for a lecture—and drew up short at the look of open approval.

"Well, well, the pretty Prince continues to be full of surprises. Where did you learn to pick locks?"

"I started by reading about it in a book," Johnnie replied, disconcerted by praise from so unexpected a source. "Curiosity got the better of me. It has proven to have its uses."

Bergrin smiled. "I do not think I want to know all the times you have made use of it. Strange, no one ever mentioned that skill in their reports."

Johnnie scowled. "Reports?"

Snickering, Bergrin pushed the front door open and slipped inside. Still glaring, Johnnie followed. The house was a disaster; it had been torn apart quite thoroughly. Shelves, tables, and chairs had all been overturned. Papers, knick-knacks, and other miscellany covered the floor. The contents of an enormous desk had been strewn across the study, nearly covering the carpet. The workshop was a mess of broken glass, spilled liquids, powders, and dried herbs. Closing the door to the workshop, Johnnie strode back to the study. He stood in the doorway, examining everything carefully. At last he said, "I do not think they found what they wanted."

"I agree," Bergrin said, looking amused.

Johnnie shot him a disgusted look. "You already found what we are looking for."

"Yes, but to be fair, I *am* good at finding things."

Annoyed, Johnnie examined the room again, then strode to the bookshelves built into the far wall. They went floor to ceiling, wall to wall, made of a heavy, sturdy, dark-stained wood with a hint of red to it. The centermost set of shelves were all covered by doors set with stained glass, meant to swing up and down and lock into place.

Someone, likely the draugr, had broken the glass, the locks, literally torn the doors from their hinges, then pulled all the books and papers inside off the shelves and cast them to the floor. Someone else, to judge by the excess of wet and muddy prints, had come along and retrieved the very same items.

Dismissing the special shelves, Johnnie moved to the other shelves—in particular, a set of three shelves where practically none of the books had been disturbed. The books here were a mishmash of scientific journals, personal journals, history books, and herbalists. Pulling all the books off the shelves and stacking them neatly on the floor, Johnnie next tested the actual shelves. Unsurprised to find them loose, he pulled them off and propped them against the wall. He studied the bare wall remaining, reaching out to touch, looking for a hidden release.

He jerked in surprise when something pressed up against him from behind, sending a frisson of awareness through him, slicing down his spine, making his muscles tighten in anticipation—

But then he saw Bergrin's hand join his own on the wood, pressing in two places, and the section of wall popped out the slightest bit. Drawing a sharp breath, wondering what in the *hell* was wrong with him, Johnnie pulled the panel all the way open.

Inside the hidden cache were three journals and a stack of letters tied with twine. The hot thrill of secrets uncovered poured through Johnnie, making him forget all about the odd, confused moment when Bergrin had stood so close.

Taking the letters and journals, he pulled out his phone and summoned his car. Moving to the front hall, he tucked all but one of the journals under his arm. "Written in code," he said, unsurprised. Alchemists—any magic user who kept such journals, which was nearly all of them—always used code. "This code looks particularly complicated. It will take me some time to break it."

"Oh?" Bergrin asked, mildly curious as he came up and glanced over Johnnie's shoulder. He swore loudly.

Johnnie turned his head slightly, quirking one brow. "Is there a problem?"

"I know this code—I mean, I can't read it, but I

know whose code it is, and it's not that of the dead man."

"Then whose is it?" Johnnie asked.

"My father's," Bergrin replied. "Why the fuck is another alchemist using my dad's code to write his journals? Not even *I* can read my dad's journals."

Johnnie closed the book with a snap. "The answer to that is obvious—so he could be certain that someone he trusted, and *only* the person he trusted, could read whatever he has taken such pains to hide." He smirked. "I guess this means you are taking me to meet your parents."

Bergrin rolled his eyes. "Excuse me one moment, Highness. Apparently I need to make a phone call."

Snickering, Johnnie sat down on the steps leading upstairs and pulled out one of the letters. They were old, to judge by the date on one. Twenty-odd years old. The envelopes were unmarked, save for a single letter—M—on the front. Another letter—T—was on the back. So the letters had likely been sent by magical means.

They, too, were written in the same code as the book. At a glance, it looked like T had been relaying to M some of his experiments. He wished he could read it, but it took him weeks, if not months, to translate such journals. There was still a small pile of them in his library, just waiting their turn.

Folding the letter, Johnnie slid it back into the envelope, then replaced it with the others. He clearly would need to figure out the identity of 'T', but if they had been using the code devised by Bergrin's father, then likely he could tell Johnnie who T was. The real question, however, was what all of this was leading—

He jumped as the door slammed open and four

men spilled inside, jerking to his feet even as he took in two wolves, a human, and... his blood turned cold as he watched the fourth turn into a dragon. Johnnie turned, but tripped over himself on the stairs, stumbling hard but refusing to let go of the journals and letters. He regained his footing and bolted up the stairs—

Only to be yanked back down, head slamming so hard into the stairs that, for a moment, everything grayed out. He struggled to his feet, to get his bearings, protesting helplessly as someone drove a fist into his gut. He dropped like a rock, unwillingly letting go of the items to which he'd so stubbornly clung.

The world started graying out again as someone kicked him, struck his face, and said something he did not catch. Someone screamed. Johnnie struggled to get control of himself, but his head throbbed and he felt as though he was going to be sick. Another scream, like nothing he had ever heard in his life.

It all became too much, and Johnnie finally passed out.

~~*

He stirred briefly, drawn from unconsciousness by warmth. Arms, he thought hazily. Someone was holding him. He could not seem to muster the strength to open his eyes, but that was all right. He liked the dark. Johnnie pressed deeper into the warmth, murmuring in approval when the arms tightened.

"Johnnie? Are you all right?" an urgent voice asked.

There was power in that voice, Johnnie noted. There was also something familiar. Scents he knew teased at him, but he could not quite catch them. He would know the hot-toddy quality of that voice anywhere, though. "Eros?" Johnnie muttered, and then fell back into unconsciousness.

~~*

Johnnie groaned and tried to lift a hand to his aching head, only to find his arms were trapped by something. Cloth. He dragged his eyes open and saw that he was lying on an old couch, covered by an afghan.

He did not recognize the house. Sitting up slowly, annoyed by just how much effort that required, he looked around. It was a small, cozy sort of room, filled with old but well cared for furniture, more knick-knacks than he could count, afghans, pictures, paintings, little bookcases stuffed nearly to the point of overflowing.

He froze as a picture on the end table nearest him caught his eye. The man in the picture might have been Bergrin, save he was several years too old. Bergrin was obviously the little boy standing next to the him. So, he was in Bergrin's house?

What had happened? His head throbbed, and Johnnie bit back a cry of pain. He swung his legs off the couch and tried to stand. When the world tilted alarmingly, he thought better of it and sat back down.

He could not remember what had happened. Johnnie gingerly touched the place where his head throbbed, feeling a knot. He had hit his head on the stairs, he recalled that much. Men had shown up, attacked him. Why? He could not remember. They had beat him...

Then what?

Johnnie simply could not remember.

Sound drew his attention, muffled voices, then he heard someone in the hallway, coming towards him. Bergrin filled the archway between the living room and the hallway, and Johnnie's thoughts stuttered, stopped. A nasty bruise had forced Bergrin's right eye mostly shut. It glistened wetly, like some sort of ointment had been smeared on the bruise. His left upper arm was heavily bandaged, and there were long scratches on his impressively-muscled chest that he had not bothered to treat past washing them. Bergrin's curly hair was a mess, going in at least twenty directions, and he wore loose sweatpants that only barely clung to his hips.

Johnnie swallowed, unable to deal with this new perspective on his bodyguard. Shaking himself, he asked, "What happened?" He scowled at the raspy, unsteady quality to his voice.

"You don't remember?" Bergrin asked, a slight frown on his face.

Johnnie shook his head, then winced. "Not really. Men came in. They attacked me. I hit my head. Then nothing."

Bergrin's frown deepened. He turned his head and called down the hall, "Hey, Pop! Bring a glass of water!" Down the hall, Johnnie could just hear a muffled reply. Bergrin walked into the living room, shoved the discarded blankets aside, and sat down next to him. He was warm, Johnnie noted. How had he never noticed all the heat Bergrin radiated?

Dismissing the strange observation, he asked, "So why are we in your parents' house?"

"Because it's safe. Familiar to me, but not to

anyone who might try to come after us. Plus, I knew once you were awake and functioning you would demand to come here anyway."

"You are hurt," Johnnie blurted, then wondered what in the *hell* was wrong with him. Clearly the hit to his head had addled his brain.

Bergrin grunted, looking briefly annoyed. "I got cocky. Remind me *never* to get cocky where dragons are concerned. I haven't been hit like that in years. Those fucking tails come out of nowhere." He twisted slightly, and Johnnie noticed the massive bruise spread across a good portion of Bergrin's back. "But you're safe now, Johnnie," Bergrin continued. "I told your father what happened—I had no choice—"

Johnnie nodded. "It is fine. What did he say?"

"Several rather interesting words I've never heard the Dracula use," Bergrin said dryly. "Beyond that, to keep you out of sight and safe until he found some bodies in need of having their heads removed."

Johnnie made a face, but he was prevented from replying by the appearance of an older Bergrin. Gray peppered the man's brown curls, and glasses framed his hazel eyes. He had a thin scar on the edge of his chin, curving along the bottom of his cheek. He wore a brown sweater and worn jeans, and held out a steaming mug to Johnnie. "I thought this might be better than water."

"Thank you," Johnnie said, accepting the mug. "You are clearly Bergrin's father. I am sorry to have intruded upon your home like this."

The man laughed. "My son is right: you do have a very pretty way of speaking." He snickered when Bergrin scowled. "You're no bother, my boy. I'm glad you seem all right. How is your head?"

"It is fine," Johnnie said, then hid a grimace of pain by sipping what proved to be chamomile tea.

"You are awake and functioning, that is a good sign. My name is Alec. It is quite the honor to meet the son of Dracula Desrosiers. Your father is a good man."

"Thank you," Johnnie said, pleased to hear his father given such praise. "I really hope I am not putting you out." He glanced at Bergrin, then said. "I am sorry, too, that your son has taken such injury on my behalf."

Alec snorted in amusement, casting his son a dry, fond look. "He's done worse all on his own and no doubt will again." He reached out suddenly and ruffled Bergrin's hair, laughing when Bergrin glared again and jerked away. Turning back to Johnnie, he asked, "Do you feel up to food? I've some vegetable broth on, maybe with some crackers?"

"Stop mothering—" Bergrin started to grouse.

"That sounds wonderful," Johnnie cut in, drowning Bergrin out, smiling. "Thank you, again."

"Of course," Alec said and left to get the food.

Bergrin sighed and raked a hand through his hair, making the curls wilder than ever. "I need to apologize, sir, for failing you. I should have been there, and you never should have been hurt." He reached out and lightly touched fingers to Johnnie's face, and only then did Johnnie realize he had a bruise on his cheek.

"First Highness and Prince, now sir?" Johnnie snapped, jerking away from the touch, immediately regretting it when the world tilted. He held his head gingerly in one hand, closing his eyes. "If you are going to say stupid things like that, I prefer you keep your mouth shut."

Laughing softly, Bergrin said, "Yes, Johnnie."

"Better," Johnnie said. "It seems strange to call you

Bergrin and your father Alec."

"No one uses my first name on pain of death," Bergrin said, then added, "Except my mom, because she gave it to me. Don't bother asking, Highness, because I'm not telling. Nor is it somewhere you can sniff it out."

Johnnie made a face at that and said nothing. He looked around the living room again because otherwise he would just stare openly at Bergrin's smooth, bare chest. He really wished Bergrin would go put on real clothes.

It was only then Johnnie noticed *he* was not wearing his proper clothes. Had it really taken him this long to notice? Like Bergrin, he wore sweatpants. He also wore a long-sleeved gray t-shirt. Both were far too big for him. "Where are my clothes?"

"We were soaked through when I got you out of there," Bergrin said. "Your clothes are packed away to be properly cleaned later since I like living too much to even attempt to clean your threads. Your father said he would see that fresh clothes were brought to you. He also said he sent word to Brennus you were here in his territory."

"Good," Johnnie replied, because in addition to everything else, he really did not need to inadvertently offend a demon lord. "The journals," he said, suddenly reminded of why he had wanted to come here in the first place. "The letters."

"All here," Bergrin said. "I even grabbed your sword stick."

Johnnie relaxed slightly. "Good. Thank you."

Bergrin grunted in reply and leaned back into the couch, looking suddenly exhausted.

"Are you certain you are all right?" Johnnie asked.

"I'm fine," Bergrin said. "My dad is right—I've survived way worse than this. But when this case is over and we're back at the Bremen, you'd better let me have a *real* nap in my corner."

Johnnie nodded, but could not, for whatever reason, form a reply. They lapsed into silence, and Johnnie leaned back into the couch himself. His eyes grew heavy, try as he might to keep them open, and eventually he gave up resisting. The last thing he remembered was his head resting against something firm and warm.

~~*

When he woke, it was to the crackle and pop of flames and the feel of something shifting and rubbing against him. Jerking completely awake at that, Johnnie fell off the couch and onto the floor with a hard thud, barely avoiding knocking his head on the floor. He scowled furiously, first at the hard floor, then up at the reason he had fallen in the first place.

Bergrin, fast asleep and snoring softly, his back against the couch, and Johnnie had obviously been pressed against him. His face was... softer, when he was asleep, but until that moment, Johnnie had never thought Bergrin's face hard.

Someone, probably Alec, had covered them in an afghan and lit a fire. Face hot, Johnnie turned away from the sight of a bare-chested, dead-asleep Bergrin, and sat with his back against the couch, facing the fireplace.

Ugh. What was wrong with him? He did not even know, anymore. He shivered slightly and pulled down an extra afghan at one end of the couch, wrapping up in it as he continued to brood. This was by far the strangest case he had taken yet. It should have been a simple matter of finding who had raised the draugr and why. He was not supposed to have wound up with the world's worst headache, more people dead because they had tried to come after him, and the knowledge that his babysitter had a damned fine body beneath his unremarkable clothes.

Johnnie pinched the bridge of his nose and wondered if he could simply finish the job his assailants had started when they had slammed his head into the stairs. He should be back in the Bremen right now, drinking vodka and reading or shooting pool, not sitting on the floor in Bergrin's father's living room because he had tumbled there after realizing he had fallen asleep on the couch with Bergrin.

His gust twisted, sharp and sudden, painful. Johnnie did not know why. He frowned, staring at the rug, wishing his head would stop hurting so damned much so he could *think*.

"You look as though you've lost your whole world," Alec said, startling him.

Johnnie looked up, then looked away again and shrugged. "I have the oddest sense I am missing something or have lost something, but I have no idea why." He sighed. "I am sorry, that makes no sense."

"No," Alec said softly, moving into the room. He stood at the arm of the couch and reached out to brush strands of hair from Bergrin's face. "I know the feeling, believe me. But I did not realize it was there until I saw Bergrin's mother." He smiled faintly. "A man came by while you were both asleep. He brought you clothes; they are in my bedroom, down the hall. You can use my bathroom to clean up, as I am sure you would like to. Once you are set to rights, we can discuss the things you've brought me. They and the letters certainly make for interesting reading."

Nodding, Johnnie stood, grateful that at least things seemed to have stopped tilting every time he moved. "How long were we asleep?"

Alec laughed. "You've been asleep for some time. It is Friday, just after ten in the morning."

"I see," Johnnie said, grimacing. They had left the Bremen almost fifteen hours ago. "You said down the hall?"

"Yes, all the way at the end, on your left," Alec said with a smile. He slapped Bergrin's cheek lightly, snickering when Bergrin groaned in his sleep. "I'll rouse the bear while you clean up."

Smothering a smile that was wholly inappropriate, Johnnie ducked from the room and went down the hall to the indicated bedroom.

An hour later, he felt much more like himself. Whoever had delivered the clothes had dropped off one of his favorite outfits—black pants with violet pinstripes, a black silk shirt, and a violet vest with gold and silver dragons. The same someone had even brought the proper tie and all the matching jewelry. Even the correct shoes. It must have been Lila. She was the only one who ever got everything correct the first time.

Refreshed and restored, he ventured back down the hall to the living room, but his steps slowed as he heard voices that were trying hard to stay low but were too heated to succeed.

"—I swear to god, you need to be knocked upside the head! Do you have any idea what you're doing?"

"No, I don't," Bergrin said bitterly, "but I'm asking

you to leave it the hell alone."

"You need to tell the—"

"This discussion is over, Pop."

"It's a long way from over. I did not raise you to behave this way."

Johnnie hovered in the doorway, reluctant to break in when he saw that Alec and Bergrin were practically toe to toe and all put poised to start swinging. At some point, he saw, Bergrin had showered and dressed as well. He wore stonewashed jeans now and a light green shirt that did startling things to his hair and eyes—and did he really need to notice such things? Did he not have enough problems?

Alec started to say more, but then saw Johnnie. "My, my, boy. No wonder Ber calls you 'Prince'. If I didn't know better, I'd bet my life savings you were a vampire."

"Thank you," Johnnie said, unwilling to be rude to Alec, even if that observation set his teeth on edge the same as always. "Am I interrupting? I apologize."

"No," Bergrin said, shooting his father a look. "We're done."

Alec looked as though he strongly disagreed, but let Bergrin have his way. He smiled at Johnnie instead. "I reheated the broth from last night, and today I actually had time to make fresh bread. It's in the kitchen, we can eat there while we talk. It's much warmer than the dining room."

Johnnie nodded and followed them into the kitchen, taking the seat Alec indicated at a large oak table that was as worn but well cared for as everything else in the house. Alec set a bowl of blue and yellow porcelain in front of him along with a matching plate piled with slices of fresh, warm bread.

Directly across from Johnnie, Bergrin was making short work of his own food. He smirked at his father. "If you weren't such a good cook, Pop, you'd be a much better alchemist."

Alec rolled his eyes. "I think that, in the long run, it is all to the good that I am a better cook than an alchemist." He laid a hand on the journals and letters he had set nearby on the table. "Now, as to your mystery, Johnnie."

"Yes?" Johnnie asked. "What do the journals say?"

Sighing softly, Alec said, "This will actually take quite a bit of explaining and some background. I have lived in this city my entire life. When this house was first built, it was the only one for miles around. Now it is the oldest in the little neighborhood it inhabits. Ber tells me that he told you I was an oddity in my family; minus my unfortunate ancestor, I am the only abnormal. But I grew up aware of my abnormal neighbors. My two best friends growing up were of alchemist-caliber, and as they got older, that is what they became. Their names were Mike and Tommy."

He smiled wryly. "I confess, I mainly became one because that was all I knew, growing up alongside them. While I am passable, my friends were much better. Anyway, we drifted apart as we finished school and moved on, though for a while we kept in touch.

"Almost thirty years ago now, I learned that a woman had entered Tommy's life. He had never mentioned a word about it before, but suddenly I received a letter from him telling me he was married. I wrote to Mike, asking him about it, but he didn't know where she'd come from either. A few months later, I received another letter. It was several pages long, but explained one very simple thing—Tommy and his wife were going to live as normals for the safety of their child. They didn't want their son or daughter growing up facing all the dangers and peculiarities that came with being abnormal.

"After that, I never heard from him again. Figured he dropped off the face of the earth exactly as he'd wanted. I should have looked into it more closely, but by that point, my own life was in upheaval." He smiled warmly at Bergrin as his thumb rubbed across his wedding ring in such a familiar way, Johnnie doubted Alec knew he was doing it.

"The point of this story, however," Alec continued, "is that Tommy did not quit his alchemical studies the way he had said he was going to, and he might have lost touch with me, but he kept in touch with Mike. The letters, unfortunately, are nothing but reports that Mike later transcribed into the journals. I had hoped they would offer up more information, but it looks like Mike kept them only because he was still working to transcribe the ones in the bundle.

"It's all frustratingly vague, but my understanding is that Tommy accidentally made something he should not have even attempted, and he and Mike were trying to figure out what the hell to do about it. What he made, I wish I knew, but they very carefully do not say. The information they left was for me to figure it out eventually, I suppose, but never explicit enough for anyone else to piece it together. However, one of the letters does seem to indicate he destroyed it. I hope he did. Accidents in alchemy almost never have a happy ending." His face softened briefly, and Johnnie rather thought that Alec had made a mistake and it *had* ended happily.

But he was far more concerned with all that Alec

had just told him. His chest felt tight, made it hard to breathe. It felt like he was freezing and on fire all at once. "You said the one who tried to give it up—his name was Tommy?"

"Yes," Alec replied, frowning in confusion. "Tommy Fitz."

"What—what was his wife's name?"

"I don't remember," Alec said. "It was a bit unusual, I remember that. I think it began with a 'C'."

"Cordula," Johnnie said, closing his eyes briefly. "Her name was Cordula. They—they must have changed their surname when they moved to Desrosiers territory. Excuse me." He stood up and fled the kitchen, fled the house, finally stopping when he reached the large, wrap-around porch, falling into a porch swing around the side of the house.

He stared blindly at the rain, thinking numbly that it was strange the rain was falling as hard here as it had been back home. Except, he recalled, Brennus was a storm demon, so such weather was typical here.

Secrets, he thought bitterly. He hated secrets. His own parents had started the tangle of lies when they had tried to be something they were not. Ontoniel was obviously keeping their secrets still.

Then there was Eros.

Something flickered in his mind, a voice he loved and loathed, speaking to him, but then it slipped away like quicksilver and Johnnie was left with only a headache.

His parents. They had fled Brennus territory, changed their surname, and started a new, normal life. Except it would seem his father had kept secrets of his own and not given up his alchemy after all. But what had he made, and why were men only now trying to obtain it? Johnnie frowned in thought, clinging almost eagerly to the mystery, gratefully shunting other problems to the side.

Something had changed, he surmised. Something new had come to light that provoked the seekers into action. Or perhaps it had taken them this long to figure out that his father had spoken to someone, and who that someone was. He could not be sure, though, which was irritating. He simply did not have enough information to paint a clear picture. He was stumbling around in the dark, and what good had that ever done him?

His body tightened with memories of all the good that had been done to him in the dark, but Johnnie forced those thoughts aside. Frustrated, he cradled his head in his hands and tried to think. Normally, he was good at that. Why did it seem like he was falling apart now?

Just the facts.

Someone had raised a draugr, provoking it to go after its 'treasures.' But the draugr had not, in fact, led them to the real gems—the journals and letters hidden in the secret compartment. Johnnie had found them and subsequently been attacked.

The journals were written in a code that only Alec would be able to easily read—and apparently only Alec had ever stood a real chance of figuring out what Tommy had accidentally created. The two dead friends had known whatever Tommy had made was dangerous, or at least problematic, but important enough they had left clues for an old friend. Yet Mike had hidden them away, or maybe he had simply died before he had been able to send them off.

What had Tommy created? Why was it all only

coming to light now? Because Mike had died only recently? Had he managed to repel all attention in the matter while he lived? Johnnie's head throbbed, and he grimaced in pain.

Why had no one ever told him about all this? Had his father really done or made something that important? What? They were his parents, damn it, he had a right to know what they had really been.

The door opened, but Johnnie ignored whoever had come to talk to him. "So you are Tommy's son," Alec said. "I feel I should have figured that out. All G—Ber told me about you was that your parents were killed and Dracula Desrosiers adopted you."

Johnnie nodded.

"Your father was a good man, for what it is worth. Quiet, I believe he took up teaching. He was a good alchemist, better than me. He had a knack for creating magic-infused items."

Latching on to that, Johnnie asked, "So he probably created a relic of some sort? Do you have any clue as to what it was?"

"No," Alec said. "I was nothing like them, not even close. My greatest moment in alchemy was a fluke, a one in a billion chance that could only ever be done by mistake. It brought me something I never thought I would have, but after that, I swore off real alchemy for good. Your father, however... I was truly surprised to hear that he was giving it all up. I am not at all surprised to learn he went right back to it."

Johnnie nodded but said nothing.

"As to what he made, it could be anything—literally. Your father chased the impossible relics like damn near every alchemist under the sun, and I doubt he ever gave that up. He liked tinkering with them too much." The impossible relics: magical items that were written about again and again but were impossible to make. They were nearly as sought after as the ability to cross the planes at will.

As in so many things, the wants and wishes had found their way into stories, passed down through the generations until they seemed only stories, and like the Cinderella slippers, no one really knew if it was the stories or the wish for impossible things that had come first.

The tale of twelve princesses who traveled to another world, where they danced the night away—the ability to cross planes at will. Snake leaves—the ability to bring the dead back to life. A mirror that could answer any question put to it. Fish that granted wishes, objects and foods that granted immortality, geese that laid golden eggs, the ability to turn straw into gold: the list of absurdities went on and on.

Only stories, but they were enough to inspire generations of magic users, especially alchemists, to try to create them anyway. History was rife with the tragedies that too often resulted. It did not really surprise Johnnie that his father might have been amongst those fools. Was it better or worse that he had been killed by a blood-crazy vampire before his own obsessions had killed him? "So the journals only contain copies of my father's experiments?" Johnnie asked, just to break the silence.

"Yes," Alec said. "I think that they believed I could follow them, that I would attempt it far enough to learn what Tommy had made, but I have not done real alchemy for nearly thirty years. All I do now is silly stuff, parlor tricks. But recreating his experiments does not mean I would ever recreate his mistake, or mistakes, and so I'm not quite certain why they wrote it all out in my code. But perhaps with more time I can figure it out. Whatever it is, I really do hope they destroyed it."

"That would be too easy," Johnnie said. No alchemist ever destroyed a creation, especially not one that caused this much trouble. He would have to speak with his father. Ontoniel would have answers, but getting them would be no easy task. Johnnie was not looking forward to the conversation.

Did this all tie back in to the way that spell had rebounded, he thought suddenly. Perhaps Tommy had done something to him. But if that were the case, why would Ontoniel not simply say? Because Ontoniel knew what it was, damn it.

"You look as though you are drowning in your thoughts," Alec said softly.

Johnnie grimaced. "I think I am, but I will sort them out. I must speak with my father, I think, to learn anything about my birth father."

"At that, I think you must be going soon. Ber was on the phone, speaking with your father, I believe." Bergrin was speaking directly to Ontoniel? Usually people dealt with his father's secretary. Precious few were the individuals who had Ontoniel's direct line.

Johnnie tucked the thought away for later and simply nodded. "I thank you again for your hospitality, and most especially for your assistance—and your patience. It is in extremely poor taste to arrive uninvited and injured, and I have not much improved since. But it is nice to have met you; Bergrin is a great deal like you."

"He's even more like his mother," Alec said with faint smile.

"I am sorry I did not get to meet her," Johnnie said, meaning it. Having met the father, he was even more curious to meet the mother.

Alec smiled more widely. "I believe you will meet her eventually. There is no need to fall back on formality with me, and you are always welcome here, Johnnie."

They both turned as the door opened, and Bergrin joined them on the porch. He wore a black leather jacket and the silly cap his mother had given him and held out Johnnie's coat and hat. "We need to get going, Pop. Sorry to bleed, eat, and run. If you see Mama before I do, give her my love."

"Of course," Alec said, giving his son a fond, warm look before adding softly, "Try to be a little careful, for me?" He chuckled as Bergrin rolled his eyes, then said more sternly. "Think long and hard about what I said."

Bergrin nodded impatiently. "Let's go, Prince. I called Peyton to let him and the others know what's what, but you and I have been summoned to your father's house."

"Naturally," Johnnie said and pulled on his coat and hat, then accepted his cane as Bergrin held it out. "Is there a car coming?"

"No," Bergrin replied. "Your—"

But even as he spoke, Elam appeared at the bottom of the stairs, as cold and hard and beautiful as ever. He motioned impatiently. "Come on, John. You have caused enough problems for one week."

Johnnie bit back a retort, bid Alec a last farewell, then preceded Bergrin down the stairs. "Long time no see, Ellie."

Elam ignored him and simply grasped their arms, and with a faint pulse of magic, they were gone.

Case 006: Danced to Pieces

They appeared in the entryway of Ontoniel's home. It was familiar and strange all at once. Just a short time ago this place had been home. A part of that lingered, but all he really wanted right then was to be back at the Bremen.

He was still pondering that realization when Ontoniel appeared, looking more exhausted than Johnnie had ever seen him. "Father."

"John," Ontoniel said, frown deepening as he took in Johnnie's face. Johnnie was startled to see real anger flare in Ontoniel's eyes, but then it eased as he asked, "How is your head?"

"Fine," Johnnie replied, and when Ontoniel gave him a look of disbelief, said, "It hurts and I will probably have a headache for days, but that is all. I am fine. I am sorry to have caused so much trouble."

Ontoniel sighed. "I thought you told me all this mystery solving would not be dangerous. I believe I am now fully within my rights to say I was wise to assign a bodyguard full time?"

Johnnie bristled. "Indeed. Yet I feel there would be less danger to my person if the people I am supposed to trust were not keeping secrets from me."

Ontoniel's mouth tightened. "I think we had best adjourn to my office."

In reply, Johnnie only strode past him and down the hall, into the west wing where Ontoniel's study was located. There, he took his preferred seat, a wing-back chair set before a massive stained-glass window. He tried not to be painfully aware of the way Bergrin took up position beside and just behind him, leaning against the wall beside the window.

Ontoniel sat behind his desk, looking for all the world like a king on his throne. Elam sat in a chair closer to the bookshelves, a distinctly sullen air about him. Johnnie suspected they had pulled Elam from his piano practice.

Before anyone could say anything, Lila arrived with a tea cart and briskly went about serving tea—rose tea to Ontoniel, Earl Grey to Elam, chamomile to Johnnie, and after asking, chamomile to Bergrin as well.

When she had gone, Johnnie decided to let someone else break the silence. It was Ontoniel who finally did so, but he surprised Johnnie by addressing Bergrin. "So you are the Enforcer guarding my son and who saved Elam, but whom I have never properly met. Bergrin, right? I cannot believe it has taken this long for me to properly meet you. You are powerful, but I cannot get a feel for your nature."

"No one really has a name for me, my lord," Bergrin said. "I'm good at finding things and taking beatings. That's about all anyone knows."

"Mmm," Ontoniel said thoughtfully. "Your abilities must come from the mother you do not know. Your file says she ran off shortly after you were born?"

"Yes, my lord."

Johnnie sipped his tea. Why was Bergrin lying? He and Alec had talked quite freely about her—Alec had said Johnnie would likely meet her at some point. Bergrin had just been given a birthday present from her and seemed to regard both his parents with much love. So why was it on record that she had run off and no one knew anything about her?

It was also intriguing that they had been so honest with *him* when, until recently, he and Bergrin could not even stand each other. He did not have the answer for why, though.

"Thank you for protecting my son. It does look as though this latest case cost you dearly," Ontoniel continued.

Bergrin laughed. "Hardly, my lord. I was on assignment once to find a missing person. Lacking status and wealth, my only way into the Pits where he was trapped was to sign up as a fighter. I went five rounds before I found him, and then we had to fight our way out. This was easy."

Ontoniel's laughter joined Bergrin's. "So that was you. I cannot keep track of who does what, there are so many problems and so few Enforcers. Very well done, indeed."

"My lord," Bergrin said, giving a half-bow. Though he tried to hide it, Johnnie could see he was startled and pleased by the praise.

"So you believe this was another kidnapping attempt?" Ontoniel asked.

"Yes, my lord," Bergrin said. "They had every intention of taking Johnnie alive but leaving me for dead. I can think of no other reason they would bring a dragon—and a black one at that."

Ontoniel nodded.

"I am not convinced kidnapping the son of the Dracula was the primary objective, or an objective at all," Johnnie said. "If they wanted to take me, there were better opportunities. I think that taking me could have been a bonus, and that is assuming they recognized me." He frowned in thought. "At that, I am known for translating such things. That alone would have provoked taking me along with the journals. As to the dragon, that could have been as much for the draugr as for Bergrin. Heath never said the persons responsible for the draugr knew it had been destroyed. Our assailants saw movement in the house, and they probably assumed it was the draugr until they were upon us."

Ontoniel started to speak, but Johnnie did not give him the chance. "What interests me, however, is not the near-kidnapping. What interests me, Father, is that the journals and letters I found were records of experiments sent to Mike by one Tommy Fitz."

Something flashed in Ontoniel's eyes, and Johnnie's anger finally got the best of him. "You are not surprised! You knew my father was still experimenting. You knew he had not gone completely normal."

"Not for a long time," Ontoniel said. "Not until after they were dead. I found letters from Mike to your father. I destroyed them and everything else I could find."

Johnnie slammed his cane against the floor. "Why would you do that!"

"It was for the best," Ontoniel said quietly. "I did not want anyone to try to recreate his experiments."

"What did he make?" Johnnie demanded.

"I do not know," Ontoniel said. "The letters were enough for me to determine that whatever he had been doing, it was a mistake. I destroyed everything and left it all behind. I had enough to deal with already." When Johnnie opened his mouth to respond to that, Ontoniel said, "I had a wife to bury and a new son to raise. Do you really think I gave a damn about the experiments of a man too dead to continue them?"

Johnnie subsided, his temper thoroughly extinguished.

Ontoniel sighed after a moment, then said more quietly, "I suspected he was doing such things because I have never encountered an abnormal who was completely capable of living normally. Then again, your mother never seemed to have any problems." He sighed again. "It was not my place to interfere, however. He was not hurting anyone. I did try to say something, anyway, for your sake." He shrugged, then quoted, "It is easier to stay out than get out."

By the books, silent until that moment, Elam made a rough, derisive noise.

Johnnie shot him a look. "What is your problem?"

"Nothing," Elam said coldly. "This little argument has nothing to do with me, and I have better things to do with my time." Without another word, he strode from the room, closing the door sharply behind him.

Ontoniel stared after him, expression troubled.

"Is something wrong?" Johnnie asked.

"No," Ontoniel said after a moment. "I think the betrothal and the pending wedding, only six months away now, are making him more mercurial than usual. It will pass, or I will make it pass."

Johnnie nodded.

Shaking his head, Ontoniel said. "I know you do not like being kept in the dark, Johnnie. You resent secrets. I did not keep the knowledge secret to hurt you, only to protect you. Your parents wanted you to live as normal a life as possible. In adopting you, I went quite explicitly against their wishes. But I am trying to respect that wish by leaving the past where it lies. You should do the same."

"I should simply abandon any thoughts of knowing anything about my real parents?" Johnnie snapped.

Something flickered across Ontoniel's face, and Johnnie was taken aback to realize it was hurt, but all Ontoniel said was, "They wanted you to be happy, Johnnie. Dredging up the past will not make you happy. The life you have is not what they wanted for you, but I like to think it is not a bad one. Why can you not be content with it?"

Johnnie frowned. "It is not—"

A sharp rapping at the office door cut him off, and Ontoniel curtly called for the knocker to enter. The door swung open wide and an imp servant entered, bowing slightly to Ontoniel before saying, "There is a lady here, my lord, claiming she had an appointment."

Ontoniel sighed and nodded. "Send her in, then."

"Yes, my lord," the imp replied and departed.

Silence passed for a moment as Johnnie tried to reform what he had been about to say, but then the door opened again and a woman stepped inside. She was a beautiful, striking woman, tall and slender and graceful. She wore a black pencil skirt with a fitted white blouse, diamonds at her throat and wrists, and black high-heels that she walked in with the ease of a woman who wore nothing but heels.

It was her hair, however, that was the most impressive. Johnnie remembered it well from the few times he had encountered her at the few places where he shopped. She had it pulled back in an elaborate twist of braids and curls, beautifully accenting the lines of her face and her long, graceful neck.

Sitting on her shoulder, clinging tightly, was a pixie.

The woman's eyes fell on Johnnie and her face lit

up with surprise. "Well, well, if it isn't Johnnie Desrosiers. I was hoping I'd run into you here."

Johnnie stood and crossed the room, taking the hand she held out and kissing the back of it—then leaning in to kiss her cheek, as she kissed his. "Phil. Long time no see. I remember those diamonds; they look beautiful."

"Thanks," Phil said. "You get prettier every time I see you, Johnnie." She looked over his shoulder and giggled. "Who's the handsome fella scowling at me?" She shifted her gaze to Ontoniel, who had stood and moved around his desk to join them. "You must be Dracula Desrosiers." She moved away from Johnnie and offered her hand to Ontoniel.

Like Johnnie, Ontoniel did not shake, but kissed the back of it. "How does my son come to know so beautiful a woman?"

Phil smiled. "He has excellent taste in his dress, something I can see he learned from his father. It is an honor to meet you, my lord. Few Dracula have your reputation for generosity and open-mindedness."

Ontoniel waved the words away as he finally released her hand. "You may call me Ontoniel. Would you like something to drink?"

"Tea would be lovely," Phil said, seeing what they were all drinking.

"Do you care for rose tea?" Ontoniel asked as he hit a button on the phone on his desk to call for a servant.

Phil nodded and accepted the seat he motioned she should take. "Yes, I do."

Johnnie quirked a brow at the way Ontoniel was offering up his own personal tea to someone he had just met but said nothing. He indicated Bergrin. "This is Bergrin, my bodyguard."

Bergrin nodded, but made no move to leave Johnnie's side. Phil smiled at him. "Nice to meet you." She laughed suddenly and reached up to touch the pixie on her shoulder. "Jester says you are 'gloomy magic', but I'm afraid that I do not know that one. You're powerful, I can see that." She tilted her head thoughtfully. "Beyond that, I simply cannot tell."

"Bergrin is unique," Johnnie said when Bergrin made no reply himself. When Phil nodded and let the matter drop, Johnnie returned to his own seat and drank his chamomile, chatting about inconsequential things until Phil was settled with her tea. "So why have you come to see us, Phil?"

Phil set her tea aside and rested her hands on her crossed legs. "I don't think it ever came up, the few times our paths crossed, Johnnie, but I'm part of a detective agency in Sable Brennus's territory. It's owned and run by Sable's consort, Christian. A few weeks ago a woman came to see us about the death of her daughter. Since taking that case, I have discovered six more murders exactly like the one I was hired to solve."

"A serial killer?" Johnnie asked, setting aside his surprise that Phil was a detective—with an agency and everything. He sincerely doubted that, as 'generous and open-minded' as his father might be, Ontoniel would ever allow him to do something as formal and final as open an agency.

"Yes, I suppose so," Phil replied. "The problem is the nature of the murders. We say murder, but honestly, we are not entirely certain what is killing them." She sat back in her seat and folded her arms across her chest.

Johnnie's skin prickled as the thrill of a mystery rushed over him. "What do you mean?"

"They look as though they died from exhaustion," Phil said. "According to all the accounts, each girl was last seen going to bed, or in bed or otherwise asleep. Three were in their beds, two fell asleep on their respective couches, one was last seen in a bathroom preparing for bed, the other in the kitchen getting a midnight snack before going back to her room. Four were wearing pajamas, one was dressed only in panties and a camisole, two were still in their day clothes. Yet upon discovery of the bodies, all were in dancing dresses, complete with hair, makeup, and shoes. All witnesses say it looks like they had gone to a party, but they know for a fact the women had done no such thing. They also looked as though they had been at their parties for hours and hours—the dresses showed extensive staining from sweat, their hair was matted, makeup a mess, and their shoes were nearly worn straight through."

"That is peculiar to say the least," Johnnie said, then quoted, "There was once upon a time a King who had twelve daughters, each one more beautiful than the other. They all slept together in one chamber, in which their beds stood side by side, and every night when they were in them the King locked the door, and bolted it. But in the morning when he unlocked the door, he saw that their shoes were worn out with dancing, and no one could find out how that had come to pass."

Phil's mouth quirked with dry amusement. "Indeed, and it gets worse. Each of the girls belonged to a special club, and like a sorority, they stay members for life. It's called the Princess Society."

Ontoniel and Johnnie both jerked in surprise at the same time.

"But—that is headquartered here," Ontoniel said. "My late wife was a member. I still donate large sums of money to it every year. Why am I only now hearing about these murders?"

Phil looked at him and said, "I doubt anyone has made the connection until now. I have been on this case for just over a month, and it was only a few days ago that I found the connection between them. These women are scattered all over the United States. Only sheer luck led me to discover the other six, and it is quite possible I simply have not found others. If these were normals, I think I would have found them much faster, for their membership in the Society alone should have drawn them together faster..."

"But abnormals are notoriously private," Johnnie finished. "So strange a death, and probably all on the higher end of the social scale, they preferred to hush it up and deal with the matter discreetly."

"Yes," Phil said. "That is the crux of it." She looked at Ontoniel. "The moment I found the connection between them, I contacted you to schedule this appointment."

Ontoniel nodded. "I thank you for the courtesy."

Phil smiled, slow and mischievous. "Courtesy nothing, my lord. I knew from various rumors that your son was a fair hand at detective work himself; I was hoping for both a connection to get me into the territory and a friendly face to assist me with the work."

Ontoniel laughed, then smiled at her, the friendliest Johnnie had ever seen his father with someone he had only just met. "Well played, my dear.

But as it happens, I may be able to offer you some help myself. My son's fiancée, Lady Ekaterina Salem, belongs to the Princess Society. Perhaps she can offer you some information you do not already possess?"

"Yes, quite possibly," Phil said, smiling at him. "That would be splendid. Thank you."

Nodding, Ontoniel hit another button on his phone.

"Yes?" Elam asked, his curt voice chilling even through the phone.

"I would like you and Ekaterina in my study immediately," Ontoniel said, then hung up.

Johnnie's mouth quirked in amusement, but he said nothing. A couple of minutes later, Elam and Ekaterina arrived. They made a beautiful couple, Johnnie thought—then his breath caught in his chest in surprise as he realized what he had just thought.

And, more importantly, how he had not been troubled by the thought at all.

He looked at Elam again, but saw only a mildly annoying elder brother. Elam was beautiful, cold, a perfect match to his stunning fiancée. Only months ago, Johnnie had fled because it tore him apart to see Elam go to someone else.

Now... now he simply did not give a damn.

What did that mean?

"Ekaterina," Ontoniel said. "I am sorry to disturb you. My son and his friend here are cooperating on a case, one that appears to involve the Princess Society."

Ekaterina's brows rose in surprise, but she only moved to sit in the chair before Ontoniel's desk, next to Phil. Ontoniel made the proper introductions, and Phil recounted her case. When she was finished,

Ekaterina digested the words in silence for several minutes, absently smoothing back her perfect, straight brown hair with long, elegant fingers painted with violet nail polish.

Finally she said, "I knew all those women. I did not know all seven of them were dead." She fell silent again, looking sad, but then continued, "Three of them were several years older than me, two were my age, two were younger. I knew them all, as I said, but only in passing. I am not certain what help I can offer, but I will certainly do what I can."

"Whatever you can tell me about them would be useful," Phil said. "Their families and friends were not forthcoming, more interested in protecting the dead than in finding their killers."

Ekaterina pursed her lips in thought, then said slowly, "I do not think they were all terribly well-to-do families, if that makes a difference. They were part of the Princess Society, but in the last hundred years, the standards for entry were greatly lowered. Only a little over a century ago, they would not have qualified for entry. It's a very old-fashioned sort of society, meant for the elite and only the elite, to see that certain standards and traditions are remembered and maintained. Abnormal society is, as you well know, very old-fashioned in many respects."

"Yes," Phil said. "This territory is one of the most advanced I've seen in terms of abnormals who fully utilize technology. Back home, we don't really bother."

Johnnie said nothing to that. He was no small part of the reason his father strongly supported technology and worked hard to see it was adapted to magic so that it could be utilized by abnormals, who in general tended to adversely affect such things. Completely lacking in magic, it was easier for him to employ phones and the like rather than constantly rely upon relics and spells cast by others.

"Not to mention," Phil continued, "the way that the Dracula adopted a human child, which is not something I know ever to have been done in vampire history. You also surrendered a very old territory in Europe to move here to indulge your first wife, and I know you kept connections with the DeLovely family after they caused a scandal of their own."

Ontoniel laughed. "Making a female an Alucard, you mean? That is not so terrible a thing, and it is a scandal fourteen years old now. I will be interested to see who she finally marries, who is willing to play consort to a female Dracula. I believe the former Alucard Zachariah also works under Consort Brennus, yes?"

"Yes," Phil said, smiling. "Zach is currently working a case up north, otherwise he probably would have been the one to deal with this matter, as he is more familiar by far with the upper echelons of vampire society than I."

"I sincerely doubt that. You seem as well verse as any of us," Ontoniel said with a smile.

Johnnie had never seen his father smile and laugh so much in the course of one afternoon, never mind at a complete stranger. Really, he just wanted to go back to the Bremen and play at normalcy for a bit.

"Anyway," Ekaterina cut in. "I do not know what the women had in common, past their membership in the Princess Society. They had nothing much in common, from what I remember. They have very different interests, were years—decades—apart, lived in different parts of the country—"

"I think we are focusing on the wrong thing," Johnnie cut in, losing all patience.

Everyone turned to look at him—Ekaterina and Elam in annoyance, Ontoniel with a faint smile, and Phil with amusement. Beside him, Bergrin made a noise that sounded suspiciously like a smothered laugh. Ignoring him, Johnnie said, "The main problem here is not that they are all from the same Society, though that obviously will be pertinent later. What intrigues me more is the nature of the deaths, what they were wearing when they went to bed, what they were wearing when they were found dead, and the fact they were clearly exhausted to death. Do you know the tale of the Shoes That Were Danced to Pieces?"

"It's a fairytale," Phil said. "About princesses who snuck out every night to party so long and hard they wore holes in their shoes every night. I remember there were forests in it, of gold and jewels and something else."

"Mm," Johnnie said. "The mystery in the tale was always how the princesses managed to escape and sneak off to their party. They were sealed into their bedroom every night, with no way in or out once the bolts were thrown. A soldier manages to follow them, through a secret passage into another world."

"Plane crossing," Ontoniel interrupted. "That story has long been studied by abnormal scholars as a tale that secretly recounts a way to cross from the mortal plane to the dream plane at will. Of all the planes, the path from mortal to dream is the easiest to travel. Many plane scholars believe that if the trick of crossing from one to the other while awake could be achieved, the key to traveling *all* planes at will could be discovered."

Johnnie smiled at his father, taken by surprised. He had never known Ontoniel knew so much about such things. "Precisely. The tale of the dancing princesses is believed to contain a key to it, some secret code—or it could simply be a taunt, from the one who discovered it to those who read the tale and know what it means. It is largely believed that the 'princes' in the tale who lure the princesses into their world are not demons but incubi."

"So we have seven women, all dead of dancing, and who had all fallen asleep," Phil said. "You think they were pulled into the dream plane. But if they were pulled in while asleep, that is hardly impressive."

Spinning his cane, then rapping it sharply on the floor, Johnnie said, "Except they were found in their dancing clothes."

Phil rolled her eyes. "Duh me. I've been doing this for how many decades?" She frowned in thought, then said, "I think perhaps this problem is even bigger than I had first feared."

"I would agree," Ontoniel said.

"I think it sounds a fine mystery," Johnnie said and rose. "We need to go speak with Micah. Come on, Bergrin. Phil?"

Phil stood up, then turned to Ontoniel. "Thank you, Ontoniel, for all your assistance. I promise to see to it your son is returned in one piece, though I think his bodyguard there has the matter well in hand."

Ontoniel rose and extended his hand, kissing Phil's again when she placed her own in it. "I am happy I could help. Please take care of yourself, as well. Johnnie, come and see me when this is all over."

"Of course," Johnnie said. "Our conversation is far

from over. Lady Ekaterina. Ellie." Holding out his arm to Phil, Bergrin shadowing just behind him, Johnnie led the way from the study.

A servant stood waiting for them in the entryway and helped them into their coats and hats. Outside, a car was already waiting, no doubt summoned by his father after they had left the study. "It is a four-hour drive into the city," Johnnie warned Phil.

Phil only shrugged, and settled into her seat with a smile. "I wouldn't mind the chance to rest. I've been traveling all over kingdom come via magic for days straight. A nice car ride will not break my heart." She reached up and lifted the pixie still cradled on her shoulder, settling it into her lap. Swirling eyes stared at Johnnie and Bergrin, wings rustling restlessly, tiny little gargoyle-like hands making motions.

"Huh," Phil said, petting the pixie. "He continues to repeat that Bergrin is gloomy magic, and he says that Johnnie is 'better vampire'. I have no idea what either of those two things mean, and after so many years, I thought I'd heard it all."

"Better vampire?" Johnnie echoed. "I am not a vampire at all, how could I be a better one?"

"You are a normal and only twenty six years old," Bergrin said. "Yet I know plenty have mistaken you for a vampire, and many vampires concede you do it better at twenty-six they did at one hundred and twenty-six."

Johnnie said nothing, merely turned his head and stared out the window.

Phil laughed softly. "So what does gloomy magic mean, then?"

Bergrin shrugged. "I have not the slightest; there is nothing gloomy about me."

Though Johnnie agreed, he did not say it.

Laughing again, Phil asked, "So who is this Micah we are going to see?"

"A friend of mine, and a regular at the bar I own and live above," Johnnie replied. "He is an alchemist who specializes in plane-crossing relics." He rubbed his thumb along the runes carved into the top of his cane. "We will see what he says about this matter, unless you have another expert in mind?"

Phil shook her head. "Not me. I know experts on any number of subjects; I'm even friends with a very powerful sorcerer and his angel. Plane crossing, though—that's powerful mojo. The closest I've ever come to that is probably Chris's Black Dog."

Johnnie glanced from the window at that, attention truly captured. "A Black Dog? Who is this Chris—you mean the Consort?"

"Yes," Phil said, giggling. "Chris worked a case a couple of years ago where the ghost of this child was haunting some fancy little gated community. They'd let the child die of neglect, and he turned into a ghost. His agony was great enough to summon a Black Dog, and after Chris figured out the problem and punished the people in the complex, the Dog stuck with him. He's fascinated by the way Chris is half-ghost."

"I have heard that before," Johnnie murmured. "I did not know the veracity of it. That territory is on the opposite side of the country, and we have little reason to interact with Lord Brennus."

Phil grinned. "You're welcome to drop by anytime—just make sure you bring an umbrella. I heard you were there recently, weren't you?"

"Yes," Johnnie said, nodding toward Bergrin. "I was at Bergrin's home briefly."

Phil looked toward Bergrin in surprise. "Oh? I did not know you were from my neck of the woods. Where do you live?"

"The historic district just outside the city. My father owns Shale Estate."

"Ah," Phil said, smiling. "It's a beautiful district. Shale Estate is the oldest house there, I believe. How remarkable. I did not even realize you were that Bergrin."

Bergrin shrugged. "We've always preferred to live quietly; my father is very private."

Phil nodded. "Of course." She turned to Johnnie. "Do you know his family history?"

"I know there are precious few abnormals in his family tree, and that they have been in Brennus's territory for a long time," Johnnie said, annoyed and not entirely certain why.

"They helped settled the territory, even before Sable arrived and staked a claim," Phil said. "They were the only law in the area for a very long time."

Bergrin shrugged. "If by law you mean shooting first, hanging second, asking questions later on."

"So babysitting runs in the blood, as well as finding things?" Johnnie asked. "You never mentioned your prestigious history of enforcing."

"That is because it amounted to very little," Bergrin said with a shrug. "It was a matter of survival. It hardly made us rich or famous, and it killed as many Bergrins as it did supposed criminals. All it amounts to is being able to say we're as old as the territory itself. I have always been more interested in the abnormal aspects of my family, rather than the normal."

Johnnie nodded. "Certainly it is the abnormal bits of one's family history that seem to cause the most trouble." He frowned, pensive mood returning as he brooded over all that his father had said—and what he still refused to say.

What could Tommy have made that was so awful no one wanted to admit what it was? Had he managed to make one of the impossible relics?

No, that was illogical. They were called impossible relics for a reason. In situations like these, it was always that the alchemist had made something he had never thought of and that he did not know how to accidentally make a second time.

He drummed his fingers on his cane, his other hand bracing his chin as he stared out the car window again.

"You look lost in some serious thinking," Phil said. "I haven't looked that unhappy since I broke up with my last serious boyfriend ten years ago. Abnormal men are even more annoying to date than normal, let me tell you."

Johnnie laughed, even if the words stirred an ache in his chest. "I agree wholeheartedly, milady. That dance is tricky enough without feeling as though you are dancing in the dark to music you do not know."

"That is perfectly said," Phil said, then smiled faintly. "You and your father are the first real gentlemen I have encountered in some time, but like all gentlemen, you are not for me to touch." She sighed. "Ah, well. So it goes. What had you frowning so, Johnnie?"

"Secrets," Johnnie said. "Everyone likes to keep secrets and leave me out of them. I am tired of it."

"Is that what you were discussing when I intruded?" Phil asked. "I am sorry. I know how frustrating it is to be kept in the dark. It's been, oh, more years than I like to count since someone tried to use me in a demonic ceremony. I didn't know what was going on, no one would tell me, and I felt like they were all treating me like a child—my father, Chris, everyone I pestered. But I pushed and pushed, and here I am, past fifty but still young looking." Her smile was bittersweet. "I buried my father, a few friends, and I am careful to avoid the rest until all that remains of my normal life finally fades away. I love my life, and do not regret my choices, but I better understand now why everyone tried to keep me in the dark."

Johnnie shrugged impatiently. "I ceased to have a normal life the moment my parents were murdered; I am tired of people trying to keep me normal."

"Well, from what little I know of you," Phil said, "if no one tells you the truth, you will uncover it yourself. Just be careful, Johnnie. Better to dance in the dark than be devoured by it."

"I know," Johnnie replied quietly. "Believe me, I am all too aware of what can happen in the dark."

They lapsed into silence then, and Johnnie slid a brief look at Bergrin, sitting directly opposite him. Bergrin, to his surprise, seemed troubled. A deep frown cut hard lines into his face, and for once he seemed completely oblivious to his surroundings.

Johnnie hesitated, then reached out with his cane and struck Bergrin lightly on the leg. "What has you looking gloomy, babysitter?"

"Hm?" Bergrin asked, then his eyes cleared as he left his thoughts to focus on Johnnie. "Uh. Nothing of importance. I apologize."

Rolling his eyes, Johnnie struck him again with a little more force. "Fine. If it is nothing, stop scowling." He withdrew his cane, and laid it across his lap again, then resumed staring out the window. The car lapsed into silence, save for brief, soft laughter from Phil.

They arrived at the Bremen four long hours later, and Johnnie gave Phil his arm, wondering with amusement how the others would react to his guest.

Inside, the entire room stopped, several pairs of eyes locked on Phil. Hanging up her coat, Phil smoothed her hair, then beamed at all of them. She strode to the bar, heels clicking on the floor, shockingly loud in the stunned silence, and leaned on the counter. Smiling at Peyton, she said, "Hey, there, wolf. Could I get a whiskey sour?"

"Sure thing," Peyton managed and went to make the drink, pausing only to slide a shot of vodka across the bar for Johnnie.

Johnnie picked up the shot and tossed it back, then turned to the rest of the room and said, "Stop gawking. Walsh, you are about to set something on fire with that cigar."

Jerking into motion, Walsh set the cigar hastily aside in a tray, then moved with the others almost as one.

Heath snickered from the far end of the bar. "Johnnie, Johnnie. However did you wind up with a woman clearly too good for you?"

Phil laughed, then thanked Peyton as he brought her drink. "Hello, boys. It's nice to meet you. What an interesting mix you've got here." She glanced at Heath. "You're Heath Etherton."

Johnnie's eyes snapped to Heath. "Are you really?"

"I was, yes," Heath said tersely. "I was disowned. I like it here. You didn't come here to discuss me."

"No," Phil said. "We came to meet with Micah."

"That's me," Micah said from one of the tables, lifting his beer in greeting. He smiled at Phil, then glanced at Johnnie. "What do you need from me?"

"Everything you know about plane crossing," Johnnie said. "Let us talk upstairs." He walked across the bar to the door leading up to his rooms, not giving anyone a chance to argue.

Phil murmured a thanks and a farewell to the other men, then followed along with Micah and Bergrin. "Nice place," she commented as she sat down in one of the leather chairs in the living area. "And above a bar. I've got a nice penthouse these days, but it lacks the charm of this place."

Johnnie smiled briefly in thanks as he sat down in his favorite place on his leather sofa. Bergrin sat down next to him, startling Johnnie. He fought an urge to shift—and hated he was not certain if he wanted to move further away or closer in, and *why* must he be noticing his damned babysitter this way? Life had been much easier, even with all his recent complications, before his awareness of Bergrin had become sexually charged.

Micah sat down in the other leather chair set next to Phil's, with a table between them. "So what can I tell you, Johnnie?"

"We have had an interesting string of murders," Johnnie began and told him all that Phil had earlier related.

"Yeah, that sounds like plane crossing," Micah said when he had finished. "Sounds like they were pulled into dreaming while half-asleep and gradually woken still trapped there, then thrown out of it—or possibly they fell out of it when they died."

Bergrin stirred at that. "Bodies do not typically move from the plane in which they died. Souls do, but not bodies."

Johnnie's brows rose. "You sound certain of that."

"I am," Bergrin said.

"How can you know that? No one knows much of anything about traveling the planes, let alone what happens when a person belongs to one plane but dies in another."

Bergrin did not reply, and in fact, looked sorry that he had spoken.

One more secret, Johnnie thought bitterly. One more stupid, infuriating secret. "Fine, keep your precious secrets. Everyone else does." Not giving Bergrin a chance to reply, he turned back to Micah and said, "How could one do that?"

Micah shrugged. "There are spells, but generally they're a one-time only sort of thing. Summoning a demon from hell, calling down an angel, bringing forth a jinn—any of it. Once their binding is broken, or their power grows too great in the case of a demon, back they go. If they die, they're gone, they don't return to their planes so far as we know, G-man is right on that count. In the case of normals and less powerful abnormals jumping planes, it's most often a one-way street. It's... too taxing, I guess, except in the case of the dream plane. And, well, how well do normals or even abnormals remember their dreams?"

"I would not know," Johnnie said. "I do not dream."

"Probably you just don't remember them at all," Phil said. "Many don't."

Johnnie disagreed, for he had read enough about dreams and dreaming over the years to know for a certainty that he did not dream, but he did not press the matter. "So what is one way to get a regular abnormal from the mortal plane to the dream plane without them being completely asleep?"

"Powerful spell work," Micah replied. "You probably already knew that. It's definitely nothing I could do, not without getting into the sort of alchemy that no one should get mixed up in. You're talking powerful sorcery, and then only if it's a damned good sorcerer. A necromancer could do it, too, though that's less likely. It would be similar to how that cane was made actually." He nodded at the cane Johnnie still held.

Flourishing it, Johnnie examined the runes, then said, "Explain."

Micah did not look happy, but he said, "An item that can cross all the planes must be made with the lifeblood of a creature from every plane. That is why I do not make more of them. That is why I do not want anyone else to have it. That is why I will die before I shared the secret with anyone who might abuse it. You three already know more than any other living person, and I tell you only because I trust you, Johnnie, and am willing to trust your friends."

"No one will ever hear it from me," Phil promised.

"It is not possible to capture a creature from every plane," Bergrin said. "Most can be summoned, but not all. No one even knows for certain how many planes there truly are, which ones are myth, which ones are fact."

Micah shrugged. "The secret of the cane's making has been passed down orally through many generations. The finer points of it, we have purposely lost. My father always surmised that the one who actually made the cane must have had help from a sorcerer who was able to summon forth all the necessary creatures. Demon, angel, whatever dream creature—I do not know them all. I only know the cane exists and that to make it required murdering each of those creatures and binding their essence to the cane."

Johnnie grimaced as he examined his cane again and quoted, "He that increaseth knowledge increaseth sorrow."

Beside him, Bergrin grunted. "I shudder to think what they did and tried before finally getting the experiment correct."

"I agree," Phil murmured. "So how does all of this tie in to the dead women, you think? Someone is trying to step it up from objects to living persons?"

Johnnie frowned, thinking, then pulled out his phone and punched one of the speed dials. "Come see me," he said, then hung up.

A moment later, Rostislav appeared by the window. He smiled at Johnnie in amusement. "You summoned, Master Johnnie? You are lucky I was not otherwise occupied."

"Jesse is always in meetings this time of day," Johnnie said dismissively. "Nothing else you do now is more important."

Rostislav laughed, then crossed his arms over his chest and leaned against the window. "So how might I serve, oh lord and master?"

Johnnie rolled his eyes. "You said once that there were rumors of someone interested in plane crossing."

"Yes," Rostislav replied slowly, pushing away from the wall again, hands falling to his side. "Someone is hunting plane crossing relics, through fair means and foul. Mostly foul—extremely foul. No one knows who or why, only that lately that sort of thing has been highly in demand. Word is that if you have one, guard it heavily or demand generous recompense. I also heard that same someone was hunting plane-crossing creatures, but I can't imagine there are many, if any, of those just floating around. There is no creature that can simply cross the planes as they please."

"Do you know anything else?" Johnnie asked.

Rostislav shook his head. "No, unfortunately. Just as the rumors were beginning to reach me, I was exiled with Jesse. I can try to investigate, but it will be more difficult now."

"I can look into it," Phil said. "Rumors aren't hard to dig up."

"Just be careful," Rostislav said. "All the rumors I *have* heard agree on the nastiness of the person behind it all. Ruthless, that's the word I kept hearing."

Phil nodded but did not seem concerned. "I've dealt with worse."

Johnnie glanced at Micah. "I wish now we had held onto that imp who was hurting you. He may have known something about this."

"You think?" Micah asked, frowning in thought. "I thought he was just after the money."

"I would not be surprised to learn that is not entirely true," Johnnie said. "So now we are looking for a talented alchemist or a powerful sorcerer, and quite possibly a rather devious imp."

Rostislav made a face. "I will see what I can do, but it's hard when visiting you is about all I can do without getting people up in arms."

"Cinderella, Cinderella," Johnnie taunted, smirking when Rostislav glared at him. "Return to your Prince Charming, then. I have other resources, though if you do hear something, by all means let me know."

"Of course," Rostislav murmured, then vanished as

suddenly as he had appeared.

Phil rested her chin in the palm of one hand, elbow propped on the armrest of her chair. "I still wonder what the girls themselves have to do with it," she mused. "There is some relevance to that, but damned if I've been able to find it." She looked toward Johnnie, then continued, "The only connection I've found between them is the Society. Otherwise, they vary in age, type of abnormal, interests, money, you name it. I would almost swear they were chosen at random, except they all belong to that damned society and they were all new wealth, so far as the abnormal world is concerned."

"That is probably all that they need to have in common," Johnnie said, idly running his thumb over the head of his cane, tracing the lines of the runes. "The point is twelve sisters, lost in a world that hopes to steal them away forever. Some people believe that the key to plane travel is in the tale itself. Whoever is doing this is clearly recreating the tale in hopes of finding that key. I would wager the women are being killed from youngest to oldest? I would also bet the youngest was talkative and easily frightened. Should all twelve die, you will likely find the oldest to be the strongest and wisest."

Everyone looked at him, with varying degrees of amazement on their faces. Finally Micah asked, "How do you know that?"

"Yes," Phil said. "You're as sharp as Chris, and he's at least twice your age."

Johnnie motioned impatiently, then stood and strode across the room to his library. Flicking on one of the Tiffany lamps, he strode to the proper bookcase and pulled down the book he wanted. Returning to the living room, he set it down upon the coffee table for everyone to see. "*An Analysis of Plane Travel in Classic Tales*. I have others." He resumed his seat next to Bergrin, wishing suddenly that he had not moved as his head had decided that was grounds to resume throbbing.

Phil leaned over and picked the book up, then sat back in her seat and began to thumb through it. "Impressive. No one has ever mentioned studies like this to me. I thought fairytales were fairytales." She laughed softly. "That seems so silly, of a sudden. Of course they would be more than they appear: that is the nature of abnormals."

"Quite," Johnnie agreed. "Someone else has read this book, I would imagine. It is quite old, but still the best source on the subject. Anyone interested in studying plane travel would begin with this book." He gripped the top of his cane and scowled. "I do wish now I had not simply let that imp run off, but at the time, the matter seemed closed."

"He can be found again," Bergrin said. "If it really matters that much, Prince, he can be found again."

"How can you find him?" Johnnie asked. "He is an imp. He could change his appearance, and you were not even there..." He sighed when Bergrin only smirked. "Of course you were there. Why did I think otherwise?" He rolled his eyes. "So why did you not save me that day?"

Bergrin only smirked again and said, "Highness, you will never know just how close I was to taking care of the matter. How close I was, period."

Johnnie cast him a withering look, then said, "Fine then, braggart. See the imp from that day is found. We will see what information he can provide."

"It will be done," Bergrin said. "After you are in bed and I have called another Enforcer to watch you in my absence."

"I truly hate you," Johnnie groused, only further irritated by the way Bergrin merely continued to smirk.

Phil laughed. "You two are cute. I think I will leave you to your imp hunt, Johnnie, and see if I can't catch a lead on the rumors Rostislav mentioned. Hopefully one of us will come across something, or stumble into it. Be careful, though, huh?"

"Of course," Johnnie said and stood up, taking her hand when she held it out and kissing the back of it. Then he kissed her cheek. "Be careful yourself, milady."

Patting his cheek fondly, Phil took hold of Jester, and then was gone, leaving Johnnie with Micah and Bergrin.

"You're getting into some dangerous stuff," Micah said quietly. "This is much worse than one stupid imp causing me grief, if you really think he's involved. No one should be trying to do what my stupid damned ancestors managed."

Johnnie frowned. "What concerns me is that they have not troubled you further, Micah."

"I've always played dumb," Micah said. "We claimed to be studying the cane to learn its secrets; we were never dumb enough to say we already knew how it was done. I don't even want to *think* about what would happen were the wrong people to learn how to make objects that can travel the planes. I fear that once they achieved that, it would not take them long to learn how to do it with people."

"They already have," Johnnie said. "If the seven

dead women are any indication, then they can move them from mortal to dream, at least while they are partially asleep, and can move them completely from dream to mortal." He twirled his cane back and forth in his hands, thinking. At last he posed, "To work this hard, to take such a risk as these murders, whoever it is must have a specific goal in mind. Risks are not taken for abstracts; they are taken for definites."

Bergrin sighed. "Why can't you take cases finding lost cats or something?"

Johnnie smacked Bergrin's leg with his cane. "That would be a waste of my intellect."

"I think you mean your ego," Bergrin groused, and his scowl was not at all diminished by the fact his right eye was still more closed than open, the livid bruise surrounding it worse than ever. "Honestly, going on an imp hunt will be cake next to babysitting you." He shifted slightly, as though making to stand, but a faint grimace overtook his face, and he did not move.

As suddenly as that, Johnnie was reminded of the scratches on Bergrin's chest, the nasty bruise across his lower back, his bandaged arm—all injuries incurred saving Johnnie.

"Just forget it," he said flatly. "You need rest, or you will be completely useless as a babysitter instead of mostly useless."

Bergrin's mouth tightened, and he stood up slowly, stiffly. When he was standing, Johnnie was suddenly, painfully aware that he was close enough to touch—to kiss—and he fought a strange urge to laugh at the idiotic observation. But that didn't keep him from vividly recalling how Bergrin had looked half-naked, and how soft his face had been in sleep, the way Alec had brushed the hair from his face in a way that Johnnie certainly could not.

How deeply he had obviously slept alongside Bergrin, despite the limited confines of the couch.

He did not want these thoughts; he certainly did not need them. He was still sorting out his hot to cold feelings for Elam and the mystery of Eros. He did not need to lust after a bodyguard whose regard was still low enough he seldom called Johnnie anything but 'Highness' and 'Prince'.

"I'm fine," Bergrin bit out. "I haven't failed in my duties so far, Highness—"

"No, you have not," Johnnie snapped, cutting him off, irritated beyond all reason by that fucking 'Highness'. "You perform your duties perfectly, right down to the letter, babysitter. If hunting imps would provide you with a welcome respite, then by all means, go hunting. Summon your replacement and be on your way." Not waiting for a reply, he turned sharply and stalked off to his bedroom, closing the door sharply behind him. Then he locked it.

Alone, he tossed his cane on the bed and stripped out of his clothes. He contemplated a shower, but that would require going back out into the main room. Being a prisoner in his own bedroom grated, all the more because he had done it to himself, but seeing Bergrin right then grated more.

Making a face at himself, Johnnie propped his cane beside his bed and crawled beneath the blankets.

Though he had expected to toss and turn, he was asleep within moments.

He woke some time later, feeling warm and disoriented. A moment's fumbling, however, revealed his own bed and a familiar weight pressed against him from behind, arms wrapped firmly around him.

"Eros?"

"Johnnie," Eros rumbled, voice heavy with sleep but still rich with that hot-toddy quality that drove Johnnie wild, even though he hated admitting it had that sort of effect. Eros's mouth trailed along his throat, soft kisses interspersed with sharp bites, and Johnnie was suddenly very much awake.

Eros rolled enough away to lay Johnnie out flat on the bed, then moved close again, straddling him, bending to take his mouth in a kiss that was soft and slow but made Johnnie ache all the more.

He wanted to say no, enough, stop—he was so tired of only being fucked in the dark—but he could not bring himself to do it. Instead, he simply looped his arms around Eros's neck and held him close, kissed him deeply, spread his legs eagerly when Eros demanded it, whimpering for more as Eros prepared him.

When Eros finally slid inside and began to fuck him, slow and hard and deep, Johnnie could only dig his fingers into hard muscle, whimper and moan and cry for more, muffle his scream in Eros's mouth as he came.

They lay panting in the dark, skin slowly cooling, until Johnnie shivered and Eros drew the blankets back up over him.

"Will there ever come a day when you will stop hiding in the dark?" Johnnie asked wearily. Was this how whores felt, night after night? But that was nonsensical and melodramatic, and he dismissed the thought irritably.

"No," Eros replied. "I like you in the dark. Only I can see you, and you have no choice but to focus on me."

Johnnie said nothing, merely pulled the blankets

up higher and buried his face in his pillow. He felt a soft kiss pressed to his cheek, and then he was alone again.

Bitter loneliness made his chest hurt, and he tried to burrow still further into his bed, his blankets. He was so damned tired of secrets.

~~*

Johnnie was sipping tea and pouring over every book on plane traveling he owned when he felt a sudden prickle of awareness. Looking up, he set his tea down so hard he half-expected the cup to shatter. He glared at Bergrin.

Bergrin only smirked. "I found your imp, Highness. Did you want him brought to you, or did you want to go see him?"

"We are going to see him," Johnnie said. He finished his tea in one swallow, then rose, adjusting his red shirt and black and silver paisley vest, moving swiftly to the bedroom to fetch his jacket and going out clothes.

Back in the living room, he eyed Bergrin. "You look exhausted. At least your eye looks better."

Bergrin looked briefly startled, but then simply shrugged. "I'm fine, Highness. I sent the temporary bodyguard home. Should I call him back?"

"Did I say that?" Johnnie snapped. Honestly, he had never even bothered to go and see the replacement. He had absolutely no interest in meeting the man.

"Should we summon your friend?" Bergrin asked. "Phil?"

Johnnie shook his head. "Let us see what we can do ourselves. Hopefully, there will be no further kidnapping attempts."

"I should be so lucky," Bergrin muttered. He tugged on his cap. "Would you at least try—"

He broke off as his phone started ringing and pulled it out, eyebrows going up as he glanced at the caller ID. Before Johnnie could ask, Bergrin answered it with a, "Hey, Pop." He fell silent, listening as his father spoke, face growing increasingly grim.

A moment later he hung up and returned the phone to his jacket pocket. "My dad says that while he's not one hundred percent certain, he is eighty-five percent certain that your father didn't destroy whatever the fuck he made."

"He did not destroy it?" Johnnie echoed, suddenly feeling cold.

"No," Bergrin said. "My dad thinks he simply hid it."

"Damn it," Johnnie said. "I wonder if my father knows that."

Bergrin shrugged. "We can ask him later. Right now, we still need to go speak with that imp."

Johnnie nodded. "Where is he?"

"Relatively close, actually. About nine blocks northeast, in a neighborhood even I avoid when I can. So if I tell you to do something, Highness—"

"I know," Johnnie snapped. "Do not worry, babysitter. I will try to avoid your getting injured a third time in the line of duty." He turned sharply on his heel and strode out of his apartment and down the stairs.

"Good morning, Johnnie," Peyton greeted. "G-man."

"Peyton," Johnnie greeted. "Would you tell Micah, whenever he shows, that we went to go speak with the imp who troubled him before? I do not know how long it will take."

Peyton nodded. "Sure thing. You two take care, huh? Ain't no fun seeing you so worn out and beat up all the time."

Johnnie shrugged and settled his fedora more firmly on his head. "It is the inevitable result of being a dashing detective and his arrogant bodyguard."

"I'm arrogant?" Bergrin demanded. "Who wears two thousand dollar suits in the low-rent district of the city and doesn't see a problem with that?"

"And what?" Johnnie retorted. "I should wear jeans and a goofy cap?"

Bergrin glared. "My *mom* gave this hat to me, so shut up about it."

"It is a very cute hat," Johnnie said in his haughtiest tone, then strode out of the bar amidst Peyton's laughter. Outside, he asked, "Which way?"

"This way, Highness."

Johnnie fell into step alongside Bergrin, gripping his cane in one hand. "How did you find him? I know you excel at finding things, but how do you do it?"

"It is not something I can really discuss, Highness."

"But you told me about your mother," Johnnie said, feeling hurt for no good reason. "Even my father thinks she ran off, when obviously she did not." He felt even worse when Bergrin offered absolutely no reply.

He had missed something, Johnnie thought, and that irritated him. He was smart, he was observant—and he had thought after all that had recently happened, since waking up in Alec's house, that something had shifted between them.

It seemed he had been wrong, however. Foolishly, humiliatingly wrong. Since last night, it seemed they had slipped back to the way they had been at the start. The silence in regards to Bergrin's mother seemed to indicate any reply would be an unpleasant one.

He had thought it a show of real trust that Bergrin had talked about his mother—but it was quite obviously something he regretted.

"Do not worry," Johnnie said bitterly. "Whatever misgivings in sharing the confidence, I will not share your secret. I might despise them, but I understand when it is not my place to share one."

When Bergrin turned to look at him, Johnnie jerked his gaze away, really not interested in whatever ice would be in those damned hazel eyes. A hand fell on his shoulder, but Johnnie pulled away, snapping, "Do not touch me."

"Johnnie—"

"Oh, look at that," Johnnie said, rounding on him. "It knows my name and can actually use it."

Bergrin's mouth tightened. "It?"

"If I am to be a Highness, you are an It," Johnnie retorted.

"Why are you so mad at me?" Bergrin demanded. "I'm still bruised because of you, I got maybe two hours of sleep because of you, and if your father finds out I'm taking you straight into danger *on purpose*, he'll gut me and all I get from you is snapped at and called It?"

He reached out again, but Johnnie stepped out of reach. "All you do is whine about me being a burden; all you do is shove in my face what an onerous duty I am. I thought—" He bit down on the words, refusing to be so weak as to admit that he had thought they might be friends. "I am sorry I am such a bothersome charge, and I am sorry that I invaded your home because of duty, and I am definitely sorry you told me about your mother when you obviously regret doing so. If I am nothing but one travail after another to you, by all means, recall your replacement and make him my permanent babysitter."

He stormed off down the street, but remembered as he reached the intersection that he did not know where they were going.

"Damn it, Johnnie—"

"Twice in a row, wonders never cease," Johnnie muttered, then looked up reluctantly as Bergrin reached him. "You are still here?"

"Goddamn it, Johnnie—"

"Three times in a span of five minutes, it is a miracle."

To his everlasting astonishment and outrage, Bergrin reached out, grabbed him by his arms, and shook him—hard. When he was released, Johnnie swung out with his cane, only further annoyed that he only hit Bergrin because Bergrin allowed it. "Do not do that again," he hissed. "I told you not to touch me."

"Stop being such a fucking brat and give me a chance to speak!" Bergrin snapped. "I can't fucking apologize if you're not going to stand still to let me!"

Johnnie stood rigid, glaring at him.

Bergrin let out a long sigh, yanking off his hat to rake a hand through the hopeless tangle of his curls, then shoved the hat back into place and finally said, "I'm sorry, all right? I was just trying to harass you. I never meant for you to think I actually hated watching out for you. I don't. You *are* the most difficult job I've had in a long time, but that doesn't mean I dislike it."

"Fine," Johnnie said, even though it was not because all Bergrin had really done was clarify that

Johnnie was not a bad job. "But if I become too cumbersome a duty, by all means, let me know."

"Oh, for—" Bergrin yanked his hat off again, somehow managing to still hold onto it as he sank both his hands into his hair. "Johnnie—I'm not watching out for you because I have to, you have to know that. I don't get beat up and almost killed just because it's my job. I mean, yes, okay, it's damned hard to tell the Dracula *no* and live to tell the tale, but if I could not stand you, or being with you around the clock, I'd tell him no."

The knot in Johnnie's chest eased a bit at that, even if he did not completely believe what Bergrin was saying. "So what about your mother?" he asked, and he did not want to ask because he was going to hate the answer—but he needed the answer, even if hurt.

"You don't like secrets," Bergrin said. "I thought—" He stopped, mouth tightening. "You get so angry about secrets, and I thought maybe involving you in the secrecy surrounding my mother was simply one more thing you resented."

Johnnie's ire eased at that. "It is the only secret anyone has told me without my having to dig it up or throw a fit about it first."

Bergrin rubbed the back of his neck, looking briefly embarrassed. "Uh—I didn't really think about it. Just seemed like I should tell you. Um. I'd tell you more, I think, but I'd have to talk to my folks first. I might be their kid, but it's ultimately their secret first."

Johnnie nodded, able to understand that even if he wished Bergrin would just tell him—but sort of happy that Bergrin wanted to tell him. He would take that, for now. Dismissing the matter, he cleared his throat, then asked, "So where are we going, exactly?"

Bergrin hesitated a moment, as though he was not quite certain he was finished with the conversation, but only said, "Turn right here, then down three more blocks. It'll be a dumpy looking brown building; our friend is on the third floor, in the back apartment."

Nodding, Johnnie led the way across the street, then down the three blocks. He was painfully aware whenever Bergrin lightly touched his back, a protective gesture as they traveled into the increasingly seedy neighborhood.

He tried not to wonder what it might be like to be touched that way affectionately, out in broad daylight where anyone could see and his companion would not object to being seen. More and more, though, he was realizing that was not ever going to happen.

"Something is wrong," Bergrin said as they reached the brown building they sought and stepped inside. He motioned for Johnnie to remain just inside the door and wandered deeper into the building himself. It was so rundown it should probably have been condemned. The rats were not even bothering to be sneaky as they crawled across the floor. The whole place smelled of piss and stale booze and overall rot.

"Something?" Johnnie echoed dryly. "I would hazard to say the list is a good deal longer than that."

"No, not that," Bergrin said, looking up the stairs then back to Johnnie, an odd timbre to his voice as he said, "I smell death."

"What—"

But before Johnnie could say a word, the few lights in the hallway went out, leaving them in near-absolute darkness.

And suddenly, there on the floor, visible only in the dark, was the spell cage into which Johnnie had unwittingly stepped.

Some of the lights came back up, then, leaving the spell cage partially visible. At the end of the hall, a man stepped out. He reeked of so much magic that Johnnie barely pulled out his handkerchief in time before he was sneezing into it—once, twice, thrice.

Eyes watering, he kept the kerchief over his face, muttering through it. "Sorcerer."

Movement at the top of the stairs briefly drew Johnnie's attention, and he looked up to see two figures—a man, and the ominous shape of a dragon—still lurking in the shadows.

Bergrin moved protectively in front of Johnnie, suddenly holding the knife that Johnnie never actually managed to see him draw. The smell of magic grew stronger, too strong for Johnnie to smell it properly—all he could do was sneeze.

"So you are the dream child I have heard so much about," the sorcerer said, looking at Johnnie. "I was told that getting to you was difficult, as there was a particularly vigilant guard dog with you these days." He flicked a glance at Bergrin and sneered. "Not so difficult at all." He snapped his fingers, and the man and dragon at the top of the stairs slunk down them. The dull yellow light of the stairwell lamps made the dragon's black scales gleam.

Johnnie barely noticed, more interested in what the sorcerer had just called him. Dream child? But he did not voice the question aloud, not wanting to admit to ignorance and reveal a weakness.

The spell, he thought suddenly. It had been a *nightmare* spell that had bounced off him. Johnnie glanced down at the spell cage holding him, the lines of it only barely visible in the yellow light. It included marks to keep in dream plane creatures. But that was absurd—this was the mortal plane. There were no dream creatures here.

Except the sorcerer had called him dream child.

And a nightmare spell had bounced off him.

And Johnnie did not dream.

That was too much coincidence.

Johnnie was yanked from his thoughts when the sorcerer spoke again. "So, guard dog. How would you like to die? I can tell you that after the last time, the dragons are dying to make you lunch."

Bergrin only laughed. "The method does not matter to me. If you are trying to scare me, sorcerer, you're failing miserably. Death does not scare me; certainly the threat of death does not."

The sorcerer sneered at him. "You talk big, dog, but all men fear death."

"I have nothing to fear," Bergrin reiterated, "but by all means, give it your best shot."

The dragon snarled and lunged—only to crash into the cage that held Johnnie, snarling in fury. But even as it turned to try again, the dragon screamed in fury and absolute agony.

Johnnie's eyes went wide as he saw Bergrin drop the body of the dragon's owner, the man's throat sliced open. He had never seen so much blood.

Tearing his eyes away from the grisly sight as Bergrin dealt with the dragon, he watched the sorcerer approach him. "How did you know we would be here?" he asked.

"You're smart," the sorcerer replied. "After being brought up to date on everything, I knew you would come this way in due course." He lifted a hand, and Johnnie sneezed, realizing that part of the man's power came from a ring on his right middle finger. The sorcerer murmured something, and power rippled over Johnnie.

"My, my," the sorcerer said. "It's true. There is no touching you, not when the spells are that old and cast by Solomon's line. I suppose I will have to return—" He cried out in sudden pain, and Johnnie jerked, wondering when the hell Bergrin had killed the dragon and how neither of them had noticed.

Bergrin grabbed the sorcerer by the hair, yanking his head to the side at a painful angle, then said in a soft, quiet voice, "You will not be returning, ever." But rather than kill him there, Bergrin abruptly threw the man against a closed door, so hard the man went through it, then followed him inside.

Then all Johnnie heard was a terrible scream, followed by an even more terrible silence. At his feet, the spell cage fractured, then faded away. Johnnie looked up again as Bergrin reappeared, blood-spattered and bruised, his mouth a grim line, his eyes dark. Johnnie looked at him, stepped closer, and started to reach out—but then was not sure he should, or even could.

"Are you all right?" he asked instead.

"I'm fine," Bergrin said. "I'm sorry I led us right into a trap. I should have seen it."

Johnnie shook his head. "Forget it. They obviously knew how to make certain we did not. We need to go see my father and figure out what in the hell is going on, once and for all." He started to reach into his pocket to pull out his phone when Bergrin abruptly stepped forward and grabbed hold of his arms again—but instead of shaking him, power flared, and they vanished.

They reappeared in the entrance hall of his father's house.

"I did not know you could do that," Johnnie said, hastily letting go before he did something stupid like continue to hold on.

Bergrin shrugged. "I don't advertise it."

Johnnie nodded, then turned and motioned to the servant passing down the far hallway. "Where is my father?"

The servant jumped, obviously not having expected anyone to call him. "Uh, the uh, the main library, Master Johnnie."

"Thank you," Johnnie said, and led the way there.

Ontoniel sat in a chair in his favorite corner of the immense, two-story library of his home, reading a book that was probably written in French.

"Father," Johnnie said tersely. "Would you like to explain why the sorcerer who just attacked us—"

"What—!"

Johnnie nearly had to shout to be heard over Ontoniel's angry cry. "Why did he call me a dream child?" When Ontoniel fell silent, he pressed on. "Why did a nightmare curse rebound when it struck me? Why do I not dream? What is going on!"

Ontoniel said nothing, but for a moment, he looked every bit his six hundred thirty odd years.

"Why?" Johnnie demanded.

Sighing, Ontoniel motioned them both to sit. "Tell me what happened."

Though he did not want to delay getting his own answers, Ontoniel's tone brooked no argument. Johnnie recounted their attempt to go see the imp. When he finished, Ontoniel lapsed into silence again. When he finally spoke, his tone and face were grim. "I would be much happier, Johnnie, if you moved back home. You would be safer here."

"No," Johnnie said. "What am I?"

"Awake? Nothing," Ontoniel said wearily. "As you are now, you are one hundred percent normal—minus, perhaps, your exceptional beauty."

Johnnie frowned. "Awake?"

"Should you fall asleep and dream, or somehow otherwise access the dream plane, then in the dream plane you would likely take on more of your mother," Ontoniel replied. "She was a succubus, brought from the dream plane by your father." His voice turned flat as he continued, "It was the first and last good spell he cast."

"What—" Johnnie's mind reeled. "I am—my mother—"

"Your mother was a succubus. I never knew the details of how they met and managed to grow close. I do know that the Consort of Sable Brennus had a hand in it. I know that shortly before you were born, they decided to give up abnormalcy and live quietly as normals, and asked if they could live here in my territory."

Bitter anger filled Ontoniel's face as he went on. "But did they? No. He slunk back into alchemy, like an addicted fool, desperate to recreate the greatness he had achieved in pulling your mother out of dreams. Your mother would not put her foot down and stop him—" He broke off and sighed, scrubbed his face, then continued tiredly. "And it cost lives. I ordered him to stop before more were lost. By then, of course, it was too late. They used my wife to kill your parents and spared your life only because they had no choice. You want to know about *real* parents, John? They were too selfish to give up the one thing that most endangered their lives—and they died leaving you in even greater danger."

Johnnie looked at him, too stunned to think—by what he was hearing, by Ontoniel's anger, the comment about Sariah. "What—what danger am I in, exactly?"

"He didn't destroy it," Bergrin said, his face a thundercloud. "He didn't destroy it, and I'd bet my fucking life it's hidden where only Johnnie can get to it."

"Yes," Ontoniel said quietly. "They kept Johnnie alive because they realized at the last moment that Cordula had hidden the object somewhere on the dream plane. I think they would have stolen Johnnie that night, except they realized it would have been fruitless—because the only unselfish thing your damned parents did was see that a spell was cast upon you that blocked *all* access to the dream plane."

"That is why I do not dream," Johnnie said. "Can the spell be broken?"

Ontoniel shrugged. "In theory, yes, but the reality is that the spell was placed on you before you were even born."

Johnnie winced. "I see." A spell that had been placed on him while he was still in the womb... That made it as much a part of him as blood and bone. That was why no one ever sensed magic on him. It was too much a part of him. If someone tried to remove the spell, there was a very good chance the trauma of it would kill him.

"So what is this fucking object they want so badly?" Bergrin asked.

Ontoniel shook his head. "That, I can honestly tell

you I do not know. I do not even know who is behind the hunt, though I have kept watch over the years, hoping the culprit would somehow reveal themselves."

Johnnie felt too many things to sort them all out. He was an incubus? But only when asleep? His parents had been murdered—"But I thought it was an accident, that your wife—"

Old pain and guilt cracked what little remained of Ontoniel's carefully stoic expression. "I loved—still love—Sariah deeply. She was my other half for nearly four hundred years. She began to go blood crazy after three hundred and fifty years. That last night, I simply needed a break." He closed his eyes, pressing the tips of his fingers to his forehead. "I loved her, and I wanted her to get well, but there is no cure for blood madness. After nearly fifty years of taking care of her, I just wanted a break—"

He broke off, and Johnnie bit back his own urge to speak. What words could he possibly offer to soothe such a pain?

After a few minutes, Ontoniel resumed. "I arranged with Jesse to have her stay a couple of days in his casino. Magic, at least strong magic like transporting someone, exacerbates the condition, so I arranged for a car to take her there. All seemed well—but not an hour after her departure, I received a call from my then Captain of the Enforcers." He fell silent again, then finished. "Three days later, I buried my wife, and I have tried ever since to let the entire damned tragedy die with her."

Johnnie had been ready to say a hundred things a moment ago—now he could think of nothing. "Father—"

Ontoniel let out a sharp, short laugh. "Do you know how long it took me to get you to call me that? I doubt you even remember how determined you were to dislike me and have nothing to do with me. To this day, I do not know what finally changed your mind."

"You bought me a book," Johnnie said softly, for he remembered it very well. "It was not one I had to borrow from this library or steal from Ellie, or sneak into the stacks of books that were bought for the household. It was just for me."

He had been so damned happy, he had run off to his room to read it and wound up crying all over it. The pages to this day were wrinkled where he had gotten them wet. He had thought it meant he belonged, fit in. That one stupid book, bought just for him by Ontoniel, for no good reason at all. He had thought it meant he really was a son and had a family again and a place to belong.

A party a week later had shattered that illusion, but by then, he did not know how to stop referring to Ontoniel as 'Father'.

"A history of famous supernaturals throughout normal history," Ontoniel said, looking amused, more like himself. "That book was primarily about thieves and other such persons. Why do I think I am to blame for your lock-picking skills?"

Johnnie jerked in surprise and whipped around in his seat to glare at Bergrin—

"I didn't say a word," Bergrin said, holding up his hands. "Wherever he learned it, it wasn't from me."

Johnnie scowled at Ontoniel. "How?"

Ontoniel only smirked. "A father always knows."

Johnnie made a face.

"On that note," Ontoniel said more seriously, "you

need to close this case you are on."

"But—" Johnnie bit the protest off, though he hated doing it, and simply asked, "Why?"

Ontoniel looked at him in surprise, then smiled briefly with rare, open approval. But the smile faded away again as he explained, "Seven women are dead, so far as you know. But I knew what else to look for—eleven women are dead in total because of the experiments in plane crossing, and I fear it is probably too late to save the last one. They were all killed roughly a month apart."

"And Phil's case came to her about a month ago," Johnnie said, gut twisting. "The last woman is dead, or will be soon. Damn it. What—what did you look for?" But before Ontoniel could reply, he answered his own question. "Early failures."

Ontoniel nodded. "Yes. I will say the early results were decidedly unpleasant. I may drink blood, but that does not mean I enjoy the sight of it in all situations."

Johnnie slumped in his seat, suddenly feeling tired. He had thought... what? That he would feel better? More included? By finally knowing the secrets he had a right to know that he would better belong?

But it seemed secrets worked as well as books at giving him a proper place.

He had read that stupid book cover to cover every single day for a week straight. All these years later, he still had portions of it memorized. Back then, twelve years old and still with no real understanding of the new world in which he lived, he had wanted only to make friends, to find people who understood him. At that point in his life, he would not meet Rostiya for a couple more years.

So he had tried to impress the few other children

at the party by telling them everything he knew about them from what he had read, especially from the book his father had just bought him.

That had not ended well for his nose, or his brand new tuxedo—or his freedom, after Ontoniel grounded him for a month for refusing to identify the bullies.

Fourteen years after that, Johnnie still did not fit in well, not unless people were telling him he made an excellent imitation vampire.

"I am sorry," Johnnie finally said.

Ontoniel smiled, tired but genuine. "All I wanted for you, John, was a semblance of the normal life that your parents promised you but did not provide. You have never made that easy. I do not like you at that bar, not while whoever nearly killed you seventeen years ago is actively hunting you again. At least lay low for a time, and *please* keep close to Bergrin. And when I finally order you to come home—"

"I will," Johnnie said, and it did not seem so terrible a concession to make, suddenly, not when Ontoniel visibly relaxed at his words.

"Thank you," Ontoniel said. "You do recall your brother's formal betrothal ball is a little over a week away, yes? Try to stay out of trouble at least that long."

Johnnie rolled his eyes but nodded.

Looking to Bergrin, Ontoniel said, "Keep him safe."

"With my life, my lord," Bergrin replied.

Ontoniel nodded. "Then go. I have things to do now. John, we will have dinner tonight, at the Beach Club."

"Yes, Father," Johnnie said, and rose. He and Bergrin left, silent and pensive as they waited outside for a car to pull up. Questions filled his mind, emotions pressed down on him. He finally had his secrets;

something, at least, was no longer a mystery.

Johnnie glanced up at the sky and murmured softly, "And when they saw that they were betrayed, and that falsehood would be of no avail, they were obliged to confess all."

Somehow, the victory felt very cold.

Case 007: The True Bride I

"Keep your hands there."

"And if I do not?" Johnnie asked, but his attempt at defiance was ruined by his moaning as Eros wrapped a hand around his cock and gave a hard tug.

Eros chuckled. "Then I won't suck you off before I fuck you."

Johnnie gasped as the hand began to move in earnest, Eros's mouth sliding across his skin. "My hands are where they should be—why is your mouth not?"

Eros laughed again, then his hands were gone, and his mouth slid down Johnnie's body to replace them on his cock, hot and wet and talented.

It took every bit of self-control Johnnie had left to keep his hands gripping his headboard and not fumble in the dark to sink his hands into Eros's hair. He was not quite able to hold back a cry when he came, absently grateful that he had noticed the time was 3 a.m. because there would be no one downstairs to wonder why he was screaming.

He was still gasping for breath when Eros spread his legs and thrust inside him, stealing what little breath Johnnie had managed to gather, drinking down his startled cry with a ravenous kiss. His tongue fucked Johnnie's mouth as surely as his cock thrust again and again into Johnnie's body, and Johnnie could only cling to the headboard for dear life.

By the time they finished, Johnnie was completely

exhausted. Eros had appeared shortly after he had gone to bed and fucked him until they had passed out in a sweaty tangle. Then, right around three, Johnnie had been woken up to be treated to a second amorous onslaught.

Something about the entire night seemed unsettling. Eros was as passionate, as satisfying, as ever—but the desperate edge that always hovered seemed stronger and sharper.

Johnnie had given up asking questions and making demands. He was still trying to reconcile with all that his father had told him a week ago; he simply did not have the energy to face the mystery of Eros as well, even if he hated this secret above and beyond all the others.

If lying sated and sweaty in the arms of someone he had never seen—and never would see—felt hollow rather than filling... he tried to convince himself at least the sex was something.

~~*

"Hey, Johnnie," a handful of voices greeted as he entered the bar.

Johnnie returned the greetings, one brow quirked in the direction of Chuck and Nelson, who were cooing and all but fondling a brand new pool table. "That explains the booming and banging."

"Sorry, Johnnie," Peyton said, bringing him a cup of tea. "Didn't mean to wake you."

"You did not," Johnnie replied. "I did not sleep much."

"Up late reading again?"

"Yes," Johnnie said because he was fairly certain

Peyton did not want to hear that his lack of sleep was due to an excess of fucking. "Nice table."

Nelson grinned. "You have excellent taste, Johnnie."

"Clearly," Johnnie said dryly. He had told them to buy a new one, that was it. "Do I want to know how expensive my taste is?"

A derisive snort came from the table behind him as Bergrin said, "Whatever it cost, I would still lay good money that the clothes you're currently wearing cost more."

Johnnie reached out with his cane and struck Bergrin's table. "You are to be seen and not heard."

Bergrin smirked, then went back to his coffee.

"Wanna come try it out, Johnnie?" Walsh asked. "We got something else for you to try. With our money, not yours."

Johnnie's brows went up at that. "Oh?" He finished his tea and handed the cup back to Peyton with a thank you, then wandered over to the new pool table, slate with blue velvet, the new wood bright and glistening. It really was a beauty.

Micah smiled and set a long case on the table, accepting the cane in exchange when Johnnie gave it to him. Opening the box, Johnnie smiled at the contents—a custom cue stick. It was glossy black, overlaid with a paisley pattern in blue, gray, and silver.

He removed the two pieces and screwed them together, then set it on the pool table. Removing his sapphire cuff links, he tucked them into a pocket of his blue vest and rolled the sleeves of his black-striped shirt up to his elbows. Retrieving his cue stick, he ordered, "Rack'em."

They played pool for hours—one on one, two

against two, across both tables, until coffee and tea became beer and vodka, and even Peyton and Bergrin were coaxed into playing a couple of games each.

Johnnie tossed back a shot of vodka, then sank another ball. Peyton approached with a tray of fresh drinks for everyone, laughing at something Heath had said—

—When the chiming of the door drew them all up short. Almost as one, their heads turned toward the sound. Johnnie paused, attention immediately grabbed by the woman's obvious distress.

Peyton immediately set down his tray of drinks and strode to her. "Hello, Miss."

She was a vampire; probably not over a hundred years old, or not by much. She had a winsome, old-school sort of beauty. Her mahogany hair was upswept in a careful arrangement of curls, held in place by gold hairpins, and she wore a long, pretty winter dress of dark green wool with touches of black and gold. It fell to just past the top of high, glossy, black leather boots. She clung to a matching purse, a handkerchief in her other hand.

The clothes were good quality, but not great, and all her jewelry was plain gold, small, simple stuff. A vampire from a minor, non-noble family.

"Um—" the woman fumbled with her kerchief, wiping her eyes and nose, then tried again. "I need help finding someone. A woman told me that I should come here, to the Bremen, and ask for Johnnie Goodnight."

Surprise rippled through Johnnie, and across the room, he saw Bergrin tense. Motioning for Bergrin to stay put, Johnnie moved closer as Peyton laughed and took the woman by the arm. "That's Johnnie, right there. I'll get you a glass of wine. Just sit here and don't cry. Johnnie will help you."

Handing off the pool cue he realized he still held, Johnnie slid into an empty seat at the woman's table. "I am Johnnie Goodnight."

"Rita Bauer," the woman replied. "I hope I am not being a bother, sir."

"Not at all. You said you were trying to find someone?"

"Sort of," Rita said, sniffling again. After a moment, though, she regained control of herself and said in a low tone, "It's a bit of a long story, I'm afraid."

Johnnie smiled and took the wineglass Peyton brought over, pushing it across the table to her. "That is not a problem. Simply start at the beginning and tell me everything."

"We met twenty years ago," Rita said, talking more to her hands and the wine than to Johnnie. She smiled sadly. "Scandalous, in vampire years, to be so absolutely certain of someone after only two decades. My parents knew each other for nearly sixty years before they began to even think about marriage. He was on vacation, and I had just moved there. We met by chance at the resort where I was working and immediately hit it off. He could not stay long, but every few months he came to see me again—sometimes for a couple of days, sometimes for a week, twice he stayed an entire month."

Tears trailed down her cheeks, and she reached up absently to wipe them away with gloved fingers. "The last time we were together, he said he wanted to marry me. All he needed was to get his father's permission. When he said that might take time, I of course understood." She finally looked up at Johnnie.

"He is nobility, you see. I have never known everything about him; I do not think I even know his real name. He seems to prefer not to be nobility when he is around me, you know?"

"I understand completely," Johnnie murmured.

"I only knew to come here because of some of the things he said, and process of elimination, but—" She wiped more tears away. "You see, he promised me that, good news or bad, he would return in two months. It has been six. I was worried about him, so I tracked him this far. I was not certain I was correct in my guesswork until yesterday."

"Yesterday?" Johnnie asked.

She nodded, then burst into tears, sobbing into her hands. "He looked straight at me! He met my eyes and did not recognize me! He said he loved me and gave me his mother's ring, and when he saw me, he might as well have been looking at a stranger! I want to know what has happened to the man I love!"

Reaching across the table, Johnnie took her hands, gently rubbing his thumbs across the back of them. "I promise to help you," he said. "Tell me what you know about him. What name did you use? Where did you see him yesterday?"

"I—I have a picture," Rita said, sniffling. She wiped her eyes and nose again, then fumbled with her purse. Swearing softly when she could not manage the clasp with her gloved hands, she set the purse aside and yanked off the gloves. Throwing them on the table, she reached for the purse again.

But by the time she pulled the picture out, Johnnie did not need it.

On the ring finger of Rita's left hand was a beautiful ring with one large sapphire surrounded by diamonds and pearls. The ring was an heirloom, passed down for centuries from mother to son, to be bestowed upon the next bride. In her will, following tradition, Sariah had bequeathed the ring to Elam.

Johnnie took the picture as she held it out, and the hopeful look in her eyes hurt. He glanced at the image, briefly startled by it.

The man in the picture was not the stiff, cold Elam he knew. The pictures of Elam around the house were of a cool, reserved, proud Desrosiers. This picture showed Elam in a sweater and jeans, hair tousled, smiling fondly at whoever held the camera. He looked softer, kinder. Almost like a stranger. Turning the picture over on a whim, Johnnie was not surprised to find something written, though the words were nearly as startling as the picture itself. *Love you, Ree. Ellie.*

Johnnie set the photo on the table. "Your lover is the Alucard Elam Desrosiers—"

"What!" Rita burst out, then clapped her hands over her mouth.

"I am afraid, my lady, that he is to be formally betrothed tomorrow night at a ball our father is hosting. He is my brother, you see."

"Betrothed—" Rita's face crumbled into a tangle of misery and pain, the heartache so apparent that Johnnie nearly winced. She folded her arms on the table, then buried her head in them and began to sob uncontrollably.

Standing, Johnnie moved around the table and sat down next to her. "Rita—" He urged her to lift her head a bit, then grasped her chin and forced it all the way up. "Rita, I think something is seriously wrong with my brother." He retrieved the photo. "My brother looks happy here. He never looks happy, trust me. Do not give up. The key is in your encounter and in the promise he made you."

"Wh-what do you mean?" Rita asked.

Johnnie pulled out his own handkerchief and handed it to her, then said, "Ellie would never pretend not to know someone. If he had decided not to marry you, he would have told you so. If he had come across you in public, he would have acknowledged you. Anything else, he would consider crass and dishonorable. He also would never break a promise. Never. That is two things he would never do that he has done. And I reiterate—he looks happy in the picture *you* took of him. Ergo, something is wrong. Do not yet succumb to despair."

He nudged the wine closer. "Drink that and fortify yourself because I am afraid you will have to tell your story to someone else."

"Who?" Rita asked.

"Our father," Johnnie said. Standing again, he moved to the bar and signaled Peyton for a drink. Pulling out his phone, he dialed his father's number.

"John?" Ontoniel answered immediately.

"You need to come see me immediately," Johnnie said. "We have a major problem concerning Ellie."

The line went dead. A moment later, Ontoniel appeared in the bar by the front door.

Rita drew a sharp breath and flushed bright red. "Oh, my—you look—you look just like him."

Ontoniel's sharp, pale eyes immediately snapped to her—then widened slightly as he saw the ring she wore. Stalking toward her, he held out his hand, gently clasping hers when she gave it. Rubbing his thumb over the ring, he asked softly, "Where did you get this ring, my dear?"

"El—Ellie gave it to me, six months ago," Rita said. "He—he said that he was going to seek his father's permission for us to marry."

"I see," Ontoniel said, voice still soft, pensive, his face inscrutable. He looked at Rita for several long moments, then lifted her hand and kissed it. "I would have given it had he approached me. He never did."

He released her hand and glanced toward the bar. "Peyton, was it not? Your best scotch. John, how do these puzzles always simply fall into your lap?"

"A talent," Johnnie said.

"Or a curse," Bergrin added.

Ontoniel laughed. "I think I must agree with your bodyguard. Come and sit with us, John. Let us try and figure out this very curious dilemma."

Pushing away from the bar, Johnnie obediently went to join them, taking the scotch Peyton held out with him and sliding it across the table to his father. Sitting down, he said, "Rita, tell my father everything you told me."

"Yes, sir—uh, Master—"

"Johnnie is fine, please."

Rita nodded, glanced shyly at Ontoniel, then finally began to recount again how she and Elam had met, their engagement, how he had never returned—and how he had not recognized her when they met on the street.

"Someone has cursed my son," Ontoniel said when she had finished. His voice was level, calm, but Johnnie knew from the darkening of his eyes that whoever was behind this had only days left to live.

"That was my supposition," Johnnie said. "It is possible we are looking at two curses. A love spell, obviously, and tied to that could be a spell to forget all other lovers. That is tricky work, though."

"All other passions," Ontoniel said grimly. "I cannot remember the last time Elam played the piano or even walked around with sheet music. At first, I thought he was actually obeying me and trying to pay attention to his new fiancée—but it was beginning to concern me, and now I hear this."

Johnnie's mouth dropped open briefly. Elam not playing piano was like Johnnie not reading. "Tell me more about Ekaterina and her family. They are the likeliest suspects."

Ontoniel frowned. "I just do not see why they would bother. Even if I had broken the arrangement so that Elam could marry Rita, Ekaterina comes from a good family, and I do not doubt they turned down other offers to accept ours. To be honest, most would consider any of those offers better; I am counted too radical these days."

Johnnie nodded, feeling guilty—most of the 'radical' changes Ontoniel had made in the last two decades had been directly related to him. Ontoniel had caused quite an uproar adopting a human child, even if he had done so out of a sense of responsibility. Then he had gone and changed so many things about his daily life and territory... "So why did they accept?"

"Because I may be radical, but I am also extremely wealthy," Ontoniel said dryly. "My money is old world, brought successfully to the new world. My territory is ideally situated, featuring a prosperous city, a fine stretch of beach, and of course, there is Jesse's casino. My wife was very old world, so our family has, as they like to say, a fine pedigree." He shrugged. "This is why it confuses me anyone would resort to such tactics. There was no reason for them. Elam agreed to the marriage, yes, but if we had broken it off, there were better options waiting in the wings—and all would sympathize with Ekaterina being yet another victim of my radical tendencies."

"Perhaps they want something more, or need this match for some reason unknown to us," Johnnie said.

"Perhaps," Ontoniel agreed. "I did a thorough background check, of course, but I am not as rigorous as some. Every family, after several centuries, has things it does not like to discuss. I try to respect that. If we are to look into this further, I ask only that we keep it as discreet as possible."

"Of course," Johnnie said. "We do not want further curses cast, after all. I should go speak with Rostiya. He will have the best advice regarding the curses."

Ontoniel nodded. "Very well. I fervently hope that Ekaterina and her family are not behind this, but I do not see who else could be."

Johnnie shrugged. "The ball is tomorrow. We can observe everything then, yes? Especially if we bring Rita along. If the forgetting curse is tied to the love spell, then it should degrade and fray as he sees her more and more. But I will verify that with Rostiya."

"I will leave it to you, then," Ontoniel said. "But please, John, have a care. I apparently have one cursed son; I do not need to hear that the other has been attacked and nearly kidnapped a fourth time."

"Yes, Father," Johnnie replied. "What are you going to do?"

"Nothing, for the moment. I do not want to alert anyone and scare them into doing something worse. I want them nice and dozy until I choose to kill them." He stood up and held his hand out to Rita, kissing hers as she gave it to him. "My dear, I am very sorry for all of this. I look forward to properly meeting you when the trouble is over. Tomorrow night we will hopefully set all of this to rights. Johnnie, use my funds for Rita, however you see fit."

"Yes, Father."

Ontoniel nodded and rose, then looked briefly to Bergrin, still casually slouched at his own table. They seemed to share some silent communication, which annoyed Johnnie to no end. Then, Ontoniel was gone.

Around the room, everyone seemed to release a pent-up breath all at once. "I cannot believe the Dracula himself has been here *twice*," Nelson said.

"No shit," Walsh agreed.

"That man is scary as hell," Chuck added.

Johnnie glared at all of them. "My father is not scary."

Micah laughed. "So says Dracula, Jr. The Alucard might *look* like his father, but everything else about that man went to you."

"What—" Johnnie cut off as, of all things, his face flushed hot. The men all laughed, and beside him, even Rita burst into giggles.

"It's true," she said with a gentle, pretty little smile. "I had heard before that Dracula Desrosiers had adopted a human, but I never believed it. If not for the fact you are definitely human, I would have sworn the two of you were related. You're very close, aren't you?"

"Uh—" Johnnie did not know what to say to that. He and Ontoniel close? That made no sense. Elam and Ontoniel were closer by far.

A hand dropped on Johnnie's shoulder, then Bergrin's mocking voice chimed in, "Very close. The Dracula spoils him rotten."

Johnnie rolled his eyes at the absurdity of that statement, then stood, dislodging Bergrin's hand. He said, "I am going to get ready. We are going to the Last Star."

"Yes, Highness," Bergrin replied.

Johnnie cast him a withering look, then stopped. "Oh, one more thing." He turned back to Rita, "The formal ball tomorrow night—have you anything suitable for it?"

Rita shook her head, looking embarrassed. "Nothing fit for the Dracula's home, and I brought none of my formal clothes with me, anyway."

"I will have a friend of mine take you around," Johnnie said and pulled out his phone to call Phil.

An hour later, he and Bergrin arrived at the Last Star after sending Phil off with Rita to put a dent in his father's checking account.

Johnnie stepped back, away from Bergrin, wishing quietly that he had just one small excuse to remain close. "I admit, babysitter, you are vastly more useful now I know you can do that."

"I live to serve," Bergrin said dryly, tugging at the brim of his cap. He looked up at the impressive monolith that was Jesse's casino. "So this is the Last Star, huh?"

Johnnie looked at him in surprise. "Have you never been here?"

"Only once," Bergrin replied, something in his tone oddly tense. "I was working, so I didn't really see much, you know?"

"Mm," Johnnie agreed.

"Plus, it's not exactly my kind of place. I don't make enough money to gamble it all blithely away, and I'm not exactly crème de la crème."

Johnnie batted the words aside. "As if that matters." He hesitated, then spoke before he could change his mind. "We can always come again, sometime, when we are not working."

"You lead and I shall follow," Bergrin replied.

Johnnie nodded and turned away, stifling his disappointment. What had he expected, really? For Bergrin to say yes?

He was spared from thinking further on the matter as Jesse appeared from a conference room. Pleased surprise filled his face, and he handed over the portfolio he was carrying to one of his assistants. He shook Johnnie's hand as he reached them. "Hello, Johnnie. We did not expect to see you today. What a pleasant surprise."

"I wish I was here for pleasure," Johnnie replied. "Unfortunately, I need Rostiya's help with something."

Jesse's levity faded into concern. "Of course. We can speak upstairs." He led the way to the elevator bay, and they rode up in silence. In Jesse's penthouse, Rostislav was stretched out on a leather sofa, dressed only in a faded blue pair of lounge pants. He was pouring over books and papers, which were scattered around and on him.

He looked up at the sound of the door opening, smiling warmly. "Jesse, I didn't think—Johnnie?" Papers tumbled and spilled everywhere as he hastily stood up. Rostislav grinned. "I guess I'd better get dressed."

Johnnie smirked. "You are not offending me, Cinderella."

Rostislav rolled his eyes and went to get dressed.

Jesse bent to retrieve and tidy up the fallen books and papers, asking over his shoulder, "Can I get either of you some refreshment?" He stacked everything neatly on the coffee table, then stood and looked at Bergrin. "So you are the bodyguard I have heard so much about."

Bergrin nodded, but said nothing.

"So, refreshment?" Jesse asked. "You can set your coats and all there."

"I am fine, thank you," Johnnie said and removed his hat and coat, giving them and his cane over to Bergrin.

Rostislav reemerged from the bedroom dressed in dark denim jeans and a cream sweater. "So what brings you here, Johnnie?"

"It is Elam," Johnnie said, sitting down in a leather chair opposite the couch, Bergrin taking the seat next to him. "He has been cursed." Settling more comfortably in the chair, he explained everything.

Rostislav looked furious as he finished. "Someone should lose their head for that. It is one thing for me to 'cast' a love spell on myself, but to ruin so many lives like that—it is sheer dumb luck that Elam had a lover because otherwise..."

Johnnie nodded, not bothering to speak. If not for Rita, his brother would likely have lived the rest of his life under the love spell. Hopefully, because he loved Rita, it could be broken.

"I think you are correct in thinking it is two spells," Rostislav continued. "Though normally the love spell is more than enough. The forgetting curse almost seems like overkill, unless they had reason to put such an extreme safety measure in place. Do you think they knew about Rita?"

At that, Johnnie laughed. "No, I do not. If my father did not know about her, I sincerely doubt anyone else did. No, I think whoever did it wanted to drag Ellie away from the only thing he would have obsessed over, love spell or not."

Jesse laughed. "I do admit, I am impressed there is anything that could drag Elam away from his precious piano. But his obsession has always paid off—he is masterful. I miss his performances here." He looked briefly sad, but in the next moment, it was gone. "So what do you plan to do?"

"We need to confirm the curses and determine why they have gone unnoticed."

Rostiya folded his arms across his chest and leaned back against the couch, legs stretched out in front of him, just barely pressed shoulder to shoulder with Jesse. "That's an easy one. Did anyone give him a betrothal gift, say, a piece of jewelry? I would hazard it has a very strong, very obvious, completely harmless spell on it that covers up the two curses also set in it. The moment he put that on, it was over."

"I do not know," Johnnie said, "but I will definitely look into it."

Jesse spoke up, "I know we were not invited, for obvious reasons, but would it help if Rostiya went anyway?"

"No," Rostiya and Johnnie said together, then Johnnie continued, "Rostiya has a well-earned reputation as a curse-breaker. If he were to suddenly show at the ball, despite his exiled status, it would immediately tip off whoever cast the curses. It will be safer if we continue to play ignorant. Hopefully seeing Rita throughout the night will do the breaking."

"Who knew Ellie had a secret lover?" Rostislav said. "Or enough spine to carry on a secret affair." He tilted his head and looked at Johnnie hesitantly. "I—

I'm surprised you're not more upset."

Johnnie shrugged irritably, not wanting to discuss why he was suddenly uninterested in someone he had claimed to love for almost twenty years. Not when that reason had just politely turned down the offer to spend a carefree day with him. "I want whoever is doing this to stop hurting my family. But he will suffer for it plenty when my father learns his identify." He sighed. "I just wonder at the motive—there is no good reason to go to such extremes."

"Who knows," Rostislav said. "I have learned never to underestimate why people do anything."

"It could simply be precaution," Jesse suggested. "If it is not Ekaterina who did it, then it could be her parents. It is not at all unusual for vampires to take lovers, and she could have been reluctant to give hers up. Perhaps she is the true target of all of this. I have never heard much about her, which could be a good thing or a bad thing."

Bergrin stirred in his seat, speaking for the first time in a while. "So why not make her the victim of the spells? It wouldn't make sense to place the curses on Elam if she is the true target."

"More believable that way," Johnnie said slowly, thinking it through. "She could have been against the marriage the entire time, for one reason or another. Hers is a good family, but not as prestigious as mine, or several others around. So she may have had a lover, or simply no interest in marriage. Unusual, but not unheard of. But what person would not immediately soften and change her mind when she finds herself the object of complete focus from someone like Elam—to the point he gives up even his precious piano. Yes, I rather like it for a working theory. Thank you, Jesse."

"Always a pleasure to help our local detective," Jesse said teasingly, though he looked distinctly pleased.

Rostislav smiled. "So what are you going to do until the ball?"

"Pick up my new tuxedo and a betrothal gift," Johnnie said.

Bergrin groaned. "I hope by 'pick up' you mean we go in, get it, and leave. If we spend more than ten minutes in that place, I'm going to kill you myself, Highness."

Johnnie glared and just to needle him, gave a dismissive shrug and said, "I do not know. I would be more comfortable with one last fitting."

"I swear to god you spend more time and money on clothes than every person I've ever met, combined."

Johnnie sneered. "Because your method of spending ten minutes a week on clothes works so well." The damned thing was that it *did* work well for Bergrin, the silly baseball cap aside. But Johnnie would never admit it, especially now, after being so firmly, if gently, turned down flat.

"Your threads only work for you because I scare off all the lowlifes that contemplate mugging you every time you walk down the street, Prince."

Scoffing at that, Johnnie retorted, "They probably feel sorry for you in that silly hat."

"Stop making fun of the hat my mom gave me," Bergrin said hotly.

Johnnie pretended to think about it, then said, "No."

Bergrin just looked at him in disgust.

Rostislav burst out laughing. "So do the two of you

always bicker like children?"

"No," Johnnie said, affronted. "We most certainly do not bicker like children, and we do not always bicker."

"You can't tell because you're always childish," Bergrin said to Johnnie, smirking.

Johnnie rolled his eyes and did not deign to reply to that.

Rostislav laughed again, Jesse chuckling next to him. "I see."

"You see what?" Johnnie asked.

"Nothing," Rostislav said with a smirk. "If I can be of further use to you, Johnnie, by all means, give me a call."

"I will," Johnnie said, eying him, wondering what he was missing that made Rostislav smirk like that. "Thank you for the help you have provided, both of you."

"Our pleasure," Jesse replied. "It is nice to see friends, whatever the reason."

Johnnie stood. "Once this mystery is solved, and my idiot brother is set to marry his true bride, he will owe me a favor—a big one. I will see to it that you are invited to *that* betrothal ball, as well as the wedding."

"It is too bad he would never consider having the ball here," Jesse said, and though he tried to hide it, he could not completely keep all the wistfulness from his voice.

Rostislav grinned. "No worries, love. Once Johnnie has cause for such celebration, *he'll* have his ball here."

Casting him a withering look, Johnnie said, "As you command." Him, a betrothal ball. Ha. Johnnie did not think a more ridiculous idea existed.

Bergrin stood and fetched their coats, holding Johnnie's so that he could shrug into the long, heavy, wool trench coat. Bergrin settled his cap on his head as Johnnie slid his fedora into place.

"Farewell for now," Johnnie said as Bergrin took hold of his arm.

In the next moment, they vanished.

~~*

"You look beautiful, my dear," Johnnie said. "Even more so than usual."

Rita flushed but smiled and lifted her chin. "I don't think I can hold a candle to you, Johnnie."

Johnnie scoffed at that and finished pinning a deep red rosebud to the lapel of his tuxedo. Comments about his beauty were more vexing than ever now that he knew his beauty *was* supernatural in origin. He did not know what to think. *Better vampire* Jester had called him.

Funny the pixie had known all along, and if Johnnie had paid any real attention...

But even then, who knew? It would not have made sense to him, not then. Detractors often referred to vampires as watered down incubi, half as pretty and too independent to do better than blood for sustenance. It was only because he was in the mortal plane, and not the dream plane, that he did not have full incubus powers.

He could not begin to imagine how different his life might have been if he had grown up half-incubus.

Johnnie turned toward the door when it opened, watching as Bergrin slipped inside, closing the door again behind him. Only barely did Johnnie remember to return Bergrin's polite nod of greeting, and he nearly dropped the corsage he held ready to affix to Rita's gown.

Bergrin was not wearing a tuxedo, but he had taken care to be a bit more dressed up than usual. He looked damned good. He wore black jeans, of such quality they almost could have passed for slacks, except that slacks never hugged quite that well—and they definitely clung in ways that Bergrin's usual jeans did not. He wore a soft-looking black sweater as well, and boots that held a polished shine. His curls had even been tamed, falling in a pretty tumble that made Johnnie want to sink his hands into them and muss them thoroughly while he kissed Bergrin senseless.

Jerking his gaze away before he was caught staring like a half-wit, he focused on pinning a spray of gold rosebuds to Rita's gown. The bright, rich yellow complemented the sapphire blue gown perfectly, drawing out her rich, dark brown curls, the diamonds and pearls and sapphires at her throat, her wrists. She was many times more beautiful than even Ekaterina, and Johnnie did not doubt that if they had known of Rita, Ekaterina's family would have cast a curse. "My idiotic brother will return to his senses before the night is out, mark my words."

Rita smiled, though it was a bit unsteady. "I hope so. Thank you for believing me—for helping me, Johnnie. You and all the others. Especially your father. He certainly would have been fully within his rights to send me away."

"Nonsense," Johnnie said. "Ellie gave you Sariah's ring—my father could never turn you away, not after seeing that."

Bergrin stirred where he was leaning against the

wall. "I'm surprised your father never asked about the ring. Surely it would have been a problem that Elam never produced it."

Johnnie shook his head. "My father would never ask, not about that. It is Ellie's ring, to give or not give, as he so chooses. Marriages are often a matter of business, but vampires do try to make love matches, or matches they think could turn to love, eventually. The ring is a love token—my father did not give it to his wife until he loved her, and that was a few years after they were married."

"But wouldn't Elam have tried to produce it when he fell in 'love' with Ekaterina?" Bergrin asked.

Again, Johnnie shook his head. "He had already given the ring to Rita, whom he truly loves. When the forgetting curse was cast, he probably forgot about the ring since it was irrevocably twisted up with his memories and feelings for Rita."

Rita smiled faintly, looking at her finger, where the ring sparkled. "Should I remove it?" She asked reluctantly. "Would it cause trouble?"

"It is a private family tradition," Johnnie said. "No one else would know about it, and seeing it on your finger might fray the curse that much faster. Leave it where it belongs."

There was a knock at the door, stalling conversation, and then it opened to reveal Ontoniel—followed by Phil and a vampire Johnnie had seen on only two previous occasions. His hair still fell all the way down his back, a beautiful cascade of blue-black. "Phil," Johnnie greeted, then turned to the vampire. "Lord Zachariah?"

"Master Johnnie," Zachariah greeted with a smile. "Zach, please. You are becoming quite the investigator, I hear."

Johnnie shrugged. "I like mysteries and solving them."

Phil laughed. "Your father invited me, and as Chris and Doug are away on a case, leaving Zach all alone, I brought him along as my date. Whatever help we can provide, just say. I told Zach what was going on after I got your father's permission. We can definitely work the crowds for information, keep a covert eye on things, since I am certain you will have your hands plenty full."

"The help is most appreciated," Johnnie said.

"Our pleasure," Zach said, pushing back strands of his hair.

Johnnie turned back to Phil. "Where is Jester?"

"He was still wrung out from a case we wrapped up the day before yesterday, and crowds like this can fluster him, so I just left him at home," Phil said with a smile. "He is probably passed out in front of the TV like every other man I know would be."

Johnnie laughed. "I see."

"That pixie is spoiled rotten," Zach said teasingly.

"No more spoiled than your imp," Phil retorted.

"Yeah, but the imp gives me sex. Pixies just take up space." He winked, then cocked his head, listening. "I believe I hear the music starting up—shall we to the ballroom?"

"Of course," Ontoniel said and offered his arm to Rita. Phil hooked arms with Zach, and Johnnie offered a teasing smirk to Bergrin as they followed along behind the others. "I should have ordered you to wear a dress."

Bergrin snorted. "I think *you* would be in the dress, Highness."

"I enjoy my suits far too much," Johnnie said, then turned more serious. "Do you expect a lot of trouble tonight?"

Bergrin laughed. "I always expect trouble. Where the rich and powerful are concerned, I expect double the trouble. Where *you* are concerned? I expect trouble in quadruple amounts."

Johnnie bristled. "I do not cause you that many problems."

"You make everything difficult, Johnnie," Bergrin said, so quietly that Johnnie only just barely heard him.

Before he could ask what that meant, however, they were in the ballroom and amidst the throngs of guests—hundreds of them, filling the grand ballroom that occupied the greater portion of the north wing of the house. Johnnie fell immediately into the role of host alongside his father, smoothly dealing with all manner of abnormal guests, though he tried to keep a watchful eye on Elam, Rita, and Ekaterina and her parents.

It was exhausting work: welcome toasts, betrothal toasts, speeches by friends, mingling, dancing briefly here and there with people he had no interest in even speaking with, food and drinks and music...

But after a little over two hours of work, Johnnie was able to slip away to a discreet corner mostly shielded by lush plants and take a break. Leaning against the wall, he watched the dance floor.

Bergrin appeared at his side, until then having tucked himself out of the way to watch Johnnie as well as those under suspicion. The entire time, Johnnie had not once seen him—but he had never stopped feeling Bergrin's eyes.

"See anything interesting?" he asked.

"Your brother definitely keeps looking at Rita, in a 'where have I seen you before' sort of way. Ekaterina seems impatient with him when she is confident no one else is paying them any mind. He is ever attentive of her, but Ekaterina certainly does not return the gestures or the sentiments behind them. Not unless they're being watched."

Johnnie glanced toward Ekaterina, who stood with one hand in the crook of Elam's arm. They were standing together, smiling and chatting with the people around them, occasionally looking at each other and smiling fondly.

But Johnnie knew his brother, and he knew the man across the room was his brother in full 'I would rather be anywhere else' social obligation mode. From time to time, just as Bergrin said, he glanced away from the crowd. Each time, his gaze fell, faintly puzzled, on Rita, or on the baby grand piano on the far side of the room.

Johnnie really could not wait to harass Prim and Proper Elam about all of this later, when it was finally over.

"What of Ekaterina's parents?" he asked Bergrin.

"They seem almost falling over grateful their daughter and Elam get along so well. Bits of gossip I've learned lead me to believe she has had trouble in the past contracting a spouse. No one would quite say why. Theories abound, but those who do seem to know for certain would not say."

"Well, I know she is a good fifty years older than Ellie," Johnnie said. "I was rather surprised to learn she was not already married. Perhaps she is picky or difficult—there are any number of reasons, and I think we had best find it."

He glanced over the ballroom again, lifting one brow in amusement when he saw Phil ask his father to dance—and his father say yes. They reached the dance floor just as the strains of a waltz began to fill the ballroom.

The mood in the room shifted then. Nearly all of the inhabitants present had come through many centuries, living through the darkest of times, the roughest, to make it to what they called 'these much softer days'. They clung to many old traditions and beliefs.

Dancing and old-fashioned parties were amongst those things to which they clung so fiercely. This was nothing like the vibrant, flashy, thoroughly modern affairs that Jesse enjoyed so much. This was a ball, with all the old world touches that word evoked. Nostalgia was thick on the air now as they all danced.

Johnnie watched them move through steps as old as the dancers themselves, steps they knew as well as they knew their names. It made him feel... isolated? Out of place? Even though he knew how to dance and could do it well, and he knew everyone present, to one degree or another.

Maybe it was the ease with which they moved: the affection between them—especially the true couples on the floor, dancing as only lovers could. No one had ever asked him to dance who did not either want to curry favor with his father, mock Johnnie, or simply fulfill some social obligation.

He had never danced with a lover, never had one he could ask or who would ask him. Johnnie wondered what it would be like to be on the dance floor with a lover, one more happy couple dancing to music that had survived centuries when so much else had faded away.

"Johnnie—"

Bergrin's voice startled him, and Johnnie turned his head to look at him, and then his heart started pounding in his chest. A hesitant, uncertain look was on Bergrin's face, and Johnnie had the sudden, wild, unexpected realization that Bergrin was going to ask him to dance. He just knew it. His breath lodged in his throat in anticipation, his chest tight with that sudden burst of joy—

"Nothing," Bergrin said, shoulders slumping ever so slightly, and he turned his head away from Johnnie, muttering, "Never mind."

The tight knot of anxious hope in Johnnie's chest turned into a sharp, twisting ache of crushing disappointment. He felt like a fool, so stupid and delusional he could not stand it. Bergrin asking him to dance! What had he been thinking? He cringed away from his own rampant stupidity.

It hurt. Worse than anything he had ever felt. Because damn it, he had wanted Bergrin to ask him to dance, and he had been so *certain* that Bergrin was going to—and then he had not. Had he changed his mind? Why?

But Johnnie knew the answer: Bergrin might have shared the secret of his mother, but he still thought of Johnnie as nothing but trouble—*quadruple* the usual amount of trouble. Johnnie had asked him to spend a day at the Last Star, and Bergrin had essentially turned him down. And for every 'Johnnie', there were at least twenty 'Highness'. He thought Johnnie's clothes were stupid, he did not much care for nobility, and until he got stuck with Johnnie, playing bodyguard had not even been amongst his primary duties.

Johnnie pushed away from the wall, unable to endure it a moment longer. Why was he never good enough for anyone?

"Hey, Johnnie—" Bergrin stopped him. "Where are you going?"

"To get some air," Johnnie snarled, jerking away. He glanced at Bergrin, feeling stupid and wretched and—

And heartbroken, he conceded. He hated to admit it, but there was little point in denying it now. He had ceased to care about Elam because Bergrin consumed all of his attention. Even the mysterious Eros did not draw him as Bergrin did. Bergrin, who had just made it painfully, humiliatingly clear that he did not want to dance with Johnnie.

"Leave me alone," Johnnie snapped, and stalked off, fleeing the ballroom as quickly as he could without drawing attention to himself.

Finding an empty room, he fell into the nearest chair, braced his elbows on his knees, and buried his face in his hands. Really, he thought bitterly, he was a great fool. What sort of man constantly attached himself to men who did not want him around, or even necessarily liked him?

Elam was his brother and decidedly cool about it. Eros was one hell of a lover, but wanted nothing to do with him outside a darkened bedroom. Bergrin saw him as a job first, and maybe some sort of friend second—and that was a very big maybe.

All three had power they used against him in some fashion. Elam never tired of reminding Johnnie that *he* was the real son, the Alucard, and Johnnie was not. Eros used his powers to keep Johnnie literally and figuratively in the dark, and Bergrin used his to harass and babysit.

All three kept secrets—

Johnnie froze, mind flipping back to his previous thought.

Power.

Eros had immense power, power that Johnnie had never been able to identify. He did not fear magic of any sort, ignored wards, did not fear consequences, he came and went with no effort, and could see perfectly in the dark.

Bergrin could come and go as he pleased, as Johnnie had recently learned. No one knew where his immense power had come from, other than his mysterious, 'unknown' mother. He had walked *over* the very same cage that had trapped Johnnie. Why had he not noticed that before?

They were both middle class and had no real love for the upper class. Neither was beautiful in the conventional sense.

And Bergrin had been around every single time Eros had appeared, except that very first night in the Casino. But no... Bergrin had said he had been in the Last Star once before, on a job. He must have been working that night Johnnie had met Eros.

Both had muscular builds. Both had curly hair. Both were half a head taller than him.

Johnnie's heart began to thunder in his chest as he thought about it. He tried to tell himself he was imagining things, but the more he thought about it the more he realized he was right.

Why had it taken him this long to figure it out?

He laughed bitterly, feeling like the world's greatest fool. No wonder Bergrin had not asked him to dance—why should he when he was already getting the only thing he wanted?

The door opened, startling him, and Johnnie looked up as a light flicked on—then everything he was feeling coalesced into a bright, white-hot fury.

"Johnnie, are you all right?" Bergrin asked.

Slowly, Johnnie stood up. "What is your first name?"

"Huh?" Bergrin asked, looking completely baffled. "What's wrong?"

"Not going to tell me? Fine," Johnnie bit the words out. "How about I guess? Is your first name... oh, how about... Eros?"

Bergrin paled, and Johnnie's gut twisted to see the plain proof that he was right. "Johnnie—"

"Stop calling me that!" Johnnie snarled. "Do not fucking dare! You played me for a fucking fool!"

"No—"

"Shut up," Johnnie snapped, then laughed, bitter and half-hysterical and so goddamn miserable. "Did it amuse you? Babysitting me, making me think we could be friends by day, then turning around and making me moan and beg for you at night? Did it? You must have gotten one hell of laugh from that."

"You don't—"

"Understand?" Johnnie finished. "I understand—you used me and mocked me and must have enjoyed the hell out of it. Here I am, supposed to be so smart, and you proving me a fucking fool."

Bergrin shook his head. "That's not—"

"Why did you not just admit?" Johnnie bellowed. "Why lead me on? Why hurt me? Why use me like that?"

"I was scared—"

"Liar!" Johnnie raged, beyond caring that they

could probably hear him in the ballroom by now. "You brag about not being scared of death, but you are scared to admit you are the man who has been fucking me in the dark?"

"Johnnie—"

"I thought we might actually be friends. I thought I actually mattered that small bit past being your fucking job, just a little." He picked up a heavy china owl from the table beside his chair and threw it as hard as he could, enjoying the sound of it shattering against the wall behind Bergrin—but his anger only increased. "I fucking loved you and all you have wanted was to use and mock me."

"What—" Bergrin's jaw dropped, but in the next moment, his face clouded, and he was decidedly cool as he said, "In love with a shadow? I seriously doubt—"

"I did not say I was in love with Eros!" Johnnie shouted, so loud his throat hurt.

The door slammed open then, a furious Ontoniel filling the doorway—but he stopped abruptly as he looked at Johnnie. "What is wrong?"

Johnnie could not take anymore. He just—he was done. His eyes burned as he strode to the door, desperate to get away. "Fire him."

"John—"

"Fire him!" Johnnie said, then stormed off, fleeing to the only place that had been his sanctuary as he grew up in a world that did not want him, had never even tried to make a place for him. His library was short several shelves of books, but it was still his, still familiar, still soothing.

He did not bother to turn on any lights, simply walked through it in the dark by memory, until he reached the table where he had spent so many hours reading, writing, translating. Sitting down, he folded his arms on the table, buried his head in them and simply sat there, alone in the dark.

When the door opened some unknown length of time later, Johnnie tensed and shied away from the thin line of yellow light that cut into the dark of his library.

"Your bodyguard is gone," Ontoniel said quietly. "Did you want to discuss it?"

Johnnie wiped at his face, grateful for the dark. He did not need his father seeing him look even more pathetic than he had already proven to be. "No," he said, voice hoarse, throat sore from all the shouting he had recently done. "It is over. There is nothing more to be said."

"I think perhaps that is not true," Ontoniel said gently. "But I think you also need time. Gather yourself, John. When you are ready, let us solve this mystery surrounding your brother. Focusing on that will clear your head, help you get your feet back."

"Yes, Father," Johnnie said.

Ontoniel hesitated a moment, then simply left. Johnnie took several long, deep breaths, trying to restore his shattered equilibrium.

He would manage. He would get past this humiliation, this... disaster. He had never needed anyone before, he would be just fine by himself from this point on. He most definitely did not need Bergrin, who only—

Johnnie cut the thoughts off, refusing to think about *him* for one single moment longer. He was gone. There would be no more Bergrin, no more Eros. That was the end of it all.

Standing, he fixed himself as best he could in the

dark, on the chance he met someone in the halls. He would go upstairs to his old room, wash his face and tidy up his clothes, put himself back together. Then he would fix Elam's problems. After that...

He did not know, and he was too worn out to think about it right now.

Johnnie strode to the door, bracing himself to endure people again, muttering softly to himself as he went. "I have sworn thee fair, and thought thee bright/Who art as black as hell, as dark as night."

Case 008: The True Bride II

The number of guests had greatly diminished by the time Johnnie returned to the ballroom. The remaining were all old friends of Ontoniel, a few Elam had known for decades, though he was not the sort to have close friends.

That made him think of Rita, and he looked around the ballroom until he saw her holding a glass of champagne and speaking shyly with Ontoniel.

Movement caught his eye, and he turned to see Phil and Zach approaching him. He hid a grimace, not at all in the mood to speak with anyone, but he had little choice—his brother still needed saving.

But instead of the dreaded sympathy or kind words he had braced for, Phil only said, "Something interesting happened while you were gone."

"What?" Johnnie asked.

"Elam finally went to speak to Rita. They had not been speaking two minutes before Ekaterina approached them and, after a couple more minutes, all but dragged Elam away on some trumped up excuse. Since then, she has kept them firmly apart."

Johnnie frowned. "She showed no such possessiveness earlier in the evening. She was clingy, but not that rampantly possessive. What tipped her?"

"Elam smiled at something Rita said, then laughed. He hasn't shown that much enthusiasm for anything the entire night; he's been little more than a bored, obedient boyfriend, really." Phil rolled her eyes. "I know the type, believe me. Even love doesn't make a man enjoy a party, and definitely not when it's a curse-made love."

Zach smiled wryly. "Just so. I am glad I gave up my title; hundreds more years' worth of parties and never mind blood crazy—I would have gone plain crazy."

Ignoring that, Johnnie glanced casually around the mostly-empty ballroom, landing on where Elam sat at a small table, Ekaterina all but wrapped around him. She could not look more possessive if she tried.

"I've picked up some intriguing gossip starting about half an hour ago," Zach said. "Once everyone else had filtered out, those women there," he pointed to a group of vampires who had to be several centuries old, not merely a few, "began to gossip like it was going out of style. Apparently they do not approve of Elam Desrosiers marrying what they call an ugly duckling."

Phil's brows rose. "I got none of that, and I worked the floor the entire night."

"They do not speak with humans much," Zach replied. "They lived through some dark times, and members of their family were hunted down."

Johnnie frowned in thought. "An ugly duckling?"

"Yeah," Zach said. "Apparently not all vampires are born beautiful. It's less common than the blood-craze, but you can only imagine how well that would go over."

"Indeed," Johnnie said. Beauty was everything to vampires—everything. Vampires had not always relied so heavily on beauty, but as the years and decades and centuries passed, it became safer and more effective to draw the prey in rather than go out and actively seek it. As the method of hunting and feeding changed, so too had vampire society; it revolved around beauty and wealth even more so than normal society.

Major portions of the abnormal world were divided into territories amongst the great three territorial races: demons, vampires, and werewolves. Of the three, vampires were the weakest in power, demons were nearly unbeatable in terms of magic, and wolves had numbers on their side. Vampires had more magic than werewolves, and longer lives, and outnumbered the demon lords, but far more vampires had been slaughtered by normals throughout history than the other two combined.

So an ugly vampire, a vampire lacking in the one thing that vampires had over everyone else... That would be even more shameful to a family than a relative gone blood-crazed. At least the latter was a disease and could be dealt with to a point. Ugliness in a vampire...

"She is certainly no ugly duckling now," Johnnie said.

"A mix of old magic and modern science, I would imagine," Zach said. "Apparently her family kept her tucked away for longer than I care to think about. That would certainly explain why she is only now getting married."

Phil frowned. "That seems so cruel. No wonder she appears so clingy and desperate—hell, I can almost understand why she might cast the curse and add the forgetting one just as a precaution. She shouldn't have done it, but I can understand why she felt she had to."

"Maybe," Zach said. "Me, I couldn't bear to live with the thought I was only loved because my spouse was under a curse. That's not love."

Johnnie *really* was not in the mood for discussions on love. He would give anything to have never met Bergrin. But he would give *everything* to know Bergrin was still to his right and one step behind him. That was the hardest thing to face.

The lingering silence drew him from his thoughts, and he realized Phil and Zach were both looking at him expectantly.

"I am sorry, what?"

Phil continued to regard him uncertainly but said, "I asked, should we let this drag on indefinitely, or should we try something more drastic?" She hesitated, then said. "Johnnie—"

"I do not think drastic measures are a good idea," Johnnie cut in, desperate not to have to listen to advice or sympathy. "We do not know enough about her or her abilities. For example—did she cast the curse herself, or pay someone to do it? If the former, then she is in possession of necromancer skills that should have been mentioned to my father but were not. Worse, I have not smelled any magic on her, which would mean she is capable of hiding it. If she hired someone, then who, and what else could we learn from that person? I also want to know if her parents are ignorant of all this, or party to it."

Zach looked across the ballroom. "Well, I can certainly work on the parents. Willingly or unwittingly, they will tell me something."

"I wish I had brought Jester after all," Phil said with a huff. "He would have marked her magic immediately—but then again, he did not say anything that day in your father's study." Frowning, she dug into her little beaded clutch and pulled out her cell phone, scrolling through numbers as she said, "I may be able to tell you her abilities, anyway. To the best of my knowledge, all necromancers must be registered, and legal or not, they would have to go through the registered necromancers in some way to obtain certain skills or knowledge. I have connections with one of them. Give me a few minutes."

"That is fine," Johnnie said, looking across the ballroom again, weighing his options.

"What are you thinking, Johnnie?" Phil asked, thumb hovering over the call button, giving him a curious look.

Johnnie pursed his lips in thought, then nodded, decision made. "I believe I will go and speak with my brother." So saying, he nodded at them in parting, and strode across the room to where his brother still sat, Ekaterina clinging to him.

"Ellie," Johnnie greeted lightly.

Looking up from where he had been speaking with Ekaterina, Ellie regarded him coldly. "Come to throw another Princess fit, or are you done with tantrums for the evening?"

Johnnie quirked one brow.

"Do not play coy with me," Elam snapped. "The entire ballroom could hear you shouting. Disgraceful and pathetic, and how like you to show no concern or regard for anyone else. Even during *my* betrothal ball, it is poor little Johnnie that Father must run off to attend."

The words should have hurt. Only yesterday—only a few hours ago—they probably would have. Nothing, however, could hurt more than the empty space at his side, the void left by Bergrin's betrayal. There was not a person in the world who could hurt him more than Bergrin had with whatever game he had been playing.

Johnnie sketched a half-bow, dipping his head low in apology. "I apologize. If I had known I would wind up—" he faltered briefly, then forced himself to rally, "—getting into an argument with my bodyguard, I would have picked a better time and place. I hope I did not ruin the evening entirely." He turned toward Ekaterina and sketched another bow, taking her hand and kissing the back of it. "My lady, I do apologize for disrupting your ball."

Ekaterina smiled warmly at him and gently squeezed his hand. "Do not trouble yourself over it for another moment, my dear. These things happen. I meant to ask you, by the way, about that little case you were working on when last we spoke. Did you figure out who was killing all those poor girls?"

"No," Johnnie said. "I am afraid we hit a dead end. But thank you again for your help."

"Of course," Ekaterina replied. "You will have to tell me all that you do know of it some time. There is a meeting of the Society next month, and I know it will come as quite the shock to hear that twelve of our members are dead, and by such horrible means. It will be a comfort to them and the families of the deceased to hear that Desrosiers's son spent some time investigating the matter."

Johnnie kissed her hand again. "As you wish, my lady. But if you will pardon me for now, I need to steal my brother for a few minutes."

Ekaterina smiled. "Of course. I will go and get a fresh drink and speak to my parents briefly. You gentlemen behave." With that, she gathered up her skirts and swept off.

Taking the seat she had vacated, Johnnie sat down and faced his brother. His mind, however, was completely distracted by what Ekaterina had just said—*it will come as quite the shock to hear that twelve of our members are dead.*

When he had spoken to her, they had only known of seven deaths, and his father had only later confirmed eleven. How had she known the number was twelve? He did not think Ontoniel would bring the matter up again in front of her, but if she had asked, he might have explained more of it. Johnnie would have to double check that.

But if Ontoniel had not told her, how could she know?

Johnnie did not like the implications. He also did not trust that she would be so careless. Either she was not as smart as she thought, or she was, and the latter was by far the worse.

One problem at a time. Saving Elam was the priority; the rest he would figure out later. Refocusing his attention, Johnnie said, "Jesse is having a small party next month. He wanted me to ask if you might be interested in performing at it."

Elam shrugged irritably. "I really do not have any interest in such things these days, never mind that Jesse is under house arrest and lucky to still be part of the territory no matter what Father says. He has taken up with a human, in case you forgot that, though I find that hard to believe seeing as you were *there.*"

"There is nothing wrong with humans," Johnnie said, bristling. "I am one, in case you forgot that, which I do not find hard to believe."

"You are an incubus," Elam retorted.

That threw Johnnie. "You—you knew?" he demanded angrily.

Elam smirked in his cold, superior, infuriating way.

"I was eighty-nine at the time. Young, but old enough I had to be kept apprised. But Father being Father, and utterly besotted with his new son, he forbade me to ever mention it to you. A normal life," he imitated in mocking tones. "Poor Johnnie has suffered enough, the past should be left to its own devices, blah blah blah, and so the entire Desrosiers world was made to stand upon its head for precious little Johnnie. Spoiled, ungrateful, know-it-all yet completely ignorant Johnnie."

"I am ungrateful for nothing," Johnnie snapped. "My ignorance was never of my own choosing, and if I am spoiled, then you are so beyond spoiled it is ridiculous. As to know-it-all—"

"Spare me," Elam cut in coldly. "From the moment he first saw you, held you, it was Johnnie this and Johnnie that. He might have been devastated to lose Mother that night, but he was not at all upset to get *you* out of the deal. Down one blood-crazed, dying wife, but up one bratty little child."

Johnnie recoiled, taken aback by Elam's words, the bitterness to them. This was not the reason he had come over here. "Ellie—"

"Shut up," Elam snapped. "As if all of that was not enough, my father turned into someone I scarcely knew practically overnight. Decades of tradition, tossed right out the window, all to accommodate precious Johnnie."

"Whatever you think I am," Johnnie said quietly, "I will never be his blood, his eldest, his pride and joy, his *Alucard*. I am ungrateful? You are nothing but a stiff, cold, unbending, whiny brat who throws a tantrum every time something does not go precisely his way! You only ever bothered to leave your damn piano to freeze someone with a look and remind him of his place."

They sat in cold silence, glaring at each other, before Elam finally broke the ice. "Say what you came to say, and then leave, John. You already caused a spectacle with one argument; I will not permit a second one. Father can spoil you and fawn over you all he likes. I no longer care. I have Ekaterina now."

Johnnie bit back further barbs, reminding himself he was here to help Elam, not succumb to a childish urge to punch him in his damned face. "I was honest in what I said—Jesse would like you to perform at the small, private party he is hosting next month. I refuse to believe you will not do it. You never turn down an opportunity to display your piano skills and be fawned over."

"As I said, I have Ekaterina now. I do not care about anything else, least of all a silly obsession. These things always pass."

Johnnie might want to punch Elam, but he wanted to kill Ekaterina. He and Elam had never gotten along, even when he had believed himself in love with Elam, but Elam did love piano, heart and soul. To take that from him was beyond cruel.

Never mind poor Rita, stoically carrying on the entire evening while the man she loved fawned over another woman and treated Rita as a stranger.

He looked at Elam in disgust and said, "You giving up piano is about as likely as me giving up my mysteries."

Elam sneered. "Ah, yes, something dear, dear Johnnie would never dream of giving up. Why should he care Father sits around in his study, worried sick for hours after being told you have nearly been killed or kidnapped yet again? What Johnnie wants, Johnnie must have." Elam raised his glass in mocking toast. Then he set it down and smirked in a way that never boded well for his victims. "Oh, but wait. I am mistaken. You seem to be missing a shadow. I guess Johnnie did not get everything—"

Johnnie was up and around the table before he had even realized he had moved, yanking Elam up and shoving him hard into the pillar by their table. Elam's eyes popped open wide, but Johnnie only knocked him against the pillar again when he tried to speak.

"Shut up," Johnnie hissed. "Just shut the fuck up."

He shoved Elam roughly aside, not caring as he spilled to the floor, then turned sharply on his heel and stalked from the ballroom, ignoring the cries of his father, Phil, desperate to get *away*.

Out in the hallway, he tucked himself into an alcove. Slumping against the wall, he buried his face in shaking hands and tried to draw slow, deep breaths. He could not *do* this—pretend as though everything were normal when it felt like some piece of him had been torn away, when he kept expecting to see a familiar smirk whenever he turned his head.

But the smirk was gone, along with the hazel eyes, the curls, the silly cap.

How *dare* Elam be so damned malicious when Johnnie had spent this entire wretched night trying to *help* the ass—

Would the night never end? Or was he going to be forced to live this nightmare forever?

Let the bastard rot. He would not endure being mocked and ridiculed because he had fallen in love—

Johnnie cut the thought off and tried to think of something else.

A soft touch made him jerk, and Johnnie slammed his head and elbow against the wall, swearing.

"Sorry!" Rita said, wincing. "Are you all right, Johnnie?"

Rubbing his elbow, Johnnie mustered a smile. "I am fine. Can I help you with something?"

"I wanted to be certain you were all right," Rita said, frowning. "The very moment he remembers me, I am going to give him a piece of my mind he will not soon forget. I cannot believe that is how he treats his brother!"

Johnnie smiled more genuinely at that. "Thank you, but I am afraid it would do no good, and to be fair, I am not much nicer to him. Elam has never cared for me, and I never figured out how to fix that—then I simply stopped caring."

"He's just jealous," Rita said. "Honestly, I've never seen him so, but it pours off him in waves. He is over a hundred; he should know better. I will speak with him, and if he does not apologize—well, he will wish he was still cursed!" She patted his arm. "Meeting you, and knowing some of the things he has said, gotten upset about, it is not really surprising to see that he is jealous of you. So many of the things that trouble him come so easily to you. Still, that is no excuse. For now, on his behalf, I do apologize, Johnnie. He went too far."

"As I said, we excel at hurting each other," Johnnie replied. "But thank you. If you *do* yell at him, only let me witness."

Rita laughed. "As you wish."

"Thank you," Johnnie said and took her hands, affectionately kissing the knuckles. "I think you will be a fine sister."

"I hope so," Rita said. "I still cannot believe my

lover is the Alucard Desrosiers. I fear I should have figured it out, and feel rather stupid that I did not."

Johnnie flinched. "I can tell you quite honestly that it is very easy to miss what is right in front of our faces, especially if we are half-hoping never to know it."

Rita looked at him in understanding and more kindness than Johnnie could bear. She reached up to hug him. "I truly am sorry he hurt you, and I am so very sorry indeed that something has gone so wrong between you and your bodyguard. I know—I know what it is like to love someone who is never wholly honest with you, who always holds something back. I hope that everything is soon set to rights."

Not trusting himself to speak, Johnnie only nodded as she drew back. When he could speak again, he said, "I do hope the idiot comes to his senses soon. I admit I cannot wait to see his face."

Laughing, Rita said, "I am not honestly certain with whom he will be most displeased. Oh!" She clapped her hands together. "I remembered what you said, about an object probably being what put the curse on him. I saw him wearing a watch. It was very large, very heavy. Ellie hates such things because they must be taken off whenever he wants to play or otherwise they get in the way. It was handsome, but not at all Ellie's style."

"He probably wore it once just to please Ekaterina and sealed his own fate," Johnnie said. "You have a good eye." He buried self-recrimination until he could face it because there just was not time now to hate himself for failing so miserably in so many ways.

He leaned against the wall again, sinking himself into the mystery. "I wish we knew the motive, for I feel that it cannot be as simple as making certain she married him for the title and wealth. There are better families."

"But none that would take her," Rita said doubtfully. "Some of the older ladies spoke to me; they kept saying I was much prettier, and I had not needed to wait for modern science to make me so. And for all that he is a Dracula, her father is not all that he could be, at least according to the Established Traditions." She rolled her eyes. "So, you say she could have done better, but I am not so certain of that." She shrugged, then added wryly, "Not that I have much room to talk. If I had not been playing Chopin's *Fantasie-Impromptu* that night, I would not now be attempting to win back my secret Alucard lover."

Johnnie latched onto that, kicking himself for not asking sooner how *exactly* they had met. He really was losing his touch—if, he thought morosely, he had ever had a touch at all. "What precisely is it you do where you work?"

Rita smiled. "I play piano. Most of it is the silly stuff you always hear at resorts and other such places. At night, I back up the singer. But before the show starts, and late in the evening, I am permitted to do as I like for the most part. It was during one of those late hours that he walked in." Her smile softened with memory. "I saw him well before he saw me; I was just finishing up a silly little piece I like to play before I moved into the *Fantasie-Impromptu*. When I finished, I looked up and saw him watching me. Right there beside the stage; I half-thought he was going to jump up *on* the stage. But he only asked if I would play him *Music Box Dancer*, and then he asked if he could buy me a drink."

"Mm," Johnnie said, "and you have been putting up with him for twenty years? I am duly impressed."

"He is not half so tense with me," Rita mused, then grimaced, suddenly looking afraid. "I worry now that maybe he never meant for me to be here—it may be that I am the one he is most angry at when he comes out of the curse—"

Johnnie laid a hand on her shoulder, reassuring her gently, "My lady, I sincerely doubt that. If he wanted to marry you, and was going to ask Father about it, then he planned on bringing you here. I promise you that when he comes out of the curse, the first thing he will do is throw a tantrum. Then he will attempt to murder Ekaterina. Then he will round on me, simply because he will not be able to tolerate that you came to me for help."

Rita rolled her eyes and muttered, "He had better be too busy with me for all that nonsense."

"But it is very interesting—and good for us—that you play," Johnnie went on. "I should have asked before because, of course, Ellie would never settle for less than a lady who plays as well as he." Johnnie took her hand and tucked it into the crook of his arm, then turned to lead her back to the ballroom. "I think, my lady, that when the time is right and you play—that will be all we need to break the curse. But I do not want to upset the balance too much before we know what we are dealing with."

"Of course," Rita replied, but before she could say anything further, Phil and Zach came spilling out of the ballroom, and from the looks on their faces, they had some interesting news to share.

"She could be a necromancer," Phil announced as they reached Johnnie and Rita. "Phoenix—"

Johnnie startled at that name. "You know Phoenix—never mind. Not now. What did you learn?"

Phil smiled briefly, then said, "Phoenix said he had heard rumors lately of a rogue necromancer, but he doesn't take pupils, and neither does Ceadda. He also got in touch with some necromancers he knows in the UK, but no luck there either."

"Ekaterina's family lived in Italy for half a century," Johnnie said grimly. "She could have learned it then, and no one there would breathe a word. She would have been rather young for a necromancer, though, especially one of the skill it would seem she could be." He frowned thoughtfully.

Zach added, "Her parents mentioned Italy, how much they all loved it and were loath to return home for her father to properly take up the mantle of Dracula. They said Ekaterina especially was livid over their departure. But out of nowhere, she suddenly loved it here. Her mother said it was like she hated it one day, adored it the next. They were relieved and did not ask questions. I cannot tell you how many times they told me she is 'mercurial, but a good girl'.

"If they are party to all of this, then they are damned fine actors. Myself, I suspect they are merely severely strained parents who are almost too grateful whenever she is happy and do not know her even half as well as they think, and they admit their daughter makes no real sense to them. Though, who knows, at that. They knew enough to know she was almost universally hated by her sisters. Really, though, that is no surprise. More than half the women in that Society are pretentious little snots."

The back of Johnnie's neck prickled. "You do not mean the Princess Society, do you?"

"Yeah," Zach said. "Our false bride was hated by a good number of her sisters."

Johnnie closed his eyes, pinching the bridge of his nose, and quoted, "The female of the species is more deadly than the male."

"What does that mean?" Rita asked.

"That we've got trouble," Phil said. "It cannot be coincidence that we wound up with twelve dead Princesses and she is a secret necromancer hated by all of them. Why did I not see that connection before?"

"You did not have access to her parents, and they would not have spoken to you of the matter, anyway," Zach replied. "We did not know to look there."

Phil shook her head. "I don't even see what my case has to do with this mess, though. What in the world is the connection?"

"Dreaming men are haunted men," Johnnie said softly, then turned to Rita and said, "My dear, I think it is time you played something for us." Break the curse and at least that problem would be solved. If she saw they were on to her, perhaps she would retreat—or at least she would be revealed, and they could face her head on. He glanced at Phil and Zach. "I think we had best resort to drastic measures. If she is this sly, there is no telling what else she can and will do. Best to have done and face her now, and hopefully, in doing so, gain ourselves some sort of advantage."

"I still would like to know what she is really after between the dead girls and all this nonsense," Phil said.

"Me," Johnnie said. "I believe she is after me." He strode off, back into the ballroom, ignoring Phil and Zach as they called after him.

In the ballroom, he looked around for his father. Spotting him standing near the buffet tables, Johnnie strode across the room to join him. "I think that Rita can finally break the curse," he said. "She is going to do it now. But we believe Ekaterina to be a necromancer—and I am completely convinced she is behind the murders of those twelve women from the Society."

Ontoniel's expression did not change, and he only nodded in reply, but Johnnie knew he was silently communicating with the various guards and other personnel scattered around his manor. "Despite your falling out," he said quietly, "I do rather wish your bodyguard was still about."

Johnnie did not reply, but he could not help but think *me too*. He hated himself for the weakness, but there was no denying he wished desperately that Bergrin was there. He turned his head slightly as music filled the air, watching Rita at the baby grand piano that Elam would normally kill *anyone* for daring to touch.

He recognized what she was playing only because he had learned by age eleven that not knowing what Elam was playing was tantamount to death. Currently, Rita was playing Liszt's *Liebestraume Notturno* No. 3. It was one of Elam's favorite pieces.

Someday, he would have to tell Elam that Rita looked better sitting at a piano than he did. The thought made him smirk—but then reminded him abruptly of what Elam had said to him only moments ago. Johnnie swallowed against the rawness scraping his throat and tried to focus on the matter at hand.

But he really just wanted the entire damned affair over so he could return to the Bremen—

Could he return to the Bremen, he wondered suddenly, gut clenching. That had been Bergrin's stomping ground first, had it not? It would not be fair for Johnnie to take it from him—but he did not want to return to Ontoniel's house, either.

Later. He would deal with all of it later. Johnnie looked around the ballroom, at all the people whispering in admiration, eyes on Rita before sliding to Elam. Everyone present knew his obsession and his possessiveness, when it came to his pianos.

Elam still sat at the table where Johnnie had left him, but he was paying no attention to the fiancée trying to get his attention. Instead, his gaze was riveted on Rita. He pulled irritably away from Ekaterina when she gripped his arm, then impatiently stood up when she tried to speak again. He continued to watch Rita, clearly enthralled.

There was also a growing confusion on his face. Like a man not entirely awake, he slowly crossed the room to the small stage where the piano rested. Rita paid him no mind, merely focused on the music, clearly pouring everything she had into the playing.

As the last strains of music finally faded away, Elam's voice, soft and unsteady, said, "Ree?"

Rita looked up, tears streaming down her face, and said, "Have you finally remembered me, you great big jerk?"

"Ree—" Elam surged onto the stage and yanked her from the bench, holding her tightly. "Oh god, Ree. I can't believe—I'm so—"

The words were abruptly cut off as Elam and Rita dropped unconscious, crashing into the bench, the piano, before finally landing in an awkward heap on the floor. The sound of thumping, breaking glass and crashing chairs created a cacophony throughout the ballroom as all around Johnnie, everyone collapsed.

"Father!" he said in a panic as Ontoniel fell right

next to him. He dropped to his knees, examining Ontoniel frantically. "Father!" He looked around at everyone else, then sneezed hard. Magic. His eyes watered from the smell of it—he had never smelled magic so potent, like something sweet had cooked too long and burned.

The sounds of heels clicking on wood drew him, and he looked up, unsurprised to see Ekaterina standing there, as cold and hard as ice. Slowly he rose to his feet. "What did you do to them?"

"The Princess shall not die, but fall into a deep sleep for a hundred years," Ekaterina replied, then laughed in a way that made Johnnie want to take several steps back. "Except, you did not fall asleep, did you, Beauty? Still wide awake, doomed never to dream when it should be your fate to walk freely in dreams. Your bitch mother saw to preventing that, though. She told me right before Sariah made a snack of her jugular."

"Shut up!" Johnnie snarled, balling his hands into fists to still their trembling—though whether it was from fear or anger, he did not know. "Why—why the fuck are you doing this? How did you do this? Wake them up!"

"No," Ekaterina said. "I tried to warn you off, but you did not listen."

"Warn—twelve," he realized. "When you mentioned *twelve* women, you were trying to warn me off."

Ekaterina laughed in that chilling way again. "As usual, little Johnnie Goodnight does not listen to those wiser than him, too busy thinking he knows everything because he's read a lot of books. How smart do you feel now, little Johnnie?"

"Why?" Johnnie asked, fighting despair. They were all so still—his father, his brother, Phil, Zach. They could have been dead, and if they slept too long, there might be no pulling them back out of the dream plane.

"Because I want something that only you can bring to me," Ekaterina said. "I have tried to obtain it myself while waiting until I could get access to you again, but the quest has proven to be extremely difficult on both counts. Did you know, dear Johnnie, that I wanted to put the love spell on you first?"

"What?" Johnnie asked.

"Except there was one already on you, and to judge by the look of it, the spell must have been cast when you were a child. I sense Ontoniel had some noble purpose there, knowing that idiot—but it worked because I could not cast one on you. So I had to settle for your brother instead, and that only after pushing my parents for years to negotiate my betrothal to Elam." She fell silent, obviously fuming over old memories.

Johnnie's mind spun. A love spell? Cast on him? Since he was a child? But...but that would explain why at only nine he had been hopelessly in love with his brother. What in the hell had they been thinking?

What the fuck did it matter now?

Johnnie tried to get a hold of himself, but he was already ragged from his fallout with Bergrin—

He closed his eyes and swallowed, missing Bergrin so much right then it was a physical ache, a weight upon his chest that made breathing almost impossible. He had messed everything up, had done not one single thing right, and now his family and friends were going to die, or worse, sleep forever and lose themselves in dreams.

"You want the object my father made?" he finally asked. "No one even knows what it is—and even if I knew where in dreams to find it, I cannot get it for you. I am completely spelled against ever entering the dream plane."

"Then I suggest you find a way to break the spell," Ekaterina said. "Let me explain everything to you so that we understand one another perfectly. I want that object. I was prepared to handle the matter quietly until you chose to poke your nose into matters too far. Your behavior has forced me to play my hand and resort to extreme measure. This entire house has been set with the Sleeping Beauty curse. Anyone who enters the house will fall victim to it. If you try to find and tamper with the spell key, they will be lost in dreams forever. You will go into the dream plane and bring back the object your father made."

"But I do not know—"

Ekaterina laughed. "How sad that not a one of you truly appreciates the accidental brilliance of your stupid father. An impossible relic lies in dreams, just waiting for you to take it, and you don't even know what it is."

"An impossible... No, that cannot be," Johnnie said. "No one has ever actually made one of the impossible relics."

Laughing again, Ekaterina then recited, "Looking-glass, Looking-glass, on the wall/Who in this land is the fairest of all?"

"You are mad," Johnnie said. "There is no such thing as a magic mirror."

One moment Ekaterina was standing several steps away—the next Johnnie could feel blood tricking down his stinging cheek from where her nails had scraped it when she slapped him. "You will bring me the mirror, and you will do it in three days, or everyone you know and love will suffer a fate worse than death. When you have the mirror, contact me. Until then, I suggest you do as you are told, and do not attempt heroics. No one but me can break the spell and wake those who sleep here. Bring me that mirror, or else."

Then she was gone, with nothing but a small, pale pink business card lying where she had stood. It bore only a phone number. Feeling numb, Johnnie bent and then tucked it into a pocket of his tuxedo. Then he knelt beside Ontoniel, staring miserably at the proof of his abysmal failure.

What was he going to do? How could he fix this when he was the one who had ruined everything? It was because of him that people had been hurt, had been killed—and now this. How could he set all to rights when he had set it wrong?

Johnnie tried to think, but his mind simply refused to work. He was done—done with everything. He was no brilliant detective, he was not a good son, he was definitely not the sort of man anyone would want to call lover. No wonder Bergrin had not wanted him beyond what he could give Eros.

He wiped his face, furious with himself. They had trusted him to help, and this was what he had done! Pulling out a handkerchief, Johnnie wiped his face, blew his nose. At the very least, he could make them a bit more comfortable.

First he straightened Ontoniel until he was laid out neatly on the floor, hands folded on his stomach. Then he stood and went around the ballroom, slowly dragging, shifting, and arranging all the others until they were lined up neatly in two rows in the center of the ballroom. Then he went through the rest of the house, making certain the scattered servants were all right. When he was finished, he made certain the house was locked up, then returned to the ballroom.

They looked, he thought miserably, like corpses.

He hated the sight of Ontoniel like that the most, and he could not even bear to look at Phil and Zach. They had only wanted to help him, and now he would have to find their friends and tell them what he had done. What he, and he alone, would have to do to save them.

Alone. He had thought he was alone before, never quite fitting in no matter how hard he tried. But this—standing by himself in a room full of almost-corpses with no one to help him lest he hurt still more people.

This was feeling alone, and it made him want to hide away in despair.

But his mind would not stop churning, working; against his will, he started sifting through the myriad versions of the tale of the notorious Sleeping Beauty and the truth that lurked, all but forgotten, behind them. It, too, had started with jealousy.

A king eager for a child and angry that his queen would produce none, had taken a lover—a witch. That affair had lasted for years, but she had failed to produce a child as well. Then, one day, his queen produced a child. Ecstatic, the king cast aside his useless lover.

Days after it had been born, the child was struck with a curse that she would die on that same day in fifteen years.

From that moment on, the king and all in his kingdom worked to break the terrible curse. They did all that was within their power to break it, to soften it, but to no avail—none but the witch herself was able to break it, and she had not been seen since eluding capture on the day she cast the curse.

As her birthday drew ever closer, the king and queen grew more frantic, more desperate. The kingdom despaired, and all who had come to love the princess wept, for soon she would be gone from them forever.

One night, several days before her birthday, the princess went to sleep.

She never woke, nor did the inhabitants of the castle. Those who came to visit the castle soon fled in fear of the terrible magic and what it had wrought. One by one the inhabitants passed away, unable to tend themselves while trapped in a terrible sleep. Then, one day, as the cock in the palace yard crowed, the princess drew a last breath, and died on the day and the hour of her fifteenth year.

As time passed, the kingdom was lost, preserved only in tales and a rare true accounting written by an unknown source.

What troubled Johnnie most was that Ekaterina had somehow duplicated the curse. It had been done before, but by sorcerers and necromancers of greater experience, and only as an experiment under tightly controlled conditions.

He did not want them to die. But he was overwhelmed by what he would have to do—somehow, he would have to break the curse that had been laid upon him and hope it did not kill him. His best chance of avoiding death was to find the sorcerer who had originally cast the spell.

And assuming he actually managed the feat, he would have to go into the dream plane and figure out where the hell to find the magic mirror.

He felt sick just thinking about it. A magic mirror. It could not be. There was no such thing as a mirror that would tell a man whatever he wanted to know. Whatever his father had made, it must come close, but it was not an actual magic mirror.

So he had to break his spell, learn how to get into the dream plane, then find a mirror that could be hidden anywhere.

And he had to do it in three days.

He needed help, but there was no one to help him. He dare not go to Rostiya, or even the Bremen, for fear of what Ekaterina might do to them. Bergrin—

Johnnie covered his eyes with the heel of his hands, and tried to laugh, but it only came out a sob. He wanted Bergrin, but Bergrin was gone and it was his own stupid fault. But what could Bergrin do? It was not as though he could help Johnnie retrieve the mirror, and he did not want to endanger Bergrin either.

No, he had to do this alone. No one else was able to access the dream plane. No one else would be able to find the mirror.

He had made this mess and he would have to find a way to fix it, whatever the cost.

The first step was to get a clear head. He would not be able to think clearly while standing there staring at his family and friends, feeling sorry for himself.

Turning sharply on his heel, Johnnie forced himself to leave the ballroom. Out in the hall, he weighed his options, then headed for the end of the house where Ontoniel's study was located. Though he had expected it to be locked, as the house was full of guests, the knob turned easily beneath his hand and Johnnie slipped inside. He flicked on a single lamp on the desk then hesitantly sat down in Ontoniel's chair.

He swallowed against the wave of sadness and shame that washed through him. He would yell at himself later, but right now he had to focus.

Ontoniel was meticulous. He might have destroyed all of Tommy's papers and equipment, but he would have kept what he needed to ensure Johnnie's safety. But where would he keep them?

The desk was enormous, a modern L-shaped desk but designed to look antique. All the drawers were locked, and heavily warded with magic—including against normal tampering, Johnnie noted with frustration, as he was magically zapped in warning with every drawer he tried.

Frustrated, annoyed that Ontoniel clearly knew him far too well, Johnnie sank back into the chair and fought despair. There had to be something, damn it all. He would find it.

Thoughts of finding, of course, immediately led to thoughts of Bergrin, but Johnnie was not going down that path. But memories of the night when everything with Bergrin had changed spurred him to look around his father's study with the eyes of a detective rather than the eyes of a frantic son.

It was still the eyes of a son that drew him to the chair where he most often preferred to sit, in the chair before the massive stained-glass window. It gave a clear view of the rest of the room and provided plenty of rainbow light by which to read—not that he had ever simply kicked back and read in Ontoniel's sanctuary.

What would Bergrin immediately see, with those sly, unknown tricks of his, that Johnnie would take longer to notice? He glanced around the room again, but his eyes kept returning to his little corner. Was something about it actually nagging him, or was it simply that he was drawn to the familiar comfort of it? Because he did not like sitting in Ontoniel's chair—it felt too much like he was accepting Ontoniel was going to die.

Hastily standing up, he strode over to his corner but did not sit. He continued to frown at it, thinking. Something was bothering him, he decided, but what and why now? He had sat here a thousand times and never noticed anything; hell, he was the only one who ever sat here. Everyone else used the leather chairs in front of the desk or the sofa and chairs in the little seating area arranged in front of the bookcases.

No one else ever bothered to sit all the way over here, where it was easier to see without really being seen. Out of the way. The few times he had been called in here growing up, he had preferred this corner. In fact, he realized suddenly, it had not always had a chair. That had been added later, but he could not honestly remember when. But he remembered being younger and called in here to get reprimanded—but Ontoniel would often be on the phone, or speaking to Elam first, and Johnnie would stand over here and wait, anxious and afraid, for his turn.

To distract himself, he had examined everything about the corner. The stained glass window, the intricate squares of paneling that ran along the bottom edge of the entire study but were most visible here. Each panel depicted the Desrosiers rose crest. He had traced them over and over, memorizing the pattern until he had known it in his sleep. He had thought Ontoniel would be impressed he knew the family crest so well, but Johnnie had never worked up the nerve to tell Ontoniel. It was only one of many stupid, pointless things he had done because he had lived in terror for so long that he would lose his second family, too.

He slumped in his chair and raked a hand through his hair. He had been good at this sort of thing, once, or at least stubborn enough to delude himself. Could he not do it just one more time? He looked around the study, trying to think, to *see*, but nothing presented.

Sighing, he stood and then knelt by the panels he had traced a thousand times—and sneezed hard as he bent close to one. He sneezed again and reached for his handkerchief before remembering with a grimace that he had already used it thoroughly.

Tossing it aside, he sneezed against his sleeve, then tried to focus on the panel. Definitely magic upon it, but so tightly confined to *just* the panel that he had never noticed it mingled with the low level of magic perpetually running throughout the house.

Reaching out, he felt all over and along the panel carefully. It was a rich, dark, red-brown color, meticulously cared for over the years, dusted and oiled, lovingly maintained like every other piece of the house. Ontoniel took great pride in his home and would not tolerate anything less from his servants.

It was only on his tenth pass, as he was growing so angry he was tempted simply to fetch an ax and hack the thing apart, that he felt it. A slight *shift* in a small bit of the fancy ivy pattern that bordered the panel. One of the leaves. It took him a couple more minutes to figure out how exactly it twisted—but when it finally moved and revealed a keyhole behind it, Johnnie cried out for joy so loudly that Ontoniel would have given him a reproving look.

He stood up and half-ran, half-tripped his way to the desk where he had left his lock-picking tools. Scooping them up, he returned to the secret keyhole and hesitantly tried his picks—and almost started crying from relief when magic did not push him away.

Ontoniel had seen this panel was warded, but he had not warded it against Johnnie's tricks.

It took him only a few minutes to pick the lock and another minute to pull the panel open to reveal a small, secret cabinet. It contained nothing but a small stack of papers and a folder—and, he noticed belatedly, a pair of rings.

He took everything out, then after a moment's consideration, took it all back to Ontoniel's desk. The rings clinked together as he sat, and Johnnie reached out to pick them up. They... they were obviously wedding rings. Simple, the sort of rings a middle-class couple would be able to afford. The woman's ring had only a single small diamond set in gold. The man's was a plain gold band. Ontoniel had these? But why, and why had Johnnie never seen them? He had no mementos of his family minus a single album of photos his parents had kept, and which had not been destroyed along with everything else.

Forcing himself to set the rings aside, he focused his on the folder. It was plain, made of good, heavy stock dyed dark brown. Opening it, he saw immediately it was a formal case report—or rather, he realized after a moment, a copy of one.

The first page was a printed form, the top portion of it listing several bits of information that had been filled in by whoever had written the report. Whoever it was had a brisk, tidy hand.

Case Number: 041 (Sweet Dreams)
Client: Tommy Fitz
Primary Detective: Chris
Secondary Detective: Doug
Summary: Man trapped in dreams.
Resolution: Case solved.

Johnnie drew a sharp breath as he realized he was reading about his parents. As he read, he realized the case was about how his mother had finally entered the mortal plane after his father was nearly killed by another succubus.

He set it hastily aside, the whole thing suddenly too much. It was not what he was looking for, anyway. Except, as he picked up the first of several pages of loose paper, he realized perhaps the old case was more pertinent to the present than he realized.

Because those names kept coming up—Chris, Doug. He knew those names. Chris was the Consort—Phil's boss. Doug was another detective. But he had seen them somewhere else, too. The first piece of paper he picked up was a detailed explanation of the spell that had been cast on Johnnie, elaborating on what it would do, how long it would last, and what could happen if it was ever removed.

A later letter, from someone named Jed, detailed the love spell that Ekaterina had mentioned and about which Johnnie had surmised. It had not actually been a proper love spell, according to the letter. Ontoniel had wanted him protected from such things, as he was not entirely convinced the threat was gone forever. By infatuating him with someone—his brother—he would be unharmed but safe from the tampering of others until the spell should naturally cancel upon his actually falling in love.

Johnnie tried to be angry, but he was simply too damned wrung out. He no longer cared what Ontoniel had done to him. He just wanted his father and everyone else back.

Who was Jed? The sorcerer? But other than that one letter, there was nothing more about him. Johnnie read through all the papers, but at the end of it all, the only sure bit he had to go on was that Chris had been the initial mastermind in all of it—rescuing his father, helping to bring his mother into the mortal plane, helping them move to Ontoniel's territory, and later setting them up with Jed.

Mixed in with the various papers was a business card for one Sable Brennus. On the back of it, however, was Chris's name and a phone number. It was a starting point, and he could do nothing but hope that it took him to this Jed he obviously needed to find.

Pulling out his phone, he quickly punched in the number, sick with anxiety while it began to ring.

After the fifth ring, just as he wanted to scream in frustration, a sleepy, husky voice said, "White Detective Agency."

"Hello," Johnnie said. "I apologize for calling at so terrible an hour—"

"So you do realize it is two in the morning?" the man asked, voice dry with amusement.

"Yes," Johnnie snapped, losing what patience he had managed to retain. "I am all too well aware of the hour, but it is a matter of life and death. Unless you relish the idea of being party to the death of the Dracula Desrosiers and his family, I suggest you cease with your ill-timed attempts at humor and provide some genuine assistance."

There was a startled silence, then a soft laugh. "Yes, my lord," the man said teasingly. "One moment, I will fetch Christian." Johnnie heard the man set the phone down and could just barely hear him speaking to someone else.

After another minute or so, another voice came on the line, sleepy sounding but more alert and markedly more serious than the first. "This is Chris. What's wrong?"

"My name is Johnnie Desrosiers," Johnnie said. "I do not know if you remember me—"

"Of course I do," Chris said, suddenly sounding completely awake. "Your parents were good people. Phil mentioned you yesterday, and I finally realized her 'friend Johnnie' was you. What's wrong? Phil and Zach went to help you with a case tonight."

Johnnie laughed because otherwise he would simply lose his mind. "They were—they are—they tried, but everything has gone wrong."

"I'll come right over—"

"No!" Johnnie shouted desperately into the phone. "You cannot. If you enter this house, you will fall under the same curse. She put a Sleeping Beauty—"

"Meet me outside the house, then," Chris said. "I'll fetch you, and you can tell me everything, and we'll figure out what to do."

Johnnie started to tell him that there was no time, that what he needed was to talk to Jed, but all that came out was, "All right."

The phone went dead, and he closed his own, then rose shakily to his feet. Gathering up all the papers, he strode to the main entryway and pulled out a leather case to put them all in. Then he pulled on his coat, hat, and retrieved his cane.

Outside, he locked the door—then turned around and jumped, seeing someone who had not been there a moment ago.

He was handsome, if dressed in clothes that clearly had seen better days and needed to be retired. Blue, blue eyes, tousled gold hair, and the power of a demon poured off him in such strength that Johnnie once more found himself sneezing so hard he thought he would break something.

"Johnnie Goodnight," Chris said softly. "You have grown up well—but I can see this is neither the time nor the place. Come on, we'll go to my place and figure it all out."

He sounded so calm, so certain, *steady*, that Johnnie did not even think about, simply took the hand that Chris held out and let him teleport them away.

They reappeared in a room that was simple in design, but no less elegant and classy for that. A black leather sofa dominated the space, facing a massive fireplace in which a fire had obviously been recently lit. Windows ran floor to ceiling along the entire length of the room, looking out and down onto a rain-soaked city many stories below.

Leaning against the windows, half in shadow, was a striking man with dark, wildly curly hair and eyes the color of thunderclouds. Unlike Chris, he was well dressed in dark slacks and a gray sweater. The magic and power radiating off him was so great that Johnnie went right back to sneezing. When he finally got control of it, he could only gasp out, "You are the demon lord Sable Brennus, are you not?"

"Guilty as charged," Sable said cheerfully, moving toward them and immediately kissing Chris's cheek, ignoring the scowl that got him. "You are the one who just took me to task. Johnnie Desrosiers, formerly Johnnie Goodnight. That is a name I remember well, though I have not heard it in more than passing for over fifteen years."

Johnnie could not think of a reply to that.

"Sit here," Chris said and took his coat and hat—but Johnnie would not relinquish the cane.

Moving obediently to the couch, he slumped down in it and wished he could simply go to sleep.

"Would you like something to drink?" Chris asked. "Coffee, tea...?"

"Whiskey, brandy," Sable added more playfully. "Perhaps the best of both worlds. My housekeeper makes a mean hot toddy."

Hot toddy—Johnnie bit back more sobbing laughter, burying his face in one hand. He would give anything to hear a certain hot toddy voice right now, anything and everything. "N-n-no," he finally managed. "I am fine. I-I apologize for the unseemly hour."

"Forget it," Chris said. "Tell me everything."

Johnnie looked up at him, staring for what seemed an eternity—then the dam finally broke, and he spilled out all that had happened.

At some point, Sable pressed a drink into his hand, but it was not until he finally finished recounting everything that Johnnie bothered to take a sip of it. Scotch, and his eyes burned because it was his father's favorite kind.

He took another sip, and by the third it actually managed to be soothing.

"What a mess," Chris said with a long sigh, raking a hand absently through his hair. "I think you are right, unfortunately—getting Jed to break your spell and sending you into dreams is the most effective route, at least for now. We will work on other things, anyway, but she sounds like she was too thorough for anyone's peace of mind. If we can't enter that house, then we can't find the spell key to destroy it and break the curse. It sounds like it is rigged against tampering, anyway. So, you will have to go into dreams, if only to break the spells on them that way."

Johnnie nodded. "But first we must break the spell, and there is every chance that doing so will kill me."

"Maybe, but this is Jed we're talking about," Chris replied. "He's not your usual caliber of sorcerer. I'll give him a call. He should be here by morning, and we can further discuss the matter."

"No—we need to do this now—" Johnnie stood up, then abruptly sat back down again, feeling horribly dizzy and suddenly exhausted. He looked up at Sable. "What..."

"Sleeping spells might not work," Sable said with entirely too much cheer, "but drugs work on everyone, and you need to rest. You can't save the world if you're exhausted."

Johnnie glared at him, or tried to, but it was suddenly so very difficult to keep his eyes open.

The last thing he remembered was the sound of soft laughter and two voices quietly talking.

Case 009: Beauty in Repose

Johnnie woke with a jerk, then slumped over, feeling groggy and heavy-headed. Where was he? Not the Bremen. Not his father's home.

Father.

He jerked up, memories flooding back, and remembered he was in the home of Sable Brennus. Voices drew him then, and he slowly stood up and turned, looking over the couch to where a group of men were gathered.

Chris and Sable he recognized, but not the other three. One was a short man with red hair and freckles. Harmless looking, but Johnnie had long ago learned to mark that unidentifiable *something* that designated an imp. Recalling all that Phil had ever said about her comrades, this must be Doug.

The other two he did not know. Of the two, one was just barely taller than Doug, about even with Chris—definitely not as tall as Sable or the other man. He was quiet, studious looking, with glasses, mussed hair, and wearing a blue and black flannel shirt over a black t-shirt, and faded stone-washed jeans. Power radiated off him, and nearly made Johnnie sneeze, except this time he was braced for it.

Nearby, the last man stood watching the studious one with open fondness. He was handsome, almost pretty—and there was an unmistakable collar around his neck. Of all the enslaved races, only one wore collars imbued with so much magic. "Angel," Johnnie said, too surprised to remember to be quiet.

Almost as one, the five men turned to look at him.

"You're awake," Sable said drolly.

Johnnie glared at him. "You drugged me."

"Children do not always know what's best for them," Sable said mockingly.

"I do not think you have room to be calling anyone a child," Johnnie said coldly.

Chris and Doug burst out laughing, and Chris slid his lover a smirk. "He has you there, Sable."

"You never take my side," Sable complained, but then gave Johnnie an approving smile. "You are precisely as we have always heard—as cold and beautiful as any vampire. Given you're a human, and barely into proper adulthood, I would say you are a better vampire. Then again, you are half incubus."

Johnnie said nothing, merely moved around the couch to join them, looking at the other two men.

The shorter, more studious one smiled in a friendly, easy manner and held out a hand. "So you are Johnnie Goodnight, all these years later. My name is Jed."

"Oh," Johnnie said, surprised even though he knew he should not be. "My father's notes were not terribly helpful in finding you. I surmised it was because you are so powerful, which I am more convinced of now."

Jed looked at him in surprise. "You can tell my power level?"

"I can smell it," Johnnie replied. "You and Lord Brennus both smell very strongly of magic; if I do not watch it, you will cause me to start sneezing."

"Fascinating," Jed said. "I've never known someone who can *smell* magic. What an intriguing way to—"

"Master," the angel cut in, smiling fondly, "you can study him later."

Jed laughed and shook his head, then smiled sheepishly at Johnnie. "Of course, forgive me. Charlie is right. We have been working on the problem of the spell I put on you almost twenty-seven years ago. Even with my skills, it is no easy matter to strip away a spell that was laid on you before you were even born. Casting it took me hours; breaking it without killing you..." He shrugged and spread his hands. "I just don't know."

"We do not have a choice," Johnnie said, "so the point is moot. So long as you *can* break it, the rest is up to me. I am not going to die."

The angel—Charlie, had Jed called him?—laughed. "You are quite stubborn."

Johnnie said nothing, merely stared at him coolly. What did they expect, that he would simply let his family, his friends, wither and die because he was too scared to risk death himself? He had lost Bergrin; he was on the verge of losing his family. He quite literally had nothing left to lose. What did he give a damn about risking his own life if there was a chance to save the people who mattered to him?

Sable clapped his shoulder. "As I said, better than any vampire. Let him see the different circles you have been sketching out, though I think it does not matter which one you go with. I believe him when he says he will not let himself die."

"I think you are both reckless idiots," Chris snapped. "No one can endure the breaking of such a spell easily—do not be flippant."

"Yes, beloved," Sable replied, but he winked at Johnnie before going to get a drink.

The sound of a soft woof drew Johnnie's attention, and he turned to see a massive black dog padding into the room. It came straight toward him, ears pricked up, pushing and rubbing in obvious curiosity, groaning and chuffing and woofing as if asking questions Johnnie could neither understand nor answer.

Chris frowned. "That's interesting. He's not normally so friendly with strangers—at least not living ones."

"I could not say," Johnnie said. "I do not hang around the dead, or the undead. There just must be traces of something interesting on my clothes." He pet the dog one last time, then pushed it gently away.

"Speaking of clothes," Sable called from the table where he was pouring himself coffee. "I had some fresh clothes brought for you, figuring you would not want to be stuck in that tuxedo indefinitely. Phil always mentions running into you when she is out shopping, so I tracked down where you two overlapped. Your tailor put something together and sent it straight over."

Johnnie looked at him, surprised—and more grateful than he could possibly put into words, for something as stupid as fresh clothes, and *his* clothes. "Thank you."

"I am always happy to help those willing to yell at me," Sable said with a smile, his eyes shining like lightning behind clouds.

Chris rolled his eyes, then reached out and stole Sable's coffee. To Johnnie, he said, "Get dressed, then we'll show you the various spell circles."

He indicated a room, and Johnnie headed immediately toward and into it. He shut the door behind him, then simply leaned against it for a moment, breathing deep and slow, getting his bearings, trying to gather himself.

All he really wanted was for everything to be normal again.

The room was a guest room, as near as he could tell, complete with its own bathroom. Stripping off his tuxedo, he threw it into a corner—he had no intention of wearing the damned thing ever again. If he could, he would burn it.

In the bathroom, he made the water as hot as he could possibly stand, then simply stood beneath it for several minutes. Only reluctantly did he finally begin to wash, and he was able to make himself do it quickly only because he was already down several hours. He probably did not have much more than two days left.

Clean, he returned to the bedroom and quickly dressed in the clothes waiting for him—a black suit with gray pinstripes and a vest of various shades of gray, touched with silver in an oriental flower pattern, over a white shirt with black opal buttons. The tie was pale, shimmery gray-green, with a black opal pin and matching cufflinks—his tailor really had remembered everything, right down to a pair of shoes to match.

Feeling much more himself, even if he continued to feel like a piece of him was missing, Johnnie rejoined the others in the main room.

"I still don't see why we can't try something!" Doug said furiously "Zach—" He cut off, then tried again. "Zach and Phil are in that house, Chris."

"I know," Chris said, "but whoever this woman is, she's trapped them good and tight. But..." He trailed off as he saw Johnnie.

Doug turned around, a scowl still on his face.

Johnnie flinched. "I am sorry. I underestimated her

abilities. I had no idea she had a Sleeping Beauty curse rigged as a failsafe."

"It's hardly the worst we've ever faced," Chris said. "And it's not entirely your fault. Zach and Phil are both experienced detectives. They are as responsible for this mistake as you—they both have dealt with necromancers before, including one ruthless enough to drain fellow vampires. So they should have known." He shot Doug a look.

Doug grunted, then grimaced. "True enough. I don't know what Zach was thinking." He sighed and said more quietly, "I hope this works, and that he'll be okay."

"He will be," Johnnie said, recognizing that look, that tone of voice.

It was not fair, he thought miserably. Even in the middle of this mess, too many things continued to remind him of Bergrin. He had greater concerns. He should not keep going back to that selfish desire. Bergrin was gone; Johnnie did not see how or why he would ever come back.

"Show me the circles," he said, moving to Jed and Charlie.

Jed handed him three pieces of paper. Johnnie looked at them, duly impressed. They were extremely intricate, denoting a skill the likes of which he had *never* seen. He read through them thoughtfully, only growing more and more impressed.

"This one I thought would help with the shock and pain—"

"But it sacrifices force," Johnnie said. "It may not be strong enough in practice, though it is in theory, to completely break the spell, and leaving the job half done could be worse, in the long run, than one clean break."

Jed looked at him, clearly surprised. "You can read spell circles?"

"You make it sound difficult," Johnnie replied, and moved on to the second, then the third, and finally the fourth. Then he went through all of them again before handing them back to Jed. "I would go with the third myself, but reading them does not make me an expert upon them. You are obviously the resident authority, so whatever you feel is best."

"A pity you cannot do magic," Jed said thoughtfully. "I think you would have a fair knack for it. The third was my vote. It will be, as you called it, one clean break. It will also be excruciating."

Johnnie thought of the near-corpses lined up neatly in the ballroom, lives ticking away because he had made too many mistakes. Then he thought of Bergrin, and the anger he had earlier felt was now only a crushing pain. "I do not care."

"No, I can see that you don't," Jed said, looking at him with such sincere sympathy that Johnnie could not stand it.

He turned sharply away, asking, "So when are you doing it?"

"Now," Jed replied. "Give me an hour to draw the spell circle."

Sable leaned against one of the floor to ceiling windows. "My maids are going to kill me when they see I have chalked up my expensive, imported wood floor yet again."

Chris snorted. "Johnnie, would you like something to eat?"

"Not really," Johnnie said, "but I suppose I should eat something."

"I'll order something up," Sable said, and Johnnie could tell from the way he fell silent that he was communicating with someone elsewhere in the building.

Leaving Jed to the spell work, knowing it was best to get out of the way, he returned to the couch where he had earlier slept and finally asked, "How long was I asleep?"

"About eight hours."

So, all told, he had lost about twelve. Sixty hours left. Johnnie winced. He doubted that was enough time to do all that he needed—assuming he was still alive in an hour. Johnnie would really prefer not to think about that, but he could not seem to stop.

He wanted to be back at the Bremen, he thought. Playing pool or simply reading while the guys chatted around him, looking up every now and then because he was *certain* Bergrin was watching him—but never able to catch him in the act, never seeing more than the bill of that stupid cap.

What was Bergrin doing now? Back at the Bremen, slumped in his corner? Or had he gone to his parents' house? Maybe now that he was free of the burden of babysitting Johnnie, and did not have even the compensation of fucking him, he had already found someone else to enjoy in the dark—

Johnnie tore away from that thought, fighting an urge to throw something through a window. He drew a deep breath—and jerked as someone touched him, looked up sharply, then froze, and relaxed. "My apologies," he muttered.

"No worries," Chris said and set a tray holding a plate heaped with fettuccini alfredo and a glass of red wine. "Eat."

Johnnie ate, but only because he wanted all the help he could get when the spell was broken. He had read enough, and listened enough, to know it was going to be hell. The wine was good, and he enjoyed it far more than the food. Setting it all neatly aside when he was done, he stood and returned to the group. "Thank you," he said to Chris and Sable.

Chris shrugged. "Your parents were good folks. I'm sorry everything went so wrong with them." He looked Johnnie up and down. "But I can see that Ontoniel has been good to you, not that I ever doubted he would be."

"I should hope not," Johnnie said, irritated that anyone would even consider the possibility of Ontoniel being anything less. "My father is a good man."

Sable laughed. "Yes, he is. Any man so staunchly defended by his son must be, but I have met him on a few occasions. I will say, though, that the Ontoniel I knew a couple hundred years ago would never have considered adopting a human."

Johnnie did not bother to reply to that.

Chris drove an elbow into Sable's gut. "Behave. Johnnie, will you be able to handle the dream plane?"

"Do I have a choice?" Johnnie asked, tired of stupid questions and comments. This was the notorious Sable Brennus and his consort? He did not see what all the fuss was about.

"I'm serious," Chris snapped. "Plane traveling is no small matter, and you're only half-incubus—there is no way of knowing how it will affect you, what might happen to you."

"My question remains!" Johnnie snarled right back. "I must go there to retrieve that damned mirror or find a way around her curse. I am hoping for the latter, as so far I have been given no clue as to where the former is located. It does not matter if I am ready, if I think I can handle it. Theoretically, I should be fine. I am half-incubus; the dream plane is in my blood.

"My father said that while I am awake, I am completely normal, but that in the dream plane I am probably much more my mother. I know as much as anyone on the mortal plane can know, possibly more. I stand a better chance than everyone in this room. But theory and practice are two very different things, so we will not know until I die trying or manage to come out of it alive."

Chris threw up his hands. "That is not quite what I meant, but I suppose it will have to suffice."

"That reminds me," Johnnie said. "Where is my cane?"

"There," Sable said and pointed to where it leaned against the wall near the fireplace. His lip curled. "It's a beautiful specimen on the surface, but it's filled with corrupted energies. Someone murdered a great many beings and tore their energies away to make that."

Johnnie picked the cane up, feeling better to have it in his hands again. He pushed the hidden release and drew the sword—and could see from the faces of Chris, Sable, and Doug that none of them had known what the cane hid. "Yes, the process that made it was terrible, for which I am sorry." he said and sheathed the sword. "It can cross the planes, and was given to me for safekeeping."

"No wonder you would not let go of it," Chris said. "When it finally slipped from your grasp, we were astonished."

"It was a gift, from my second case," Johnnie said

quietly, thinking of Micah, the others. Wishing he were with them. Though this world was his, this steel and glass palace thirty stories above the rest of the world, he liked his humble dive better.

Especially, he thought miserably, when it had included the most infuriating man he had ever met.

"What was the case?" Chris asked.

Johnnie looked at him, genuinely surprised by the question. "Uh—it was not much. A man's wife had been kidnapped because the imp who wound up being behind it wanted this cane. It turned out the wife had been turned into a rosebush. The man, Micah, gave the cane to me in gratitude, and because he trusted that I would take care of it and keep it out of dangerous hands."

"Huh," Chris said. "You'll have to let me read over the case file sometime."

"Case file?" Johnnie asked. "I do not keep anything so formal. I am not a real detective. Where is my coat?" When Sable pointed to a closet, Johnnie strode to it and pulled out the journal he always carried with him. Returning to Chris, he presented it after hesitating only a moment. "I called it 'The Riddling Tale'. It was only a few months ago. You can read it, if you really want. My cases cannot be half so interesting as all of yours must be."

Chris snorted. "I doubt it. They are never half so interesting as one hopes. And I have certainly never pissed off a necromancer so bad she cast a Sleeping Beauty curse on my home."

"No, you just—" Sable grunted as Chris drove an elbow into his gut a second time, "—get yourself into bigger messes," he finished in a somewhat petulant tone.

"Stop whining," Chris retorted. "I will read the case and take care of this until you can retrieve it. Thank you."

Johnnie nodded and started to say something, though he was not quite sure what, when he was interrupted by Charlie. "We're ready."

Hiding a grimace, Johnnie gripped his cane more tightly and strode toward Jed, who stood by the elaborate spell circle he had just spent the past hour drawing on the floor He wiped his chalk-dusty hands on his jeans and smiled at Johnnie. "If you'll step inside, I'll chalk the last mark and seal you in."

Nodding, Johnnie looked over the spell circle, thought of all the people who needed him to do this, and stepped inside.

Jed knelt and drew in one last mark. "There," he said, standing and wiping his hands again. He smiled gently. "If anything goes awry, it will be contained. I have woven in what pain-counters I could without sacrificing the power of the spell." He sighed and pushed his slipping glasses back up his nose. "I hope this works."

Johnnie said nothing, only watched him until Jed finally nodded. "Here we go, then." Kneeling once more, he began to mutter softly beneath his breath—then his hand abruptly flashed out and slammed down on the circle, activating the spell.

For a moment, Johnnie felt nothing but a sudden lance of shocking cold—like being hit by a cold freeze and suffering a particularly painful jolt of static shock all at once.

Then it felt like gentle heat spreading through him, a sip of brandy that warmed him to the core.

But as he drew another breath, and the counter-spell began to undo a spell set nearly twenty-seven years ago, the pain started.

Johnnie heard himself screaming, but he could comprehend nothing more than that, could barely understand that he was screaming. All he felt was the searing pain, like someone cutting him apart, burning him, shredding him, from the inside out.

He screamed and screamed and screamed, feeling pain, tasting blood, hitting something—he thought for a moment, somewhere in there, that he might have thrown up.

Then he just gave up.

~~*

Johnnie woke up shouting—and realized abruptly he was lying in his bed. At the Bremen.

What?

He pressed the heel of his hand to his forehead, grimacing as the pain of a headache caught up to him. He felt like shit. Stumbling out of bed, Johnnie slowly made his way to the bathroom, flicking on the light and looking in the mirror.

Which showed him nothing but a gray, misty, indistinct wash of colors.

Mirrors do not work on the dream plane he remembered with a sharp, nasty jolt. He—it—the counter-spell had worked. He was in the dream plane.

And now that he was aware, Johnnie began to notice all the little details he should have caught before. The apartment was almost perfect, but there were minute details missing, bits and pieces here and there. Like his mind had not been able to fill in all the details.

Johnnie shuffled through his memories, calling up all that he had read on the limited subject. The dream plane was a composite plane. It was made of the memories of the dreamers, creating a world that was close to the other planes but not like any of them—and it was always shifting, changing, as minds were added, subtracted, attention swerved. Of all the planes, the dream plane was the easiest for anyone to access, but that was largely because it was the most undeveloped, the most fragile, and therefore, the most unstable.

Only the natural inhabitants were constants, creatures so strongly believed in that they took on a life of their own—or so it was said, but no one would ever be able to say for certain.

That, in turn, reminded him of what *he* was here. *Incubus.*

Mirror, he thought with another jolt, jerking his head back up to stare at the useless bathroom mirror. They did not work in the dream world because everything in the dream world was subjective, uncertain, ever changing. Mirrors could only reflect reality, cold hard truth. That was why mirrors did not work here—there was no cold hard truth to reflect.

But, Johnnie thought, a magic mirror would probably work just fine. If it had been brought successfully to this plane, then it had been rendered capable of that. So it would probably work here, however it *did* work.

Striding back to his bedroom, Johnnie looked around—and smiled in relief to see that his cane had come with him. No one and nothing in the dream plane would be able to manipulate or otherwise tamper with his sword stick here. All the rest of what he saw, what he wore, might be the workings of the dream plane, but the cane sword would remain untouched by all of it.

Leaving the apartment, he strode downstairs and through the bar, which proved to be deserted, and out into the streets of a city that passed muster at a glance, but failed miserably upon closer inspection. He could not believe he was actually here on the dream plane. Was he merely asleep—but no, the cane had come through, so after Jed broke the spell he must have simply vanished and wound up here.

At least he was not dead.

Johnnie walked the streets, trying simply to get comfortable with the idea that he was on another plane. And he was an incubus here. What did that even mean? How would that affect him?

He would have to learn as he went, because he did not have the luxury of time to stop and figure it all out more methodically.

That also meant he needed to figure out where to go. Where would his mother have hidden the mirror? Johnnie realized then just how little he knew about his birth parents. He had been desperate to know their secrets, but he did not even know the most basic things about them.

He had been grief-stricken when they died. A nine-year-old boy thrown into a nightmare world who had found out in the worst possible manner that monsters were real. But then he had thrown himself into that world, desperate to please his new father, terrified that Ontoniel would vanish as well.

Where had they lived when he was a boy? He had vague memories of the street he'd grown up on, the house, his old friends. They had liked to play at the park at the end of the road. Cops and robbers, he remembered suddenly, and laughed. He had always been a cop. But where had that been?

All he knew was that they lived in the district largely populated by abnormals who preferred to be as far from abnormal life as possible. So he should head that way, and... what? Explore miles upon miles of streets in the hopes that he would stumble upon the right one? There must be an easier way to go about it, but damned if he knew it.

Stifling a sigh, he turned right at the next corner and briskly made his way out of downtown, headed towards the suburbs where, in the mortal plane, the normals of Ontoniel's territory all lived. He had walked for what felt like ages when he heard voices, jarring him from his thoughts. Until then, the world had been eerily silent.

"Hey, slut," one of the voices said, and then a handful of shadows separated from the dark edge of one building, coming toward him with hostility written into their every movement. Four of them, Johnnie counted, and scrambled to think what they were.

Bogeymen, he decided. The litter of the dream plane, but not to be underestimated. Their sustenance was the fear born of nightmares, as opposed to incubi who fed on lust, and baku, who were the carrion eaters of the dream plane.

Johnnie tensed as they approached him.

"This is our territory, slut," the ringleader said. "You can't come here."

"Passing through," Johnnie said coolly. "I have no interest in your territory."

"Something funny about him," one of the others muttered. Like all bogeymen, or at least like Johnnie had read, they were roughly human in appearance, but...oddly indistinct. Detailed shadows, nothing more. Somewhere in the dream city, people were dreaming terrifying, awful things—a bogeyman would find that, merge with the dream, and dine like a king.

If Johnnie were a true incubus, he would do something similar, but his venue would be lust, not terror.

Right now, he would simply settle for knowing his way around the dream plane—or to have someone with him who did. But even—

He cut the thought off. There was no one who could help him, and that was that.

The ringleader reached out and grabbed him. Johnnie gasped and tried to jerk away, startled by all that single touch was telling him: the bogeyman wanted him, and Johnnie knew the best way to enthrall it, make it succumb.

He also noticed a sharp, gnawing ache, like being so wrapped up in his work he did not know he was hungry until he smelled food.

Johnnie wanted to feed. He tore away, shaken, stumbling back, desperate to get away until he could better understand this new, strange part of himself. He did not want to feed on anyone, especially not by fucking them.

"Holy shit," one of the others said. "He's a roamer."

A roamer—that was another word for a lucid dreamer.

"But he's an incubus, too," the ringleader said, and Johnnie could see the puzzlement on the thing's face, shadowy though it was. "Only the sluts look that fucking pretty."

Envy, Johnnie realized. The bogeymen were

jealous, and hated that they wanted him too. Was it always like this for incubi? Had his mother faced such things?

"Let's just kill him," said the third one.

"Yeah," the ringleader agreed. "He's in our turf anyway."

Then, as simple as that, they lunged.

Johnnie managed to dodge the first swing, and he got in one good, solid hit before his cane was snatched away and the ringleader got a grip on him, throwing him into a wall that felt a lot harder than Johnnie thought it should.

He crashed to the ground, then fumbled to pick himself up, struggling futilely as he was yanked to his feet and punched hard in the gut. He dropped again, tears of pain blurring his vision, and cried out as someone kicked him.

Bullies, he thought bitterly. They did not change from plane to plane, it seemed. And it would also seem years later, in another world entirely, he was still a favorite victim.

Someone back handed him, and Johnnie tasted blood. All the lessons, all the schoolyard beatings he had overcome—and now he was right back where he had started. He was so fucking tired of it. He had driven others back without ever having to lift a hand. He had learned how to stop the hits from ever coming.

He reached out, fumbling, catching someone in the face, then grabbed another, digging his nails in, holding fast—gasping in surprise as he felt *something* shift, a slight tug that seemed to move from him to his victim. Lust, control—he could feel something in his mind stirring, waking.

More terrified of that than bullies, Johnnie

wrenched away and tried simply to run—but they caught him, and threw him down again, and he simply did not have the energy to keep fighting. Blood stung his eyes, and Johnnie realized someone had cut his face.

He flinched as one of them grabbed him, reaching by pure instinct to take the man's wrists, stop him somehow, but he could not see well and he recoiled as that *tugging* feeling that he could not control came again—

And then someone screamed. It was a terrible, awful, gut-wrenching scream. Johnnie let go of the man he was holding to instinctively cover his ears—and abruptly realized he knew that scream. Or rather that type of scream.

He could also suddenly smell myrrh and musk roses. But that was impossible. He must be imagining it.

Then the man holding him was abruptly gone, and Johnnie fell back onto the street, disoriented and confused. He struggled to sit up and wipe the blood from his eyes at the same time, finally managing to get to his knees. His hands were wet and sticky with blood, and he could feel it drying all over his damned face—but he could see again.

But what he saw, he could not believe.

It... it was... but there was no way it was Bergrin.

He stood over the man who had been holding Johnnie, facing away. He held the bogeyman's face in his hands, as if staring at him—and the man's eyes were definitely meeting Bergrin's, but they were wide open and terrified, and he was screaming so loudly, and with such terror, that Johnnie could not begin to imagine what he was seeing.

Then, as abruptly as he had started screaming, the bogeyman stopped. Johnnie realized in the next moment that he was dead. Bergrin dropped the body—but then did not turn around.

Slowly, wincing at the aches and pains a beating always left, Johnnie stood up. "B-Bergrin?"

Bergrin did not turn around, though Johnnie saw his shoulders tense.

What was going on? "Bergrin—" Still Bergrin did not turn, and Johnnie finally snapped. "God damn it, Bergrin! Do not fucking ignore—"

Johnnie forgot what he was going to say as Bergrin finally turned around. His eyes. Johnnie stared in disbelief, mouth open. Gone were the pretty hazel eyes he had so admired, so missed. Gone were his eyes entirely, replaced by... They were completely and totally white—more like a pale, almost shimmery gray. Unbroken, perfect, like his eyes had been replaced with orbs of frosted glass.

"I can't—I can't hide my eyes here," Bergrin said, sounding miserable. "The mortal plane I can, but—"

That stirred Johnnie from his trance. "What are you doing here? How are you here? Damn it, Bergrin—"

"I couldn't stay away," Bergrin said miserably. "A thousand times I've tried to stay away from you, Johnnie. You're not for me to touch—you're so far out of my league—but I—" He stopped and took off his cap, that stupid, silly grim reaper cap that Johnnie never thought he would see again. Bergrin raked a hand through his hair, then shoved the cap back before finally saying quietly, "I could not stand that you thought I had used you, meant to hurt you. I never—I would never want to hurt you, Johnnie. I just wanted a chance to say that, so I went back to find you, even though your father told me to wait a few days."

He sighed, then continued before Johnnie could figure out what to say. "I saw everyone asleep, and I found a spell key hidden in the green room. Then I realized you were nowhere to be found in the house and picked up your trail. It took me awhile to find you in my hometown." He smiled ever so briefly. "But I finally tracked you to the Tantalus, and then saw the spell circle, or what was left of it. When I realized you had gone to the dream plane, I came after you, but you didn't do it the right way, so it took me longer than I liked to find you."

"What—the wrong way?" Johnnie asked, not certain he was ready to ask the other questions spinning through his head.

"Yeah," Bergrin said and smiled hesitantly. "Everyone else sticks to the path, Johnnie. You decided to veer off the path and take a shortcut and got jumped by some big bad wolves."

Johnnie bristled, but then smiled and said sweetly, "Well, thank you for the help, Red Riding Hood."

Bergrin scowled. "Huntsman. I'm the Huntsman."

"If you say so, bab—" Johnnie broke off, faltering, realizing abruptly that it had been far too easy to slip back into their habitual bickering. He looked away, all the anger and hurt flooding back. "What are you doing here, Bergrin?"

"I couldn't stay away," Bergrin said miserably. "I tried. But I—I wish I could stop. Stop—stop loving you." Bergrin paused, then continued. "I wish I could just walk away like I should have right from the start, but I can't. If I have to spend the rest of my life watching you, and watching over you, from the shadows, then I will."

Johnnie's breath caught on the words, and the ache in his chest hurt so damned much. He stared into those strange, strange eyes. "Why? Why the lies? The deception? You say you were not using me—"

"No!" Bergrin burst out. "I never meant you to think that. I kept trying to tell you that, but you never listen, Johnnie. You're so smart, but there are so many things you refuse to hear or see."

"Then why?" Johnnie demanded. "Why be Eros? Why lie? Why, damn it?" He went to wipe at his face, and only then remembered he was covered in his own blood. What a sight he must be making, bloody and dirty and soundly beaten. He fumbled in his pockets for a handkerchief—then jumped when someone touched him.

He looked up, and those white eyes were even more eerie up close. Johnnie found it hard to breathe, and harder still as Bergrin cupped the back of his neck, tilting his head and holding him firmly in place, and then began to wipe Johnnie's face off with a damp cloth. Where had he gotten it?

Johnnie swallowed and stood as still as a statue, heart thudding in his chest as Bergrin cleaned his face, his hands, then returned to his face again, finishing by slowly dragging a corner of the cloth across his mouth.

The words slipped out before Johnnie could even think to hold them back, a trifle unsteady as he spoke. "What do you want?"

Bergrin stilled, then slowly pulled the cloth away. He traced his thumb along Johnnie's bottom lip and said quietly, "To be with you in hell."

Johnnie laughed, shakily, and replied, "It would seem your words/Bode neither of us any good."

"Tell me how men kiss you," Bergrin said, voice soft, a hint of desperation, sadness, in it, sounding every bit as miserable as Johnnie felt. "Tell me how you kiss."

Unable to bear it any longer, Johnnie pushed up and covered Bergrin's mouth with his, wrapping his arms around Bergrin's neck so tightly he would not have been surprised to learn Bergrin was choking.

But if he was, Johnnie could not tell it from the heat and fervor of Bergrin's kiss. It was laced with desperation, with fear, but it was definitely Eros who was *Bergrin* and *here* and Johnnie had never felt so deliriously happy in his life.

When they finally broke apart, Johnnie said, "I—I am sorry I did not give you a chance—"

Bergrin cupped his face, stopped his words with his thumbs. "Johnnie, shut up. You don't owe me any apologies. *I'm* the one who should be saying sorry, and I do—I mean—I am sorry. So damned sorry."

"Why did you not just tell me the truth?" Johnnie asked because the hurt of that would not quite die.

"I was scared," Bergrin said.

Johnnie frowned. "Scared? Of what?"

"You."

"That is ridiculous," Johnnie snapped. "I have seen you face what other people would call certain death, why—"

Bergrin laughed, but there was nothing happy in the sound. "Death does not scare me. Death will never scare me. The only thing that scares me is you. Because you're so far out of my reach. Because you're beautiful. Because everyone *sees* you, and I cannot afford to let anyone ever truly see me. My entire life was spent learning how to be invisible, go unnoticed. I don't know how to handle being seen—and then I fell in love with someone who is always seen, who deserves to be seen. You are not for me to touch, Prince, but I cannot seem to stop myself."

Johnnie hit him.

"Ow!" Bergrin said, rubbing his bruised chest and giving Johnnie a wounded look. "What was that for?"

"For being a fucking idiot!" Johnnie said, then just because it had felt good, hit him again. "And that is for being a coward and not asking me to dance!" He hit Bergrin a third time.

"And that one?" Bergrin demanded.

"Just because," Johnnie retorted. "Why did you not ask me to dance? You were going to. I saw it in your face."

Bergrin sighed. "I was scared. Practically everyone in that room could not stop looking at you, and your father was only a few yards away, and I could not imagine that with so many better options in the room you would settle for me." He looked at Johnnie and touched his cheek lightly, as though not certain he was allowed. "And I knew that if, by some miracle, you said yes, I would admit to everything, and I was terrified I would lose you." He looked away. "Then I lost you anyway."

Johnnie relaxed, the last of his turmoil bleeding away. He took on a haughty tone as he replied, "Well, you found me again, babysitter. Which is good because you do like to brag about being good at finding things. It would have been quite beyond the pale if you had *not* found me."

Turning back to him, Bergrin smiled—a slow, happy, *real* smile, the likes of which Johnnie had never really seen. "I did. Not sure that I will be allowed to keep you, but I did find you."

"You are keeping me," Johnnie said imperiously.

Bergrin leaned close, so that their noses were all but touching. Johnnie thought he was already getting used to those unusual eyes. "Yes, Highness."

"How long have you meant that as an endearment?" Johnnie asked quietly, wondering why he had never noticed before.

"Always," Bergrin said. "I tried to mean it as an insult, to put up a barrier, but... well, I fail at being intelligent where you're concerned."

Johnnie could think of no reply to that except to take the kiss he really wanted, and so he did.

Bergrin groaned and bundled him close, and Johnnie really could not think of anything better than finally having Bergrin. "I really should still be punching you," he managed when they broke apart to breathe.

In reply, Bergrin only resumed kissing him—mouth, cheeks, jaw, forehead, as if he could not get enough, and Johnnie was not going to protest. "Whatever you want, Johnnie. Just so long as you never send me away again. I just want to be with you, no matter what role I have to take."

"Your only role is to be mine," Johnnie said. "I do not want a secret lover." Bergrin nodded and kissed him again, but after a moment, Johnnie pushed him away. "Speaking of secrets—I believe you still have two, and I want them."

"Two?" Bergrin asked, but Johnnie could see Bergrin knew exactly what he meant.

"Yes, two," Johnnie replied. "What are you? And what is your damned first name?"

In reply, Bergrin merely smirked. "Come now, detective. Are you telling me you have not figured me out?"

Johnnie scowled at him but pondered it. "You entered my father's home without trouble, and the first time we *met*," he glared at Bergrin, "you were not impeded by the wards. You walked over that spell cage that trapped me. So, magic does not affect you. I think, perhaps, it does not *account* for you. Whatever you are, you do not fear death. You can teleport with ease. And somehow, someway, you can cross to at least the dream plane."

"All planes," Bergrin said. "I can access all planes."

"You do not exist," Johnnie whispered as one entry and one alone came to him from his bestiaries of mythical creatures.

Bergrin ducked his head, tugging on his cap, and Johnnie stared at it. "Once upon a time," Johnnie said, "there was a poor woman who had two children. The youngest had to go every day to fetch firewood. One day, when she had gone very far, another little child appeared to help her. The child helped the girl carry firewood home, but then simply vanished. The girl told her mother all of this, but the mother did not believe her. One day, the girl brought home a rose and told her mother what the strange child had said—that when the rose bloomed, the child would return one last time. The mother put the rose in water. One morning, she went to wake her daughter and found she had died in the night. But there was a smile upon her face, and the rose on the table was in full bloom."

"A pretty story," Bergrin said, "if fanciful."

"So-you—you are what—a grim reaper?"

Bergrin laughed. "More like a shepherd."

Johnnie hit him.

"Stop that!" Bergrin said, rubbing his arm.

"Baby," Johnnie hissed. "So you are death?"

"Half-death," Bergrin replied. "That's why my eyes are only strange here. In the mortal plane, I'm mostly my father's son, though my powers are quite extensive. But on every other plane, I am mostly my mother's son, and practically all of her comes out in me. I can maintain my human shape, but the eyes I cannot control."

"Dark is as day to mine eyes," Johnnie quoted softly. "That is why you can see so well, no matter how little light there is."

"Yes," Bergrin said.

"Death as something with a corporeal form is not real," Johnnie said. "Even amongst abnormals, you are a myth."

Bergrin smiled ruefully. "My father is a crappy alchemist, like I told you—like *he* told you. But he got upset one night, was totally despondent at the mockery leveled on him by his peers. So he decided he'd summon an angel and show them all."

Johnnie winced.

"Exactly," Bergrin said. "He fucked up. Instead of summoning an angel, he got my mom. Very long story short, they fell in love. I don't need to tell you how bad it would be if the wrong people ever got hold of me or my mom."

Nodding, Johnnie said, "I like your eyes. They are... eerie, but pretty. Your hazel eyes are prettier, though."

Of all things—the very last thing Johnnie expected—Bergrin turned red. "Whatever," Bergrin mumbled, then said more clearly, "No one can hold a candle to you, Johnnie."

"I am an incubus," Johnnie said. "I cheat."

Bergrin cupped his face. "That only accounts for physical beauty."

Johnnie swallowed. "Shut up."

Laughing softly, Bergrin kissed him, and Johnnie really wanted to *kill* him for keeping them from doing this for so long.

Several kisses later, he finally asked, "Do not think I have been distracted from your remaining secret. What is your name?"

Bergrin turned red again. "I would really rather prefer not to mention my stupid name."

"Fine," Johnnie said tartly. "I will keep calling you Eros, in front of everyone."

"That would probably be better," Bergrin muttered, then glared when Johnnie hit him again. "Ow! How about I start beating you?"

"I have already been beaten today," Johnnie said haughtily. "Clearly, you are still in need of one."

Bergrin glared so fiercely then that Johnnie almost recoiled. "Those fucking spooks will not be beating you again, that is for certain."

Johnnie stared at him, startled by the vehemence of his tone. Then he remembered the way the men had screamed, how terrified the one had looked, before he had finally died. "What did you do to them?"

"It is the lot of those of us called Death to find those souls that go astray," Bergrin said, and his voice picked up that Eros-timbre, that hot-toddy timbre Johnnie loved. He shivered. "We travel the planes, looking for the souls that have lost their way. We see souls, can touch souls—something no other creature can do without suffering. I show them their own souls, and that is something no one so foul can ever endure. It always kills them. Painfully," he finished flatly, and then his white eyes seemed to ease some, and he looked again at Johnnie. "No one is allowed to hurt you."

"Certainly I cannot think of a better babysitter than death," Johnnie replied. "I still am lacking a name."

Bergrin groaned. "All right, all right. My mother—uh, she was summoned once before. A very long time ago, by um... the Norse. They decided she must be a Chooser of the Slain."

"Your mother was thought to be a Valkyrie?" Johnnie asked with a laugh. "How fascinating."

"Yeah, except she's obsessed," Bergrin muttered, "and my idiot father let her name me, so now my name is Grimnir."

Johnnie blinked—then laughed. "You are a grim reaper named Grim?"

"We aren't *reapers*," Bergrin said hotly. "If you ever use my name, I'll kill you."

"I am allowed to call you Grim," Johnnie decided.

"No one—"

"I am," Johnnie repeated, then just because he was not above fighting dirty, added, "Eros."

Bergrin glared at him. "I really do not like you."

Johnnie smirked. "Whatever you say, Grim. I cannot believe that is your name."

"It's one of the names of Odin," Bergrin said defensively. "My mom—she means well, but she's, well, you're always making fun of my hat. She thinks it's cute. She thinks my name is cute. I think she just likes torturing me."

Laughing, Johnnie curled his fingers into the front of Bergrin's shirt and titled his head up in blatant invitation. "They are both exceedingly cute, Grim," he assured.

"Shut up," Bergrin muttered and took Johnnie's mouth.

"I cannot believe it is you," Johnnie said softly when they parted. "I cannot believe you are *here.*"

"Yeah, well, I can't believe you're kissing me," Bergrin said and took another quick kiss as if to reassure himself. "Speaking of here, though—what is going on? What the hell happened after I left?"

Johnnie tensed as he was abruptly reminded of everything he had neglected, ignored, since seeing Bergrin again. "I screwed up," he said, withdrawing, tensing—only to be yanked forward and held. Johnnie froze in surprise, then abruptly relaxed. Being held was nice, he thought, resting against Bergrin's chest, soothed by the weight of the arms wrapped around him—still reeling from the realization that Bergrin was back, and his, and he did not think he would ever grow used to that.

"Tell me what happened," Bergrin said. "Whatever it is, I can fix it."

"Arrogant," Johnnie said. "Like I said, I screwed up. I have just over two days left to find wherever my mother hid the magic mirror my father made or she will kill everyone she put to sleep." Slowly, he explained to Bergrin everything that had happened since he had left.

When he had finished, Bergrin said. "We need your father, then."

Johnnie frowned.

"Ontoniel will know where she hid it," Bergrin continued. "I could try to find it on my own, and probably would eventually, but getting Ontoniel would be faster. If we can wake him, we can find the mirror and destroy the damned thing."

"But if we tamper—"

"Only from the outside, right? If we can find him here in dreams, then we can wake him from this side, and he will be able to tell us where to find the mirror so we can destroy the damned thing. Then I will find that bitch and destroy her."

Johnnie nodded. "So where do we find my father?"

Bergrin snorted in amusement. "Honestly, detective, where a king is always to be found—in his castle. You should know that. Why are you over on this side of town anyway?"

"Because," Johnnie snapped irritably, "I was alone and have no magical ability to simply *find* things and I had to find the mirror—"

Bergrin cut him off with a soft kiss. "I'm here now, yeah? I can help where no one else can."

Johnnie hit him again, then turned away, looking around the street. Spotting his cane, he went to fetch it, calling over his shoulder, "It took you long enough."

"Stop hitting me," Bergrin groused. "Come on, Highness, let's go find His Majesty." He took Johnnie's hand and they vanished.

They reappeared in Ontoniel's home—or an attempt at it. The house seemed gray and washed out, like an unfinished image. "Why is the house like this?" Johnnie asked, looking around at the gray walls and floor, the random bursts of color and detail.

"Fewer minds dream of this place," Bergrin replied. "The more minds, the clearer the image. The dream plane is... complicated, and if you ask me, far more dangerous than even hell. I hate the dream plane, but all too often this is where souls wind up."

Johnnie turned from examining an oddly intriguing, incomplete version of one of his favorite paintings and looked at Bergrin. "So you actually do that? Find lost souls?"

"Sometimes, not often," Bergrin replied. "I feel them more now than I used to, though. Being Death is equal parts being angel and demon. My mother did not have form until, like an angel, she was summoned and given form. But like a demon, it takes my dad as her 'anchor' to keep that shape and stay as human as she will ever be." He pointed to his eyes. "Her eyes are like this even on the mortal plane."

"That is why I did not see her, that one day at your father's house. You could not risk me meeting her—but your father said he thought I would meet her soon."

"Um—" Bergrin rubbed the back of his neck, looking embarrassed. "My father figured out I, um, had more than a professional interest in you. Then he bullied the whole sordid tale out of me and went off on me. That's the argument we were having when you walked in."

Johnnie shook his head. "You really should have listened to your father."

"That's funny, coming from *you,* who defies his father at every possible opportunity."

"I do not defy my father at *every possible opportunity,"* Johnnie said. "I merely resent that he wants me always near to hand and sets babysitters upon me." He turned away, headed toward Ontoniel's study, adding, "Even if the babysitter is good in bed."

Bergrin's laughter chased after him, followed a moment later by the man himself. "So does that mean I am allowed back in the bed?"

"That depends entirely upon who else you save, Red Riding Hood."

"Huntsman," Bergrin said.

"Yes, Grim," Johnnie said, then reached out to grasp the doorknob.

Bergrin came up behind him, reaching around to grasp his wrist. "Don't do that."

Johnnie froze, then let go of the knob. "Why not?" He glanced at the door. "It is different. Sharper—it looks exactly as it should. Why?"

"This space has been overtaken by dreaming," Bergrin said. "Whoever is dreaming, and we obviously know who, knows this place well enough to fill out every detail subconsciously."

"That would definitely be my father," Johnnie said. "So—what? We cannot go in?"

"We cannot charge in and disrupt the dream," Bergrin said and took his hand, lacing their fingers together. "But we can watch and wait for the right opportunity."

Johnnie just looked at him. "So we wait out here? For what?"

"I didn't say we were going to wait out here," Bergrin said. "Don't let go of my hand."

"All right."

Bergrin smiled, and Johnnie sneezed as the scent of myrrh and musk roses surrounded them—the smell, he realized, of Bergrin's magic at its strongest, or when he was not banking it.

Johnnie startled as he realized he could barely see Bergrin—like a ghost, he was completely translucent. But it was not until he glanced at their clasped hands that he realized he had gone translucent as well. "No wonder you are so good at sneaking around, and no one would ever think to account for *death* in their spells. So this is why you're always able to follow me unseen."

"Yes," Bergrin said. "My mother says that once, a long time ago, people *did* account for death in their spells. Life, she said, was much more dangerous back then. But over time, they attributed more and more to superstition, to the unfounded fears of the primitive and uneducated. So, it is much easier to be me now."

"Stalker," Johnnie muttered. "You are nothing more than an abnormal stalker."

Bergrin did not reply to that, only tugged on his cap with his free hand and said, "Come on, let's get this over with." He stepped toward and then *through* the door, and it was the wildest thing Johnnie had ever seen—until he did it himself, skin prickling and it seemed so *wrong*.

He started to ask a question, then recalled he should not. He looked around the office, frowning thoughtfully. It was different than the study he knew: some of the paintings were different, his little corner did not have its chair. The books were different, the curtains...

Beyond the windows flashed thunder and lightning. Rain drummed against the window panes and combined with the single lit tiffany lamp in the room to give the entire space a horror-story ambiance. Movement caught his eye, and Johnnie turned to see that Ontoniel sat at his desk.

Johnnie's eyes widened with dismay. Ontoniel looked awful. His hair, usually so neatly combed, was disheveled, falling over his fingers where his head was buried in one hand. His other hand was curled lightly around a snifter of brandy.

His arms were the worst. Every now and again Johnnie would catch a glimpse of the scars, but

Ontoniel almost never rolled up the long sleeves of his shirts. Here, in this dream or nightmare, the wounds were fresh—evidence of the blood-crazed madness consuming his wife.

Blood-craze was the fear of all vampires: a disease that seemed to come from nowhere, creeping up and creeping up until there was no denying its presence. Blood-craze was the gradual loss of the ability to process human blood and turn it into what was needed for the vampire to live. Johnnie had only ever read about it because it was extremely rare that vampires would talk about it at length with anyone not strictly necessary. Over time, the vampire's body simply forgot how to use human blood. To counter that, in the early stages, vampire blood could be used as a refresher, a reminder—a starter—and the body could copy that.

But gradually the problem worsened, until the only way to keep the afflicted alive was to feed them vampire blood.

Unfortunately, the craving for human blood never went away. It too grew worse and worse as the body increasingly wanted something it could no longer have. It would not have been hard, the night Johnnie's parents died, for someone to kidnap Sariah and manipulate her into the feeding frenzy that had killed his parents.

To judge by the surroundings, this dream was of a time when Sariah had still been alive—but later on, when Ontoniel would have been feeding her his blood almost exclusively. The wounds on his arms were too fresh for it to be otherwise. Johnnie could not fathom what a nightmare that must have been, and he winced, thinking of the argument he and Ontoniel had gotten into not so long ago.

The door opened, then, and a servant slipped inside.

"I gave orders that I was not to be disturbed," Ontoniel said.

"Yes, my lord," the servant replied, "but I thought you would like to know that Mr. and Mrs. Goodnight are here and have brought their son with them."

"The baby was born?" Ontoniel said.

"They would understand, my lord, if they had to come back—"

"No," Ontoniel said. "Of course I want to see them. Thank you. Bring them to me."

As the servant left again, Ontoniel tossed back the last of his drink, then rolled down his sleeves and straightened his hair. Thought not quite as neat as usual, he looked much more like the Ontoniel Johnnie better knew.

The door opened again, and Johnnie's eyes suddenly burned—somehow, it had not struck him what the servant had said. Mr. and Mrs. Goodnight.

His parents.

He knew them from pictures, from his few memories, but this was not the same. Not at all. He really did look exactly like his mother, but dark where she had been fair. Johnnie did not realize how tightly he had been gripping Bergrin's hand until suddenly he was pulled back against Bergrin, an arm around him. Johnnie could not tear his eyes from his parents, the way his mother held him, little more than a pile of blankets in her arms.

"Thank you for seeing us, my lord," Tommy said.

"Not at all," Ontoniel replied. "I am happy to see you are settle, and that your son has made it into the

world, alive and healthy. May I?"

Cordula beamed and gently handed her son over. "Of course, my lord. Given everything you've done to help us settle here, we thought you would like to see him."

"Yes," Ontoniel said, gently holding the baby, smiling ever so faintly. He moved across the room to the seating area and sat down in one of the leather chairs, settling the baby more comfortably in his arms. After a few minutes, he looked toward Tommy and Cordula, seated on the couch now, holding hands and watching Ontoniel holding their son. "What did you name him?"

"Actually—" Cordula smiled shyly. "After all that you have done, all the trouble you have gone to for us—for him—we thought it would be fitting if you named him, my lord. I mean, if you would like."

Ontoniel looked at them in genuine surprise. "Me?"

Tommy nodded. "We would be honored, my lord."

"The honor is mine," Ontoniel replied softly, and looked down at the baby again. "I think something simple and innocuous for you, something to help you live the normal life your parents want so badly for you." He fell silent a moment, then said, "John, I think. That suits perfectly."

Cordula smiled. "John it is."

Johnnie did not know he was crying until he realized he could no longer see. Ontoniel had named him? Why had no one ever told him? He stared at the image, of Ontoniel holding him, talking to him, while his parents watched, until the image suddenly blurred and grayed—

"Wait here," Bergrin abruptly said and let go of him, surging to where the figure of Ontoniel was still just visible.

Everything shifted, changed—and Johnnie realized as the study started to fill in again that the whole thing was starting over.

Then Bergrin reached out, to where a lone Ontoniel was standing by a window that was still forming. Bergrin grasped his face, tilted it up, and his eyes seemed to shimmer as he simply said, "Wake."

As suddenly as that, Ontoniel was gone. Bergrin strode back to Johnnie. "I had to wait until the dream changed or restarted so that I did not interrupt it and cause some sort of harm. He should be awake now and free of the curse, having broken it by waking up. It's time for us to go."

Johnnie frowned. "The spell on me is broken—does that mean I will now fall prey to the Sleeping Beauty curse?"

Bergrin shook his head. "I don't believe so. You're an incubus. That should make you immune to such spells."

He held out his hand, and Johnnie took it. "I hope this works."

Bergrin smiled in a way that made Johnnie shiver, and looking into those strange white eyes, he could see why people had preferred to believe that death as a corporeal being was a myth. "It will work. Nothing and no one hides from death forever."

Johnnie nodded and held tightly as Bergrin took them out of dreams.

Case 010: Paragon of Beauty

Johnnie looked around the ballroom in surprise, disoriented for a moment, unused to the sharp clarity of the real world after the blurred unreality of the dream plane.

But then one of the bodies on the floor moved, and he raced over to Ontoniel, dropping to his knees. "Father! Are you all right?"

Ontoniel pressed the heel of his hand to his forehead, eyes closed in a grimace. "I am fine. My head hurts something fierce. What happened, John?"

Johnnie's words caught in his throat briefly as the new significance attached to that name washed over him, but now was not the time. "Ekaterina cursed all of you," he said, and helped Ontoniel stand as he began to explain everything.

"I see," Ontoniel said when he had finished. "What a mess. But I am pleased you found the papers, John. I knew you would, should you ever need to. I always meant to give you those rings, but I never got around to it." He shook his head. "A magic mirror. I cannot believe that idiot—" He broke off and let out a sigh.

"How did she even know about it?" Johnnie wondered aloud, frowning. "I never even thought to ask that until now."

Ontoniel frowned. "She was there, the first night I learned your father was doing things he should not have been. I had arranged for someone to check on them from time to time, to ensure that they were being permitted to settle into a normal life, that abnormal problems were not bleeding into it. I truly wanted their attempt at a new life to work, for them—for you, John." He sighed again. "But that night, I had Ekaterina and her family over for dinner. They were only recently returned to the States, and I had not had anyone over since Sariah took a turn for the worse. She had been fairly calm that entire week, however, so I felt obliged to invite them to dinner to welcome them home."

Johnnie thought of the fresh wounds he had seen in the dream, Ontoniel weary and all but broken, sitting so alone at his desk.

"At some point late in the evening, one of the guards I had set to watch your parents came to me. We spoke at length in the hall, just outside the parlor where Elam was playing." He closed his eyes and pinched the bridge of his nose. "It would not have been hard for her to eavesdrop if she so desired. Why she would have bothered, I do not know, but if she heard enough to intrigue her—"

"She could have kept tabs on Tommy's work herself," Johnnie finished. "For that matter, she could have discreetly encouraged him. I do not think we will ever know. When she decided to take the mirror from him, and they hid it from her, she lashed out with the one thing into which no one would ever look too closely."

"Yes," Ontoniel said. "Most would have hushed the matter up quickly and moved hastily on, eager to forget that a blood-crazed vampire murdered people. But I did look deeper, enough to know something was wrong. But I was blind to the fact that one of my own was behind it—and I nearly let her marry one of my sons."

He glanced over to where Elam lay on the ballroom floor, fast asleep, so still he might have been dead. "Thankfully, that did not come to pass. Why did she even drag Elam into this? Simply to get closer to the family, I suppose," Ontoniel mused.

Johnnie scowled. "She said she had wanted to cast the love spell on me—"

Ontoniel winced.

"You *did* see that a love spell was cast on me," Johnnie said. "Why would you do that?"

"To protect you," Ontoniel said. "It was meant to be much milder than it proved, and I regretted it the moment it was done. I did not want you running away, and I greatly feared you would, as unhappy as you were in those days." He smiled briefly, looking between Johnnie and Bergrin. "I have never been happier to see someone fall truly in love, believe me. I am glad the two of you seem to have reconciled."

Johnnie's face heated. "Why do you sound so smug and unsurprised that—"

"That my Enforcer is breaking rule number one and yet still employed?" Ontoniel said dryly, sliding Bergrin an amused look. "John, you have always been very good at seeing everything but your own reflection."

"What is that supposed to mean?"

"It means any idiot watching the two of you could see that you were in love—but the two of you could not see it short of a shouting match at a betrothal ball."

Johnnie shot his father a disgusted look. "If you were anyone else, Father, I would tell you to shut up."

Ontoniel chuckled.

"Not that I'm not grateful still to be breathing,"

Bergrin said, "but we need to know where Cordula might have hidden that mirror."

"I am surprised the journals your father has do not say," Ontoniel said, frowning. "But maybe Cordula showed some sense in never telling him where it was—not that he could have gotten to it anyway. Who knows. Those two never—" He cut himself off and fumed in silence for a moment. "Your mother was smart, if soft. She would have put the mirror in a place only she knew about, some place that was special to her."

Johnnie thought for a moment, then said, "It would have to be a memory of something after she left the dream plane since that is the only way I would ever have a chance of figuring it out. Some place, I suppose, that is special to her and my father."

"When they first met," Bergrin said. "That would be something only the two of them knew, something only she would think of."

"But my parents are dead," Johnnie said, "and those memories would have died with them. So it would have to be someplace still there, still sustained by other people."

"Where they met for the first time in the real world, then, or maybe where they lived before moving to your territory," Bergrin suggested. "A memory of that. Whatever the place, it would be common enough to still exist on the dream plane."

Johnnie frowned in thought.

"Applewood, that is where they used to live in Sable Brennus's territory," Ontoniel said. "I remember them talking about it. They seemed almost ashamed; I remember thinking it must be a poorer district. That sort of thing always makes people uncomfortable around me."

"I remember that name," Johnnie said. "It was in the file. Before they moved here, they lived in Applewood Apartments."

"I know the place," Bergrin said. "That's an old complex, up on Lace Street. Applewood Manor used to be there, way way back in the day. But the owner went crazy, burned it to the ground. The lot was vacant for decades until the apartment complex went up. Bad side of town. They call that area the Woods because all the streets around there are named for trees—Apple, Plum, Oak, Elm, Peach, Birch, Maple. That place is rife with nasty types. Rumors are there's even a damned D-pit somewhere, though no one has ever been able to find it."

"No wonder Tommy and Cordula wanted out," Johnnie said.

"It's a starting point, at least, so we had best go see if the mirror is there," Bergrin said. "I would go by myself, but I suspect your mother made certain that only you could actually retrieve it."

"All right," Johnnie said, but he was suddenly loathe simply to leave Ontoniel. He would not soon forget the way Ontoniel had just *dropped* when the curse was cast, or how miserable he had looked sitting at his desk in the dark, fresh wounds on his arms from where his wife had cannibalistically fed.

The way Ontoniel had smiled as he gave Johnnie a name.

Ontoniel lifted one brow. "Do not say you are worried about me, John. I assure you, I will be quite all right by myself. Stop frowning so."

Johnnie meant to snap that he knew that, that he was not worried, but all that came out when he opened his mouth was, "I did not know you named me."

Surprise filled Ontoniel's face, and then he smiled softly. "Now how did you know that?"

"It—it was the dream we woke you from," Johnnie said, feeling guilty and awkward.

"I see," Ontoniel replied. "It was a bright point, in the midst of Sariah's growing madness. I always hoped a normal name would help give you a normal life."

Johnnie did not know what to say to that, all the words clogged in his throat, but at last he managed, "I like the life it did give me, even if that life is not normal."

Ontoniel smiled, but said only, "Get going. The hours are ticking away."

"Yes, Father," Johnnie said and took Bergrin's hand as he held it out.

In the next moment, they were gone.

~~*

"This switching between planes is disorienting," Johnnie said, closing his eyes for a moment to adjust to the disjointed, fuzzy feeling of the dream plane. "How do you just hop between them?"

Bergrin smiled. "I've been doing it since I was a kid. Until I was about ten or so, I was almost totally normal. But as I got older, my real powers began to manifest. Some of us could not afford to have fancy sorcerers cast spells on us."

Johnnie rolled his eyes.

Snickering, Bergrin continued, "One day, I did it by accident. Had no idea I'd just leapt into the dream plane. I just knew something was wrong. So I did what any smart boy would do in my situation."

"Cried for help?" Johnnie guessed.

"Screamed for my mommy," Bergrin affirmed, grinning. "She found me pretty quickly, and after that, I started getting lessons. Followed by more lessons. And after that, more lessons. Then even more, until I wished I had no abnormal powers whatsoever."

"Obviously that stance changed," Johnnie said dryly. "Do I even want to know what changed your mind?"

Bergrin looked around briefly, then motioned, and they began to walk. Johnnie only passingly recognized the dream version of Brennus's territory. "His name was Harold; he was pretty, rich, and thought I was lower than dirt."

Johnnie bristled, something dark and thorny twisting through his stomach. "So, what? You have made a lifelong habit out of stalking and molesting wealthy nobles? Just how many—"

He tried to push Bergrin away when Bergrin slid an arm around his waist and not give in to the hard kiss, but he sensed it would be easier to give up breathing.

"I did not stalk and molest him," Bergrin said when they parted. "I scared the living shit out of him for being a jerk to me. Then I vowed I would never again, under any circumstances, fall for a spoiled little rich brat."

Johnnie eyed him, only slightly mollified to hear he was not simply the last in a very long list. "What changed your mind?"

Bergrin smirked. "Getting called into work on my day off."

Losing all patience, Johnnie swung out with his cane and hit Bergrin. Hard.

"Stop abusing me," Bergrin said, rubbing his arm where Johnnie had struck it.

Johnnie only scowled.

Bergrin chuckled. "Like I said, I was off duty. But I got a call from my boss—not your father, but the woman below him who's basically Captain of the Enforcers. All the usual bodyguards for Johnnie Desrosiers, she said, were otherwise occupied. A simple job, I was told. The kid was going to a party—"

"The kid?" Johnnie said.

Bergrin grinned. "The kid was going to a party at Adelardi's casino. Go and keep an eye on him, job should be cake. I was offered double pay for it, since it was my first day off in a long time, so I went."

"You only met me because you were going to get paid double time?" Johnnie asked. How dull and disappointing. But what had he expected, something dashing or romantic? Then he frowned thoughtfully. "I did not even realize you were at that party. So the one and only other time you have been in the Last Star, that job you mentioned, was to babysit me?"

"Yes," Bergrin said, peering at him, expression pensive and a bit hurt. "So you don't remember me at all? You looked straight at me."

"I did?" Johnnie asked. "Rostiya called me to that party to help him locate a Cinderella before something bad happened. I did not pay attention to anyone who was not a likely Cinderella. Where did I see you?"

Bergrin shook his head, laughing softly. "Did you know that before that night, I had never seen you? I saved your brother the one time, but some way, somehow, I had never encountered the infamous Johnnie Desrosiers. I was sent your picture after I agreed to the job, and thought you looked like a typical rich brat. Then you walked in..." he drifted off.

Johnnie frowned. "I walked in...?"

"You were beautiful," Bergrin finally said, clearly lost in the memory. "You and Rostislav stood at the top of those stairs like royalty. You made a pretty pair, like night and day. I could not take my eyes off you. Then, a few minutes later, you came toward the bar and sat right next to me, only one stool between us. I could not believe it. I smiled at you, and was going to talk to you—"

"But Jesse showed up," Johnnie said, remembering. "I recall it. There were four people at the bar—two masked, two unmasked. You were one of the unmasked. You were wearing all black. But I had quickly determined none of you was Cinderella. Then Jesse came up and asked me to dance." He slid Bergrin a look. "A little while later, I was molested in the dark."

Bergrin pulled his cap down low over his eyes. "I still cannot believe I did that. And kept doing it."

"Neither can I," Johnnie said. "Then again, I can't believe I kept letting you. Really, you should be fired, like my father clearly failed to do."

Bergrin tugged at his cap again. "He said the only reason he did not fire me—or kill me—was that he knew real heartbreak when he saw it. He told me to take a few days off, then talk to you again."

"I think my father cannot help interfering the way you cannot help stalking."

"I'm not a stalker," Bergrin said hotly.

Johnnie lifted his brows. "You secretly follow me around, then used your job to follow still more closely, and made a habit of molesting me in the dark. I would say you qualify as a stalker."

"It's not like you really protested. If you had I

would have stopped," Bergrin muttered. "I can't help that you're more addictive than any drug on the planet."

"Good answer," Johnnie said. "As you pointed out, I hardly protested. I should think it was rather obvious I enjoyed Eros thoroughly."

Bergrin smirked. "You definitely never—ow! Stop hitting me!"

"No," Johnnie said. "Where are we going?"

Shooting him a look, pointedly rubbing his chest where Johnnie had just smacked it with his cane, Bergrin motioned. "It's just over there, couple more blocks down."

Johnnie looked where he indicated. It was a small apartment building, four stories high, forming a sort of squared off 'U' around a tired looking private courtyard. In the center of the courtyard was a broken fountain in the shape of an apple tree.

Beside Johnnie, Bergrin was staring intently up at one corner of the building. The apartments looked to be about five across at the wide part of the U, and the sides were about two apartments wide, five deep. Johnnie kept watching Bergrin, trying to let him do whatever it was he was doing, but curiosity eventually got the better of him. "Grim—"

"Hmm?" Bergrin asked, the faint glowing of his eyes fading as he turned to look at Johnnie.

"What is it you see, exactly?"

"It's hard to explain," Bergrin replied. "But—demons see what they call 'energies', what others call 'auras'. Basically, the different energies that make up a person and attach to them over the course of their lives. Different groups tend to have predominantly one color: normals have a neutral sort of cream, vampires are most often red, abnormal humans green, so on and so forth. Demons see these energies on each person; it's how they read people, the reason they are hard to trick, how they so often know the best way to kill. I see... further than that, deeper than that, and I can see not only the energies of a person, but I can see where else those energies have been. I can see one person, and then who else that person has been with, affected, what they've touched. I see the energies in greater detail and in more places."

"Incredible," Johnnie said.

Bergrin smiled at him. "For example: you are technically normal, on the mortal plane, but there are absolutely no normal energies in you. Instead, you're a rainbow of colors. Greens, reds, splashes and touches of other colors. Um—lately, a good deal of black is clinging to you, and that's actually becoming part of you."

"I wonder why," Johnnie said, giving him a look.

Making a face, Bergrin continued, "Here in the dream plane, there's a good deal of pink on you, from your mother, I guess. I'm surprised that element of your nature has not affected you more."

"It has—did—" Johnnie stopped, then tried again. "Those bogeymen, I could feel they wanted me. I probably could have—" Drained them, he finished silently, not able to say the words. "But I do not know how to use my... abilities. I do not really want to know, honestly. Hopefully I never need to do—that."

Bergrin made an odd, growly sort of sound, yanked Johnnie close, and kissed him roughly, reminding Johnnie of so many kisses in the dark. "If you need a fix, incubus, all you have to do is say."

Johnnie nodded. "Trust me, I will say—though I do

not feel that odd pull or awareness when I touch you, and I know you want me."

"It could be because I'm your lover," Bergrin suggested. "Incubi don't feed on their mates typically. They can, but they don't."

"I have no interest in feeding on anyone," Johnnie said, cringing away from the idea, then added quietly, "The only one I want is you."

"Well, me you have," Bergrin replied. "Speaking of that, and energies, you're so soaked in my black that anyone who can perceive such things will know—"

"Exactly who is sleeping in my bed?" Johnnie finished for him, amused. "You said they were becoming part of me, so they will see a great deal more than that." His amusement faltered under a sudden thought. "Do you not want them to know?"

"You're the one who could do better than the likes of me," Bergin replied, reaching up to lightly touch his fingertips to Johnnie's face. "Why do you think I was too ashamed and embarrassed to admit I was Eros?"

Johnnie huffed. "Are all grim reaper as stupid as you?"

Bergin's eyes narrowed. "I'm not—"

"You are exceptionally so if you thought for a moment I would ever hesitate to want or acknowledge you as my lover. I hope I have made that perfectly clear by now." He lifted his cane in warning.

Bergrin grabbed it and reeled him in, dropped a hard, possessive kiss on his mouth. "Crystal Clear, Highness. And I was going to say, I'm not a reaper."

"So you were not going to deny your stupidity?" Johnnie asked, smiling against his lips.

"I am starting to question my sanity in falling in love with a brat prince."

Johnnie kissed him again, unable to form more words, content to revel in Bergrin's. When they finally drew apart, though, he did manage to say, "Do not be absurd, that is the only smart thing you have managed to do."

"Brat," Bergrin muttered, and kissed him one last time before drawing back.

Johnnie smoothed his rumpled clothes. "So are energies all you see?"

"Like I said, it's hard to explain, and it changes slightly depending on the plane. I don't see half so clearly on the mortal plane as I do here—and I see better still on other planes. Right now, I can see traces of your energy, or rather your mother's, lingering here. It's faint but true." His eyes started to glow again as he focused on things only he could see. "A back corner apartment, I think."

"You can see through walls?"

"I can *go* through walls," Bergrin replied and led the way into the building and then up the stairs. "It's just taxing, if I do it too long. Only ghosts can really do that sort of thing with zero effort."

"Hmm," Johnnie said. "You would make a fascinating study, even if I could not ever publish it."

Bergrin glared at him. "I am not your lab rat."

"Not even if I paid you?" Johnnie asked, leaning in close enough to splay his hands across Bergrin's chest, and oh how he was looking forward to seeing Bergin naked, to enjoying his Eros in full light.

"Maybe," Bergrin conceded.

Johnnie snickered, but his amusement faded as they reached the dull, flat, poorly fleshed out apartment that was all that remained of his parents' first home.

Except that as they passed from the kitchen and living area into the one bedroom, it became fully fleshed out. Like Ontoniel's study, every minute detail was filled out.

"This should not be possible," Johnnie said. "Only my parents would remember this room with such clarity."

Bergrin said nothing, but the set of his mouth was telling.

"What?" Johnnie asked, and when Bergrin did not reply, snapped, "Tell me."

"This is a dying dream, or a death dream," Bergrin said reluctantly. "It means that your mother came here while she was dying, probably slipping out of consciousness and into the dream world. When she died, she was still here, and her dying energy... cemented this. It will probably remain here, exactly like this, for a long time."

"I see," Johnnie said and looked around the room. It was a worn out, run-down apartment, but effort had been made to cheer the place up and make it a home. The walls had been painted a calming blue, with blue and yellow curtains at the single, small window. An old, full-size bed took up most of the room, with a bureau, two night stands, and an old chair the only other pieces of furniture. The blankets and sheets on the bed matched the curtains.

The night stand on the right side of the bed was cluttered with alchemy books, an old pair of reading glasses, and a man's watch. The other one held a wedding picture and a romance novel. Next to that night stand, an old blue upholstered chair was shoved in the corner. Books were piled on it, covering a range of subjects.

Johnnie realized he remembered most of them—library books, he recalled. His mother had gotten them from a library when they were throwing away old books to have space for new ones. He had never realized she had gotten them so long before he was born.

One in particular drew him, and he went to the haphazard stack, moving several aside to get at the one he sought. "I remember this book," he said softly.

Bergrin moved to his side. "I did not see it until you touched it."

Johnnie barely heard him, attention only for the book. It was an old, sorely and heavily used, barely held-together edition of Grimm's Fairytales. It had been published, he knew without having to look, in 1917. By the time he had been old enough to read it himself, the poor thing was mostly just a bunch of loose pages kept together by a large rubber band over the cover, removed only when someone wanted to read the stories. His mother had held the book dear. "She used to read this to me. I had forgotten that until now."

"It holds a great deal of her energy," Bergrin said. "But, like I said, until you picked it up, I could not see it."

Nodding, Johnnie flipped the book open—and nearly dropped it in surprise when he saw that a hole had been cut in the pages. Someone had hollowed the book out. And there in the hole was something wrapped in a woman's scarf. Silk, Johnnie realized. He wondered if it had been a gift, once, from his father to his mother.

Pulling the wrapped object out of the book, he set the book aside and then began to unwind the scarf.

When it was unwound, he dropped it to the floor and focused all his attention on the object in his hands—a cheap, plastic compact with a poorly imitated tortoiseshell pattern and lettering too faded to tell the brand of makeup.

"Surely not," Johnnie muttered and opened it.

The smell of make-up powder was faint but there, though the powder itself was long gone. In its place, someone had used paint to write runes of protection, preservation—and in what must be his mother's blood, marks to carry the compact into the dream plane.

"*That's* the magic mirror?" Bergrin asked.

"I suppose we are about to find out," Johnnie said and then recited, just because it seemed the thing to ask, "Looking-glass upon the wall/Who is fairest of us all?"

The mirror, cloudy until then, shimmered—reminding him briefly of Bergrin's eyes—and then, of all things, showed him an image of Bergrin.

One of Johnnie's favorite memories, in fact, of after he had woken up in Alec's house, and Bergrin had strode into the living room, barely dressed, bruised and battered, somehow irresistible and unforgettable.

"So who is fairest of us all?" Bergrin asked.

"You," Johnnie said and closed the compact, slipping it into his pocket.

"Ha ha," Bergrin replied, looking hurt.

Johnnie moved closer to him, titling his head up to meet Bergrin's strange eyes. This close, he could just barely smell the myrrh and musk rose scent on Bergrin's skin. It made him feel warm—hot—and like his skin was too tight, too small, too confining. "The mirror does not work; it shows me what *I* think is most beautiful."

Bergrin stared at him a moment, then flushed and shook his head. "Then clearly you need more than just reading glasses."

"Shut up or I will hit you again," Johnnie said. "The mirror is subjective rather than objective. That is why it works here in the dream plane, despite not being a true magic mirror." He laughed, feeling sad. "All that death, all that misery, for something that does not even work the way it should. I tried to tell her there is no such thing as a true magic mirror. No mere object can see everything. Every 'near success' of magic mirror making has resulted only in these subjective mirrors."

"Hell," Bergrin said, "that actually sounds more dangerous than a true magic mirror."

"They are," Johnnie said. "Snow White is not the only tale of a magic mirror, only the most common one—and over time they gave the story a happen ending, though that is not how the reality played out."

Bergrin grimaced. "I think I liked fairytales better when I believed they really did all end happily ever after."

"Me too," Johnnie said softly.

"We have the mirror," Bergrin said, "and obtained it more easily than I had dared hope. If we can just take care of Ekaterina, we can manage some sort of happy end of our own."

Johnnie grimaced as Bergrin wrapped an arm around his waist. "Unfortunately, the hardest part is still to come."

"All I need is to get close to her, and she's dead," Bergrin said. "That's the easy part. For now, though, back to your father's house."

"I really wish I could cross the planes as you do."

Bergrin smiled, slow and hot and promising. Johnnie shivered. He liked that smile at least as much as he liked Bergrin's simple, truly happy smiles. "Why should you need to when I'm always happy to take you wherever you want to go—for a price."

Johnnie rolled his eyes, but splayed his hands across Bergrin's chest. "We will discuss that later."

"I'll look forward to it," Bergrin said, and took them back to Ontoniel's home.

They appeared in the main entryway, and Johnnie clung to Bergrin for a moment, adjusting to the change. He wondered how long it would take him to get used to it. "I am never going to adjust to the shift," he said when he finally felt he could stand on his own without falling over.

"I don't see that you'll have much reason to grow used to it," Bergrin replied, "unless you plan to spend a great deal of time in the dream plane. But you do get used to it, trust me. On the bright side, you don't have to learn all the planes."

"How many are there?" Johnnie asked.

Bergrin looked sheepish. "I'm not sure, to be honest. I rarely go beyond all the usual ones that any book will list. My mom says that's a good thing. Even now, she prefers to be with me when I visit certain ones. 'Only twenty-nine' she says, is far too young for most of the 'darker planes'."

"Twenty-nine?" Johnnie said. "You are three years older than me?"

Bergrin smirked.

"Oh, shut up," Johnnie said, and turned away, leading the way back to the ballroom.

When they got there, however, it was empty—

completely empty. Turning, Johnnie left the ballroom and headed to Ontoniel's study.

Rather than his desk, Ontoniel sat in a chair situated by the massive bay windows and the bookshelves, sipping a glass of blood wine and reading a book. One of Johnnie's books. "That is the Sleeping Beauty study."

"Yes," Ontoniel said, closing the book and setting it aside. "I did not think you would mind my borrowing it."

"Of course not," Johnnie said.

Ontoniel asked, "Did you find the mirror?"

"Yes, such as it is—merely a subjective magic mirror."

Ontoniel took the compact when Johnnie held it out, looking unsurprised, sad, and cynical. "After six hundred years, it is hard for anything to surprise me, but I am amazed at what people will do for things that will never exist." He opened the mirror and looked at it, then closed it again. "Let us finish this so the others may finally wake up."

"Did you move them?" Johnnie asked.

"Yes," Ontoniel said. "My magic is minimal but enough for that. I could not bear to leave them all on that hard flooring."

Johnnie nodded, then took the mirror back when Ontoniel held it out and slipped it back into his pocket. He reached into another pocket and pulled out the business card Ekaterina had given him. He turned it over and over in his hands, pondering. "She will never let any of us live. She cannot afford to do so."

"It does not matter," Bergrin said. "Once I find her, I can kill her before she even knows I'm there. I do not think it will be difficult to pick up her trail. Hell, we could avoid calling her and try to find her my way. We have more than a day left—nearly forty hours."

"No," Johnnie said. "She has something more up her sleeve, I know it. You did not see her after she cursed everyone and forced me to do this. She hates me—hates all of us. She is devious. Look at how long she has waited to get what she wanted."

"Call her," Ontoniel said. "So we at least know the next step, and can plan our move."

Johnnie nodded, grimacing, and took out his phone. He punched in the number on the card, then waited while it rang.

Ekaterina picked up on the fourth ring. "Dear Johnnie, never say you have my magic mirror already?"

"Yes," Johnnie said. "Free them from the curse."

"Not until I have the mirror."

"Then come and get it," Johnnie replied, voice flat.

Ekaterina laughed. "Dear Johnnie, I am not so stupid as that. You will bring the mirror to me at your childhood home. You will come alone. No tricks."

"Fine," Johnnie said.

"You have two hours."

"Fine," Johnnie repeated.

"Oh, and Johnnie—"

Johnnie said nothing, merely waited.

Ekaterina's voice was sweet—as sweet as only poison could be. "If you, or anyone else, are thinking of killing me, it may behoove you to know that all those sleeping beauties will die with me. Ta."

Johnnie closed his phone then threw it across the room, uncaring as it shattered against the heavy oak study door. "If we kill her," he said in clipped tones, "the others will die with her. I am to go and meet her—

alone—in two hours."

"Damn it," Bergrin said. "That is why so much black energy is mixed into the spell key. I thought it was only because the Sleeping Beauty curse is so often fatal."

Ontoniel frowned. "Energies? But you are no demon—how can you see energies?"

Johnnie hastily said, "I'll explain later, Father. How are we going to save everyone, then? We cannot tamper with the spell, and we cannot kill her."

"We'll have to save them the same way we saved your father," Bergrin said. "There's no other way. Freeing them from the inside out is the only way it will work."

"But—that is almost thirty people," Johnnie said. "We will never find them all in two hours, and really, it is less than that now."

"You won't be looking for them," Bergrin said. "In a case like this, I can do it faster without you."

Johnnie nodded reluctantly. "But that is still a lot of people for one person, even you, to find in less than two hours."

Bergrin tugged at his cap, smiling faintly beneath the brim. "I'll get my mom to help."

"Speaking of secrets and keeping them from those who need to know," Ontoniel commented dryly from his chair, "why do I seem to be the only one getting yelled at for it?"

"Uh—" Johnnie winced, abashed. "As I said, we'll need to talk later."

Ontoniel snorted in amusement. "Indeed. I am going to check on everyone. Johnnie, do not leave without telling me. Bergrin, good luck." Standing, nodding to them, Ontoniel left.

Johnnie rounded on Bergrin. "You cannot possibly

find twenty-eight people in two hours! Less than that! Grim—"

"I really hate that name," Bergrin said, "but not when you say it."

"Stop trying to distract me," Johnnie snapped.

Bergin made a face. "Sorry, wasn't trying to. My mom is loads better at this than I am. I'm twenty-nine; she's like, a trillion years old. Don't tell her I said that. Two hours is a good start. If you can buy us another one, three should be plenty of time for us to get the job done."

Johnnie nodded, suddenly feeling scared again. He had not felt afraid, he realized, since Bergrin had returned.

"Don't look so unhappy, Highness," Bergrin said and closed the space between them, pulling Johnnie into his arms. "Just look haughty and arrogant; it drives me crazy when you act that way, like you really are some proud, untouchable prince. I want to shake you senseless and fuck you senseless all at once."

"I seem to recall you doing both," Johnnie replied.

Bergrin smiled. "Mmm, and both were fun, though I have a strong preference for the second option." He leaned down and fit his mouth to Johnnie's, cutting off any reply.

Johnnie had no problem with that; he liked kissing Bergrin, and liked even more that Bergrin wanted to kiss him. He really wished the nightmare would end so he would have the opportunity to finally see and know his lover, enjoy that they were no longer lovers only in the dark.

He wrapped his arms around Bergrin's neck and kissed him until there was no room for fear, for thought, for anything but Bergrin. He absolutely hated it when they finally had to part. Johnnie swallowed. "Be careful."

Bergrin laughed. "Sweetheart, I'm not the one going into danger. *You* need to be careful, even though I know all too well that being careful is not in your nature. Just try to behave until I can come for you."

"I will be fine," Johnnie said. "Just—just hurry. And—and I love you." Three stupid words had never been so fucking hard to say, but the last time he had said them, he had been furious and had spoken them in the past tense.

The surprise and delight in Bergrin's face almost hurt, it was so genuine and just—just plain *happy*. He could not understand why *he* was the one putting that look on Bergrin's face, but he would be damned if he ever let anyone else do it.

Bergrin kissed him again, long and slow and sweet. "I love you too, Johnnie."

"Good," Johnnie said quietly. "Then you are not allowed to do anything stupid, and you had better come for me as soon as possible."

Bergrin gave him a look. "*I'm* not allowed to do anything stupid? We just had this discussion: you are the one who needs a bodyguard, Highness."

"Oh, really?" Johnnie countered. "What sort of grim reaper allows his ass to get kicked by one measly dragon?"

"I am not a *reaper*," Bergrin said, almost sounding petulant.

Smothering a laugh, Johnnie replied, "My mistake. What sort of grim *shepherd* allows his ass to get kicked by one measly dragon?"

"That dragon did not kick my ass," Bergrin said hotly. "It got in *one* hit before *I* killed *it*. And the second one never laid so much as a claw on me. You are nothing but an ungrateful little brat."

"I remember the one hit," Johnnie said, smoothly ignoring the brat comment. "I woke up on your father's couch and tried not to get caught staring when you walked in the room half-naked shortly thereafter."

Bergrin opened his mouth, then closed it again, face flushing as he finally said, "You, uh—I never thought you noticed anything about me. Until, you know, too late."

Johnnie thought of that moment, when he *had* finally started noticing—and appreciating—Bergrin. The very bare, very broad, very well-muscled chest. "Believe me, I noticed."

Bergrin grinned.

"We also fell asleep on the couch together," Johnnie recalled. "I must have realized, on some level, that you were Eros, but my subconscious was not sharing the news with my conscious."

"We did?" Bergrin asked.

Johnnie glared at him.

"I sort of remember dozing off, but then all I remember is my father beating me awake. I figured you'd gone off to sleep or read or something. No wonder Pop pegged me so fast," Bergrin said. "I never bring people home, for any reason, and I definitely never dozed off with anyone on the couch."

"Acceptable explanation," Johnnie declared, then said reluctantly, "I guess you should get going."

Bergrin grabbed him, dragged him close, and kissed him so hard Johnnie's lips bruised. "Be careful, Highness. I have plans for you later."

"Be quick," Johnnie said. "I bet we have the same plans."

Laughing, stealing one last quick kiss, Bergrin smiled and then was gone. Johnnie stood in the study, tired of learning new meanings of the word 'alone.' Life had been easier, simpler, safer, before he had met Bergrin.

But it had not been as bright.

Sighing, he tried to stop thinking about Bergrin and focus on his pending meeting. Bergrin knew what he was doing. Johnnie had not a single clue as to what he would be facing when he went to meet Ekaterina, or how he would stall her for at least an hour.

Leaving the study, he went to go find his father. He did not even have to think about it but went straight to Elam's bedroom. He had only been in Elam's room a small handful of times, and usually at Ontoniel's request, to fetch Elam for one reason or another.

Ontoniel had pulled an armchair alongside the bed, legs stretched out in front of him, hands tangled together, elbows braced on the armrests. On the bed, Elam and Rita lay side by side. If he did not know for a fact they were merely asleep...

Johnnie looked away and contemplated Ontoniel instead, not certain what to say.

"They are a beautiful couple," Ontoniel said quietly, "and obviously well suited. It is my fault entirely that he would not come to me about her."

"I do not see why," Johnnie said with a frown. "It is not like you would have ever said no."

Ontoniel laughed, sounding rueful and tired. "Because twenty or so years ago I would have been highly displeased. Fifty years ago I would have told him no. We will not go back further than that." He sighed and stared at Elam and Rita. "Six hundred years is a very long time. The world as I knew it when I was born no longer exists. You cannot fathom what has been lost, what has been gained. So much has changed, John. There are no extensive histories written by abnormals because precious few of us want to dwell that much on the past. In small ways, in many traditions, yes. But the overall picture we prefer to let be swallowed by time.

"Elam was born one hundred and six years ago. Shortly after his birth, Sariah began to show the barest signs of the blood craze. She would not be seriously struck with it for another fifty years. She always thought she hid it from me, in those early days." He fell silent a moment. "She was afraid I would turn on her, lock her up or kill her. A couple hundred years ago, it would have been the safest thing to do. Back when we first got married, three hundred years ago, it would have been expected of me."

"But you loved Sariah," Johnnie said. "You never would have killed her or locked her up—and a lot of vampires still do that, but it is stupid to think you would act like them."

Ontoniel's mouth twisted. "It was the first reason they started to call me radical. I did not care, but with Sariah's fate sealed, I was overprotective and harsh in regards to Elam. I eased up eventually, but too late, it seems."

"I disagree," Johnnie said. "He was going to speak to you. He had finally reached a point where he thought he could. The love spell was the only thing that stopped him."

"We will see when he wakes," Ontoniel said. He fell silent again, then said, "I do not like the idea of you going alone."

Johnnie made a face. "Neither do I, honestly, but

she holds nearly all the cards right now. Until we hold the better hand, we must play the game her way. Grim said he would come for me. I can stall until he does."

"Grim is it?" Ontoniel asked, looking amused, but he only said, "You are being overly confident, John."

"No, I am not," Johnnie said. "Ugliness in vampires is one of the main taboos, third only to the blood-craze, which is second only to taking up romantically with a human. She has worked hard to make herself beautiful, to give herself power and place. I suspect desperation and ambition alone made her a masterful necromancer. She tried to align with our family, but only as a stepping stone. All the real power, the old power, is back in Europe. I would imagine, as reluctant as she was to leave, she wants very badly to return. She is vain, cruel, ruthless, and under it all, desperate not to lose all that she has gained. A magic mirror would be all she needs. Someone like that... It will not be much more complicated to keep her talking than it would be to get most any vampire to wax ad nauseum about themselves. I only have to last an hour or so."

Ontoniel laughed, tired and sad, but with a thread of real amusement. "You have Tommy's sharp mind."

Johnnie hesitated, then said quietly, awkwardly. "But you were the one who taught me how to use it."

For a moment, there was only silence. Then Ontoniel said raggedly, "Go, John. I want this over with, and I want my sons back home, safe and sound. Do not be reckless."

"Yes, Father," Johnnie said. "I will see you in a couple of hours." He turned sharply around, pulled the door shut behind him, and left.

He would get Rostislav to get him close and go the rest of the way on foot. Hopefully this entire mess really would be over in a couple of hours.

~~*

Johnnie stood on the sidewalk and regarded the house that had once been his home. He barely remembered it.

He had preferred to forget. It had hurt, it had felt like a betrayal, but he could not both cling to his dead life and live his new. It had been easier to throw himself into what had seemed a living nightmare at the time than it had been to cling to a life that, with every passing day, seemed more and more like a dream.

It was a sad looking house now. No one had taken care of it through the years, leaving it now to look sunken, dilapidated, and forlorn. A faded and torn For Sale sign fought to be seen through the overgrown grass and weeds. At some point, someone—kids, probably—had thrown rocks through the front windows. Litter was strewn across the porch: bottles, cigarettes, snacks.

No one, Johnnie surmised, had wanted to live in a house where such a tragedy had occurred. He remembered his last birthday, when a friend whose face he could now no longer recall had gone missing. Only a week after that, his parents had been murdered.

Johnnie strode up the cracked and broken cement path, footsteps loud in the utter silence of a dead world. Most of the houses on this street looked empty, deserted. Had the poison from his house spread out, spread so far?

He reached the porch, picking his way over the

garbage, and opened a screen door that had practically no screen left. He knocked on the front door. When no reply came, he tested the knob and found it unlocked.

Having learned his lesson the first time, Johnnie glanced down, around, and cautiously sniffed the air, checking for any magical traps. But he could smell no magic, not near enough that he might be walking into a trap.

Moderately satisfied, reasonably certain that Ekaterina would not try anything until she had the mirror, Johnnie finally stepped inside. A single, small pool of light leaked from what he remembered being the living room. He did not remember the house well, but he thought it had not looked then the way it did now, neglect notwithstanding. The walls were darker than he remembered, and there was carpet in places where he remembered bare wood. No doubt the realtors had tried to cover up whatever remained of the bloody mess left behind.

But Johnnie sensed no amount of effort would ever sell the house, and the realtor had obviously figured that out a long time ago and given up even pretending to maintain the house. Johnnie was surprised they had not simply torn it down and built a new house.

In the living room, Ekaterina sat on a couch that Johnnie knew was not the couch he had sat on so many times growing up. Not that he remembered his couch well, but he knew it from photos. "You are two minutes late," Ekaterina said.

"I got a bit lost," Johnnie said. "I'm not exactly familiar with this place anymore. You couldn't pick a better place to meet? This seems tiresome and cruel."

Ekaterina laughed. "Tiresome and cruel? I merely thought it fitting." Her face was pretty and cold in the light of a single, small, magically-powered lamp. "Everything could have ended peacefully that night if your parents had given me the mirror. They chose to be fools and got what they deserved. They are to blame for what has happened to you, and it seems fitting to meet in the place where they sealed your fate."

Johnnie held on to his temper—he needed to keep her busy, keep her talking, and if he had to take such barbs to do that, he would. "I do not understand why you had to kill them. Logically, it made more sense to keep my parents alive. If you had, it would not have taken you this long to get the mirror."

"They kept defying me," Ekaterina said with a shrug. "I thought to kill your mother and force your father to cooperate, but Sariah was harder to control than I had anticipated. I only just barely kept you alive. Now, here we are, seventeen years later. That is not so long a wait for a vampire."

"I suppose not, considering you must have waited almost a century for medical science to be good enough to supplement magic to make you just pretty enough to pass for a proper vampire."

She moved faster than Johnnie could follow, slapping him so hard that Johnnie understood the phrase 'saw stars'. He could taste blood in his mouth.

"You have no place mocking me in regards to beauty," Ekaterina hissed. "Little Johnnie Goodnight, turned Johnnie Desrosiers: a stupid, worthless normal treated like a vampire. No magic, just the ability to smell it. You're nothing but a dog with a half-wit alchemist for a father and a dream-slut for a mother."

Johnnie said nothing.

"Nothing but a dog," Ekaterina repeated, "and yet all I ever hear is talk of your beauty, your so-called talents, how much Ontoniel adores his worthless human son. A stupid fucking normal, and the Dracula Desrosiers loves you like you really were his son! You're not even a vampire!"

"What bothers you more?" Johnnie asked her. "That my father accepts me more than yours ever did, or that it is only because of you that Ontoniel is my father at all?"

Ekaterina slapped him again.

Johnnie was really getting tired of people hitting him. It was no fun at all, not like his hitting Bergrin, who whined when they both knew he had barely felt Johnnie's smacks. He wiped the blood from his lips and said, "So you would say you are bothered equally by both those facts?"

"In the fairytale she lives, and the Queen dies, but we both know that in reality, you die, Snow White."

"I am not Snow White," Johnnie said, taken aback. The story of Snow White was so legendary, no one really knew the *true* story anymore. Snow White and the woman known now only as the 'Evil Queen' were two of the most famous tragic figures in abnormal history—or in what passed for history among abnormals. As Ontoniel had said, few wanted to remember and record the long years they lived.

No one knew how Snow White and the Evil Queen had been related. The most common tales were the classic stepmother and stepdaughter, but they could have been real mother and daughter or sisters or step-sisters. Like all major pieces of the tale, the truth was lost. What *was* known was that Snow White had been an exceptional witch and the Evil Queen a great alchemist.

But Snow White had been the better of the two, and over time, the Evil Queen grew jealous. Like all alchemists, the Queen had been obsessed with the impossible relics. But she had also been highly skilled at the 'crasser' art of mere poisons.

Finally the Queen's jealousy turned into hate, and she set out to kill her rival—the woman she had once loved, once admired, once worked happily alongside. Legend went she tried various ways and means to kill Snow White, but it was not until well after the last, successful attempt, that anyone realized previous incidents had been failed attempts.

History also disagreed on how the Evil Queen died—whether she had actually been caught and killed, or if she had killed herself.

Ekaterina laughed. "No? You live mere seconds from a beach, but your skin is pale. Hair as black as ebony and even without all that lovely blood, your lips lean toward red. Perfect at everything, deserving nothing, uncaring of those around you. A mother who gave up her life for you, and your father a lonely man in his castle, too stupid and foolish to see what he let into his home."

"An evil witch who lost her magic mirror and is jealous of poor Snow White?" Johnnie asked derisively.

"Give it to me," Ekaterina said. "I have had enough of this foolishness. You are no longer protected, Johnnie, by anyone or anything. I can kill you in more ways than you could possibly imagine."

Johnnie shook his head. "I am not giving you anything until I know that my family and friends will be safe. I am not stupid, Evil Queen. You cannot simply leave us alive. Did you think I would believe that you would simply take the mirror, take your parents, and leave the rest of us alive?"

Ekaterina laughed. "Whenever did I say I gave a damn about my parents? They did not give a damn about me until I made myself beautiful. If they are not dead yet, they will be dead soon; I've no further use for them. When I return to Italy, it will be alone. Give me the mirror, Johnnie, or I will start killing."

"You kill anyone," Johnnie said, slipping his hand into his pocket to wrap it around the mirror, "and I will destroy the mirror. It will not take much to do so, and I can do it before you can get it away from me. You get nothing until I know they will all be safe."

She glared at him. "I see there will be no peaceful resolution to this. Are you trying to stall until your little guard dog can get in here to kill me? I am surprised you did not bring him along, but actually listened to me and came alone. A fascinating specimen, your dog."

Johnnie did not reply, but the control over his temper started to fray. If she dared to even think of hurting Grim—

"I will make you a bargain, dear Johnnie," Ekaterina said. "Truly, I am going too far away to care what mess I leave behind here, and no one will come after me. There is too much I could do to them. So, give me the mirror and your guard dog, and I will let the others go free."

"No," Johnnie said flatly. "Even if I believed you, I will not hand him over. He is not an object to be traded. Why do you even want him?"

"He intrigues me. Not much to look at, of course,

but he has power the likes of which I have never seen. He would suit my experiments, I think. I would not mind knowing the weight and flavor of his blood, either."

Johnnie's hand tightened on his cane as he fought against the urge to draw the sword hidden within it. "You will never touch him."

"Mm, possessive," Ekaterina purred. "Is that ugly little thing the reason your daddy's love spell finally broke? I could do to you what I did to your brother. How would you stop me? I could make you adore me, make you love me, make you forget all about—"

He swung, catching her across the side of her face with his cane. Pulling back, he stepped away as she recovered from the shock of his actually striking her.

Then she lunged and Johnnie bolted to the side, barely avoiding her. He pressed the release on his cane and drew the blade, bring it up and assuming a defensive stance. "You will not get away with this, Ekaterina. You want the mirror, you will have to kill me to get to it. If you try to hurt my family, I will see you live to regret it for a very long time."

Ekaterina laughed, and then suddenly Johnnie's eyes were watering with the effort not to sneeze. "Do you honestly think, Snow White, that you can defeat me? That is only how the *story* ends, not the reality."

She lunged again, and Johnnie swung, connecting with her arm, blocking her briefly—but then she did something and he sneezed, and Ekaterina took her opening.

Laughing again, Ekaterina shoved him into the wall and wrapped her hands around his throat, squeezing tightly. Whatever spell she had cast was keeping Johnnie from fighting her—from moving at all. He struggled to breathe, but the effort was futile.

"I am going to leave your corpse in the middle of the city for all to see, for your father to find, and I hope the pain of it kills him slowly. I will watch him bury you, bury Elam, bury all of them, and laugh. I'll string you up and leave you to bleed out slowly, leave you aware enough to wonder if the rest of your family is dead yet, to know that one-by-one they will fall in dreams, until at last your father comes and finds your remains. Then I will find your guard dog and ensnare him, and we will toast your name in Venice before I take him to my lab and make him scream in pain because he loves me."

Johnnie said nothing, simply fought not to black out.

"Now, you paragon of beauty," Ekaterina quoted mockingly, "this is the end of you."

Johnnie looked up, forced his eyes to focus, then simply smirked.

Ekaterina frowned.

"Let him go."

The voice made Ekaterina jump and accidentally let go of Johnnie—and then Bergrin grabbed her, yanked her around, grasped the sides of her face, and forced her to look into his eyes. His hazel eyes became pools of shimmering white. "Look into my eyes and see your soul reflected."

For a moment, there was silence—then Ekaterina screamed in a way that Johnnie would not forget for the rest of his life. It was terrified, broken, desperate, worse by far than all the screams he had thus far heard Grim induce.

He turned his head away and clapped his hands over his ears when he could take no more. But when the awful sound finally cut abruptly off, the heavy silence that followed almost seemed worse.

Then familiar hands grasped his shoulder, hauled him up, and wrapped around him. Johnnie held fast, voice thin and hoarse when he said, "Took you long enough, babysitter."

"I'll be faster next time, Highness," Bergrin said gruffly, hugging him tighter still.

Johnnie coughed. "You had better. Take us home."

Without a word, Bergrin obeyed.

The house, when they arrived, was, to all appearances, back to normal. A servant, arms piled with clothes and other things taken from the ball room, stopped as he saw them. "Master Johnnie, your father said that you could find them in the front room when you arrived."

"Thank you," Johnnie replied. Unwilling to let go of Bergrin's hand, he led the way to the immense living room at the front of the house.

In the center of the room, across a massive oriental rug, were two couches and half a dozen chairs. Scattered about on the furniture were Ontoniel, Elam, Rita, Phil, and Zach. "The others?" Johnnie asked.

"Sent home," Ontoniel replied. "It was not hard to convince them that the party extended into a two-day affair, and they got carried away. People tend to prefer to accept the easiest explanation handed them."

Elam stirred in his chair. "Except for Ekaterina's parents. They are dead."

"I tried," Bergrin said sadly. "My mother tried, but she said they were doomed the moment they fell victim to the curse. Whatever else might have happened, their fate was sealed."

"That is unfortunate," Johnnie said quietly. "What will become of their territory?"

Ontoniel sighed and leaned back in his own chair, a black armchair positioned closest to the enormous fireplace. "That is for me to straighten out another day. It will not be the first time I have dealt with such a mess. Elam, you may assist me if you like; it would be good experience for you."

"Of course, Father," Elam said.

Johnnie nodded and turned to Phil and Zach. "I am surprised you both are still here."

Phil tapped her forehead. "We've been chatting. Oh!" She snapped her fingers, then fumbled through the pile of jacket, purse, and high-heeled shoes next to her on the couch, finally coming up with a familiar book. "Chris sent this; he said to tell you it looks like the west is well on its way to having a fine abnormal detective of its own."

"Tell him thank you," Johnnie said, unable to say anything more. "For all his help, and Jed as well."

"We will," Phil said, "after he's done yelling at us. Maybe."

Zach snorted. "On that note, we really should be going. We're glad you've made it safely back, Johnnie. We'll see you again, sometime. Thank you both, for saving us."

"Thank you," Johnnie said. "I am sorry—"

"No need," Phil cut in. "We'll see you around, babe."

Then they were gone, leaving only Johnnie and his family.

"I hope," Ontoniel said into the silence, "that we have had enough upheaval in this family to last us for the next few centuries. I would prefer the only problems to be dealt with in the future all pertain to wedding plans. Am I understood?"

"Yes, Father," Elam and Johnnie chorused.

Ontoniel nodded. "I am certain I do not need to ask, but I will anyway—Ekaterina is definitely dead?"

"Yes," Bergrin said.

"What about the damned mirror?"

Johnnie reached into his pocket and pulled out the cheap compact, then strode to the enormous fireplace and pitched the mirror into the flames. "Destroyed," he said, turning around and facing Ontoniel.

"Good," Ontoniel said. "Rita, Bergrin. Welcome to the family. I am sorry you were introduced to us amidst so much turmoil."

"My lord," Bergrin murmured as Rita bowed her head and said the same.

Ontoniel smiled faintly, then slowly stood up. "I think we have all had quite enough for now. I am going to bed, hopefully to rest properly. I expect to see *everyone* at breakfast, nine o'clock sharp."

"Yes, Father."

"My lord."

"Good," Ontoniel said, and with a nod, left the four of them alone.

Johnnie stripped off his coat and hat, tossed them onto an empty chair, then strode to the mini-bar in the corner and poured a double. Knocking back the vodka, he then flopped down on the leather sofa recently vacated by Phil and Zach.

Bergrin sat down next to him and slid an arm around Johnnie, pulling him flush against Bergrin's side. Johnnie approved and leaned against him, wanting to crawl into bed but deciding that took entirely too much effort at the moment.

He looked at Elam, then at Rita, then back at Elam. "She is far too good for you."

Elam gave him a withering look and did not deign to reply.

Rita laughed. "He is not *all* bad, I promise."

"I will take your word for it," Johnnie said. "But in return for breaking his curse, I fully expect you to make him a nicer person."

"Then I fully expect having a bodyguard lover to make you a more sensible person," Elam retorted.

"Ha!" Bergrin said.

Johnnie scowled and elbowed him, then pulled away, knocking Bergrin's hand away when he tried to pull Johnnie back. "You are supposed to take my side. Sit all by yourself."

Bergrin smiled, eyes full of affection and a hint of wicked promise. "How about if I said I like you when you aren't being sensible? A sensible man would have refused me."

"I think you have the same amount of sense, come to that," Johnnie said, but let Bergrin pull him close again.

Elam looked at them in disgust. "Do you always act like you are twelve?"

Rita's laughter cut off Johnnie's scathing retort.

"I think you are conveniently forgetting all of our antics, dear. What about that night we got drunk and played chopsticks for hours on end?"

"You are supposed to take my side," Elam said, folding his arms across his chest and glaring at her.

Rita smiled and patted his cheek. "If you say so, darling."

Elam covered her hand with his own, meeting her eyes for a very long moment.

Johnnie turned away, giving them their space, and found hazel eyes watching him. He smiled. "I am glad it is all over."

"Me too," Bergrin said. "Please try to stick to only stupid, easy cases for a bit."

Johnnie smirked. "If you insist. I *had* thought I would simply avoid taking any for a week or two, but—"

Bergrin bit his lip, then kissed him, briefly but with heat—and promise of all the things he would do once they had the energy to do them.

Johnnie turned back to Elam and Rita as he saw them stand. Elam caught his eyes, though Johnnie did not know if it was by accident or design. They stared at each other a moment, then Elam nodded and said gruffly, "Good night, Johnnie."

"Good night, Ellie."

Then they too were gone, leaving Johnnie alone with Bergrin. "You will have to tell your mother thank you for me."

"I will," Bergrin said. "She will want to meet you and your family, eventually."

Johnnie snorted. "My father already has the dinner half-planned. That is probably the main reason he wants us all at breakfast."

Bergrin tugged until Johnnie was sprawled in his lap and then buried his face in the crook of Johnnie's neck. Johnnie held on tight, just because he could, just because it was hard to believe he could.

"I cannot believe—" Bergrin cut himself off.

"What?" Johnnie said, combing through the soft mess of curls.

Bergrin looked up. "This. You. The son of a Dracula is not supposed to pick me. The Dracula is not supposed to give his approval. After all this mess, after everything went wrong, I did not ever think I would wind up in the Dracula's living room with his spoiled brat son in my lap."

Johnnie tugged on the curls he had just been petting. "When did I ever care about all that? If my father ever cared, he does not now." He fell silent, then added quietly, "She called me Snow White. I wonder what made me that instead of the Evil Queen."

"You could never be evil, Johnnie. You're entirely the wrong sort of arrogant for that."

"It would not have been so hard," Johnnie argued. "Wanting what others have—the magic, the talent, the fitting in by right of birth—"

Bergrin cut him off with a snort. "Even if that were remotely possible, I would not allow it. You're only cute when you're *mostly* obnoxious, not entirely. All that aside, dating Death is definitely taboo, so the rest is completely moot."

"I do not care anyway," Johnnie replied, then quoted teasingly, "For thy sweet love remembered such wealth brings/That then I scorn—" His words were cut off by a kiss, but Johnnie did not mind. "Take me to bed, Grim."

Bergrin smiled and kissed him again. "As you wish, Highness."

Fin

Book Three in the *Dance With the Devil* Series:

Midnight

Lord Devlin White, Duke of Winterbourne, is the last in a long line of powerful witches who assist the Demon Lord of London by solving mysteries and settling problems amongst nightwalkers. With his proud family line all but ended, considered eccentric even by the standards of his strange world, Devlin is kept from despair by his unusual ward, Midnight.

Murdered as a child, turned into a draugr in death, Midnight is a nightwalker like no other. Neither alive nor dead, sustained by magic and a bond to Devlin, he is happy to spend his life by Devlin's side, though he longs for the day that Devlin sees him as more than a ward.

But now a powerful figure seeks the secret of Midnight's making—a secret that Devlin will die to protect.

About the Author

Megan is a long time resident of queer romance, and keeps herself busy reading, writing, and publishing it. She is often accused of fluff and nonsense. When she's not involved in writing, she likes to cook, harass her wife and cats, or watch movies. She loves to hear from readers, and can be found all over the internet.

meganderr.com
patreon.com/meganderr
pillowfort.io/maderr
meganderr.blogspot.com
facebook.com/meganaprilderr
meganaderr@gmail.com
@meganaderr

Made in United States
North Haven, CT
16 October 2022

25515492R00232